Behind the Mask

Behind the Mask

Jasmina M. Svenne

ROBERT HALE · LONDON

© Jasmina M. Svenne 2001
First published in Great Britain 2001

ISBN 0 7090 7023 3

Robert Hale Limited
Clerkenwell House
Clerkenwell Green
London EC1R 0HT

2 4 6 8 10 9 7 5 3 1

Typeset by
Derek Doyle & Associates in Liverpool.
Printed in Great Britain by
St Edmundsbury Press, Bury St Edmunds, Suffolk.
Bound by Woolnough Bookbinding Limited

PART I
1777

Chapter 1

The accident had happened only minutes before the horsemen drew up. It was Elizabeth the younger man addressed, though whether that was due to her proximity or her face, she couldn't decide. Nan, after all, was just beside her. Several other women were within calling distance, all outwardly calm so as not to alarm the children, but secretly as tense as rabbits.

Even in August, night claimed Sherwood Forest long before it grew dark out in the open and the sun was already low. Quite unconscious of the perils of footpads, cold and the dew, three fair-haired children squatted in the dusty grass, gathering pebbles in their aprons and pockets, while their older brothers, unwearied by the journey, tested the climbing potential of an oak.

'Anyone hurt?'

The speaker was a tall youth with an inquisitive gaze and an exquisitely cut coat, sadly at odds with his ancient mount. The other man was older, but sternly handsome. His coat had been blown back by the ride, revealing the still elegant curve of thigh and leg in tight-fitting breeches and riding boots. His chestnut mare tossed her head.

'Only bumps and bruises. Is it far to Mansfield?'

'About two miles,' the older man replied. His gaze rested on her a moment, registering the absence of an accent in her voice. Elizabeth shivered. To his companion no doubt they looked picturesque enough. But this man had the sort of eyes which would notice the patches beneath Nan's arms where the original material had rotted away, the much-darned clothes of the children, her own much-mended shoes. He turned to survey the scene.

The turnpike road between the oaks and birches was nearly blocked by a wagon. A mound of trunks, two gilded chairs and a wooden grave-stone, painted to look like marble, stood among the bracken. Propped against a tree was a flat of a symmetrical garden with a fountain in the centre. Most of the men of the troupe were unloading the wagon, so the axle could be mended. Only the bleary-eyed prompter sat on a stump, his hands shaking fractionally more than usual.

'Such a pretty voice, such a pretty face – where does Mr Boxall find his new actresses?' The younger gentleman leaned forward on the neck of his horse to get a better look.

Elizabeth promptly averted her face, affording him an excellent view of her dark hair, piled high as was the fashion, her hat set at a jaunty angle on top. The spark was no more than eighteen or twenty and no doubt had his own opinion of actresses and his ability to seduce them.

She had seen his eyes alight on Mrs Boxall. The leading actress sat apart from the others, half turned away but not quite far enough. A naked breast was visible above a little skull cap and a caressing claw of a hand. She was aware of his gaze, too. Elizabeth could tell from the way she arranged the folds of her full petticoats and matching jacket, opened nearly to the waist.

'I shall certainly come and see *you* at the theatre,' he said with emphasis.

'Oh, please do,' she sighed, turning up her eyes mock-innocently. 'We are the best actors in the world, either for tragedy, comedy, history, pastoral, pastoral-comical, historical-pastoral, tragical-historical, tragical-comical-historical-pastoral . . . I forget the rest, but I am not obliged to know everyone else's lines as well as my own. And we also do 'She'-tragedies, sentimental comedies, heroic tragedies, burlesques, afterpieces, comic songs and farces.'

During her increasingly breathless speech, Elizabeth became aware that the older man had fixed his eyes on her. Nan was tugging at her fan-shaped cuff, desperate for her to stop. It was necessary to tread carefully with anyone likely to be a magistrate, since they had the power to send them to the House of Correction as rogues and vagabonds. But sometimes Elizabeth forgot she was no longer a lady and felt her old sense of mischief stir within her.

'Do you plan to stay long in this area?' he asked indifferently. Nan shivered suddenly.

'About a month, sir. I hope you've no objection?'

'It'll take a few days to mend the wagon properly, if you mislike us being here,' Nan added in her rustic accent, 'and I'm sure the children would be glad of a rest.'

There was no perceptible softening in his marble features. Elizabeth groped for something to say, but the youth intervened.

'Come, come, Mr Holbrook, don't frighten the poor maidens with that scowl. You know you have been known to countenance play-acting before this.'

Elizabeth was startled into throwing a curious look at the speaker. Mr Holbrook must have been about forty and she had expected the young man to be deferential to his face, even if he was flippant behind his back. However, Mr Holbrook's face relaxed momentarily, though he replied in a neutral tone.

'My house is only a mile distant. I'll send a servant with a cart so some of your belongings and the children can be taken to the town.'

Elizabeth contented herself with a quiet 'thank you', but Nan's warm nature bubbled over and she assured him they would all remember him in their prayers that night. Elizabeth braced herself for a chilling retort that would cut Nan short, but none came.

'Are you coming, Collingham?' Mr Holbrook asked. 'I'm a busy man, even if you are not.'

This time there could be no doubt: it was certainly Elizabeth's face which tempted him to stay. Mr Holbrook's mare shied fretfully, anxious to get back to her warm stable.

'In a moment, sir,' Collingham said, still eyeing Elizabeth. 'Will you give me one little kiss in parting, madam?'

'Oh, fie, sir, how can you fluster a poor girl so?' Her lips kept twitching into a smile, despite her best efforts. 'My only fortune is my reputation and you would take that from me.'

'I'll give you a shilling.'

'Worse and worse. What kind of mercenary wretch do you think I am?' Out of the corner of her eye Elizabeth was watching Mr Holbrook. His eyebrows had contracted, producing two puckers above his nose, but there was a glint in his eye she could not define.

9

'Well, two shillings then, and not a penny more.'

'What a miser you are.' Elizabeth made a face. 'I despair of the younger generation. I presume you are married, sir,' she added, turning to Mr Holbrook, 'or else I would ask you to bid against your friend and raise the price a little.'

He uttered a bark that might have been a laugh. 'You are a merry lady.'

'There was a star danced, and under that was I born,' she quipped.

'I believe you. Come along, Collingham.' He nodded to Mrs Boxall, who had fastened her bodice and risen, and dug his heels into the flanks of his elegant mare.

Collingham saw delay was futile. He threw a wistful glance at the buxom manager's wife, winked at Elizabeth, doffed his tricorne hat with a flourish of feathers and followed his mentor. Mrs Boxall's smile vanished as soon as both men were out of earshot. 'Well, Miss Hathaway?'

'One of the gentlemen promised to send a cart.' Elizabeth managed to smile naturally.

'Humph. So you didn't succeed in offending anyone with that over-ready tongue of yours?'

'Oh, no, madam. How could you think such a thing?'

Mrs Boxall was not deceived by her innocent gaze, but she contented herself with turning on her heel and joining her husband, a hearty man barely the wrong side of forty.

'Oh, Lizzie, how can you?' Nan breathed, her round face flushed. 'Do you know who those gentlemen are? Mr Holbrook is a magistrate and Mr Collingham's father is an attorney. If you offended them or Mrs Boxall, she would have you thrown out of the company.'

'Don't fret, Nan. I know how to address gentlemen. I was bred among them.'

For all her smile, Elizabeth did not feel at ease. Mrs Boxall's jealousy had reached such a pitch, she had been in danger of being dismissed six months ago. Only the fact that Mrs Boxall had been far gone with her seventh child and Mr Boxall's persuasive powers had saved her.

'Mr B is too shrewd a manager to let me go,' she added. 'He offered me a shilling more a week when Mr Wilkinson offered to take me.'

It was not for the money she had stayed, however; she owed a debt of gratitude to Mr Boxall, for taking her into his company and allowing her to play all the leading roles while his wife was unable to perform. And she didn't like leaving Nan behind. Nan had taken care of her in those first homesick days when she was sure she would never adapt to her new way of life. It had been a huge risk, choosing to leave everything and everyone she had ever known and she was fortunate, on the whole, in having met with so much kindness.

Now sometimes she doubted she had made the right decision, placing emotion above reason. Of late, instead of progressing in her career, she had had the terrifying sensation of slipping backwards. Mr Wilkinson's company was larger, more successful and travelled across all three ridings of Yorkshire. And London managers were constantly poaching his best actors. But there was no time to brood. Having had a little rest, most of the troupe set off on foot, to save time, leaving only a few men behind to guard their belongings.

For a while they walked in silence, the baby drowsing milkily on Nan's shoulder, two small girls clinging to Elizabeth's hands. But Nan's thoughts had been running in one particular channel and eventually she broke out, 'Isn't he a handsome gentleman?'

Elizabeth's mind had been on other things, but she gathered her wits and replied carelessly, 'Which one?'

'Oh, the young one, of course. Don't tease me like that. He was much taken with you, too.'

Elizabeth shrugged, 'He thinks a great deal too highly of himself.'

'What makes you say that?'

'Oh, the cut of his coat, the style of his cravat, the lace on his cuffs, the embroidery on his waistcoat – and the self-satisfied smirk on his lips.'

'Liz, you are merciless,' Nan retorted, fascinated and horrified at once. 'Mrs B is right – you'll never be wed if you talk so.'

Elizabeth tossed her head.

'That is precisely why I fled from home – to escape match-making and petty restrictions. It isn't marriage that's on young Collingham's mind, you should know that as well as me. And if I did want to marry, Will Ramsay would marry me any day of the week.'

'You didn't ought to talk like that,' Nan chided, pulling the skull cap a little further forward on the infant's head. ' 'Tisn't right keeping Will dangling.'

Elizabeth's eyes darkened. The topic was a sore one, for all she made light of it. She had made mistakes in that business, but it wasn't wise to trust Nan with all her confidences. Not that Nan would thoughtlessly betray her. But her good nature was so universal, most people knew how to exploit it. She was too honest to tell a lie if she thought someone might be comforted by the truth. And Nan was not a good liar, even when absolutely convinced of its necessity.

Elizabeth knew her friend both admired her daring and feared it might one day lead her into a situation from which she could not extricate herself. But Elizabeth at heart was more cautious than most people gave her credit for and her ready tongue had saved her – and Nan's – skin more than once.

They passed a narrow, heavily wooded lane, winding up a hill. Elizabeth guessed it led to Mr Holbrook's house. There was no sign yet of the promised cart and she scooped up the smaller girl, who was beginning to whine, and settled her on her left hip.

'Not much further' – she tried to keep her tone cheerful – 'and then a nice little supper and straight to bed, eh, Bessy?'

'No!' the three year old declared, despite sticky eyes which she rubbed with grubby fists. 'Not tired.'

'Then you're a better man than I am; isn't she?' Elizabeth said, with a conspiratorial wink at the little girl dragging alongside her.

Augusta Boxall, named like both her sisters after George III's daughters, managed a faint smile. The Boxall children had never known any other life and, as their mother didn't pamper them, they grew hardy and uncomplaining very quickly.

'Miss Hathaway, a word with you.'

One of the men in the troupe, a broad-shouldered fellow with a tolerably handsome face, had spent the last five or ten minutes chewing his lip, turning over the contents of his pockets and generally working himself up to approach Elizabeth, had she but known it.

Her brow furrowed but Nan slipped away before she could stop her. She reconciled herself to this interview chiefly because the newcomer hoisted Augusta up on to his shoulders.

'Why so formal, Mr Ramsay?' she asked.

He failed to smile. Elizabeth sent up a silent prayer that he wouldn't say too much in front of the children in the mistaken belief they were too young to understand.

'Well then, have you decided yet?'

She was too tired to use her usual ploy of pretending not to know what he meant.

'Mr Ramsay,' she said, giving herself ample time to pick her words, 'I gave you my answer a week ago, a fortnight ago and a month ago. I may alter my mind by and by, but I must warn you it appears less and less likely every time I consider the matter.'

'Why can you never be serious about serious matters?'

Bessy winced at his tone and began to whimper. Elizabeth shushed her before answering. 'If I were demure and hardly dared say yes or no, would you still feel the same about me?'

'If I can love you when you're such an infuriating wretch, why shouldn't I love you if you behaved yourself?'

She sighed. It was pointless arguing with him. He would never understand that this was her true self and she couldn't be anyone else for any length of time. He started repeating the same arguments she had heard so many times she felt she, or maybe he, had learnt them by rote.

'Acting is a dangerous profession for a single woman. I'd keep you safe from anyone who made unwanted advances. And if you wanted to leave Mr B's company and go to London, say – well, I'd go with you and I wouldn't be jealous or stand in your light like some husbands. . . .'

She suspected he was deceiving himself on that score. Her shoulder ached. She shifted Bessy to her other hip, checking an impulse to say something rash. He was even misinterpreting the grave silence in which she was apparently listening to him as a sign she was softening.

'I love you so much. Won't you reconsider? We used to be such good friends,' he urged her. 'Something changed you. Tell me what it was. What did I do wrong?'

But that, of course, she couldn't tell him. If she was fair, she had to admit she had liked him immensely once and was grateful for his friendship. He had often helped rid her of impertinent admirers. His only crime, if she could call it that, was that he had fallen in love with her.

'Ah, Will, I foresee a day when I shall have to be very cruel to you,' she said.

He flushed. Suspicion lurked in his eyes. Was she mocking him? Her light-hearted tone, intended to sweeten the pill, only ever left him in doubt whether she was in jest or in earnest.

'You still refuse then?' he murmured sullenly.

'I still refuse. But I thank you for your kind offer and—' She bit her tongue. The ending she had intended to add – 'and I fully expect you to repeat it within the next two weeks' – might have suggested to him that she wanted him to persist.

'And?'

'And I am a shocking flirt and cannot imagine why any man would want me in all earnest.'

Will allowed himself a smile, 'You vain creature, you want to be praised for your modesty.'

The cloud was dispersed. She could breathe a little easier. Her ear picked up the sound of wheels crunching through white sand and loose pebbles and a cheer rose for Mr Holbrook's cart.

'Papa, is it true?'

Edward Holbrook raised his head somewhat irritably from his paper. 'Is what true, child?'

'Mary Parr says Mrs Collingham told her mother that Frank Collingham told her that you and he met the strolling players who are going to perform in the theatre in McLellan's yard.'

'Yes, it's true,' he replied briefly, and returned to his newspaper.

But the pretty young girl – she was fifteen, though she took care to make herself look older – would not be defeated so easily.

'And you will take me to see them before I go to Buxton with

14

Aunt Lester, won't you?' she cooed. 'I've been moped and dull these past weeks and I am out of mourning now, and. . . .'

She bit her lip and let her eyes swim. Her father shifted in his chair and said gruffly, 'I had every intention of taking you, Miranda.'

'Oh, you are the best of fathers.' She flung her arms round his neck, knocking his head against the back of his armchair.

'You needn't kill me for my kindness. But don't be surprised if it proves a frightful bore.'

He peeped at her from under his eyebrows. Her attempts at sewing seemed doomed to be as ineffectual as his to read the *Nottingham Journal*. She sank on to the hearthrug to tease the cat.

'I wish we didn't live so far away from everyone,' she pouted. 'If we lived in a town, we could go to balls and plays and masquerades all the time.' (Catch me letting any daughter of mine attend anything as dangerous as a public masquerade, Edward thought grimly.) 'Out here, we might be all murdered in our beds and the house set alight and nobody would discover it for a week.'

He did not bother to point out a blaze would be visible from a distance on the Nottingham turnpike and that there was regular traffic – postman, tradesmen, servants, not to mention visitors – between Mansfield and Woodlands, the house his grandfather had built.

He was struck again by the resemblance Miranda sometimes bore to her mother, slender, fair-haired, innocent despite a superficial sophistication. Half-child, half-woman as Maria had been when he married her. There were times when he could barely bring himself to look at her. He loved Miranda with a hidden ferocity, but feared how exposed that love left him.

For the first five years of her life she had been an angel and he frankly adored her. Maria had come to him now and then, indignant at some allegation made by another child's mother or a servant. Neither of them had believed there could be any truth in the stories, until he himself witnessed that one incident.

He supposed the other child must have been one of the Parrs. He had never taken much notice of other people's children or their games. He had been coming back from somewhere on foot and as he passed the garden, the children's voices carried in the clear autumn air.

'I'm not going to play with you any more and no one else will either if I tell them to. And I'll say you broke my doll.'

'But I didn't.'

'I'll tell them you did and they'll believe me, 'cos Papa says I'm a princess and an angel and – and he'll send you to prison. My papa can do that. He told me.'

'I don't believe you,' the other little girl said, but her voice quavered.

'Papa will do everything I tell him to. And it's horrible in prison – there are bars and chains, and puddles on the floor and when you fall asleep at night, the mice and rats and spiders and beetles and snakes all come out of their holes and eat you alive.'

She was a plucky mite, but when he came round the box hedge, she screamed and backed away before breaking into a headlong run. He was appalled to discover the second child was smaller than Miranda. It must have been Nettie Parr. Miranda herself looked frightened at his sudden appearance.

Instinct led him to pursue the little fugitive. He had a vague idea that if he did not dispel the notion at once, she would look upon him as an ogre for ever after. But running after her only made her worse. She was so terrorstruck, she seemed blind to all obstacles.

By the time he succeeded in scooping her up, she was uttering ear-piercing shrieks and writhing convulsively, so he was in danger of dropping her. He tried to tell her he wasn't going to hurt her, but he couldn't make himself heard. Maria and her visitor appeared at the door. Mrs Parr began apologizing for her ill-mannered child, promising to punish her when they got home.

At this point he caught sight of Miranda's smug little smile as she watched the scene and it almost made him lose his temper before company.

'Why can't you be a good little girl, like Miss Miranda?' the unfortunate mother scolded.

'I'm afraid it is Miranda's fault, frightening her with stories,' he intervened, fishing in his pocket for some bonbons intended for Miranda, which he offered to the sobbing child.

She only shook her head and hid her tearstained face on her mother's shoulder. Miranda protested her innocence. He could see

16

the women were inclined to believe her and he knew he would have done so too if he had not heard what had passed between the girls.

My daughter is a hardened liar, he thought, appalled. And only five years old. Well, maybe not hardened. He remembered now what he had barely noticed then, the half-frightened, half-reproachful way she sidled up to him, tugged at the skirts of his coat and said, 'I *am* your little princess, aren't I, Papa?'

He shook her off, 'You're a changeling and nothing more.'

He didn't suppose she understood the word, but his tone and the way in which he stormed away from her raised a wail of despair. The sound cut him to the quick, but he forced himself not to turn back and comfort her, but to go into the library and shut the door.

He had cooled by the time the carriage drove away and he supposed the two mothers settled matters somehow. But he shuddered to see the telltale bulge in Miranda's cheek when she passed him in the hall on her way to the nursery. He didn't want to know how she had possessed herself of that bonbon and any others she might have in her apron pocket.

It seemed to him there had never been a perfect understanding between him and Miranda since that day. Other examples of her less amiable traits crowded in on him till he felt besieged by them. The way she assumed everyone, even her father, was at her beck and call. The way she evaded punishments or prohibitions from one parent by running to the other in tears. Almost within a day he was chilled to discover he was living with a stranger in the house.

He knew that, logically speaking, Miranda had not changed in a day. It must have happened while he wasn't paying attention or was wilfully blind. Every time he wanted to indulge her, that scene recurred to him. He tried to discipline her, but his wife undermined him. Being an ogre sapped his energy. Sometimes he gave up in despair and immersed himself in his duties instead.

Then Miranda would find some trick or wile to attract his attention and he felt ashamed of himself and tried to make amends. But she would become wayward or fretful as soon as she got her own way. It confused and wounded him. Did Miranda behave affectionately towards him because she loved him, or only because she

17

wanted something? Was she really so deceitful and manipulative? He missed adoring his little girl.

Miranda had spent some years at school. He felt it was better for her to be away from the increasingly bitter quarrelling between her parents, despite the forlorn tone of some of her letters. Others, however, were full of mischief, and after Maria's death, he found a second bundle of such letters to her mother. Maria herself never forgave him for sending their daughter away.

She had been home now for more than a year, ever since her mother's illness had worsened. He was relieved at his sister's offer to take Miranda with her to Buxton. She was at an age when he felt obscurely that a girl needed a mother's care. Sophia had a daughter about Miranda's age and the two of them could spend all night whispering and giggling together.

'Is that a new gown?' he asked, interrupting Miranda's monologue to the cat. He noticed for the first time the low, square *décolletage* of her striped gown over her still flat chest.

'I told you Mrs Collingham took me shopping with Ruth.' Her tones were defensive, as she brushed off the cat. 'Naughty puss, you'll spoil my gown. I need almost everything new – you haven't noticed, I suppose, how much I have grown in the last six months.'

'And I suppose the draper, the milliner and the mantua-maker will send their bills to me?'

He meant it in jest but her bottom lip stuck out a little further, making her look six again.

'You always say I'm extravagant, but I'm not. Not half as extravagant as Mary Parr or Nettie, or Sarah Lester. . . .'

'I believe you, child. And who else would I spend my money on if not you?'

Mollified, she scrambled over to him and laid her head on his knee, 'You'll miss me when I'm gone?'

'The house will be empty without you.'

'And you'll let me start powdering my hair?'

'Absolutely not. I've told you before, I refuse to discuss the matter for at least another year.'

'But Papa. . . .'

Chapter 2

*T*he baby was crying again, but no one had leisure to attend to him. Final preparations were being made to the stage. Mrs Boxall, clad only in shift, stays and upper petticoat over her hoop, was simultaneously trying to tie back the long fair hair of all three of her older boys, while Charlotte, her firstborn, hunted for missing shoe buckles, ribbons, scissors and papers of pins.

'I've never had a baby that cried before,' Mrs Boxall had said in perplexity more than once.

Augusta, who had been patiently nursing her only doll in the ladies' dressing-room, saw Bessy's lip begin to quiver in sympathy and slid down from the box on which she had been perched with a slight thump. She padded across to Nan Kemp, who was gathering together the black folds of Elizabeth's petticoat to lift it over her head.

' 'S crying again,' she announced, tugging at Nan's skirts.

'In a moment, Augusta.'

'Bessy's going to cry, too,' she added, glancing over her shoulder.

'Go on, Nan, I can manage.' Elizabeth's voice was muffled by the petticoat.

Nan draped herself in a towel to protect her costume and picked the baby up. Elizabeth shook the petticoat over her under petticoat and tied the tapes round her waist before reaching for her matching black silk gown. The room was not large, but each lady had her own mirror and a candle and chalk marks on the floor divided what space there was in equal shares.

'Someone has stepped on your train and torn it at the back,' Nan said. 'If you'll take the baby, I'll tack it up for you.'

Elizabeth took the writhing, red-faced mite and gave him her finger to chew. She watched Augusta patter across to Bessy and, cupping her hands, whisper something in her ear.

Of the children, only Johnny, the middle of the three boys, and Augusta showed promise as actors, though it was too soon to tell about Bessy. More than once, Mr Boxall had written his own lines to show off the crystal tones of Augusta, and Johnny was always the darling of the audience as the quick-witted smaller Prince in the Tower.

They joined the others in the green room as soon as they were ready. Mrs Boxall snatched the baby, as though afraid Elizabeth might poison him. The inevitable happened. Woken out of his drowse, the baby began to cry, jarring on everyone's nerves.

Mr Boxall bustled past, a hump fastened to one shoulder under his black tunic. As was his custom he began distributing paternal kisses on the women and as many children as he could find. At first, Elizabeth had been inclined to resent such familiarity from a man unrelated to herself, but she had been so tired and homesick that first night, she had not put on her middle-class dignity. And then, the nature of her profession meant she had to be prepared to be kissed and mauled about on stage.

She managed a twitchy smile at the manager's words of encouragement. No matter how well she knew her part, she needed this sense of fear before a play, because, if she was not afraid beforehand, she would suddenly be afraid on stage and then her performance would be groping, at least in her own ears.

'Your turn will come later.' Mr Boxall winked at Elizabeth and pinched her cheek.

Yes, later, when audiences dropped off, or when Mrs Boxall finally admitted she was tired, when the baby kept her awake, or the other children proved troublesome.

Edward Holbrook smiled and nodded at what he hoped were the right places, but his mind was elsewhere. Rather fastidious by nature, he hated crowds and vulgar bustle. Tonight there was not a single space left in the old barn an enterprising innkeeper had fitted up as a theatre.

There were four small boxes, into which the cream of local society, including himself, his daughter, sister and niece, had been crammed, rows and rows of rough wooden benches and a stage across which a faded curtain had been dragged. The press of so many bodies was creating an odour of sweat, perfume, dirt, lavender and beer, the preferred Nottinghamshire beverage.

He cast only the most cursory glance at the playbill. *The Tragedy of King Richard the Third* it announced in portentously large and elaborate lettering. An ambitious choice, no doubt hacked to pieces in order to reduce the number of roles.

The play seemed to have been chosen with an eye to the glory of the Boxall family. The actor-manager was to play the lead role, with his wife as Queen Elizabeth and no fewer than four of the Boxall offspring in the various children's roles.

The other names were meaningless to him and he wondered about the raven-haired beauty whose image had intruded on him at intervals since that meeting on the road. She had been on his mind when Mr Boxall had called, ostensibly to thank him for lending them his cart.

'Being an old soldier myself,' Boxall added, 'I thought maybe we could have a benefit night for the relief of some honest soldiers, crippled in battle, or to maintain the widows and fatherless children of those killed fighting the American rebels.'

He listened in silence to the actor's pious sentiments about how he hoped, should anything happen to him, someone would take pity on his own wife and children. Boxall had measured up his audience and Mr Holbrook could see he was straying into self-parody.

'When I think of poor Macduff and what he must have suffered. . . .'

He cut Boxall short at that, amused by him, and promised to enquire about a fit object for the players' charity. As he was leaving, the actor turned back one last time.

'If you should hear of anyone, sir, both Mrs Boxall and Miss Hathaway are willing to give music lessons to young ladies' – Boxall knew perfectly well his host had a daughter – 'and when a young

21

gentleman has needed instruction in clarity of diction, if he was going into Parliament or taking orders, I have been known to give a little advice that way. All for a very reasonable fee.'

By this time Mr Holbrook had begun to grow impatient and, under the influence of his grave eye, the actor-manager made a hasty exit.

Since that interview, he had had little time for thought. Preparations for Miranda's departure disrupted the whole house. He had been asked to arbitrate in several disputes between Miranda and Mrs Morris, the housekeeper, on the subject of what should or shouldn't be packed.

Then there were protracted negotiations with his daughter about how much money it was wise to trust her with, the sum she absolutely needed to avoid debt being about twice the amount he thought would have sufficed for a much longer and more expensive holiday.

They had compromised, but not without tears, accusations, lamentations and a lecture on the value of money, the disgrace of debt and why the Duchess of Devonshire was not a desirable model for a girl of limited means.

The opening scene confirmed Mr Holbrook's low expectations of the play. Mr Boxall was not *very* bad – he had seen worse – but he was stiff and declamatory and lacked the spark of an evil genius at work. Edward could not help wishing he had chosen a comedy instead, at which he obviously excelled, judging from his performance in the library at Woodlands.

At least the crowd had grown quieter and he could concentrate on his own thoughts as his gaze drifted round the auditorium. The press and throng in the small building had made it rather warm already and he hoped he would not fall asleep.

He smiled grimly at the witticisms about Edward IV's wife and mistress. It was no easy matter to be torn in separate directions by two women. He knew that from experience. It was safer to stay aloof, because once they had you in their grasp, they moulded you like molten wax.

But although it had ended bitterly, he felt a sudden upsurge of longing for Julia. And, struggling out of the mists of time, even the memory of his wife as she had been during the first years of their marriage welled up inside him.

He knew this mood, however. If he did not crush it down he would begin to regret things, done and undone, to dwell on things that could not be changed, and did not matter any more.

It was a voice that broke him out of his bitter thoughts. There was something familiar about it, something connected with excitement. For a moment, it even struck him that it was Julia's voice. His eyes flew to the stage. Of course it was not Julia. Julia was where he would never see her again. But his eyes remained fixed on the female figure on the stage.

With a tremor, he realized that this was the one truly talented member of the cast. In response, the actor-manager changed his style, fired by her mixture of defiance, fear and vulnerability, even innocence.

He would never have thought her capable of such depth. The mocking female on the dusty road seemed only fit to play light, flirtatious roles. But her interpretation of Lady Anne Neville had a radiance that the brilliant, knowing creatures of modern comedy lacked.

He did not take his eyes from her while she remained on stage. She was not a conventional beauty. Her raven hair contrasted with a pure white skin. Her gaze was intense; her figure graceful. The crudely painted scenery faded away, the shabby costumes. Nothing else mattered.

He watched her yielding to the villain, flattered, awed and seduced by having her enemy apparently in her power, moved in spite of herself to regard Gloucester not as an incarnation of evil, but as a man capable of deep passion.

He gazed breathlessly as she discovered that even hatred did not allow her to kill in cold blood. As Richard slid his ring upon her finger, Edward Holbrook almost felt her hand between his own, her quick, warm breath upon his cheek. Then, with a half-hearted attempt at resuming her earlier contempt, she was gone and the stage was a desert.

Edward let out a long breath, glancing stealthily at his companions to see if they had noticed his absorption. The blood was coursing through his veins, yet everyone around him seemed calm and unmoved.

He remembered the mocking eyes under that high forehead and beribboned hat. She herself had suggested he might bid for her. All actresses were whores by another name; no better than they should be, as the saying went. Why should he feel so uneasy?

'I'll have her, but I will not keep her long.'

Words leapt out at him from Gloucester's soliloquy, voicing his secret desire. It was true he was much older than her – she could be barely ten years older than his daughter, maybe less – but like Richard, he did not intend to keep her long. She would warm his bed nicely during her brief stay in this area. His wife was dead. What was there to stop him now?

Tonight he was hampered by his family. By the time they had gone, it might be too late. He didn't deceive himself he would be the only man to show an interest in Lady Anne. The thought of sharing a mistress with any man, especially one younger than himself, was repugnant to him.

If he could palm Miranda off on his sister while she bad farewell to her friends for one last time, he might be able to slip behind the scenes after the play. Boxall for one would be only too pleased to see an influential patron.

> Upon my life, she finds – although I cannot –
> Myself to be a marvellous proper man.

He knew he was as good-looking – maybe more so, more distinguished – as he had been at twenty-four, the age at which he married. Maybe she preferred a mature man to a green boy like Frank Collingham. Better an old man's darling than a young man's scorn. Not that he would admit to being old. And he was rich enough to tempt most girls.

His eyes ran down the playbill. Lady Anne Neville – Miss Hathaway. He paused. It was unusual for an actress to be unmarried. Those who had not already been deserted by a feckless husband made a marriage of convenience during their first season or adopted the title 'Mrs' without having any right to it, thus preserving a veneer of respectability.

But he did not see Miss Hathaway's status as a single woman as a serious obstacle. All it meant was that there would be no jealous oaf or sycophantic pimp to complicate negotiations. If all else failed, he could maybe threaten her with the House of Correction. But it would not come to that. Since that business with Julia, he had never allowed a woman to get the better of him.

Surreptitiously he glanced at his watch. It would be a weary long time till Miss Hathaway was on the stage again. Apart from a brief appearance as a ghost on the eve of the Battle of Bosworth, she had only one more scene.

Older, wiser, embittered, yet still compassionate towards Queen Elizabeth at the death of her sons in the Tower, Lady Anne would acknowledge the folly of her marriage to the enemy she cursed. She would shrink from the bitter responsibility of being queen under such circumstances and soon after that she would be dead. He would be in a fever until her saw her again.

She picked her way through the chaos of the green room, Nan trailing in her wake. Mr Boxall was introducing a gentleman to his wife and Elizabeth recognized Mr Holbrook. She also recognized the way his eyes darted towards her and the contemptuous smile on the lips of the former beauty.

Before Elizabeth joined the troupe nearly three years ago, Mrs Boxall was its undisputed queen. She might, in time, have grudgingly yielded that title to one of her daughters, but she resented this premature usurpation.

At first glance most people would not have believed that this statuesque, fair-haired woman was the mother of seven live children and two or three dead ones. She had married young and ten, even five, years ago she must have been exquisite, but her way of life was taking its toll. The men noticed nothing, but the actresses marvelled at the self-discipline with which she had regained her figure and returned to the stage almost as soon as her youngest child was born.

Mr Boxall stopped them before they reached the dressing-room door. 'Don't go, girls. Mr Holbrook, may I present Miss Hathaway, Miss Kemp.'

Both young women curtsied.

'Charming,' Mr Holbrook remarked, 'and still young enough to blush.'

Elizabeth felt a cold finger probe beneath her chin and tilt her face to the light. But that trick worked both ways. Her eyes met his fearlessly.

'That is a malady time will soon cure.'

'I hope not,' he paused, his eyes scorching her skin. 'I wished to tell you how much I was moved by your performance tonight.'

'Thank you, sir,' she curtsied again, but allowed the faintest trace of irony to appear in her voice. Clearly he heard and understood it, since he flushed slightly.

Nevertheless, he made a joke about coming to bid for her after all, if the offer was still open. He was so obviously uneasy, she felt sorry for him, and flirted with him until he thawed. Somehow, probably with Mr Boxall's connivance, he managed to draw her aside. He lowered his voice and that in itself warned her of what was to follow.

'If I sent my carriage for you tomorrow night, would you have supper with me?'

She smiled but took her time choosing a reply. 'I suspect that might be unwise.'

'Madam, that was the wrong answer.'

'Sir, it was the wrong question.'

Mrs Boxall was watching them with narrowed eyes. There would be trouble later.

'Well, I won't take offence, since you have left me a glimmer of hope,' he smiled provokingly and cut short her reply. 'No, not another word. You might say too much and then be afraid to change your mind. Take time to consider. Goodnight, Miss Hathaway.'

He seemed suddenly in a hurry, as if he had forgotten an appointment, and it was with difficulty that he shook off Mr Boxall.

She shrugged. It was too much trouble to disillusion him about the power of his charms. Trying to justify herself might only persuade him she laid more emphasis on their conversation than she did. He would learn soon enough that she knew her own mind perfectly.

Elizabeth studiously talked of other things while she changed out of her costume. She loitered a moment after the others had gone to make sure everything was in order in the dressing-room. As she shut the door, she was startled by a voice behind her.

'I heard what he said and you're not to go.'

'Are you there, Will?' she replied vaguely, drawing her cloak closer around her. 'You'll see Nan and me safely to our door, won't you?'

'Did you hear what I said? You're not to go.'

'Will's right, Elizabeth. You can't possibly . . .' Nan began.

'Oh, how tired I am,' she yawned. 'I wonder if it is possible to fall asleep on your feet?'

'I forbid it, Lizzie.' He clenched her arm and Elizabeth steadied herself with a deep breath.

'You forbid it? And what right have you to do that?'

'By the right I have of – of loving you.'

'You presume too far. I permit you to love me, if you must, but I won't let you curtail my freedom.' It was so absurd. She had absolutely no intention of accepting Mr Holbrook's invitation. But Will Ramsay's possessiveness annoyed her.

'Then you do intend to go,' he persisted, scanning her face. 'You intend to let that man, who doesn't care tuppence for you, touch you and – and. . . .' Words failed him and he flushed scarlet at the scene he had conjured up.

'And what, pray? I am curious.'

'Never you mind.'

Elizabeth shrugged. Nan was looking at her with pleading eyes and she found it hard to steel her heart against her. But it frustrated her that, for all his boasted love, Will knew so little about her character. She plunged out into the darkness, shivering slightly. There was a hint of autumn in the air. Will would not give up.

'Why that man?'

'Why any man? Does it matter much?'

'It matters to me. And you always said you'd never marry anyone you didn't love. You wouldn't even let me kiss you, 'cept on stage, because you said you didn't love me enough.'

And yet, with all these carefully hoarded hints, he still persisted in

27

seeing the situation in his own distorted way. She pinched her lips and made her way round an unidentifiable mound of something rotting, which obstructed half the pavement. She couldn't help teasing him.

'He's old, Lizzie.'

'Not so very old. And I'm not so very young. At my age, Mrs B was the mother of five.'

'He's a widower with a daughter of marriageable age.'

Elizabeth raised her eyebrows. Will, then, had taken an interest in his rival beforehand.

'He's rich, I believe.'

'And I'm not. Is that all that matters to you?'

'If it were, do you think I would still be with this troupe?'

It was only a short distance, past the market place and along the uneven pavement, to their inn, taking care to avoid the open sewer and other indistinct obstacles. There were only about twenty lamps scattered about the entire town and many of the windows were already dark.

The smell of decay had long since ceased to trouble Elizabeth and she paid no heed to dark shapes scurrying away from the halo of Will's lantern. She had never been afraid of mice or rats and, all in all, it was admirable how quickly it was possible to adapt to rough conditions, even after a life of, if not quite luxury, then at least of comfort.

Mr Boxall had obtained rooms for his family and the two young women at the cheapest inn in the town, till they could find other lodgings. Elizabeth and her companions arrived there in time to see a ramshackle vehicle disgorging an apparently endless stream of fair-haired children, whose precious voices had to be protected from the unhealthy night air.

The landlady herself was perched on the doorstep like a bird of ill-omen, peering and counting them, as though afraid that, for unknown reasons, an additional child or two might be smuggled on to her premises. Will loitered, searching for a ploy to delay Elizabeth. She dismissed him with a curt goodnight, but it was Mrs Boxall who settled matters.

'Here, Mr B, take the baby,' she said, ' I want to speak to Miss H. Goodnight, Mr Ramsay.'

And, as though the pair had planned it together, the landlady slapped the door shut and began locking and bolting it, mumbling something under her breath.

The entire troupe, including Mr Boxall, knew those tones all too well and melted away up the staircase at the other end of the taproom. The demonic flickering of candles cast their shadows up the wall and halfway back across the low ceiling.

The landlady hobbled and mumbled her way to the kitchen to make sure all was safe there.

They were left in darkness, save for one tallow candle. The smell of melting animal fat always made Elizabeth feel qualmish. The little circle of light seemed an enchanted yet dangerous place. Finally Mrs Boxall broke the silence.

'Mr Holbrook spoke to you for a good while.'

'He was praising the play,' Elizabeth risked a lie. 'He was charmed by the children.'

Mrs Boxall's face did not visibly relax.

'I know perfectly well what Mr Holbrook wanted,' she continued in the same low, even tones, 'and I warn you, if you spurn him as you have spurned other influential men, I'll have my husband turn you off.'

It was not an idle threat, yet Elizabeth could not repress an ironic smile.

'Don't smile at me. I won't stand your impudence, with your white face and your grand airs. If you want respectability, go back to wherever it is you come from, if they'll have you. One of these days you'll push Mr B too far – don't be deceived by his easy ways, I know him better – and then you may go starve or sell your face for far less than you'd get now if you were wise.'

'I suppose that is how you manage to keep all those children, or maybe how you came by them in the first place. How many fathers did Bessy have at last count? Four? Five?'

The slap came almost before she had time to register the fire in her opponent's eyes.

'Don't you *ever* think I am your inferior,' Mrs Boxall hissed, her face very close to Elizabeth's, the candle making her cheekbones prominent and her eyes hollow.

'You mean you'll drag me down to your level any way you can.'
It was unwise to provoke her further, but Elizabeth couldn't help
herself. She wasn't going to show she was afraid.

'I won't warn you again. Displease Mr Holbrook at your own
peril.'

She turned and swept upstairs. Elizabeth was forced to follow as
she didn't care to wait in the dark for the landlady's return. Luckily
Nan opened their door at the sound of footsteps and Elizabeth
groped her way to the light.

She passed her friend without a word and threw herself face
down on the bed. She didn't know whether to laugh or cry. Mrs
Boxall ordering her to become Holbrook's mistress, Will Ramsay
forbidding it, respectable citizens decrying the morals of actors and
taking advantage of them. Her own opinions and desires of no
account to anyone, least of all Mr Holbrook. . . .

Nan sat down on the bed beside her. Elizabeth tugged at the
ribbons of her cloak in silence.

'What will you do?' Nan ventured. 'You don't intend to go, do
you?'

'No, I don't and I never said I did.' She turned on to her side.

'But why do you provoke poor Will? He loves you so much. Why
don't you marry him?'

She had never taken Nan fully into her confidence, but tonight
she needed a friend.

'Many, many reasons. Because I don't love him, that's one. And
if I did marry him for safety's sake, what would become of me if I
fell in love with someone else? And, well. . . .'

'You don't have to say any more. If you don't love him, you don't
love him.'

Nan rose to hang up the cloak from a hook on the door, but
Elizabeth caught a faint ghost of her face in the spotted mirror.

'But *you* do, don't you, Nan?' The revelation was so sudden, it
took her breath away.

Nan hid her face in her hands, so her plump shoulders hunched
up, but she said quickly, 'No, I don't. I wouldn't.'

There was no point in forcing her to confess.

'The plain fact is, I'm ambitious. I know it is an unwomanly thing to say, but I can't help it. I want an engagement in London or Bath, where all the fashionable people go.' Elizabeth sat up and began to unbuckle her shoes. First one, then the other thumped on the bare floorboards.

'If I were married to Will, maybe they wouldn't want me. Will does well enough in this troupe, but he'll never be a second Garrick. I'm afraid no company would take a wife without her husband, or at least without his permission. And I don't know if a man's pride could bear to have a wife who was richer, more successful than himself. That is, if I'm good enough.'

'I know you could do it,' Nan said. 'When you're on stage, I believe every word you say. I mean – you're not just pretending, you really are Ophelia or Goneril or Calista.'

'Goneril and Calista,' she sighed. 'Much as I relish the role, don't you see the absurdity of my playing Mrs B's older sister? And Calista – I will never be Calista again while I stay here, unless Mrs B falls a-breeding again. I cannot go on waiting for her – heaven forbid – to die in childbed. She is trying to persuade Mr B that Charlotte could play most of my roles.'

'Charlotte Boxall doesn't have a smidgen of your talent,' Nan declared stoutly, suddenly hugging her. Elizabeth returned the squeeze round her waist.

'I know that and so do the Boxalls. I had hoped that once I showed him what I could do, Mr B might let me keep some of my larger roles.'

'And he has. You know he has.'

'But not enough. I've had a taste of glory. I don't want to return to being bosom friends and sisters and cousins again unless there is a hope I might progress.'

Chapter 3

*E*lizabeth paused at the top of the stairs, hearing her name behind a door. It was a bitter night and she had run up to fetch her muff before they left for the theatre. Nan was waiting but, however painful it might be, it was impossible to take a step further.

Mrs Boxall was tearfully accusing her husband of being in love with Elizabeth, not because she believed it, but because she felt it was her strongest weapon against her rival.

'You want her to take my place.'

'Not at all. But unless we let her fret and strut her hour upon the stage, she will leave.'

'I wish she would.'

'Nay, but sweetheart,' Mr Boxall wheedled, 'you must admit we didn't lose money while you were so ill. I don't say she could replace you – no one who saw you both in the same role could ever compare you – but she did well enough and though I much prefer your style, you know there are some people who like her mannerisms and so forth.'

Elizabeth curled her lip. She told herself she didn't care if this was Boxall's real opinion or not. Either way she had no cause to thank him. Mrs Boxall was silent, apparently willing to be mollified by a little more talk in the same vein.

'Suppose some nights we let her play the heroine so you can rest. I know you're not strong yet, for all you bear up so bravely, so I shouldn't worry, and you can choose your own roles. . . .'

Elizabeth tore herself away. Her head ached. The bustle in the courtyard beneath her window had woken her at dawn, after only a few short hours' rest.

She noticed Will as soon as she entered the green room. She felt a tight knot forming within her. It was at these times, when her mask of good humour was at its frailest, that it was unwise to provoke her. She held herself at the ready, expecting that Will would try to talk to her alone. He threw her a reproachful look and turned his back on her. Somehow the simple gesture made her feel rejected. To her shock, she even felt tears rise in her eyes.

Before she could recover, Mr Boxall breezed up, kissed both her and Nan for luck and added, pinching Elizabeth's cheek, 'Tomorrow night, Miss Hathaway. Be sure you sleep well tonight – we want you to be as radiant as possible. Rehearsal at the usual hour.'

She was cheered in spite of herself. She had been unfair. If he did not fear his life would be made unendurable unless he appeased his wife from time to time, Mr Boxall would have given preference to Elizabeth above every other actress in the troupe.

Though her part in the main play was short, she played the title role of the farce which followed, Garrick's *Miss in her Teens*. She struggled to keep a straight face, while goading two inappropriate suitors into a duel to expose their cowardice. Every burst of laughter from the audience raised her spirits and when she had bounded off the stage, she caught hold of Nan and whirled around with her, despite lack of space.

They chattered merrily as they changed their gowns and wrapped themselves up. Elizabeth pushed aside the idea which had struck her in her short scenes with Will, who played her lover. He had gazed at her so earnestly, she suspected he had really been trying to woo her.

She knew from experience that Will sometimes found it difficult to believe she was only pretending on the stage. But they had spent so little time together, she could not be sure she had any cause for unease. He was waiting for her in the green room.

'Miss Hathaway, do you forgive me?'

The assignation with Mr Holbrook had almost slipped her mind in her exhilaration at her success, but she was jolted back into the nightmare. Nonetheless she smiled and assured him she was in charity with the whole world. But he would not let the matter drop, trying to extract a promise from her that she would not go to meet the rich widower.

Elizabeth felt her naturally perverse nature asserting itself. She did not like to be forced into anything. Nor did she want Will to believe he could command her whenever he pleased.

'Why won't you give me your word?' His face darkened again.

'You are in danger of repeating your earlier offence.'

'Miss Hathaway,' a voice called.

Elizabeth barely noticed, but her companion turned to look. Mrs Boxall, who had been addressed by the liveried footman, tossed her ringlets and pointed in Elizabeth's direction.

'You intended to go without telling me,' Will said slowly. 'You intended to lie to me, maybe send me on some fool's errand, so I shouldn't know you had gone to him.'

'You allow your imagination too much free rein, Mr Ramsay.' Elizabeth began pushing her way through the crowd, unaware that Nan, being less ruthless and less angry, was left behind.

'You must not go. Stay with me,' he pleaded. 'It is the last thing I shall ever ask of you.'

'I am tired of repeating this conversation whenever we meet. Let go of me.' She saw Mrs Boxall's gloating eyes, but she didn't care.

'Miss Hathaway.' The voice was closer now and she looked up. 'Mr Holbrook's chaise is waiting.'

'Oh. Oh, thank you.'

'Elizabeth!'

She was only ten steps from the carriage. She fully intended to sweep past it, but the crowd hampered her. She felt as though everyone was watching, but Will seemed past caring. He would be unendurable if she gave in now. He would dog her all the way to her lodgings. The door was open, the steps down. If she could persuade Nan to follow her, she would be safe.

It was the work of a moment. She flounced up and threw herself into the seat. The steps clattered up, the door banged with the speed and efficiency of long practice before she could call Nan's name, let alone locate her in the confusion. The carriage lurched forward almost before the footman had time to spring into his place.

Will had no dignity. He tried to wrench open the door, scrabbled at the window, still pleading, protesting, commanding. Elizabeth leaned back in her seat and closed her eyes to obliterate his face, but it remained imprinted on her inner eye.

She had been propelled by anger, but she had not completely lost her faculties. By the time they reached the market place, her heart had almost resumed its usual rhythm. They were not far from her lodgings. She pulled the communication cord. There was no response, but she would not be defeated so easily. She drew down the window and leaned out her head and shoulders.

'Excuse me! Would you mind setting me down here? I'm sure I can find my own way. . . .' They rattled on in stolid silence. 'Excuse me, will you stop a moment?'

If anything, the coachman urged his horses faster and they had turned into a winding lane of an unsavoury appearance. Elizabeth sank back into her seat, letting her breath out in a slow hiss.

The truth dawned on her. The servants were under strict instructions not to slow or stop or heed anything she said. Nothing she could offer them could compensate for their master's displeasure. She was not rich enough to bribe them and any other charms she had were confined, invisible and useless, inside the carriage.

She would have to face the consequences of her action. If nothing else, her reputation would suffer, unless she could find means to return to her lodgings within a short space of time, and crying would not do her a bit of good. At least, not while there was no one to see her tears.

She shut the window. The draught might harm her voice. Even so, the vehicle was cold. She plunged her hands deep into her muff and pressed it to her face to help her think. It would be unwise to jump from the moving vehicle and anyway, they had passed the outskirts of the town. It was too late to scream for help and the locals seemed an uncouth lot, as far as she could judge. Better to fall into the hands of a gentleman than to risk insult or assault elsewhere.

They were retracing the route by which she had entered the town only a few days ago. She peered out, hoping to see some landmark, but the trees obscured what little moonlight there was.

35

She must prepare for her encounter with Mr Holbrook. She had no illusions about what he expected from her, but she had not the slightest intention of letting him have his way. She still retained some of her middle-class values, despite choosing this way of life. She had struggled too hard to preserve her chastity and her good name to let it come to this.

She had played this part often enough, or watched or read it. But Elizabeth felt a nagging fear at the back of her mind. Stratagems to persuade a seducer to spare his intended victim worked in comedies because they were foreordained to end happily. All too often in tragedies, the woman would kill herself, or trick the man into killing her, only minutes before help arrived.

However dear her virginity was to her, Elizabeth was not sure she was ready to die defending it. But she was exaggerating. It would not come to that. Even she could see those plays had been screwed up to the highest pitch in an attempt to make audiences weep.

This time she would have to write her own lines and her confidence in her ability as an actress wavered. She could not predict how the other character in this scene would react. She had only met him twice and then very briefly. She could hardly even remember what he looked like, except for those eyes. Her hand rose instinctively to make sure her muslin handkerchief was modestly covering her shoulders and breast, despite the low cut of her bodice.

They turned off the turnpike road and were now ascending a steep hill. The chaise slowed, the horses strained. Elizabeth shivered. Sherwood Forest was notoriously full of thieves, especially on moonless nights. By dint of peering out at one window, then the other, she caught a glimpse of lights on the right. She had not much time left. Should she play the innocent, deliberately misunderstanding his insinuations? Should she plead for mercy, or try to speak to him as an equal? Or insist haughtily on being taken back to town immediately?

They passed through the gates into a yard. The house rose on one side, the outbuildings on the other. The carriage door was opened. She gathered her petticoats and her foot groped for the step. The door of the house stood ajar and a masculine shape filled the patch of light.

She had a vague impression of an elderly servant, immaculate from powdered wig to white stockings and polished shoe buckles, as she stepped over the threshold, loosening her cloak. She was in a lofty, if rather narrow hall, with a staircase bending up one side and closed doors almost indistinguishable from the wood panelling. Dark rectangles decorated the wall above the stairs, but Elizabeth could make out little of the pictures, apart from pale blobs of faces and a white column, probably someone swathed in light material.

'Shall I take your cloak, 'm?'

'Oh, I shan't be staying long.'

The words escaped her before she had time to think. How strange it was it all came back to her. But the servant was looking at her with unamused eyes and it occurred to her that she was not simply paying a morning call at the parsonage. He picked up the sole candlestick and Elizabeth clutched her muff tighter in a effort not to panic.

'If you'd follow me, 'm,' he set his foot on the lowest step.

'I believe Mr Holbrook's invitation was to supper,' she quavered.

He turned back to her with the same dead-eyed stare. 'The master thought you'd find it more comfortable in his dressing-room than downstairs.'

Elizabeth hesitated, but there was no other light and she was in a strange place. She followed with a cautious tread. To relieve her feelings, she made a face at the back of the servant and another at the supercilious man in a portrait staring his disapproval at her.

The sense of familiarity was disturbing. The feel of carpet under-foot, the mingled smell of beeswax, good food and dying flowers, the hints of opulence revealed by the fitful flicker of the candle. The knot of dread, the sense of being stifled almost overwhelmed her.

'Miss Hathaway, sir.'

The servant stood aside. Raising her chin and looking straight ahead, Elizabeth entered the room and heard the door shut softly behind her.

There were two or three candles – real wax candles smelling of honey – lit about the room and even a moderate fire, though it was early in the season. But far from being comfortable in a small room,

37

Elizabeth felt the ceiling was pressing down on her, trapping her in her old life.

Like all eighteenth-century dressing-rooms, the name was a misnomer. It was a cosy sitting-room, a retreat from the outer world, with a sofa, several comfortable chairs and plenty of book-shelves. Elizabeth thought she caught traces of the late Mrs Holbrook in the hand-made firescreen, the embroidered footstool, maybe even the watercolour landscapes on the wall.

'Good evening, Miss Hathaway. Welcome to Woodlands.'

Elizabeth curtsied without moving a step closer. He stood by the fire and now she was in his presence, she remembered his broad forehead, straight nose and rather thin-lipped mouth. He would have looked unyieldingly stern, except for the vestiges of babyhood in the curve of his cheek and his cleft chin.

'Thank you, sir, but I cannot stay long,' she said, adopting her usual mask. 'I only came for politeness' sake, to offer my excuses for not coming. And now that is done, I would be grateful if you ordered the chaise to return me to my lodgings.'

The cleft chin rose and the lower lip protruded. The strongly marked eyebrows drew closer together, but Elizabeth could see it was not a genuine frown.

'I'm afraid that will not be possible at present. My horses have had a hard day – you must allow them at least half an hour's respite,' he said, 'and as you have come all this way, it would be foolish not to have supper while you wait.'

She had not expected him to let her go at once, but it seemed promising that he was willing to use a similar turn of phrase to her own.

'It's very kind of you, but really I have very little appetite. . . .'

Like a Judas, her stomach growled in response to the tempting smells. It had been such a long time since she had eaten anything but the plainest fare.

'Won't you at least take a glass of wine?' He did not take his eyes off her face as he approached. 'Or are you in such a vast hurry as to wish to dispense with all preliminaries?'

She felt a hot wave slap her cheeks. She had to keep her head. It was a dangerous game she was playing. The tiger whose tummy she was tickling now might bite her hand at any moment.

'Thank you, you are very kind. And maybe I will have a bite to eat. It seems such a shame to waste it. The cook would be offended, I daresay, to have her efforts slighted.'

'You talk a good deal,' Mr Holbrook observed.

She set down her muff on a corner of the sofa and felt fire-warmed fingers linger on her shoulder as he helped remove her cloak.

'It's my worst fault.' She mustered the radiant smile she used for comic heroines. 'But then, you see, talking is my profession. Papa always said I should make gossiping a paid occupation so I need never starve, but I don't suppose he ever believed it was possible.'

He looked uncomfortable and she guessed he would rather know as little about her as possible, so he could think of her as a doll or puppet rather than a person.

'I must look a fright. At least, I suppose that is why you are look-ing at me like that,' she went on, to spare him the necessity of asking questions. 'Will you excuse me a moment?'

A candle had been placed in front of the mirror to reflect the light and she could see enough of herself to arrange her ringlets, straighten her lace cap and pin her handkerchief firmly to her stom-acher with her only brooch, in the hopes of deterring wandering fingers.

She caught his eyes, reflected in the mirror. She knew so little about him. Was there any danger he would forget himself suffi-ciently to become violent, when she disappointed him? Her glass had been filled and she took a sip to steady herself. She needed no more coaxing to help herself liberally from every dish set before her and she noticed he looked askance at her plate.

Throughout the meal she continued to chatter nonsense to fill the void. He did not seem inclined to talk much and was as secre-tive about his life as she was about hers. He merely picked at the food, drank two or three glasses of wine, and occasionally glanced at a clock behind her right shoulder, being too well bred to pull out his fob watch.

Disconcertingly, Elizabeth discovered her glass never seemed to get any emptier, but she was still sober enough to see he was trying to make her drunk. He finally broke his silence when she began helping herself to a second portion.

'For someone with no appetite, you eat a good deal.'

She paused, looked down at her plate and tilted her head thoughtfully to one side.

'I suppose it must look that way,' she conceded, leaning towards him across the table, 'but if you knew how often I have to satisfy myself with a scrag end of mutton or a chicken so thin, it is nothing but bones, not to mention the days when there is no meat at all. . . .'

Mr Holbrook's smile did not reach his eyes, 'A handsome girl like you should be able to secure herself a rich protector and then you could eat in this style every night.'

'Oh, but that is just what I don't want.' Elizabeth left her fork hovering halfway to her mouth. 'You see, I am proud. I had far rather eat mutton I had earned than – than venison or pheasant I had not.' She started raising her fork, but seeing he was about to speak, she added, 'I love my profession far too much to give it up.'

'I'm sure there are men who would be willing to let their mistresses appear on stage, as long as they remained faithful,' he remarked drily.

She shook her head sadly. 'I shouldn't care for that at all, to work long hours in the theatre and then be expected to dress and be amusing all the time and never complain when I was neglected or ill-treated.'

He glanced distastefully at her plate, knit his eyebrows and began beating a tattoo on the tablecloth with his blunt fingertips. He did not deign to reply and she went on, expatiating on the freedom an actress enjoyed, to travel and to be whoever she chose.

'Oh, sometimes I am tired and out of spirits and I perform badly or make mistakes, but the money I earn is mine by rights and not the result of some gentleman's whim and. . . .'

He had had enough, however, and cut her short. 'Much as I enjoy your conversation, this was not the purpose of your visit,' he said, rising.

Spin it out as long as she could, Elizabeth recognized that supper was over. Eating so late would have dire effects on her digestion and sleep.

''You are right, sir,' she said, also rising. 'It is late and I ought to return to town. If you would just ring the bell for the. . . .'

His hawk-like eyes bore into her and for the first time her voice faltered. Moreover he must have heard it, too. To her surprise, Mr Holbrook reached for the bellrope.

'Won't you take a seat by the fire until everything is ready?'

Elizabeth couldn't imagine what he meant by this apparent acquiescence, but did as she was bid. The warmth of the fire and a full stomach made her sleepy. Her feet ached to be free of her shoes, her ribs to escape the restriction of her stays. Instinctively she groped for her cloak.

The servants whisked away the remains of supper and Mr Holbrook went as far as the door to murmur something to one of them. She knew that circumstance ought to make her suspicious, but her eyes were suddenly dropping shut. Surely he had not drugged her wine? That would defeat his whole purpose.

She was roused by him sitting down on the sofa beside her.

'Well, is my carriage ordered?' She forced herself to sound sprightly.

'Presently. All in good time.' His fingertips brushed down her cheek and neck to her shoulder. Elizabeth shrank. Quite dispassionately she noted how handsome he was. Only three faint lines etched in his forehead indicated his age. And yet she felt nothing towards him, except perhaps the first tentacles of fear.

'You have a very unusual beauty.'

'My great-grandmother was Welsh. But I have intruded upon you too long already.'

His grip tightened on her shoulder, he leaned closer. She could feel his knee against her leg.

'Would it not be bad manners to leave so soon after eating?'

Her sleeve ripped as she pulled herself away and placed a chair between them, 'I hope you do not treat all your guests in this manner.' She made a last attempt at child-like innocence.

'You are no ordinary guest.' He whisked the chair away with the casualness of a conjurer performing a trick, but she took refuge behind the table. The door was not far, but she measured the distance carefully.

'All the more reason to treat me with some consideration.'

He laughed at this and came closer. 'You have an answer for everything, I see.'

41

Elizabeth bit her lips. She needed a clear head to get out of this situation unscathed.

'Or have I caught you out?' Mr Holbrook asked. 'Have I silenced you at last?'

'By no means, sir, since I have no weapon but my tongue to preserve my virginity.' The desperation was audible in her voice, but the smile, which remained fixed on his lips, suddenly looked cruel in her eyes. 'I appeal to you in the name of your daughter. May she never plead in vain against a seducer or – or ravisher.'

Even to her own ears the words sounded melodramatic. A look of boredom glazed his eyes and he sighed. 'Sweetheart, you play the virgin prettily enough on stage; there is no need to continue the charade afterwards.'

With a rustle of petticoats, she reached the door. He made no attempt to follow her, as she cast a defiant glance back at him. Her hand closed over the doorknob. 'You have no right to keep me here against my will.'

The squire sat down on the arm of a chair.

'You realize, my tempter, that you are in *my* power, under *my* roof, with *my* servants at *my* beck and call, and no transport except at *my* command?'

'You own a great many things, Mr Holbrook, but you do not own me.' Her heart quailed nonetheless, picturing the long walk back through dark woods along a half-known road. A mile was nothing by daylight, but at this hour. . . .

'This part of Sherwood Forest is known as Thieves Wood,' he added, still watching her through narrowed eyes. 'Only last week one of my horses was taken. I imagine that ruffians will be less considerate towards a tender morsel like yourself than I am.'

Elizabeth felt sick to the pit of her stomach. Her cloak was hanging from the crook of her left arm, which she pressed under her ribs in an effort to spur herself on. Every step of the way, supposing she was allowed to leave, would be a nightmare.

But better that than this, her heart whispered. She could not let him frighten her. She shut her eyes as she turned the doorknob. If she could convince him she was in earnest, perhaps. . . .

The door refused to budge. She rattled it slightly, but she knew in an instant what had happened. She thought she even remembered the telltale click as he turned the key while she drowsed by the fire.

Elizabeth leaned her forehead against the door. She discovered she was reluctant to turn and face his self-satisfied smirk. Again she felt walls closing in on her.

'If you want the key, I have it in my waistcoat pocket. Why don't you come and look for it?'

'Aren't you afraid I'll pick your pockets of other valuables too since you think so meanly of my character?' Elizabeth felt a surge of bitterness. She stayed by the door, waiting for his next move and trying desperately to think of a way out.

'Character!' he was laughing at her again. 'Oh, every actress has a *character*.'

She swished round to face him, resenting the insinuation in his voice.

'You have mistaken me for Mrs Boxall, I fear.' She tossed her head, her eyes flashing. 'Her character is indeed what you think mine, though she hides behind her marriage. There's not one of her children that doesn't have a different father, or so 'tis said. But I don't have a husband to protect me and I will not destroy my hopes of happiness and success for an ageing Lothario.'

He winced at the epithet and his eyes grew darker. She had caught him on the raw.

'I will not be insulted in my own house. I am offering a fair price for your company tonight – and the rest of your stay here, if you should suit me – but beware how you provoke me.'

'My price is above anything you could ever pay,' her voice trembled, as she backed away.

He uttered a short bark of a laugh. 'You have courage, minx. And what fabulous sum do you consider you are worth?'

'My price is love.'

There was a moment's silence. He tried ineffectually to wipe the irritation from his face, 'Well, then, sweetheart, if that be all, I love you to distraction.'

'You mistake me, sir. I did not mean your love; I meant mine. I can only belong to a man who inspires me to love him.'

A flush crept over his face as he realized the implications of her words. There was a conflict of doubt and conviction in his eyes, but doubt won out.

'And that is why you make assignations with gentlemen? To pursue your quest for love?'

'I did not come to please you, but to spite someone else. I begged your servants to let me out at my lodgings. I never intended to come – I told you that.' But she hadn't told him, or she couldn't remember doing so. Her vision was blurred. She could not read his expression.

'And I'm sorry I came.' She sounded like a pettish child about to cry. Not at all dignified or eloquent as she had intended to be. She was exhausted. That was her only excuse.

Mr Holbrook turned away impatiently. 'And what am I meant to do with you?'

'Send me home.'

'I'll send you to the devil first. You understood the terms on which I invited you. You cannot deny it. I should send you to the House of Correction as a vagabond and – and a whore.'

'Then you are a hypocrite to punish me for a sin I refuse to commit. I am not afraid of you.'

'You ought to be.'

He snatched her arm before she could get out of reach. In spite of her words, Elizabeth was too scared to look in his eyes. She could not judge what he was capable of. It ought to have been easy to pull herself away and yet she remained paralysed, watching his lips form his next words.

'Would you be something of a favourite with your company if I invoked the full force of the Theatre Licensing Act of 1737? I assume Mr Boxall has neither letters patent from His Majesty King George, nor a licence from the Lord Chamberlain to act, present or perform any play for hire, gain or reward?' As a precaution before her arrival, he had read his lawbooks till he had the whole act virtually by heart. 'You know how vagabonds and rogues are punished, I take it?'

She knew. Imprisonment, whipping, being dispersed back to the places where each individual could claim settlement under the

Elizabethan Poor Law, which was still in force 200 years after it had been enacted.

She might be spared these humiliations if she managed to send word in time to her family. But that might be the worst humiliation of all, an admission of failure, a voluntary laying of her head on the block of respectability. They would make her suffer for her rebellion.

'I believe an alderman tried to arrest an actor in Nottingham some years ago and roused the full fury of the mob against himself,' Elizabeth replied, dimly recalling a story Nan had told her. 'Abuse what little power you have. *I* cannot stop you.'

He released her with a little push which threw her down on to the sofa. He said nothing for a good while, but through the haze of a blinding headache, she could hear his angry breathing.

They were deadlocked. A clock chimed and, in anguish, Elizabeth realized it was already too late for her. Even if by some miracle she could reach her lodgings, someone would have to let her in. Everyone would know. She had been away too long. Her reputation was in tatters.

'I am not a cruel man.' Mr Holbrook cleared his throat. 'I'd treat you kindly enough. You can have anything you ask for, within reason.'

She pushed a stray strand of hair which had become uncurled off her face. She braced herself as, hitching up the skirts of his long coat, he perched on the corner of the sofa beside her.

'I apologize if I have mistaken your character, but you must admit appearances are against you,' he said stiffly. His fingers fumbled as he took her hand, almost caressingly. 'You remind me of the swans on my lake. I watch them from my window while I am. . . .'

Window. The word roused her failing faculties. She didn't hear the rest of his sentence.

'I should like to see them,' she said faintly, staggering to her feet. The room swam. He made an attempt to keep hold of her hand but she slid it free just in time.

'You won't see much at this hour,' he snapped, but he remained where he was.

She knelt on the windowseat and leaned her forehead against the glass. It misted up directly. The pond was a glimmer in the smudge of darkness, with a single white petal in its midst. Glancing up, she could see thin clouds skimming across the face of the moon.

She had the vague impression that Mr Holbrook was speaking, trying to justify himself or woo her. She wasn't sure which. She squinted down. There was a path at the foot of the house, but she found it difficult to judge what it was made of – gravel or flag-stones? – or the distance. Could she haul herself on to the windowsill and drop down? Would she be badly injured? A broken leg might cripple her for life. But at least it was a way of showing him she was in deadly earnest. It was not as if this was the first time she had climbed out of a window.

Elizabeth glanced over her shoulder. He had walked across to the mantelpiece, his head bowed on his breast, his hands clenched behind his back.

She struggled to push up the sash, but it could not be done with-out making a noise. Mr Holbrook uttered a cry. A thin stream of cold air seeped through her cheap silk gown. An arm wrapped tight round her waist, a hand forced down the sash, nearly trapping her fingers beneath.

'Are you insane?' he demanded in exasperation.

'No, I am desperate.'

The last strain of night air blew out the nearest candle.

'So am I.'

His voice was very close. She felt his breath upon her lips and at the last moment wrenched her head aside. His lips brushed against her earlobe by mistake. She twitched and her ear-ring tingled against his mouth. In the darkness their eyes met, gleaming white. His arms were locked tight around her, making it almost impossible for her to move her arms.

'Were you trying to frighten me, you little witch?' He sounded angry, as if to conceal the fact he *had* been afraid.

'If you think I won't jump, why don't you let me go?' She winced as his arms tightened still further.

'Yes, I understand now. If it became known you had leapt from my window, you could play the victim to your heart's content. And I almost believed your charade. Tell me, my dear, how large a pension are you trying to squeeze out of me in exchange for your silence?'

'I wouldn't even spit on your money.' Elizabeth's lip curled in scorn. 'But what do you suppose your wife would think if she could see us now? Or your precious daughter?'

He winced. She could see she had found a sore spot and pursued her advantage ruthlessly. 'Does poor Miss Holbrook know she is under the same roof as the sort of woman she would cross the street to avoid and wouldn't even look at for fear of tainting her reputation?'

'My daughter is away from home.'

'That makes it no better.' She drowned out Mr Holbrook's protests. 'A serpent polluting the nest in which the innocent dove usually dwells, and everyone will know it except she. Or maybe some sympathetically malicious soul will tell her how you profane the memory of her poor mother. This was her room, wasn't it?'

He wrenched her to her feet so suddenly her heel caught on the hem of her petticoat. She heard the lowest flounce rip away. She would have overbalanced if he had not still held her.

'Aye, tear my clothes, do. I have precious few left, but don't let that trouble you.' Elizabeth had become so angry she had almost lost her fear of him. 'I suppose Miss Holbrook has so many clothes, she only wears each gown twice before giving it to her maid.'

'I wish to God it was still possible to duck scolds,' Mr Holbrook's voice was bitter, 'but I'll break you in other ways.'

'Will you, la? Oh, I quake in my shoes. Save me, save me.'

She fought to free herself, but he managed to drag her some distance towards the bedroom door, near which the candles still flickered.

'I won't be defied by a chit like you.'

'I pity your wife for marrying a man who regards all women as his slaves. But I warn you, I won't give way tamely. I'll show everyone my bruises – white skin marks so easily.'

In the candlelight, she could see his expression. It was not what she expected. Instead of the sneer of a brute, determined to conquer by force, she saw a pang cross his face, a mixture of emotions too numerous and too complicated for her to decipher so quickly.

With unexpected force he pushed her away from him.

'Go then. Say what you will to anyone who will believe the word of an actress.'

Elizabeth did not reply. In her fall she had struck her head against a chair leg, but she sat up with a struggle, tucking her legs under her and raising her hand to her throbbing temple. There was silence save for their agitated breathing.

'I'll buy you a new gown and then I never wish to lay eyes on you again . . . but you are hurt.' He knelt down beside her, but she shook her head and resisted when he tried to remove her hand from her forehead. 'Let me see.'

'No, no, you can't deceive me, pretending to be kind.' She spoke angrily to choke down her tears of pain.

'Oh, very well, have it your own way.' He rose and tugged the bellrope. 'Go home and lick your wounds by yourself,' he growled, 'but don't imagine I won't complain to your manager about your behaviour.'

Hearing steps, she scrambled to her feet, snatching up her cloak. There was a tap at the door. Mr Holbrook unlocked it and threw it open.

'See that this young person reaches her lodgings safely.'

Elizabeth slipped out and the door slammed. She heard something kicked over in rage, but was unaware that Mr Holbrook had stooped to pick up the muff she had accidentally left behind.

Chapter 4

S*erenely* the swan glided across the lake. Edward Holbrook watched it with a jaded eye. Morning had brought no peace to him.

It had haunted him all night and ever since he opened his smarting eyes that she thought he was capable of raping her. One by one, he reviewed the events of the previous night, struggled to remember precisely what she had said, how she looked. He could no longer doubt she was as innocent as she claimed to be.

Why hadn't he gone out on to the landing and thrown the muff down after her? Instead he stood there, stroking the squirrel fur, full of self-loathing. Why hadn't he controlled his temper?

Coming to his senses, he dropped the muff on the sofa. But it looked lonely there, forlorn, and for some reason he took it with him into the bedroom, before remembering the conclusions the servants would draw from finding it there. Did he want the world to think he had seduced the girl? Or was he afraid they would discover the truth? Neither version was much to his credit.

He examined the muff mechanically. It appeared to be good quality, if rather worn, and too small to be strictly fashionable. Miranda's new muff was twice the size. In the end, he left it in a corner of the dressing-room, where it might easily have been forgotten in the haste of Miss Hathaway's expulsion.

The swan observed him with a black, oval eye, then skimmed its beak across the surface and tilted back its head to swallow.

It had not been an idle compliment. The swan in all its glory conjured a vivid image of the Hathaway girl. He could picture her in a white polonaise, with muslin cuffs and lace ruffles falling from her elbows nearly to her wrists. Her slim waist, delicate arms, long neck, every graceful contour was etched on his inner eye so clearly it made him sick with desire.

He had spent two nights feverishly undressing her. He had unhooked her bodice, unlaced her stays, untied her garters. Actresses had magnificent legs. There were so many plays which required them to dress as boys. . . . He stopped himself with a jolt. That way madness lay.

He should not have let her provoke him. Now he was battling conflicting urges, to redouble his efforts to appease her, or to cast her out of his mind completely. His pride shrank from the possibility of a second failure. He would not grovel to any woman, no matter how beautiful.

Was he really growing old? When he looked in the mirror, despite sleepless nights, he could not fault his face even in the full glare of sunlight. With darkness and candlelight to soften lines of age, surely he was still a handsome man? He could not have wasted his youth. Surely, surely. The marriage that blighted him, the doomed love for Julia Elton . . . it couldn't be too late.

What would she do? Lodge a complaint against him as she threatened to do? She must be silenced somehow. If only she wasn't staying in the town for another three weeks.

He was willing to lie, if she forced him to it. Who would listen to her, after all? A man's word was stronger than a woman's in a court of law. But gossips did not care about that. The less likely a story was, the better. How the mighty are fallen. He had disgraced himself in his own eyes. And they would resurrect poor Julia, too. She had not deserved this, even if he had.

He merely picked at breakfast; then, unable to concentrate on his accounts, he allowed himself a walk in the grounds. But business could not be put off any longer. He was too meticulous a man to delay doing his duty.

He had not been in the library long when Isaac, the elderly manservant, tapped at the door and announced that there was a young person to see him.

Edward's heart leapt involuntarily, but he had time to settle his face into an uncompromising expression before the visitor was shown in. She proved to be a plump young woman he vaguely remembered seeing with Miss Hathaway.

He elicited, after a good deal of stammering, stroking of petticoats and glancing at the door as if she wanted to bolt out of it, that her name was Ann Kemp, that she was Miss Hathaway's friend and had some inkling of what had passed the previous night. Mr Holbrook forced himself to frown to suppress a smile of relief.

'She sent you, did she, to make advances?'

'Oh, no, sir.'

'But you have influence over her?'

'No, sir,' she stammered. 'You wouldn't suggest – what you did if you knew her. I'm sure you have a kind heart. I sat up waiting for her and stole down to let her in and she was shaking and quaking. It would have melted the hardest heart to see her. She cried and tossed all night. She doesn't think I know, I kept so still, but I know.'

He assumed his coldest demeanour with difficulty as he rose. She had said nothing, then, to her roommate. But Miss Kemp's eyes continued pleading with him. 'Why are you here?'

'I – I've come to' – even her ears were red, but she persisted – 'to offer myself in her place.'

'*What?*'

The suggestion was so preposterous, he refused to believe he had understood her correctly.

'Lizzie wants to be an actress in London, with Mr Garrick and Miss Farren and everyone,' she smiled sadly, 'whereas I'll never be anything much. It doesn't signify what happens to me.'

Edward turned to the window while she spoke, but he had grown very still. He saw himself confusedly through her eyes. What did she think of him? How had he been presented to her? What she suggested was ludicrous, grotesque.

'I know I'm not beautiful or a lady like her or anything but. . . .'

'There can be no question of it. Do you think I am some sort of dragon that will swallow one maiden as easily as another?'

He could see from her reddened nose and eyes she was about to cry. She let out a shuddering sigh, 'Then – then you don't want me?'

51

'No, madam, I do not.'

'But you won't make Mr Boxall turn her off, will you? She said you said you would. She loves the stage so and Mrs Boxall is so jealous of her. . . .'

'Go home, young woman. I have not decided what I shall do next.'

He silenced her protests with a frown and she vanished like a rabbit down a hole. He sat down and took his head in his hands. He could not think clearly. He was angry with Elizabeth Hathaway for rejecting him after raising his expectations and with himself for putting himself in this absurd position, but he still desired her.

He was uneasy about the picture of her distress Miss Kemp had conjured up. He had not intended to frighten her so much. But fear was a weapon, if he chose to use it, as was ambition. If he furthered her career. . . . He had never done anything so unscrupulous. Wasn't he honour bound to desist his pursuit? He must make amends. He must stop thinking of her in that way.

He rose, sat down again, then strode to the window, the door, back to the desk. He wanted to see her again. Maybe then he could fathom what she was thinking. But he didn't want Miss Kemp to see him pass.

Enforced idleness irked him. He straightened the inkwell, toyed with the account book. The figures danced. It was pointless to make a blunder simply because he was not paying attention. He met the housekeeper in the hall, carrying a pile of linen.

'Mrs Morris, where are those gowns and what-have-you Miss Miranda is giving away?'

'In my room, sir.' She eyed him dubiously. 'I was just taking off the ruffles.'

Lace was expensive, so it was common practice to remove it from old gowns and attach it to new ones. Indeed, much of Miranda's lace had been her mother's, even her grandmother's.

Her extravagance made the perfect excuse for him to toss around the heap of finery. He had the vaguest notion what each item cost, but he believed he had an eye for what would look well on the stage – and on Miss Elizabeth Hathaway.

A short while later he rode out, grim-faced, without informing anyone where he was going or when he would be back.

*

Loneliness washed over her. Nan hadn't been needed at the rehearsal, but Elizabeth expected to find her in their new lodgings. They had moved their belongings that morning to a sparsely furnished room above a grocer's shop and Nan had offered to unpack while she was away.

Hairbrushes, pincushions and scripts were neatly arranged on the only table. Elizabeth's petticoat lay on the bed. Nan had begun to mend it, then cast it aside, as if a thought had struck her and she had been so anxious to be gone, she had forgotten how she left things.

Elizabeth sighed as she sat down with her sewing. There was still the torn sleeve to see to and she ought to buy fresh ribbons for one of her costumes, which was fraying and growing yellow with age.

Nan's absence left her a prey to her thoughts. The reaction set in as soon as she stepped into the chaise. Fierce shudders shook her and she could barely repress her sobs till she was indoors. Whenever she shut her eyes, she found herself grasped by strong arms, his breath scorching her skin. Had he been trying to drag her to the bedroom or simply away from the window?

All morning she waited for the blow to fall. Mr Holbrook had the power to deprive her of the means of earning a living, hoping to force her into his arms. He could not know what sort of family she came from. She herself was not sure if they would raise a finger to save her.

Her mother would defend her, and her cousin Lucy, but the latter was unmarried and neither woman had money nor a home of her own. The others would demand humility and implicit obedience as expiation, even though she had changed her name as soon as she left home.

Where could Nan be tarrying so long? The sun was beckoning to her from the window. Maybe she would meet Nan on her way to the draper's shop.

There was another customer being served when Elizabeth entered and she waited patiently, her eyes wandering over the glossy bolts of material. She glanced round as the door opened.

A middle-aged woman bustled in with two younger women. The youngest, a mere girl, was obviously her daughter, since both were short and plump. All three had chip hats perched on top of their hair and their gowns were gathered up, polonaise style, at the back.

The shopgirls flew to meet them with offers of tea or a seat, addressing the lady as Mrs Parr. The youngest shopgirl took a hesitant step towards Elizabeth, but her superior tugged her by the sleeve and muttered something. The two Miss Parrs, their attention drawn to the actress, twittered and giggled. Their mother turned a hard stare on Elizabeth and began a lecture on the immodesty of female display.

Mercifully it didn't last long. The assistants were kept busy fetching down bolt after bolt of silk, satin, brocade, damask and taffeta from the shelves and spreading them on the counter. The trio, hat ribbons bobbing, pored and squabbled over patterns and colours.

Elizabeth grew restless and tearful. She would have given anything to escape her thoughts. This demonstration of the privileges she had forfeited only served to emphasize the dangers of her unprotected position. She wandered across to the window, tempted to leave, then turned back. No, she would stand her ground. She needed that ribbon.

The door opened again.

'Oh, Mr Francis Collingham, what brings you here?' Mrs Parr gushed, while her younger daughter spluttered over a giggle and her sister took refuge behind an arch look and her fan.

'Gloves, I'm afraid,' he laughed, 'but I'm in no hurry.'

He turned as if accidentally in Elizabeth's direction, bowed and greeted her. She returned his good morning, but was relieved when the Parrs claimed his attention. Their transaction was soon over, but they seemed inclined to stay and chat with the handsome young man. When the shop assistant asked him how she could help him, Elizabeth decided to make her retreat.

'No, no, please serve this lady first. She was here before me.'

Elizabeth murmured her thanks and spent as little time as possible choosing. She felt too distracted by Collingham hovering behind her to calculate the relative quality, prices and shades of ribbon. The

Parrs were shown to the door in great state while she fumbled in her purse for the right change. Picking up her package, she found Collingham had opened the door for her.

'Never mind about the gloves. I'll call again,' he called over his shoulder, adding in a lower tone, 'I saw you enter and waited so long for you to come out, I thought I'd go and rescue you.'

'I had begun to believe I was invisible until you hailed me,' she remarked, considerably embarrassed that he had followed her into the street. He returned her rueful smile.

'You *are* invisible except to the sharp eyes of love.'

'I was always taught that love was blind.'

In sunshine, Mansfield always looked its best. A shower during the night had washed away some of the dirt and the sandstone houses glowed warm yellow in the sun. A strange half-sweet, half-sour smell hung in the air, the smell of fermenting hops.

She did not particularly like the idea of leading Collingham to her lodgings and was forced to be direct when he steadily refused to pay attention to her hints.

'Have you no business of your own to attend to?'

'None that I can remember while you turn those beautiful blue eyes on me.'

She covered her eyes with both hands. 'Well, can you remember now?'

'Yes.'

She ought to have expected it. Two hands touched her shoulders and a pair of lips brushed against hers. A sudden revulsion seized her. She pushed his face away, feeling the rough warmth of his chin against her fingertips.

'You wicked boy, I'll tell your mama and she'll send you to bed supperless.' She struggled to keep herself in check. It was not his fault he had awoken memories of the previous night.

'Surely you didn't expect me to resist such temptation?' He would not release her and smiled provokingly as she began the painstaking process of peeling away one finger after another. Suddenly a figure hurled itself at them and pushed Collingham against the wall of a shop.

'Don't touch her, don't you *ever* touch her,' Will Ramsay cried.

He turned towards Elizabeth with flashing eyes. 'Did he hurt you, Lizzie?'

'No, of course not, don't be absurd.' She flushed deeply, aware of eyes attracted by Will's almost incoherent cry. She stooped to pick up Collingham's cane, which he had dropped at the unexpected onslaught. Will watched her with fists clenched.

'This is all the return I get for my devotion,' he growled.

'Does this gentleman have any claim on you?' Collingham enquired, brushing down the sleeves of his coat. A frown lurked behind his smile nonetheless.

'Yes, I do.'

'No, he doesn't.'

They spoke simultaneously. Elizabeth noticed Will was flushed and his breath smelt of beer. Collingham glanced from one to the other, laughed and offered his arm to her with a light word.

'I'd scorn to be such a soft thing as you be,' Will glared at him, 'hiding from a real man behind that smile and a woman's petticoats. Let go of her, will ye? I'll fight you for her.'

'You'll do no such thing,' Elizabeth intervened. 'You'll go back to your lodgings and sleep it off, so Mr Boxall doesn't dismiss you for drunkenness.'

Will watched them like an animal at bay. She knew it was a mistake to speak to him like that, but sometimes he pushed her past all endurance.

'I won't be treated like a child, Lizzie Hathaway, as if I was of no account,' he panted, 'Look at the sneaking coward. Do you really prefer him – and every other man – to me?'

'Are you surprised she dislikes you when you behave so uncouthly?' Collingham remarked, 'I ignore your aspersions on my character only because you are clearly not in your right mind.'

Elizabeth saw he was deliberately adding fuel to the flames and interposed between them. She scolded them for drawing attention to themselves and her, and urged them to beg one another's pardon, or else she would leave them to tear each other to pieces if they chose.

Both men glowered, but said nothing. She was at a loss what to do. Will was rarely easy to appease and she didn't dare favour one man above the other, for fear of their reactions. She tried chatting to Collingham, trusting him to second her attempts to change the subject. He told her he was a student at Cambridge and was staying in his father's house opposite the church during his vacation. But she sensed Will, rather than growing calmer, was offended at being ignored.

'Is no one expecting you home?' she asked, growing desperate.

Will uttered a sneering laugh. 'We wouldn't want you to get into hot water.'

Collingham pointedly ignored him.

'I should never forgive myself, madam, if I did not see you safely to your door and it was later discovered your throat had been cut by an unknown ruffian.'

One spring was all it took and both men were struggling in the street, oblivious to horses, carts and pedestrians alike.

The first steps had been taken and, though he was breathless, as if he had just passed a deep gorge, Edward felt better about the business. He wanted to be alone, to think things through, but he had promised to drink tea with the Collinghams and it was too late to send his excuses now.

There seemed to be some sort of disturbance ahead, which had brought traffic to a standstill. A clamour of voices rang in his ears and he eased his spirited mare between a drey of beer kegs and a half-empty farm wagon.

Two men were keeping tight hold of a third. Frank Collingham, barely recognizable with his curled hair – only old men wore wigs – hanging lankly about his ears and his cravat askew, sheathed his sword. He stooped to pick up his tricorne hat and began brushing it with his sleeve with a look of disgust.

But Edward Holbrook's eyes were drawn to a different figure. She, too, had been seized by rough hands, though she made no attempt to escape as far as he could see. She had not seen him yet, her white face turned aside, her eyes dropped or shut. He could not tell which.

Others had seen him, however, and called on him to intervene as a Justice of Peace. At the sound of his name, he saw the flash of terror in her eyes as they met his, then she shut them again in apparent resignation.

He sensed there was something unpleasant about this affair, that he of all people should not be involved. But he was the only magistrate present and to refuse would be to raise questions in the minds of the onlookers.

He recognized one of Miss Hathaway's captors as the keeper of a nearby inn and rode across to him. The innkeeper was only too pleased to offer him a private room at the Crown, hoping for increased custom now and subsequently when everyone would want to hear his story.

That was in the nature of the case and he would not have cared if Miss Hathaway had not been involved. Would she say something damaging? Would she suffer from being the subject of gossip? He was quite willing to pity or protect her as long as she did nothing to harm him.

The entire mob would have forced itself into the whitewashed parlour if it had been permitted. It took all Mr Holbrook's authority to reduce the number to himself, Collingham, the two actors, the innkeeper, the town constable and two other men to keep the irate actor in check. His eyes still glowed, though Collingham looked bored and Elizabeth Hathaway weary.

'Well, Collingham,' Mr Holbrook began, 'I gather you have been brawling in the street like a framework knitter's apprentice.'

'I was defending my honour, and that of this young lady.'

'Honour!' the actor spat out the word, looking directly at the magistrate. 'I know what a gentleman's notion of *honour* is.'

Edward stiffened. This man was dangerous. He knew too much. He had to be silenced at any cost. 'Keep a civil tongue in your head, or I'll send you to the House of Correction.'

'Aye, aye, you'd like that. Then there'd be no one to protect—'

'You are not helping me, Will. Can't you see you are exposing me to lies and gossip?' Miss Hathaway's voice was hoarse, as if she had been forced to raise it too much during the brawl.

Edward frowned to hide an upsurge of desire. He could have gazed at her for hours in her simple blue gown, open to reveal the petticoat and gathered in a polonaise at the back. It was probably cheap enough material – he was no judge of such things – but it suited her admirably, making her eyes look bluer and her skin paler. A black ringlet rested on her breast. He must find a way of dismissing the others so he could talk to her alone, reassure her.

To hide the direction of his thoughts, he cross-questioned the combatants and witnesses. According to Collingham, Ramsay had made an unprovoked attack on him, forcing him to draw his sword and assert his superiority as a gentleman, while the actor declared he had been saving Miss Hathaway from the hands of a libertine.

'And what have you to say, Miss Hathaway?'

Her lips parted, but as she hesitated, Ramsay leapt into the breach. 'Nay, you needn't ask *her*. She doesn't know her own mind no more and must be rescued in spite of herself.'

Edward felt an icy knot tighten within him. 'Well, madam?'

'Well, sir, Mr Collingham and I were conversing—'

'You let him kiss you!' Ramsay's voice cracked.

Elizabeth shuddered and looked away. Edward's fists clenched and he dared not glance at his rival. Collingham. Yes, Frank Collingham had everything a young woman would want – youth, good looks, a rattling tongue. All he lacked was the means to support himself.

'Is this true, Collingham?'

'Well, yes, but it was only in fun. We neither of us meant anything by it.'

'Oh, this is too much! Can't you see, Lizzie, how little he values you?'

'Sit down, sir. I won't have such outbursts in my presence,' Edward thundered, glad of any vent for his feelings, which he suspected were not so very different from Ramsay's. She raised strained eyes to his face for the first time.

'You must excuse Mr Ramsay, sir,' she said. 'I'm afraid he – has been fond of me for some time and I have toyed with his affections, because my vanity was flattered.' She spoke heavily, as though playing a part to which she was unsuited.

'Don't beg him on my account, Lizzie. Don't debase yourself so far.'

She ignored the interruption. She took all the blame upon herself and appealed to his sense of justice. She seemed to be treading a tightrope. Mr Holbrook found it hard to decide if she was flirting with him or hinting she was in love with Ramsay and begging for his compassion. The actor buried his head in his hands and moaned.

Out of the corner of his eye, Edward glanced at Collingham. He was tweaking the upturned brim of his hat, taking no apparent interest in the scene taking place before him.

'Let the fellow go, will you, sir. I bear him no ill will.'

Ramsay lunged forward, but Miss Hathaway caught his arm and gazed deep into his eyes. 'Don't, Will. For my sake. I couldn't bear it if something happened to you.'

His face softened, 'Don't sacrifice yourself to save me.'

She gave him a crooked smile. It was still on her lips as she turned to the magistrate. She took two steps, extending her arms in front of her.

'I alone am to blame,' she repeated, a note of mockery creeping into her voice. 'Should you not manacle your prisoner and take her away?'

Edward was overwhelmed by the longing to take both those wrists and demand to know the truth about his rivals with all the urgency of a jealous lover. And then, even if her answer did not satisfy him, to take her into his arms and kiss that mocking smile from her lips.

'That will not be necessary,' he said, knotting his fingers behind his back.

Instead he bound them all, including Collingham, over to keep the peace, threatening them with the full severity of the law if there was any more trouble. His eye rested on Ramsay. The fellow was obviously easily provoked and inclined to drink. Resentment and suspicion lurked in his face. Only Miss Hathaway's influence prevented him from breaking out again.

Another flame of jealousy seared him. His reason told him she was only playing a role, but his heart refused to believe it. It did not matter that this man was her inferior in every way – birth, breeding, talent, intelligence. Women had married handsome fools before this and some were even flattered by displays of jealousy.

Hadn't she said she had come to Woodlands to spite somebody?

And this man played her lover, even kissed her on stage. He was poor, but he was young. If she were in love, it would be one explanation why she was impervious to his offer of wealth.

Lizzie. Ramsay even called her by a petname which he, Edward Holbrook, was forbidden to use. He had hardly patience to stay in the room till the formalities were over and he scolded Collingham on the short journey to Church Street to relieve his feelings, knowing as he did so that he was listened to with polite indifference, or maybe not listened to at all.

Once they were alone Will began babbling, promising Elizabeth he would curb his temper in future. She silenced him with a curt reply. She was tired and had barely recovered from the shock of Mr Holbrook's sudden arrival.

Some magistrates liked nothing better than to have someone who had slighted them in their power. She expected Mr Holbrook to wilfully misinterpret events, dismiss everything she or Will said in their defence, maybe cart them off ignominiously to the little town of Southwell, which, for unknown reasons, possessed a magnificent minster and the local bridewell, in which petty criminals were punished. And of course he would have offered her her freedom at a price when they were alone.

She knew Will too well to dare expect he would keep his temper and she had learned to her cost that Collingham was still too much of a boy to resist the temptation to get others into trouble while keeping his hands clean. But glancing at Mr Holbrook, she suddenly sensed he could be trusted. His aims were the same as hers. He did not seek revenge or power over her.

'I – I know it must have been an unpleasant scene for you,' Will ventured. 'I know maiden modesty forbids you to confess publicly to loving any man, but. . . .'

Elizabeth shuddered. So he believed she had saved his skin because she loved him, maybe even that she had not known how much until he was in danger. She had known at the time that Will would believe what he wanted to believe, but the contrast with her thoughts was too stark.

'Will,' she began, without knowing what she intended to say. He was gazing at her with such trust, she felt a lump rising in her throat. How could she topple his house of cards?

'Elizabeth, where have you been?' Nan panted, flying towards her. 'Oh, such news.' She drew up short at the sight of Will.

'Well, what is it?' he demanded.

'I daresay – Mr Boxall will tell you,' she stammered. 'He's come to see you, Liz.'

Nan took hold of Elizabeth's arm and pulled her towards the door. Will dropped back to let them enter and, hoping he wouldn't overhear, Nan whispered, 'I was so frightened when Mr B said he'd been to see him. I thought I'd made things worse.'

'He? Who?' Will turned on Elizabeth when Nan didn't answer. 'Tell me. What's happened?'

'I am as ignorant as you are,' she protested.

There was no time for any more. Without warning, Elizabeth was seized and kissed heartily on both cheeks.

'You're a clever lass,' Mr Boxall declared, kissing Nan, too, for luck and looking as though he might almost kiss Will, 'though he drives a hard bargain, eh, my dear?'

Mrs Boxall, to whom this remark was addressed, pressed a cold cheek against Elizabeth's. 'Well, madam, I see you excel when you choose to exert yourself. You need not be *modest* about it.'

Her ironic emphasis sent Elizabeth's heart, chill as stone, plummeting down a dark well. 'I don't understand.'

'Why bless you, child, didn't Nan tell you?' Mr Boxall winked. 'Shall we say, an admirer of yours called and offered the company his old cart. In return, he insists you should play the lead on the night of the benefit for the war widows and orphans.'

'And,' Mrs Boxall added, 'there is a parcel waiting for you in your room.'

Elizabeth's eyes flew from one face to the next. She barely had time to register the look of fury and pain in Will's eyes, before he had gone.

Chapter 5

*O*n her first free morning, Elizabeth took the package and, saying nothing to Nan, set out for Woodlands. After the cold spell, summer had returned and the sun was drawing out every putrid smell it could find in Mansfield. It was a relief to reach the shade and fragrance of the wood.

She had planned to spread the story that Mr Holbrook's chaise had taken her to her lodgings, rather than to Woodlands, but no one believed it. The parcel was the last straw. She could not explain that it was not for services rendered, but a bribe. She wanted to send it back unopened until it occurred to her it was probably her muff. Even so she left it to Nan to open it.

Her exclamation made Elizabeth look up, curious but apprehensive. It proved to be a cream silk gown with narrow, dark pink stripes. There was a letter, too, written in a firm hand, which Nan declared she could not open. Reluctantly Elizabeth broke the seal. Token of esteem – coming to the play tonight – expect to see you wearing my gift – dire consequences. . . .

It was almost a relief to discover the silk dress was a full inch shorter than her blue stuff gown and the bust and waist were so tiny that, no matter how tightly she was laced, there was no hope of squeezing Elizabeth into it.

A secret part of her coveted that gown, cast-off though it was. The expensive material brought back submerged memories. Once such a dress might have been hers by right. It was the hardest thing for her pride to bear, being forced to wear another woman's clothes.

It seemed much further to the lane branching off to Woodlands than she remembered it and she began to doubt herself as trees, brambles and ferns as tall as herself stretched in front of her. She had had a bad night. She struggled to drop her true self like a cloak in the wings. Rumour had got about. There were more men than usual backstage, come to stare at the woman at the centre of the brawl, and Mrs Boxall remarked acidly on the increase in the takings.

Elizabeth discovered from Nan there was a second reason for Mrs Boxall's resentment. The leading actress had spent the previous afternoon calling on the most fashionable ladies in town, with Augusta in tow, canvassing for their support at the benefit.

Augusta was a useful ally now that Johnny, with all the dignity of a ten year old, considered such displays beneath him. She would recite poetry on command, and sing and dance to her mother's accompaniment. Naturally, everyone was in ecstasies, and several ladies engaged the actress as a music teacher for their children, believing she might achieve similar results. She returned in high good humour, only to be confronted with the awkward fact that, to please Mr Holbrook, she would not even be on stage on the night of the benefit. She had sworn never to play second fiddle to her rival and was far too proud to make an exception.

Mr Boxall's attitude was harder to fathom. He had apparently undertaken to ensure Mr Holbrook had free access to Elizabeth, intercepting her when she tried to slip out of the green room. Mr Holbrook, however, was in no hurry to take advantage of the opportunity. The place was too public to talk openly. He seemed more at ease, but eyed her gown with deep meaning. A Mr Parr, presumably the head of the family she encountered at the draper's shop, swooped on her to lecture her on the whole art of acting. Elizabeth didn't bother listening. She caught a glitter of amusement, a silent challenge in Mr Holbrook's eye, but she did not take him up on it. Mocking Mr Parr, she sensed, would not be a wise move. He was not so stupid that he wouldn't notice what she was doing.

She had seen Mr Parr talking to Mrs Boxall and patting Bessy's head, succeeding in making the little girl cry. Obviously he was one of the men who was convinced, perhaps erroneously, that he was the father of one of the Boxall brood. The company had been in

Mansfield, so Nan said, at about the time Bessy was conceived.

She barely exchanged a dozen words with Mr Holbrook all evening, but even that did not satisfy Will.

'I suppose you've heard the stories about that Holbrook man?' he remarked, as they plodded home, Elizabeth and Nan with their skirts raised slightly to keep them out of the dirt.

'Not a whisper,' she replied, and tried to change the subject. Her heart beat faster. Since the brawl, Elizabeth had been intrigued by Mr Holbrook and she was secretly glad Will was so full of his new information that he blurted it out, proud of his ability to judge character.

'He kept mistresses while his wife was alive, some of them his own servants.'

Her first instinct was to deny the charge. Instead she shrugged and said it was no business of hers. She knew better than to believe rumours too implicitly, but she suspected they usually had some foundation. She could not overlook Mr Holbrook's reaction to her references to his wife. Was his past the reason why he was so certain she would simply fall into his bed?

Her head was throbbing and she was forced to rest before climbing the hill to Woodlands. There was a risk of meeting Mr Holbrook on the way. Once she began to imagine she heard hoofs behind her, she could hardly refrain from glancing back at every two steps she took.

She ought to have sent someone else, a stray urchin, one of the younger men of the troupe, not Will, but maybe Samuel would have been willing. Why had she imagined she was the only person capable of carrying out this mission?

The lime trees whispered, bees hummed. A sandstone wall, mottled yellow and grey, rose beside her. A jackdaw chattered, then uttered a creditable imitation of a human whistle.

There was a rustle ahead of her and something sprang out of the undergrowth. She stopped. A round white tuft of a tail bobbled across the path and vanished in the tangle of brambles, but a lithe, red-brown creature remained.

Its eyes met hers in a long, incredulous glare. Then the weasel, apparently accepting that its prey had escaped, whisked round and disappeared where it had come from. Elizabeth, shocked, tried to push aside the feeling this was an omen. The gates were only yards away, but she had to take a deep breath before forcing herself on.

She crossed the yard. She could hear men's voices, but no one was visible. The air smelt of hay, horses and leather. A young maid answered the door and, though she looked dubious, she took the parcel. Elizabeth bounded down the steps. If she could just get away safely. . . .

The suddenness of the encounter startled them both. Elizabeth shrank against the nearest wall, while the high-spirited mare swerved and skittered.

'What an unexpected pleasure,' Mr Holbrook said, lifting one hand to steady his tricorne hat. 'You won't go yet, will you? I want to show you my swans.'

Caught off guard, Elizabeth had begun to sidle towards the gate, murmuring an excuse. Why had she come herself? Had she secretly wanted to see him one last time?

He blocked the way with his chestnut mare. 'If you dare set foot outside the gates before you have my permission, I will personally hunt you down and sling you across my saddle.'

'Oh, mercy!' She stretched her eyes in mock terror. 'You will frighten me out of my senses.'

'And then, my beauty, I will carry you home and lock you up in my highest tower.'

Elizabeth squinted up at the neo-Classical house. 'There aren't any towers.'

'I shall build one. And till then, I shall keep you locked in the wine cellar, with all the spiders and mice.'

'Aren't you afraid that by the time your tower is built, I shall have drunk your cellar dry?'

Mr Holbrook let a small smile twitch at his lips, in spite of his attempts to look grim.

'A pretty sight I should be, too,' Elizabeth continued pettishly. 'My hair full of dust and cobwebs, my nose bloated and – heavens! – my eyes small and red like a mole's from sitting in the dark so long.'

This time he could not resist. Mr Holbrook threw his head back and laughed out loud, not the bitter little bark, but a real, warm laugh. The look of amusement, even affection, faded from his face and his mouth settled back into its usual stern lines.

'You assume I would be a neglectful host,' he said. 'I've a good mind to teach you a lesson.' He raised his voice and called the groom to take Juno to the stables.

He swung down from the saddle and she found her hand taken, with unnecessary force in her opinion, and tucked through Mr Holbrook's arm.

'And James,' he added, as Juno's hoofs began to thud on the hard-baked earth, 'inform Mrs Morris that I have a guest to dine with me and that I do not wish to be disturbed.'

'Will he remember all that?' Elizabeth asked, watching the retreating figures of horse and groom. 'In my experience, servants are *so* forgetful. . . .'

'He knows that any servant who forgets or disobeys my orders is in danger of being dismissed. There are poor people enough willing to take his place.'

One glance at his face convinced her he was in earnest. Although her feet were aching, she let him lead her through an arched gate. There was something soothing about the walled garden which nestled close to the house. It was protected from the fresh breeze which, even on such a still day, seemed a constant presence on the hilltop. The scent of roses enveloped her.

A second gate led to the lawn in front of the house. The grass had been recently cut and the smell suddenly brought back the green fields of Herefordshire. When she shut her eyes against the golden glow of the sun, she could see blue hills on the horizon, hear the cows lowing, see the swallows swoop almost to the ground in grace-ful arcs, as if competing with each other. Opening her eyes dispelled the illusion. The garden rolled into a valley, then rose towards wooded hills, mere hummocks in comparison with the Welsh moun-tains she had known from childhood. Neat paths intersected the lawns. Fountains, urns and statues were tastefully scattered. Three steps at the end of a path led into a shrubbery. In the valley, the shimmer of the lake and an island covered in weeping willows were visible.

Elizabeth complimented Mr Holbrook on his garden and turned to look at the house, sliding her hand out of the crook of his arm. It was a modern, symmetrical building of honey-coloured stone with a grey slate roof, large enough to be imposing and small enough to be comfortable. Her eyes ran along the pedimented upper windows, then dropped down. The path was flagged. She might have broken her ankle.

'By the by,' she remarked, 'is it your custom to press-gang all your dinner guests? Most hosts prefer to send invitations.'

'I have something to say to you and I didn't know when I should have another opportunity.'

Elizabeth braced herself. Now maybe they would reach some sort of understanding.

'I believe I promised dire consequences if you scorned my gift.'

'Oh, I don't scorn it. 'Tis monstrous pretty. Only I can't wear it.'

'I insist upon it.'

'Faith, I shall cut a poor figure if I do, with my petticoats above my ankles and every seam of the bodice stretched till it bursts asunder.'

He mustered a smile. For some minutes Elizabeth had been lovingly eyeing a bench and she suggested they might sit down. He agreed but began probing her with indirect questions. She saw he wanted to discover more about her. Someone, Mr Boxall most likely, had told him she was a lady. She was practised enough by now to avoid giving direct answers, but he persisted.

'Where does the name Hathaway come from?'

'Stratford-upon-Avon, I believe.'

'Then you are from Warwickshire.'

'Oh no, sir,' she smiled up at him. 'You surely did not believe Hathaway is my real name? My family would never have forgiven me if I had disgraced their name. I think I chose it out of revenge on behalf of poor Mrs Shakespeare, abandoned to raise two daughters and tend her son's grave. *She* could not break free, but *I* could.'

She stopped abruptly. She had not intended to tell him even this much. He leaned forward eagerly, watching her face and took one of her hands, which lay loosely in her lap.

'Is freedom so very important to you?'

His question touched her too deeply for her to be able to answer it seriously.

'Are only gentlemen allowed to crave freedom? I'm sorry, I didn't know. I'm only a poor ignorant girl. For instance, I have not the least idea why you are looking so very cross with me.'

'You know perfectly well, you impudent little chit.'

She protested her innocence and took her revenge by turning his questions back on himself. Inevitably he lost patience. He began striding towards the lake so fast she was forced to follow at a trot, musing aloud to prevent him from resuming his interrogation.

'What manner of man is Mr Holbrook? Well, he is impatient, secretive, abrupt, walks far too fast for any woman to keep up with him' – grudgingly he slowed his pace – 'and of course he is very proud. Was he born proud, achieved pride or had proudness thrust upon him?'

'That, my dear Miss Hathaway, is none of your business.'

Wings ruffled, a magnificent cob swam towards them, nodding politely. The wind swayed the drooping branches of the willows.

'Yes, I forgot that,' Elizabeth went on. 'Mr Holbrook is also prone to anger and may even be capable of violence.'

'You are in a fair way to discovering what I am capable of.'

Elizabeth glanced at him, trying to hide the fact that she was scared she had overstepped the mark. He forced himself to smile and shook his head.

'No, Miss Hathaway, you will not provoke me into forbidding you from ever setting foot on my property. I am determined not to dine alone.'

'Well, then,' she said, turning to the swan and taking a hunk of bread out of her pocket, 'since I am destined to a sumptuous meal. I might as well give my dinner to someone in need.'

At the spectre of food, a smaller swan, three half-grown cygnets and dozens of geese and mallard ducks flocked round her. The tamer birds even ate from her hand.

'You seem to know a great deal about me,' Mr Holbrook said drily, 'but though you talk so much, I know precious little about you. Could it be, Miss Hathaway, that you are hiding something behind that barrage of words?'

'All swans belong to the king, don't they?'

'And you are adept at changing the subject if I ever get near dangerous ground.'

'I suppose it could be deemed treason to hurt a swan. I've never understood why anyone would wish to hurt something so beautiful.'

'Sometimes beautiful, wild creatures hurt themselves, trying to flee from those who want to help them.' He touched her cheek and a shiver ran down her spine. She reminded herself this man was a philanderer, had no doubt been unkind to his wife, maybe broken young girls' hearts.

'So, you are another of those men, like Will Ramsay or Mr Parr, who believe they would like me better if I hadn't a spark of spirit and never raised my eyes or my voice except to lisp "yes, sir", "no, sir", "if you please, sir", "I don't know, sir", "how clever you are, sir". . . .'

'Even as a silent woman, you would be remarkably loquacious. I ought to have expected it. Whenever my wife said she wouldn't say another word on a subject, I knew I would hear of nothing else for a week.'

His bitterness startled her. Here was a different version of the tale Will had heard. She must stay on her guard. She had witnessed enough unhappy marriages to make her take the woman's part. 'Maybe she was lonely and wanted your attention.'

'She wanted her own way and nothing more.'

'Did you let her have her own way?'

'Yes, yes, for the most part, for the sake of peace.'

'But she must have seen you did it ungraciously.'

'How the devil do you know how I treated my wife?' He seized her by the shoulders, but allowed her to peel his hands away so she held him at arm's length.

'Oh, I know nothing, of course. I only wondered if you tried to bribe her into compliance.'

'Compliance! God give me strength. She forced me to submit to her every whim. And Miranda has become a copy of her mother.' He pulled himself free and turned his back on her.

'Have you ever considered that maybe what your daughter or your wife feared was that you did not love them?'

She had forgotten who she was talking to. It was her own father she had been thinking of. But she had never seen such a look of anguish and fury in her father's eyes. He turned on her, then drew back, as if he hardly trusted himself not to strike her.

'Go to the devil,' he muttered through gritted teeth.

He began striding up the hill towards the house. Elizabeth followed, overwhelmed with guilt. She had to make amends.

'I'm sorry. It's none of my business. It's just that papa was hardly ever at home when we were little and didn't seem to like us much when he was there,' she murmured. When he did not reply, she added, 'You must see that after what happened here on my first visit, I might be forced to consider the rumours about you are true.'

'Rumours!' Mr Holbrook laughed mirthlessly. 'You have no conception how miserable that woman made me. No one knows what I had to endure.'

He did not elaborate and she could only see his contracted brow in profile.

'Trust me,' Elizabeth said. 'Although I talk so much, I am adept at keeping secrets.'

She was puzzled by her motives. Breaking down barriers might bring them closer, when she ought to keep her distance. But she didn't want Will to be right. She didn't want him to be just another libertine. His eyes flickered towards her. A muscle worked in his cheek. The impetus to confide in her was over. There was only one way she could possibly appeal to him.

'I don't think it right to judge a family until I have lived with them,' she said, stooping to smell a rose. 'Everyone thought our grandmother was wonderful, but we could hardly keep a servant for more than a few months because of her.'

'What was wrong with her?' he asked, his eyes sharp and suspicious.

'Oh, she seemed so meek, but her bell hardly stopped ringing for ten minutes at a time. First she was too hot, then too cold; she wanted her medicine, a glass of water, more coal . . . it was all uttered in the gentlest of tones, but her perpetual discontent would fret a hole in a stone.'

'Is this true?'

71

'It is.'

He grasped her hands fervently. 'Then maybe you'll understand how constant complaints and jealous upbraidings without any cause might finally drive a man to infidelity.'

Somewhere behind them a duck uttered a raucous laugh.

'I swear I never looked at another woman, but she tormented and watched me and dismissed the pretty maids if she thought I spoke kindly to them. I'm sure she complained to her friends and they believed her. Oh, everyone was very polite to my face, though God knows what was said behind my back.'

He turned away in disgust. 'You are right to say I am a proud man, Miss Hathaway. I was too proud to justify myself or offer excuses. I fled from home whenever possible and the inevitable happened. That is all.'

He had shut the doors and Elizabeth let the matter drop. It would serve no purpose forcing confidences from him. He might grow attached to her, or he might resent her for knowing too much. For her own sake, she must stay detached. She would be gone in three weeks.

They had reached the house by this time and Mr Holbrook held the door open for her. Again Elizabeth was overwhelmed by a sense of familiarity. The drawing-room was much like any other she had seen, only slightly more untidy than most housekeepers would approve of.

There was faded green, striped wallpaper on the walls. The upholstery of the chairs had been scratched by the cat and there were two scorch marks on the hearthrug. The harpsichord stood in a corner and a neglected sewing-frame by the window. A mirror above the mantelpiece reflected the portrait of a pretty fair-haired child. Sharp-eyed visitors might have noticed a delicate down of dust in obscure corners.

The cat lifted its head from its forepaws and appraised the newcomer before yawning to reveal hooked fangs. Elizabeth approached cautiously and, when it showed no sign of bolting, knelt down on the hearthrug. The cat allowed her to stroke its head, then began pawing at her lace cuff as it dangled and swayed.

'Be careful – her claws are sharp.'

'So I gather.' Elizabeth shook her hand and sucked her forefinger.

'Don't expect any sympathy. Of all the things you might have admired in this room, you chose to play with that flearidden monster.'

'I'm sure the cat is very fond of you, too.' She scrambled to her feet, tossing back her ringlets and brushing herself down. A spasm of pain crossed his face.

'What's wrong?' she asked.

'Nothing.'

Chapter 6

'It must be very late.' Her voice drifted across to him from the armchair in which she nestled, eyes half-shut, amid a cloud of draperies. 'Will you lend me your carriage now that your good food and comfortable chairs have rendered me quite unfit to walk home?'

'I should not dream of sending you home in any other way,' Edward Holbrook replied, 'but are you not afraid of what the gossips will say?'

In repose, she looked as delicate as a wax doll. He had done the honours of his house, Miss Hathaway had done justice to the dinner, and they had passed the afternoon as amiably as two old friends. He even forgot to be jealous of the other claimants to her attention. She behaved as if neither Collingham nor Ramsay existed.

'Neither you nor I can stop the rumours now,' she said, opening her eyes. 'I cannot prove my innocence and I hope by being apparently under your protection, other men will leave me alone.'

'So you mean to take advantage of the situation, do you?'

'What else can I do?'

Edward sat forward, his hands resting on his knees. 'But I don't stand to benefit from this arrangement as much as you do. I am in a position to offer you anything you like; the one thing I ask of you, you refuse.'

Her pale cheeks grew pink but, rallying herself, she sprang to her feet. 'Well, if you do not find me amusing company, I'd best go and never trouble you again.'

He intercepted her before she reached the door, though he knew

74

perfectly well she did not seriously intend to go.

'Since your reputation is blasted already,' he said, taking her hand, though he really wanted to catch her round the waist, 'why not do what everyone thinks you have already done?'

'I'm sure the Devil tempts lost souls with the same argument, but my conscience would know and you of all people. . . .' She broke off and, head lowered, tried to withdraw her hand.

A cold wave lapped over him. 'What were you going to say?'

From nowhere she produced the radiant smile he had seen her use on stage. 'Oh, something shockingly rude and tactless. Please forgive me.'

The chill oozed out of him. Memories of Maria and Julia receded, like waves on the shore.

'Never in a thousand years, unless you kiss me.'

He marvelled at himself. He had not behaved so frivolously since Miranda was small. He had not thought himself capable of it any more. Everything had become so ugly and bitter, there had been times he thought he would never smile again. And, on some level, he knew he had deserved to be punished.

'Oh, you rogue,' she said, shaking her head.

He was suddenly overwhelmed by the fear of losing her. They had talked at dinner about aesthetic matters, politics, literature and it had confirmed what he had suspected since he first saw her on stage: there was an intelligent mind lurking behind her frivolous façade.

'When shall I see you again?'

'You may *see* me at the theatre any night you choose to pay Mr Boxall for the privilege.' He refused to be put off so easily.

'We could take the chaise and go for a jaunt in the country. Have you seen Southwell Minster yet?' Edward broke off. In his own ears he sounded hideously eager. She must never discover how fascinated he was by her.

Nevertheless, he persisted. He countered all her objections, assured her Mr Boxall would excuse her from rehearsing at his request, invited Miss Kemp as a chaperon and, noticing her glance at the slender walnut clock near the door, he added, 'You can go as soon as you accept.'

75

'Nay, that is impossible.'

'Why?'

'You have not yet ordered the carriage.'

He returned smile for irrepressible smile. 'Then, I will order the carriage as soon as you give me your promise – and a kiss for inviting your friend, too.'

For all she pretended to be sophisticated, she blushed again. His heartbeat quickened in anticipation. 'Very well. I suppose I must pay you now, before you raise the price.'

She put her hands on his arms to steady herself as she rose on tiptoe and planted a more demure kiss on his cheek than he ever received from Miranda. A scent of roses enveloped him. He noticed the sun had reddened her skin on her collarbone. There was barely time to resist the impulse to kiss her there before her heels lowered and he felt the clasp of her fingers loosen.

Neither of them spoke. She turned aside to inspect a copy of the *Nottingham Journal* he had left on a rosewood table. Edward, coming to his senses, turned to ring the bell. The movement brought him face to face with the clock and the unpalatable fact he had promised to discuss some legal matters with Mr Parr. There was no point in making the carriage travel back and forth and being seen with Elizabeth Hathaway would stamp his mark on her.

He ordered the chaise, then excused himself from his guest. He bounded across the hall and up the stairs to change out of his dark-green frock coat, plain waistcoat and drab breeches into an evening suit of blue silk and an embroidered waistcoat. The lace cuffs of his shirt set off his strong hands tolerably well and he took a little time arranging his cravat so it fell in frothy folds. He was vain enough to believe his tight breeches and white stockings showed off his legs to advantage and, having hurried through his preparations, he forced himself to descend slowly, so as not to appear to be in an unseemly haste. About four steps from the bottom of the staircase, he was brought up short by a sound.

Elizabeth, left alone in the drawing-room, glanced round for something to do. She examined the ornaments and pictures, then picked up the newspaper. Since the excitements of July – the assizes, the Nottingham races – were over, it was dull reading. By an effort of will Elizabeth prevented herself from unravelling the tangle Miranda Holbrook had made of her embroidery.

Nothing was left but to sit down at the harpsichord and play the pieces she knew so well she could have performed them at dead of night without the aid of a candle. It was a good quality instrument, though in need of tuning, indicating it had been banged with a good deal of vigour. Without warning the door was thrown open. One glance at Mr Holbrook's face made her stop in the middle of a phrase, her hands still on the keys. He looked haggard and his fingers twitched convulsively on the door handle.

She expected an outburst, but he only stared through her into another world. Unable to take her eyes off him, Elizabeth groped for the lid of the instrument and cleared her throat. It echoed like a thunder clap in the silent room. To her relief, she saw that look fading from his face. The steady heartbeat of the clock resumed. She rose as he came a few steps further into the room.

'I am sorry if I have done anything amiss,' she ventured.

He made a little impatient gesture, as though brushing away a fly, and remarked gruffly that the carriage was waiting. She noticed Mr Holbrook had changed his clothes and, with a lopsided smile, he informed her he had business of his own and he didn't intend to overwork his horses.

He overruled etiquette and insisted she should sit beside him instead of with her back to the horses. Elizabeth expected to have her hands or waist taken captive as payment for this privilege but, still under whatever influence had seized him in the drawing-room, he did neither.

Her attempts at making conversation fell flat. He replied in vague monosyllables and only roused himself when the carriage began to pick its way through the two- and three-storeyed sandstone houses.

'I hope you were not too uncomfortable at that inn,' he said, still gruffly. 'I wouldn't lodge a dog I was fond of there.'

Privately Elizabeth agreed but to cheer him, she recounted how she and Nan had slept fully clothed on the first night because their sheets were damp, and the battles Mrs Boxall had fought with the landlady on the subject of bedbugs, which the latter claimed did not exist, despite evidence to the contrary.

Mr Holbrook looked grim and disinclined to see the funny side of such discomfort, even when she reassured him she was more comfortably lodged now. Without warning, he pressed a large, heavy circle of metal, warmed from his grasp, into her hand.

'Sir, I cannot accept money from you.'

'I'm afraid you must.' Mr Holbrook's eyebrows drew closer together, emphasizing the puckers above his nose. 'I promised you a new gown and since Miranda's won't do, I must keep my word in some other way.'

Elizabeth protested but he cut her short. 'Would you prefer it if I took you to Mrs Green's shop and insisted you bought yourself something pretty?'

She threw him a suspicious look. Was he trying to buy her again? But he seemed perfectly sincere. He kept his hand closed round hers so she could not return or examine the coin, but she guessed from its size it was a sovereign, or maybe a guinea.

He was still holding her hand when the carriage drew up outside her lodgings. Two women were shouting at each other, each with a baby on her arm. An older child was squatting in a niche between two buildings, drawing patterns in the dust with a stick and picking his nose.

Elizabeth clambered out, but Mr Holbrook delayed her, leaning out of the window. Clearly he had taken her at her word and wanted people to see them together. Had his intentions changed since their first meeting or was this kindness just an insidious way of ensnaring her?

'When shall I call for you? It's ten miles to Southwell and ten miles back.'

Elizabeth made hasty calculations, 'I daresay we could be ready at half-past eight. Or is that too soon?'

Mr Holbrook laughed. 'I generally rise at six at this time of year.'

'Oh, but I am rarely in bed till well past midnight and might not fall asleep till two or three in the morning.'

Their presence had been noted and so they parted. Had they known it, both were equally relieved Nan had been included in the invitation. Neither knew what to expect from the other.

All the way to town, Edward had been haunted. That tune kept running round and round his head, irresistibly reminding him of Julia. It was a timely warning that he was slipping too deep into this friendship. Her behaviour at dinner had eclipsed the scene in the garden.

She had not only evaded his enquiries into who she was, she had tricked him into revealing more than he had ever told anyone. He had failed to establish what manner of relationship she had with Ramsay, or Collingham for that matter. A girl like that could easily make a fool of him.

It was dangerous to pursue the friendship any further. She would be gone in three weeks, to Retford and Newark, returning to Nottingham for the Christmas season. His sister's family usually spent Christmas at Woodlands, but he found himself plotting how he could get to Nottingham to see her, with or without Miranda.

And that was another issue to consider. What would Miranda say about his behaviour, so soon after he had come out of mourning for her mother? The child was not to know he had been mourning his marriage twelve years before Maria died.

No, he would take her to Southwell, though he had considered calling it off, but it would be in the nature of a farewell. He would be with her one last time, then cut himself off entirely.

Despite his preoccupation, he noticed the smothered giggles of the younger Miss Parr as he entered the spotless parlour. Mary Parr looked grave and slightly contemptuous of her sister's inability to control her facial expression.

Once the first greetings were over and Edward was ensconced in a chair with a steaming cup of tea, Mrs Parr enquired, 'Have you heard anything from Miss Holbrook?' It took him a moment to disentangle the question from his thoughts.

'Yes, I received letters from her and my sister Lester this morning, informing me they had arrived safely at Buxton.'

He noticed Mary Parr murmured something to her sister which made Nettie choke on her tea. Mrs Parr stared at her for a moment before urging Mary to slap her on the back, which she appeared quite willing to do. Nettie, however, moved hurriedly away.

'I shall be right again in – hum – a moment,' Nettie spluttered, her voice gargling.

Mrs Parr did not relax her stare one jot. 'Really, Esther, if you do not learn to behave, I shall be forced to send you away to school and not let you come out till you are at least sixteen.'

The prospect of staying trapped in the schoolroom for two more years sobered Nettie in an instant. Mrs Parr had obviously not noticed Mary was the cause of the disruption, but as she was not his daughter, Edward could not reprove the culprit for the rudeness of whispering in public.

He had only been in the parlour ten minutes before he became as fidgety as he usually did in such company. Mr Parr was not home yet. He was a wealthy hosier and therefore always had plenty of business to detain him. Edward found himself longing even for young Collingham's company, as Mrs Parr said he might look in for a few moments.

Edward had time to remember all the business he had left undone that day and which, due to his rash invitation, would not be done the next day either. There was the harvest to superintend, preparations for rent day at Michaelmas, when he was expected to treat his tenants to ale in the kitchen, and of course the house to run. Having a stranger in the house had made him aware of how much it had been neglected.

Miranda, when she was at home, knew little about housekeeping and her autocratic airs were liable to cause the maids to elope with alarming frequency. He had hoped Mrs Morris, a distant cousin of his wife, would be an adequate substitute till Miranda was older. But it had become clear to him since her arrival shortly after Maria's funeral that she had little command over the servants or his daughter. She wasn't used to such a large house, having lived in small lodgings with a single maid since her widowhood.

There had been hints that he ought to remarry. Mrs Collingham determinedly invited eligible widows and spinsters to stay with her in the hopes that one would do. He supposed he had been rather sarcastic with several of them and had even reduced one nervous specimen to tears without knowing how. Quite how Mrs Collingham thought such a woman would manage Miranda, let alone a household of three men and four maids, he couldn't fathom.

Besides which, he was not eager to make a marriage of convenience and he had become sufficiently disillusioned about love in the past years to doubt it was desirable at all.

And yet, he could not help a stray thought from crossing his mind. It was nonsense, of course. There could be no question of it on either side. Her reputation was in the way. She was far too young. And of course she would not want it either.

Mansfield was already bustling when they set out. Elizabeth caught a glimpse of cockades on the hats of four soldiers, indicating a recruiting party. Such sights had become commonplace. There was hardly a densely populated area in the country which did not have its local militia to guard the country and free the standing army for the war in America and the East Indies.

She teased a few terse remarks on the rights and wrongs of the war from Mr Holbrook, but nothing more. It was out of character. She had gleaned from the conversation at dinner the previous day that he had strong opinions and was not one of those men who refused to discuss politics with a woman.

Elizabeth had no better luck with Nan. She was too awed to venture more than faint remarks on the prettiness of the countryside and then glance fearfully at their host, afraid he might contradict her. Mr Holbrook was scrupulously polite to Nan, but he dismissed Elizabeth curtly before turning suddenly to the window so that all she could see was his shoulder.

At length they clattered into the small yard of the Saracen's Head Inn, having caught a brief glimpse of the twin steeples of the minster through the massive stone arch which guarded the west entrance of the churchyard.

Mr Holbrook roused himself enough to explain that this was the inn in which King Charles had spent his last night of freedom. The next morning, the local cobbler refused to make new shoes for him because he recognized the king as a condemned man in his dream.

After a little discussion, it was decided to go and see the minster first and then to return to the inn for dinner, once their appetites had been sharpened by walking.

'S'uth'll,' Elizabeth remarked, taking care to use the local pronunciation, 'is an almost absurdly pretty town.'

81

'You wouldn't say that if you were here at the meat market,' Mr Holbrook replied drily.

At present, the small market place at the crossroads outside the inn was taken up by countrywomen of all ages, selling eggs, butter and other produce which wouldn't keep. Most of the land around the town was not yet enclosed and anyone who wished had the right to lease a strip of land in the communal arable fields, or to graze a cow, a pig, a goat, three sheep or a handful of poultry on the common pasture.

Small farmers' houses and craftsmen's cottages nestled in obscure corners of the town and Elizabeth suspected that even the genteel houses, many built according to the latest style, had barns, dovecotes and other farm buildings hidden out of sight behind their serene façades.

But every building in the vicinity was dwarfed by the Norman minster. Elizabeth quailed at the sight and wondered if it would not have been wise to eat first. Her companions, however, unbent. Mr Holbrook pointed out all the important features of the cathedral, inside and out. Nan, awed by the building, forgot to be awed by the gentleman and spoke to him in her natural way.

At last they emerged from the chill interior into the sunshine of early autumn. Fascinated, Nan wandered away on her own as they explored the ruins of the Archbishop's Palace alongside the minster. Elizabeth felt Mr Holbrook's eyes on her face but as she looked up, he turned aside and made some indifferent comment which needed no reply.

'We are both very grateful to you for bringing us here,' she said.

'Say no more about it.'

Something in his tone told her he meant literally what he said. She had a fair idea how pretty she must look, her hat ribbons flapping in the breeze, her gown billowing and the sunlight on her face. She teased the tips of her shoes into a crevice in the old stone wall to get a better view.

On one level, of course, she was relieved. Will, for instance, would not have allowed her to enjoy this moment in peace and would have persecuted her with his attentions. But she wanted the matter settled, preferably in the open air where the wind could blow away any bad feelings.

'Well, what next?' she asked.

'I thought perhaps dinner first, then a walk around the Burgage Green. I doubt there'll be time to visit the Free School or the House of Correction.'

'That wasn't what I meant.' Elizabeth jumped down and turned to face him.

A muscle twitched in his cheek, as if he was trying to keep his face inexpressive. 'Well, if you mean what I think you do, madam,' he paused, 'I didn't intend to discuss this now.'

'But if not now, when? Nan will be back soon and when we return to Mansfield. . . .'

'No, of course, you are right.' The lines appeared in his forehead again. 'Well then, I haven't time to go gallivanting about the countryside and since you are not prepared to fulfil your side of the tacit bargain we made at the theatre . . .'

She winced. It felt as though she had only dreamt the pleasant afternoon yesterday. It had been poisoned because all the time he had still been plotting to make her his mistress.

'. . . it would serve no purpose to prolong our acquaintance.'

He had not even stopped for breath. She had known something was wrong all day. She was about to ask why he had bothered to drag her all this way at all, but she caught sight of Nan returning with a hesitant step.

'As you choose.' Elizabeth mustered all the coldness of which she was mistress. 'If you consider that women have only one purpose in life, that is your right, I suppose.' She drew herself up tall, conscious of the tapering pleats of her close-fitting bodice, and hastened towards Nan. Let him admire her back, if he chose. Why should she care what he thought?

No more was said. Elizabeth and Mr Holbrook remained coolly polite to each other for the remainder of the day. They could not loiter because both actresses were performing that night. Elizabeth grew restless as the minutes slipped away. If he saw her anxiety, Mr Holbrook made no attempt to reassure her on the speed of his horses or the state of the turnpike road.

It seemed an age while they waited at the tollbar between Edingley and Farnsfield, even though they had bought a ticket for their return journey. The tollpike keeper, like all men of his trade, was surly and disinclined to hurry, no matter who was waiting.

Maybe it did not take as long as she supposed. Mr Holbrook showed none of the impatience he had revealed at the Saracen's Head when a tapster was slow in carrying out his orders.

The sandstone cliffs on the outskirts of Mansfield, in which cave dwellings had been scooped for poor besom-makers, were dyed a fiery red by the setting sun. The town spread beneath them in the valley, the church tower poking out amongst the trees that surrounded it. The bells of St Peter's were just tolling as they splashed through the ford across the River Maun.

Mr Holbrook let them out at their lodgings. There was nothing left to do but thank him, bid him farewell and bustle Nan upstairs so they could dust themselves down, wash their hands and faces and make sure they had everything they needed.

Elizabeth was brought up short as she stepped out of the shop, almost bumping into Nan in front of her. Mr Holbrook's carriage was still there.

'Get in,' he said, his mouth compressed.

'Oh, but we couldn't possibly. . . .'

'Get in,' he repeated. 'It's my fault you're late.'

Nan looked at Elizabeth for advice. She nodded, her throat constricted, and Nan clambered in with no more fuss. They arrived at the theatre at exactly the same time as the Boxalls. It was worth sacrificing her pride, Elizabeth mused, to see the look on Mrs Boxall's face.

She went without a backward glance. Mr Holbrook gazed at her until the door hid her and James turned the horses for home. His fists knotted and he threw himself against the cushions.

It was over. It was better this way. Oh, Lizzie, Lizzie. What had he expected? He could not marry her. She did not wish to marry him. And as for keeping her as his mistress, if she agreed to it, there was the expense of a second establishment, not to mention Miranda and her marriage prospects, his standing in the community, his own principles. Why had he ever started this?

Infatuation. That was all it was. Infatuation and lust. What was she, after all? Hadn't she plagued and teased him? And had she not kissed him and made him laugh? He would not go into the drawing-room. It would still be haunted by her.

But he stole in there nonetheless, after supping in the library. Instead of going through his papers, he sat there as he had sat the previous afternoon, staring at her chair, doing nothing.

Chapter 7

*H*e allowed the precious days before Miranda's return slip away, one by one. At first he kept to himself, busying himself in matters concerning his property, till his servants and tenants alike began muttering behind his back that nothing was ever good enough for him.

He excused himself from social engagements, alleging he was too busy overseeing repairs to fences and roofs and fulfilling his duties as a magistrate. When he went to church, he kept his eyes fixed straight ahead for fear of catching sight of Elizabeth Hathaway.

As he was leaving, he was seized upon by Mrs Collingham. She was determined to invite him to dinner so she could introduce him to her dear friend, Mrs Tallant, who had taken genteel lodgings above Mrs Green's shop on Mrs Collingham's recommendation. Edward could find no plausible excuse to hurry back to his deserted home on a Sunday.

' 'Tis a sad story,' she sighed, as they crossed Church Street. 'When her husband died all her friends thought she would die of grief. Think of your daughter, I told her. Poor Clara has already lost a father. Not but Mr Collingham and I wouldn't take her in if she *had* been left an orphan. She has the prettiest manners for all she has no money to speak of, a few hundred a year I believe, Mr Tallant's fortune being entailed to the nearest male heir, who, to be sure, is rather a distant cousin and quite an old man.' Mrs Collingham paused for breath, but only for a second. 'And of course Clara would be company for Ruth.'

'Where is Miss Tallant now?' Mr Holbrook asked, his heart heavy.

He saw the scheme as clearly as if Mrs Collingham had drawn it on paper like a battle plan. Mrs Tallant had been mistress of a large property, so she could manage Woodlands. She had a daughter near enough Miranda's age and it would be *so* nice for Miranda to have a sister.

And it would be a chance for him to display his benevolence to take an unfortunate widow and her fatherless daughter under his wing. Not to mention the fact that Miranda was reaching that delicate age when she needed a mother to chaperon her, teach her the correct modes of behaviour, help her with her wardrobe and instruct her in housekeeping.

'I believe she is at boarding-school at present, or staying with schoolfriends.' Mrs Collingham wrinkled her brows. 'I'm sure Mrs Tallant told me, only I can't quite recall, and then, you know, I am told such a vast deal, it is not surprising I don't remember it all.'

When he came to review that Sunday dinner in the evening, Edward realized he had only the vaguest impression of Mrs Tallant, except that she was rather good-looking, about his age and still dressed in second mourning of black trimmed with white.

That was all, except that some chance remark of Frank Collingham's had made her whisk out a black-edged handkerchief and scuttle away with a tremulous excuse to recover herself in a corner. Mrs Collingham assured him she was still grieving for Mr Tallant and that she was a woman of great sensibility, but he was uncertain whether or not the display was genuine.

Sunday night was long and lonely. When on Monday he declined going to the theatre with the Collinghams, the night stretched out infinitely. He could not concentrate enough to read. For the first time the house seemed vast and empty, despite faint voices from the servants' hall.

He fought the urge as long as he could, but in the end he could not resist. He fetched the volume of Shakespeare's history plays and blew off the dust a careless maid had allowed to accumulate there.

The place was going to rack and ruin without a mistress. He couldn't be everywhere at once and if he remembered one thing, he forgot a dozen others. He was sure he was being cheated over household bills, especially expensive items like tea or coffee. He ought to compare present bills with the accounts Maria had kept, but in theory that was Mrs Morris's province.

Feverishly he found the right page and began to read and re-read both the short scenes in which Lady Anne Neville appeared. They conjured up Elizabeth's face, the intonations of her voice, her gestures. Others were watching her at this very moment, listening to her. Why hadn't he gone too? Miranda would be back at the end of the week.

No, he would only recover from this infatuation if he stayed away. He must not idealize her. She had played with the feelings of that Ramsay fellow. By her own admission she was a coquette. It was probably Ramsay she was in love with.

But his resolve was beginning to crack. Unable to endure another night alone, he accepted an invitation to a card party at the Parrs.

'And we shall have the pleasure of seeing you again tomorrow night, won't we?' Mrs Parr said in parting.

'What is happening tomorrow night?'

'Oh, you rogue.' Mrs Parr tapped him with her fan while he searched his memory. 'You yourself arranged this benefit night at the theatre, so I heard.'

A heavy weight tumbled from his breast. The benefit. Of course he couldn't stay away. They needed to sell as many tickets as possible. Now he had had time to think over this absurd infatuation, he would see her with new eyes. She would be just another woman of dubious repute in a tawdry, spangled gown, parading in front of crudely painted scenery.

And Mrs Tallant, who was at the card party, seemed a sensible woman with decided though quietly expressed opinions on the role of a wife, mother and housekeeper. It was just a pity that something, maybe her eyes or the way she smiled, reminded him of his dead wife.

She looked up expectantly as the door opened, but Nan shook her head.

'Still nothing?' Elizabeth asked faintly.

'No.' The bed dipped as Nan sat down beside her. 'I'm sure it's nothing to fret about. It's just as the post's got delayed or maybe. . . .'

A friendly arm slid round her shoulders and Elizabeth leaned her head against Nan. She could not explain the growing dread she had felt for the last two or three days.

Within a week of arriving at a new venue, she always received a crackling letter in spidery handwriting. Usually Elizabeth herself went to whichever shop or inn served as a post office in the town or city, but it was getting to the point when she hardly dared set foot outside.

Even the company of Nan did not protect her from lewd propositions. It was accepted in the town that briefly she had been Mr Holbrook's mistress, but that they had quarrelled, or he had grown tired of her, and therefore she was fair game. The accepted wisdom, since Shakespeare's time at least, was that a woman who lapsed from virtue, even if she repented of her sin, was morally in no position to pick and choose whose offer she accepted next.

Elizabeth suspected Mrs Boxall had had a hand in propagating stories, dropping hints to the ladies who invited her to drink tea with them after her music lessons were over. Audiences had grown more hostile towards her recently. Would they hiss her tonight at the benefit?

In the past Will had acted as her guardian. Now he was frequently absent and she had heard rumours of his drinking. One of the married couples sometimes took the unmarried actresses under their wing and Nan also enlisted the help of Samuel, one of the younger actors, but Elizabeth hated being a burden. Mr Boxall offered her assurances that no one would molest her, but she was beginning to suspect him, too.

More than once she had seen him talking to one man or another and she knew he was being offered bribes to persuade her to change her mind. Sooner or later, there would be one so tempting he would not be able to resist testing the water. He too, after all, believed she had compromised her principles with Mr Holbrook.

Not that she was afraid he would do more than coax her, maybe threaten and bluster a little. It was Mrs Boxall who was her implacable enemy. She had begun to have nightmares about betrayal and she dreaded sleeping. In this half-rational state, it was not surprising she was upset by the absence of mail. She shook her head at Nan's consolations.

'It's no use. Even if Mama couldn't write, my cousin Lucy would. Something is wrong.'

'You – you've never told me much about your family.'

The urge to unburden herself was strong and she knew Nan would be sympathetic.

'You must have guessed my family does not approve of my profession. My father is a very conventional man and my brothers and sister resemble him. I was always an outcast and I grew tired of being urged to marry so I wouldn't be a burden on the family. We had some amateur theatricals while Lucy was staying with us, and I enjoyed it so much I thought maybe I could earn my living that way. In any other profession I would need a letter of recommendation.' Elizabeth shut her eyes. There were some things she couldn't even tell Nan.

'Things went from bad to worse. I'd rather not talk about it. Lucy helped me escape. I didn't tell Mama I was going. I wish I had now, but I didn't want her to be forced to keep my secrets, or to come and find me. Lucy stayed behind, though she considered coming, too. My mother and I write to her and she forwards our letters to each other.'

Nan knew the rest. One evening, an unknown lady in a black cloak had ventured backstage and asked the manager to hear her recite a speech with a view to giving her a job.

'Are you afraid someone has found out?'

'Maybe. Or maybe Lucy is ill, or . . . I don't know. It just seems there are so many things that can go wrong.'

Nan rocked her gently to and fro, murmuring reassurances as if she were one of the Boxall children. Elizabeth rallied herself with an effort. She must prepare for the benefit.

She had felt it necessary to use Mr Holbrook's money as he had intended. She bought silk for a gown and made it herself with the aid of Nan. She used the money saved from not employing a mantua-maker for her costume for the benefit. But all this while he had not come near her. She wondered whether she had not, after all, made a mistake in not returning the money. What did it matter how shabby she looked by day as long as she was elegant on the stage?

Discussion about the choice of play for the benefit had been intense. Mrs Boxall placed as many hurdles in her way as possible, not wanting to be outshone. Many roles she claimed as her own or had already performed in Mansfield this season. Finally Elizabeth insisted on Otway's *Venice Preserved*, despite her rival's sulks. The role gave her ample scope as an actress, including as it did attempted rape and insanity.

The house was packed, Nan informed her in a breathless whisper. Elizabeth herself made a point never to peep through the curtains before a show. As the auditorium was generally as brightly lit as the stage, she had trained herself into a sort of selective blindness, refusing to pick out faces in the crowd when the curtains were open.

She sensed tension in the air. The crowd was only waiting for a ringleader to begin taunting her and they would all follow suit. Before she could stop herself, her eye flickered towards the boxes. She couldn't say exactly what made her certain Mr Holbrook was there, just as she couldn't explain why she knew he had not been to the theatre since the trip to Southwell.

She felt the transformation take place. She became Belvedira, disowned by her family and beset with peril. She felt she had never given such a good performance in her life. The hostility of the audience seemed to melt away and even the air, the candlelight vibrated in sympathy.

Spontaneous silence, so much more flattering and heartfelt than the most tumultuous applause, greeted one of her speeches. Towards the end she even heard audible sobs from the most susceptible members of the audience. The shaking only began when she got into the wings. She had not realized how close to breaking-point she was.

Mrs Boxall had insisted the children should have their share of the limelight and sing and dance before the comic afterpiece, to help raise money for children less fortunate than themselves. One of Mrs Boxall's patronesses bustled backstage afterwards, trailing her husband, a bewildered woman in mourning clothes and several wide-eyed children in her wake.

'My dear Mrs Boxall, I hope you are not ill?'

The fair-haired actress adopted her most saintly expression, drew Bessy to her side with one arm while cradling the drowsy baby in the other. 'I thought it best to rest my voice as I didn't think it right to deprive Miss Collingham of her singing lesson tomorrow. And the baby has been fractious – I hope you could not hear him crying in the audience?'

'Dear me.' Mrs Collingham peered at the pink-faced bundle. 'You must send for Dr Litton to look at the poor mite. And be sure to mention my name – I'll settle the bill. I remember when my pair were young. Croup and measles and mumps . . . Mr Collingham joked we ought to let out a room to Dr Litton, he was there so often. But I want you to meet one of the families which will benefit from tonight's enterprise.'

The Boxall offspring had gathered round their mother and both groups of children eyed each other mistrustfully. Mrs Collingham went through the rigmarole of prompting the widow to make a halting speech of gratitude before, growing impatient, she took over the narrative herself, with numerous asides. Mr Collingham meanwhile beamed in the background and occasionally uttered a remark, which his wife swept aside with the rapidity of her tongue.

Elizabeth had time to feel a pang that her triumph had been stolen from her. The green room was full to overflowing and Mr Boxall took one group to see the stage and its contrivances. Too late Elizabeth noticed Mr Holbrook amongst them with yet another widow clinging to his arm.

She wondered dully whether to try to talk to Will. Did she feel strong enough to be snubbed again? Even Nan had deserted her and was talking to Samuel in a low, earnest voice. Without warning an enthusiastic voice burst over her.

'By Jove, that was magnificent. Never saw the like of it, even in London or Cambridge.'

'You flatter me, Mr Collingham.'

The student reverently took her hand and asked if he could kiss it.

'If you must,' Elizabeth replied, recovering her good humour, 'though I am beginning to think from our meetings that you think of nothing but kissing.'

'I can't possibly think of anything else in your presence.'

She let herself flirt with him, ignoring possible consequences. Suddenly there was a bustle. Elizabeth found herself facing a redoubtable enemy in a black silk cloak and a calash with metal hoops, to protect a precariously high construction of real hair, false hair and grease, powdered grey and garnished with feathers and ribbons.

'Frank, where have you left your sister? Go and find her at once. I couldn't bear it if she fell into bad company, or caught a chill in this draughty, unhealthy place.'

'She is in perfectly good company,' Collingham protested, 'she is with Mrs Parr and. . . .'

'Mrs Parr has her own daughters to chaperon and – oh, there they are. Come along, Frank.'

Elizabeth had the impression Mrs Collingham had intended to lock horns with her, once her precious boy was away from this morally corrupting influence, but there was considerable relief in the matron's tone as she glimpsed Mr Boxall's party. She nodded in Elizabeth's direction and wheeled her son away, still dutifully followed by husband, widow and assorted children.

Elizabeth couldn't help noticing a trio of young women watching her, their eyes huge above the gilt paper edging of their silk and ivory fans. Miss Parr looked arch and her younger sister had caught her lower lip under her teeth, as though afraid she might laugh out loud. But the third girl, presumably Miss Collingham, was flushed and her eyes were suspicious.

A man's chest and shoulder interposed between her and them. Elizabeth found herself being warmly congratulated on her performance and being introduced to a Mrs Tallant. The widow took both her hands and gazed so earnestly into her face that Elizabeth could not take her eyes off her, despite sensing Mr Holbrook looming beside her.

'I knew the moment I laid eyes on you you were a lady,' Mrs Tallant declared, the little rays at the corners of her eyes deepening as she smiled, 'and I must confess, I never cried so much in the theatre in my life, not even when I was as young and pretty as you are.'

Elizabeth thanked her, her heart growing warm. Here was a woman who must have been lovely once, but who did not resent another woman's youth. She dressed appropriately for her age and, with her delicate bone structure, she would no doubt still be attractive in twenty, thirty, even forty years time, if she lived that long.

'I was so glad when Mr Holbrook said he would introduce me to you.' Mrs Tallant smiled up at the silent gentleman and pressed Elizabeth's hands. 'I wish my daughter were at home. Then I could ask you to teach her music and I would have an excuse to see you frequently.'

Quite so much warmth from a complete stranger, to whom she had barely said three words, made Elizabeth suspicious. Another glance at the older woman's face brought a twinge of guilt and to compensate she exerted herself to be as charming as she could.

Thinking over the encounter later, when Nan was asleep, Elizabeth wondered if Mrs Tallant had a hidden motive. Or maybe she had simply been moved by the performance and had not yet been warned about Miss Hathaway's character or her connection with Mr Holbrook.

It was strange that, though she knew Mr Holbrook had been watching them all the time they were together, Elizabeth could not remember him uttering anything of significance. She couldn't even remember if he had looked well or happy, she had been so taken up by the widow.

A possible explanation came to her the following morning as she and Nan made their way to rehearsal. She recognized Mr Holbrook's carriage even before he got out of it. For a moment she thought he had caught sight of her and wanted to speak to her. But it was Mrs Tallant he had stopped for. He doffed his hat, then sent his carriage on ahead before offering her his arm. They strolled after the carriage and, as the actresses approached, Elizabeth strained to catch a few words above the bustle of market day.

'I am sure you will be delighted to have her home again,' Mrs Tallant said. 'Fifteen is such an impressionable age.'

Mr Holbrook assented vaguely and Elizabeth missed the widow's next remark under the bawling of a farmer intent on selling his produce.

'No, no, I am early,' he assured her. 'I wouldn't dare to leave the minx waiting – heaven knows what mischief she would get up to.' His voice was suddenly very clear as Elizabeth passed him. 'And you know what these post-coaches are like, never on time.'

'How very true. Once I was delayed on the road a whole week by a blizzard. . . .'

The voices faded away. So, Elizabeth thought, Miranda Holbrook is coming home and Mrs Tallant has set her cap at Miranda's father. It was not impossible that the widow had heard the rumours and that last night was an illustration of the fact she was prepared to cast a blind eye on a husband's little indiscretions.

Chapter 8

*M*iranda burst into Woodlands like a whirlwind. Edward thought wryly to himself he could no longer complain of the house being too quiet. He no longer had time to think, but maybe that was better. Brooding only seemed to increase the confusion in his mind.

On the first day, Miranda contented herself with whirling round the house and grounds, reacquainting herself with the servants, animals and inanimate objects as if she had been gone for years and decades. She bestowed presents and kisses indiscriminately on every living being in the house and her tongue hardly stopped for a second.

Ordinarily, Edward might have let her voice drift through his head without paying much heed to her words. At present he was glad of any distraction. He guessed she only regaled him with the more respectable of her adventures at St Anne's Well or the assembly rooms.

'And Aunt Lester took us to Poole's Cavern,' Miranda rattled on. 'Everyone's been there – Dr Johnson and Mary, Queen of Scots, and the playwright Ben Jonson. The guide was a little old wrinkled woman, like an apple kept too long in the straw, and Sarah had such a fright when a bat flew past us, and when she screamed, the whole cave echoed.'

'I suppose you didn't take part in any unladylike screeching?' He felt obliged to speak, to prove he was at least partially listening.

But unchecked by his comment, she described the stalactites and stalagmites, some of which were yellow and red and blue from the metals and minerals the rock contained, and she told him about the fifteenth-century outlaw Poole whose concealed treasure had never been found.

His ears tired by the din, he was only too pleased the following day to lend her the chaise to go and call on the Parrs. Mary had been left to preside over the parlour and pour the tea. She had begged her mother for the best china but Mrs Parr had drawn the line there.

Mrs Parr herself was in the kitchen, superintending the pickling, preserving and bottling of garden produce that every autumn demanded, Nettie explained. Ruth Collingham arrived a few minutes later, having recognized the Holbrook chaise at the door.

All four were so full of their latest news, they scarcely had time to listen before another incident worth mentioning leapt into mind. Miranda, having new places and new people to describe, naturally had the most to say, but her words acted as reminders to the others.

'Oh, I've been bursting to tell somebody all about it,' Miranda sighed, ignoring the fact that she and Sarah Lester had talked almost incessantly while they were away. 'I was so desperate, I nearly told Papa. Wouldn't he have stared to discover how many beaux I had? We went to every single assembly there was and didn't sit still all night, and when one gentleman asked how old I was, he refused to believe I was only fifteen and said I must be eighteen at least.'

Mary Parr, as the oldest, fanned herself and remarked, 'You know, Miranda, you wouldn't want to look old before your time.'

'Oh, fudge, Polly,' Nettie declared stoutly. 'You know you teased Mama about having your hair up and coming out ever since you were thirteen.'

'Well, no one could ever mistake *you* for being older than you are.'

There was no time for the quarrel to develop. Miranda continued, counting up her conquests on her fingers, giving a brief history of each as she went.

'And if Aunt Lester hadn't arrived at just the wrong moment, I think Mr Prestwick would have made a declaration there and then.'

Astonished gasps greeted this. At seventeen, Mary had not yet received her first proposal of marriage and it was with difficulty she choked down her envy. However, she reminded herself that the gallant Mr Prestwick had not actually said anything and might not have intended to.

'Oh, Miranda, are you sure?' Ruth breathed.

'Well, I'm almost sure,' Miranda conceded, shaking out her striped pink and white gown. 'He asked my aunt about my family and where I lived. Sarah heard them talking. And he told me he owns land in Leicestershire and is quite independent, but he never asked how old I was.'

'Would you have said yes?' the irrepressible Nettie asked, sitting well forward.

'I don't know,' Miranda confessed, taking a judicious sip of luke-warm tea and looking almost as demure as Mary, 'but it is fun having a choice.'

She put her cup back on her saucer and set them down on a walnut table. Her voice was rather restrained as she said, 'By the way, how is your brother, Ruth? Is he still at home?'

Ruth's grey eyes darkened and the smile vanished even from Nettie's dimpled face.

'Yes, he's still here, but Mama wants Papa to make him go and stay with one of his friends at a shooting party until he has to go back to Cambridge.'

'What on earth *for*?'

Miranda felt a contraction of fear. She couldn't bear it if she didn't see Frank Collingham before he left. He might not even be home for Christmas if he was invited to one of those big, lively houseparties of students and young ladies who had come out properly and made their curtsy to Queen Charlotte.

At the age of twelve, Miranda had first noticed Frank Collingham stalking about a children's ball with a superior air. His purple coat, gold-embroidered waistcoat and slim legs encased in lilac knee breeches and white silk stockings elevated the sixteen year old far above the snivelling little boys, skulking in corners and liable to get hopelessly lost if forced to dance. Miranda had known at that moment her heart was irretrievably lost.

She had spent many agonizing nights reflecting that he still thought she was a little girl and crying over his departure to university. The terror that he might marry someone else was never far away.

When the secret became too much for her poor tormented breast, she had confided in Ruth. She was delighted at the possibility of having Miranda for a sister, though a little dubious about her brother's attractions. She had revealed some things he did and said which Miranda found difficult to reconcile with her image of the perfect hero.

Miranda begged her to keep her secret and Ruth had done so. It was Miranda herself in her most effervescent mood who revealed it to the Parr sisters, her closest friends at school and her cousin Sarah.

'They're dreadfully afraid he has thrown his heart away on an actress,' Nettie burst out.

It was her darkest fear. She staggered under it, hardly listening to their description of her rival. Although they agreed on the main features – dark hair, pale skin, quite tall and slim – there was a great deal of disagreement if she was beautiful, pretty or merely tolerably good-looking.

Miranda gathered her wits. Frank Collingham was not yet twenty-one and therefore could not get married on English soil without his parents' consent. (But Scotland was a different matter and was only three or four days' journey away, travelling non-stop in fair weather with six post horses and, after all, the woman was undoubtedly an artful minx.)

Ruth repeated her assertion that her parents would never permit anything to happen and Miranda knew from experience how determined Mrs Collingham could be.

'And then there's the business with your father,' Nettie added.

Mary and Ruth exchanged stricken looks. Both spoke at once to drown Nettie out and Mary pinched her sister viciously to keep her quiet. Miranda was seized with a sudden dread. Had the whole of her world fallen apart in the few days she had been away?

'Do you remember Ruth's mother talking about Mrs Tallant and her daughter?' Mary asked, 'Well, she – the mother, I mean – has taken lodgings above the draper's shop.'

'What has this to do with Papa?' Miranda interrupted, pushing her saucer further towards the centre of the table.

'Mama is determined to make a match of it between them,' Ruth said. 'She says you need a stepmother to take care of you and your father and the house, and. . . .'

'Papa would never do such a thing.'

At lightning speed, all sorts of frightful images darted across Miranda's mind. She had returned from her holiday full of plans about taking the reins of the house. She had spent so much time asking Mrs Lester how certain things were done – how often silver needed polishing, when to brew cowslip wine, how to stamp your authority over impertinent servants – that Sarah Lester had called her a bore and the cousins hadn't spoken to each other for a full three hours.

Now everything was in jeopardy, memories too deep and personal to be shared with anyone. She had already lost her mother; she could not bear to lose her father, too.

To have a stranger in the house, a busybody poking her nose into everything, no doubt changing the furniture, the wall hangings, curtains. Someone to scold the servants, to take away the power and freedom Miranda had been used to for such a long time.

Her mother had let her do more or less what she liked. Even her father, though he grumbled, rarely refused her anything she wanted. Miranda knew enough about stepmothers from books. She would favour her own daughter above her stepchild. She would stint her of money, saying they needed to implement a system of prudent economy.

The idea of a stepsister was too appalling even to contemplate. Miranda was startled by the savageness she felt towards the inter-lopers. She had spent her life fighting for her father's love. Even at those frequent moments in her childhood when she doubled her fists and declared she hated him, she could have cried with desolation when, from the nursery window, she saw him ride away. To her horror, she realized she was nearly crying now.

'He's always talking to her,' Nettie said, awed into a whisper by Miranda's glittering eyes, 'and they always go to the same places – card parties, the theatre.'

'I've seen them walking together in town,' Mary volunteered.

Ruth added, 'Mama always makes sure they sit together at dinner and he takes her home in his carriage, though maybe that was because he had it all to himself.'

Miranda tottered to the window. She had not realized how shaky her limbs were until she tried to move. A lean old horse ambled past, nodding at each step as though dropping asleep.

'I think she's quite nice really,' Ruth suggested. 'Maybe it would-n't be so very bad.'

'No!' She turned back towards her friends, eyes blazing. 'He *can't* marry her. He's married to Mama.' She could hardly see the room any more. 'I'll take care of Papa. We don't need anyone inter-fering. I won't let him make a fool of himself. And you'll help me, won't you?'

Ruth had one appalled thought of what Mama would say. But somehow all four girls clustered together and Ruth stifled her conscience beneath her loyalty to her friend.

Elizabeth took a deep breath before stepping out into the street, empty-handed. The long awaited letter had still not arrived.

Her tormentors were still there, a pack of half-grown youths, apprentices she supposed. The previous day notices had appeared, nailed to the door of the theatre and elsewhere, consisting of some doggerel verses, making use of every rhyme for the name Hathaway in the alphabet.

Since then one or more of the youths had fitted the words to the tune of a bawdy ballad and the whole pack, whether they could read or not, had memorized it. They had followed her all the way from her lodgings, singing out of tune, usually keeping at a wary distance, but occasionally swarming closer to jostle her.

A few months ago Elizabeth might have felt confident of her abil-ity to manage these youths, but a great many things had happened to unnerve her. For one thing she could no longer rely on her repu-tation for respectability and she had discovered conscious innocence was not as strong a shield as she had been led to believe.

She caught sight of Will, standing in the door of an alehouse. He had torn the doggerel verses to shreds, but now instead of coming to her rescue, he ducked back inside. He was not the only one to shun her. Respectable citizens, who might have intervened, crossed

101

to the other side of the road. Elizabeth dreaded that, emboldened by their success, the boys would be tempted to try something more daring.

Even as the thought crossed her mind, their coarse voices grew louder, discussing her good points as if she were a horse for sale. She could hear the scuffling of their feet, feel the warmth of their breath on her neck. She was on the verge of turning to face them, to say she knew not what. A rough hand seized her arm. There was a swish and someone bellowed in her ear.

She dragged her arm free, wondering if her eardrum had been burst. Elizabeth had paid no heed to the horse's hoofs, so convinced was she her plight would be ignored. As she raised her eyes, she was dazzled by the sun above the grey slate roof of the house opposite.

The rider let his riding-whip and his tongue loose on the lads, having caught the tallest one by the collar. The boys scattered, ducking into yards and alleys which led past outhouses on to Back Lane, a narrow, gloomy street reserved only for deliveries by tradesmen.

'Why aren't you at work, Jack Dawkins?' It was unmistakably Mr Holbrook's voice. 'I always said you were born to be hanged and I see I wasn't mistaken.'

The lad did his utmost to keep up an air of bravado and was apparently innured to physical pain after long years of hardship. Still, Elizabeth couldn't help feeling sorry at the way he screwed up his pitted face and writhed to free himself.

'Master's drunk again,' he replied.

Mr Holbrook made no reply to this and Elizabeth intervened, 'Let him go. He's only a boy.'

Jack Dawkins threw her a look of contempt and spat heartily on the ground. 'I don't need the likes of you to defend me.'

'That's enough,' Mr Holbrook cut in. 'I see I shall have to teach you some manners.'

The boy winced, expecting another blow. Mr Holbrook made no move, but he contracted his brow and chewed his lip, taking time to make up his mind.

'You can tell your friends, Dawkins, that I know every one of them and I'll be talking to their masters to keep them hard at work during business hours.'

The lad scowled back at him, shifting restlessly from one foot to the other.

'And if I ever catch them or you molesting anyone, no matter who it is, I'll find some excuse to sit you all in the stocks to cool your ardour.'

The lad showed no sign of fear or repentance, but the magistrate let him go and he slunk away, too defiant to run as the others had. Mr Holbrook was still frowning as he turned towards Elizabeth. Suddenly he extended his gloved hand. 'Get up behind me. I want to talk to you.'

Elizabeth measured the distance between the ground and the stirrup, but he pointed with his whip to the shallow steps round the old Market Cross.

It never crossed her mind to refuse. He drew Juno up beside her. Twisting round, he gripped her right hand while she grasped his elbow with her free hand. Impeded by her full petticoats, her foot slipped from his boot as soon as she attempted to lift her other foot from the top step. He made no comment, but she sensed his impatience and made another effort.

Every muscle in their arms and backs strained. For a moment she hung perilously in the air. Then she swung round, reaching for a good hold round his waist. Her breath quivered with exertion. Relieved, she leant her heated face against his back.

'There, there, my pretty,' he murmured over his shoulder. 'You're under my protection now – no one will molest you any more.'

Juno danced beneath them. As he turned the horse's head, there was a distinct 'Well, really!' nearby. Elizabeth raised her head. Mrs Parr was staring at them. Mr Holbrook raised his hat, but Juno was allowed to frisk along unchecked. Even without looking directly at her, Elizabeth saw Mrs Parr rotate to watch them pass.

Once they reached the Market Place, Elizabeth expected them to turn to the right into the tortuous Spittlehouse Gate, which passed between the stableyards of the two principal coaching inns, the Swan and the Crown. That led to Cockpit Lane and the Nottingham turnpike.

Instead, Juno picked her way across the Market Place, shaking her head as if she disdained the smells of rotting and fermenting which hung in the air. Elizabeth asked where they were going, but either he chose to ignore her or he could not hear her with his back to her.

She felt a thrill of unease as they went straight ahead down Church Street. The stone church, a mellow mixture of more architectural styles than could be counted, stood at a crossroad where two smaller streets branched off Church Street.

She had been in Mansfield long enough to recognize the houses clustered round the church; the vicarage on the corner of Toadhill Lane; solid, three-storey homes of respectable families, like the Parrs and the Collinghams; the late Mr Stanhope's house (one of *the* Stanhopes, cousin of the Earl of Chesterfield who wrote those letters), now Mrs Clarke's Seminary. Close at hand, looking small and twisted, stood the black-and-white, half-timbered Ram Inn which always made her homesick for Herefordshire where such houses were commonplace.

Mr Holbrook drew the mare up alongside the churchyard steps and looped the reins through an iron ring in the wall. Elizabeth slid from the saddle. Taking her by the hand, he hurried her up the steps and along the path between the flat table monuments and slanting headstones. The porch was on the opposite side to Church Street, but he did not stop there.

He led Elizabeth to the most secluded part of the graveyard, where the church jutted out and sheltered them from two sides. The trees along the river, which marked one boundary of the graveyard, screened them from the houses on the other bank. They were thus visible only from the grammar school, which consisted of only half-a-dozen boys, the schoolmaster and the usher.

'Now,' he said, 'what am I supposed to do with you?'

She sat down on the low wall which separated them from the river. 'You should have thought of that before you brought me here.'

He smiled, but in a grim manner. The breeze ruffled his cravat and made the heavy skirts of his frockcoat flap.

'I gather from what I witnessed today that I have become responsible for your safety.' He laughed briefly. 'I've half a mind to take you home and lodge you in one of the guest bedrooms, only I'd rather not be plagued with Miranda's tantrums and Mrs Morris's hysterics.'

'I am glad I merit something better than the wine cellar now.'

Still his features didn't relax. The remains of that frown prevented her from thanking him for her rescue. He began to say something, then at a sound he broke off and strode away. Above the rushing of the river, Elizabeth heard someone whistling tunelessly between his teeth, as he came along the path. Footsteps echoed in the porch and the massive oak door thudded.

This seemed to produce the effect Elizabeth had laboured for in vain. Mr Holbrook laughed irrepressibly and she was forced to smile in reply. Laughter made him look younger and the threatening aspect faded from his face.

'What's the joke?' she asked.

'The joke, my beauty, is that Church Street will put only one possible interpretation on the sight of a couple hurrying to church, closely followed by the vicar. Mrs Collingham was at her parlour window when we arrived and I've no doubt she is waiting to see us emerge.'

She smiled uncertainly. To her there seemed to be as many serious sides to this matter as comic ones.

'And what's more, I intend to give rise to even more gossip by keeping you here until the vicar leaves, which I hope will be long enough to convince them we have exchanged vows.'

Elizabeth sprang to her feet. The path between the gravestones was narrow; the graveyard was full to overflowing. Instead of going round a monument, she took the nearest way. She might as well have thrown herself directly into his outstretched arms.

'Don't you like my plan?' he asked, drawing her to his breast.

She could feel his warm breath on her forehead. There was a smell of newly turned earth, a faint odour of decay in the air, and lavender. His linen shirt had been stored in lavender.

'No. Let me go.'

'Why so sad and serious?' he asked, tilting her chin back. 'I thought nothing could put an end to your frolics and jokes.'

'You misjudged me.' Elizabeth made another attempt to pull free, but he clung on, though he had to let go of her face to hold her.

105

'No, I didn't misjudge you,' he said, 'I suspected there were hidden depths in you the first time I saw you on stage.'

Her cheeks were burning. She was not sure if it was her own heart she could hear or his. 'Night and day you have tormented me, forever out of my grasp, like a glint of light on the water.' Mr Holbrook's tone grew softer, almost menacing. 'And now I have you in my power I am determined to wreak my revenge.'

She raised frightened eyes at this, but got no more than a blurred impression of his face. It was too close to hers. His first kiss was awkward, half-smeared away as she turned her head, but the next instant, his hand was on her neck again, his thumb beneath her chin. He stifled her cry of protest with a second kiss.

'That's for being so maddeningly beautiful. And this kiss' – he paused long enough to print it on her lips – 'is for your chattering tongue, and this for your performance at the benefit, and this for being young enough to be my daughter, and this is for your disgraceful profession. . . .'

Elizabeth was stunned by the barrage of kisses. No matter how she strained her neck, she couldn't free her head and her other faculties seemed to have become paralysed.

He couldn't know she never allowed any man to kiss her like that, not even on stage. Will had tried, but she quarrelled with him about it. Even when briefly she had wondered if she might come to love Will, she had winced away when he tried to kiss her on the lips and let him kiss her hand, her cheek, even her shoulder so that she would not be forced to kiss him back. But Mr Holbrook gave her no choice. She found herself reciprocating his kisses, her head light, her feet floating on a cloud. Even when his hand slid from her neck, down her shoulder and back, she did not turn her face away.

He seemed at last to run out of reasons to kiss her. He uttered a deep sigh of satisfaction and she found herself nestling against his waistcoat, sheltered and unafraid of being in the power of someone physically stronger than herself. She knew the breeze along the river was cool, but she did not feel it. Torpor invaded her limbs. Moving would have involved a huge effort, though she sensed he would not detain her this time if she tried to go.

'Tell me, Elizabeth, who are you really? Where do you come from?'

She shook her head. 'It doesn't matter. I'm going away soon.'

'Trust me. You owe me that much at least.' His lips brushed against her forehead.

The smell of damp earth reminded her of home. The rain clouds swirled down so often from the Brecon Beacons and the Black Mountains, everything was always green and flourishing.

'My real name is Elizabeth Browne, quite boring and undistinguished, except for the 'e' at the end,' she said sleepily. 'I was born in Herefordshire, in a little village near Kington.'

Her voice caught, taking her by surprise. She had forced herself not to think about her past much, since the first lonely nights when she was kept awake by mice scratching beneath the floorboards. She had told herself she liked travelling, that with every journey she was growing nearer her aim of being acknowledged a great actress. And at first it had appeared to be true.

But it was not the countryside she had been trying to escape, only the stagnation of her life. Even now she could not see a dark-blue cloud on the horizon without thinking for a moment it was the Giant's Staircase or the Fairy Queen's Palace, or one of the other hills whose real name she didn't know but which she had renamed as a lonely little girl in a family of brothers. Her only sister had been born too late to be a companion.

Under Mr Holbrook's gentle prompting, she found herself telling him things, in no particular order.

'My parents couldn't afford to take us to London or even to Bath, which is no great distance as the crow flies. They did what they could, paraded us at county assemblies, hunt balls, even the assizes. But in the end I just got sick, sick, sick of all the matchmaking and tale-bearing, the assumption that if you smiled at a gentleman one week, you must marry him the next. I hated being watched as if I were some rare insect in a jar. I know what they said when girls barely out of the schoolroom were married before me. My own sister sneered at me for being an old maid who would nurse our parents in their old age, when what I really wanted was something more, something greater than her own quest for a wealthy husband.'

107

She buried her head on his breast, trying not to cry. She had told herself she did not care about the opinions of such people, but she did. Particularly members of her own family.

'How old are you, if you pardon my asking?' he asked gently.

She bit her lip, calculated, wondered if it was worth lying about. But after all, why not tell him the truth since she had said so much already?

'I'm twenty . . . five,' she said with a slight hesitation.

'Twenty-five,' he repeated. 'Just think, when you were the prettiest baby in christendom – I won't be contradicted, I know it for a fact – I was a great hulking lad of fifteen.'

She scarce heard him. The misery of not hearing from her mother or her cousin welled up inside her. She did not want Mr Holbrook to know she was crying, but she could not help herself. She uttered an audible sob and withdrew her hand to cover her mouth. With a murmur of sympathy he shushed her as if she were five years old.

It all tumbled out, bit by bit, her anxiety about her mother, her troubles with her fellow actors, the doggerel, the insinuations. He let her cry till she was calm.

'Now that's enough of that,' he said gruffly. 'You'll spoil my waistcoat and I shall be forced to pretend mottled patterns are the latest fashion and all the young sparks will try to copy it.'

Elizabeth laughed in spite of herself and felt better for it. Mr Holbrook pushed a handkerchief into her hands.

'Make yourself presentable while I tell you what I have decided,' he continued, while she snuffled and dabbed at her eyes. 'Every night, whether I attend the theatre or not, I shall send my carriage to take you to your lodgings. You are perfectly at liberty to ask Nan or the children or whoever you choose to accompany you. Are you rehearsing tomorrow morning?'

'No, but—'

'Good. I'll send for you tomorrow at – oh, let's say ten o'clock, to come and give Miranda a music lesson. Though I must warn you,' he added, to drown out her protest, 'my daughter quarrels with all her tutors and governesses. Still, it will only be for two weeks.'

Elizabeth saw he was determined to draw her under his protective wing. The speed with which her situation was changing startled her, but before she could say much, the door of the church banged shut.

'Wait a moment.'

Before she knew what was happening, Mr Holbrook strode away in pursuit of the vicar. The two men talked for some minutes. Elizabeth began picking her way through the gravestones. It struck her for the first time that Mrs Holbrook must be buried somewhere here, probably in a vault inside the church.

'Miss Hathaway!'

She raised her head. It had taken time to get used to answering to that name. She hastened her step and joined the men. She was introduced to Mr Plumptre, the vicar, had her hand pressed and, through the haze in her brain, she gathered he was congratulating her on the sum of money the benefit had raised. All this happened in full sight of Mrs Collingham's windows, Elizabeth realized, as soon as the clergyman had left them.

'Humph, well, you'll do, I suppose,' Mr Holbrook said, eyeing her, 'though you don't look much like a radiant bride. Your eyes and nose are as red as if I had kept you in my cellar for a month.'

'Thank you for the compliment,' Elizabeth retorted.

'I wish I had something to give you to protect you from danger.' He took her by both hands. 'Richard III must have had small fingers to own a ring fit to give his ladylove.'

Instinctively Elizabeth looked down at their clasped hands. She had never noticed that Mr Holbrook wore only two rings, a thin band of gold and a large mourning ring, containing a lock of light brown hair worked into the form of a weeping willow and the initials M.H. Emblems of the beginning and the end of his married life.

Chapter 9

*P*apa was reading aloud from the newspaper but Miranda had not heard him for quite a while now, despite the fact she was sitting on a footstool, her back against his knee, struggling to mend one of his shirts by the light of the same candle which illuminated the newspaper.

For one thing, sewing had never been a favourite occupation of hers and she kept pricking her fingers, despite the silver thimble her mother had given her. For another, though her position had seemed romantic when she chose it, her limbs and back were beginning to feel cramped. But most of all, her mind was too full for any more information to creep in, unless maybe Papa discovered an article on London fashion or a sensational murder.

The past days had been a trial. More than once Miranda resolved to give the whole thing up in despair. But when she considered the alternative. . . . She held up the shirt and viewed her work doubt-fully. The stitches were uneven, but would anyone see them? A gentleman never appeared in public in his shirtsleeves, unless he were fighting a duel, or maybe rescuing someone from drowning. She doubted Papa would be called upon to do either in the near future.

Miranda's plan was to surround her father with so much domesticity, he would see it was absurd to contemplate a second marriage. She had overreached herself on the first day, leaving herself no time to sit down or enjoy herself and had got little but sore feet for her pains.

Of the thousand-and-one tasks she had performed, the only one her father commented on was that Miranda had taken it on herself to order a favourite dish of his for dinner. But that was not an expedient she could use every day.

She had also fetched and carried for her father, cut flowers for the vases, darned stockings, made sure every book in the library was dusted while Papa was out, tried at least to make an account of her personal expenditure and, most trying of all, had kept a curb on her temper, no matter what the provocation.

And the provocation had been more severe than anyone could possibly guess, even Ruth. In the last days, Miranda had finally been introduced to her two greatest enemies. On the second day of her campaign of domesticity, her father announced after dinner that he had engaged one of the actresses to teach her music at the ungodly hour of ten.

Given a choice, Miranda preferred to go to bed in the early hours of the morning and sleep till midday, but every book she had ever read declared that the prudent wife, mother or daughter rose at six, at least in the summer. She was not willing to go to quite such an extreme, but in the interests of keeping Papa happy, she was prepared to compromise. Beside, there was nothing to do at midnight in the countryside apart from go to bed.

The trouble with being good, though, she thought, jabbing her finger again, was that no one noticed or praised you for it. Papa was acting as if nothing had changed in her behaviour.

It was as well they had had a card party to attend that night. Miranda had never expected to be introduced to Miss Hathaway and was bursting to talk to Ruth. She drew her friend into a window recess and demanded her advice. Ruth's reaction, however, was no comfort whatsoever.

'I heard Mrs Tallant say she would hire Miss Hathaway to teach her daughter if she were at home,' she said. 'Maybe that's why he's done it.'

Clearly this woman had a deal too much influence over Papa. They didn't remain in seclusion for long. Mrs Collingham instituted a search for them because she wanted to introduce her good friend Mrs Tallant to dear Miss Holbrook.

Miranda hated her on sight. Whenever she felt her resolve slipping, she reminded herself that this woman was trying to wriggle her way into Woodlands and take Mama's place. Even now the thought made her flush. She was not her father's daughter for nothing. In her sweetest tones, she had delivered several effectively sarcastic comments before escaping.

It had been agreed that the Parr sisters and Ruth would do their utmost to keep Mrs Tallant away from Mr Holbrook. But more than once, when she heard merry laughter from the table where the three girls and Mrs Tallant were playing for sixpences, Miranda felt a pang at being excluded. These were *her* friends. *She* should have been laughing with them, not that woman who was old enough to be their mother.

And Clara was such a paragon; Clara could do no wrong. Whereas Miranda knew her father told everyone, friend or stranger, that his daughter was spoilt and wilful. Mama had loved her and praised her, but Mama was gone.

She put Mrs Tallant to good use, however, by imitating her airs with Miss Hathaway. She even asked the actress to take tea with her after the lesson, as they both had dry throats, and Papa had come in and sat with them and seemed pleased with her.

But the battle was by no means over and Miranda could not help feeling tired just thinking about it. Miss Hathaway would be gone soon, but the greater danger still remained and heaven knows how long it would be before the war was over. Involuntarily she sighed and leaned her head against her father's knee.

'Well, missy, what is it?' Mr Holbrook finally broke off reading.

'What do you mean?'

'You needn't pretend to be so innocent. I know when you want something.' He tugged one of her ringlets and watched it coil back into shape. 'You've been good and quiet long enough, and sighed this last half-hour as if your heart was breaking. I know all the signs.'

She flushed and sat upright before twisting round to look him full in the face.

'I don't know why you think I am so very mercenary.'

'Because I've known you these past fifteen years. Now come, tell me how much whatever it is will cost me so I can bluster a little, swear a little and then let you have your way with a clear conscience.'

112

Miranda sprang to her feet, tears suddenly gushing into her eyes. 'You are cruel to say such things to me, when I've tried so hard and got no thanks for it . . .' she choked, unable to go on.

'Hey-day, miss,' her father exclaimed. 'This must be a serious case. How many thousands do you. . . ?'

'No, Papa, you are not listening. I don't want anything from you and if I was sighing it was – it was because I was thinking of Mama.' She knew that invoking her mother was the easiest way to make him feel guilty and extract promises from him.

He sighed, too, and in her inflamed state of mind, she felt he was mocking her.

'I know you never loved Mama and you were always quarrelling because of me.'

His face turned so sharply towards her that she caught her breath.

'You know that isn't true, Miranda.'

'It is, it is! Do you think I was a fool just because I was little? Do you think I didn't hear you even when you sent me out of the room? And Mama used to come to the nursery afterwards and take me in her lap and cry and say horrid things about you, but I would never, never believe them. But you believe all the horrid things anyone ever says about me.'

At first Mr Holbrook looked too shaken even to speak. He put the newspaper on the arm of his chair, but it overbalanced and dropped on to the carpet with a soft flap.

'Miranda, my child, it isn't true,' he repeated, getting to his feet.

'Do you even *like* me, Papa?'

Time seemed to echo in her ears. And yet only seconds could have passed before he grasped her tightly, murmuring, 'Oh, what a question. Of course I love you. You are Papa's little princess, remember?'

'That was a very long time ago.' Her voice was muffled by his coat and her own tears.

He didn't seem to hear her and went on, 'You are all I have, child. But what sort of father would I be if I spoilt you all the time?'

'What sort of father are you if you mock me every time I speak and never have a kind word for me?' She couldn't help sounding petulant and she braced herself for his anger.

'Come here.'

He pulled her to his chair and took her on his knee, something he hadn't done for longer than she could remember. Papa seemed different somehow, she couldn't say how. Drained, she rested her head on his shoulder, listened to his soothing words coming from deep within his chest.

She grew drowsy, but there was another feeling tugging at her like an insistent tide trying to drag her out to sea. There might never be another opportunity to talk to him, but she was afraid of being pushed out, away again.

'Papa, you are – contented, the way things are at present?' she suggested, tilting her head to catch sight of his mouth, nose and one eye. 'I am trying to learn how to keep house for you.'

'Yes, yes, child.'

Was it worth venturing? She bit her lips.

'Papa, don't be angry, but. . . .'

'But what? I hope I am not such an ogre that you are afraid to speak your mind to me.'

There was a trace of his usual irritability and Miranda drew herself upright, ready to quit her seat as soon as she was told to.

'Can't we stay like this for – for a while? Just the two of us together, I mean.'

He eyed her closely. 'Who has been putting ideas in your head?'

The heat rushed into her face.

'Somebody . . . said you . . . you might want to . . . to marry . . . Mrs Tallant.' The name was almost incomprehensible. She waited for the bitter taunt or cool remark that would confirm her fear.

'You shouldn't listen to gossip,' he said. 'I've no immediate plans to get married, and certainly not to Mrs Tallant. Will that satisfy you?'

She snuggled against him, shutting her eyes tightly.

If Mr Holbrook had hoped for a quieter life after this scene, he was disappointed. Miranda's spirits, long repressed, burst out in all directions, from sliding down the banisters to quarrelling with Mary Parr, from leaping high fences on her horse to reducing Mrs Morris to tears with her sharp tongue.

As he passed the drawing-room on his way to the library, Edward heard her playing up in her music lessons, wilfully misunderstanding instructions, singing off-key or changing the topic of conversation whenever and however she could.

It took all his determination not to interfere, despite the hint of exasperation in Elizabeth's voice. It would only undermine Elizabeth's authority and maybe alert Miranda to the fact her suspicions had been misdirected.

He could not be sure if his spur-of-the-moment decision to create a new rumour in place of the old one had worked. So far it seemed Miranda suspected nothing and he himself was the last person anyone would confront on the subject. He had chosen the graveyard for their talk solely because it was the most private spot in the bustling town. The rest was pure coincidence.

How much credence would a whisper of a clandestine marriage gain in the town? Especially as he took such pains to ensure Elizabeth was protected and had the opportunity to meet her supposed stepdaughter.

He managed to write two or three letters on matters of business, but at the end of each paragraph he paused, twirling his pen between his fingers and staring out of the window at the saplings and bushes which were almost bowed to the ground by the wind.

This was to be Miranda's last lesson. The last performance was tonight. Early next morning, the men of the troupe would load the scenery, props and trunks. Bills would be settled, children bundled up warmly against the autumn weather. And she would be gone.

When he heard the rattle of the tea service, he put down his pen, dusted the wet ink with sand, closed the lid of the inkwell and made sure his desk was tidy before shutting it. Then he let himself follow his impulse.

Elizabeth looked up as the door opened. Her pupil had been in her most frivolous mood, apparently as relieved as Elizabeth that their mutual torments were over. As far as she could judge, Miranda had only agreed to the lessons to please her father, and maybe out of curiosity.

There had been no repetition of the scene in the graveyard. Mr Holbrook contrived to meet her almost every time she came.

Sometimes when she arrived or departed he was in the hall or the yard, about to mount his horse. Occasionally he took tea with them or interrupted a lesson to ask Miranda about some household matter.

Once or twice she had had a scare. The servants had cast her some strange looks, but there were no direct references to her first visit to Woodlands. Mr Holbrook was clearly too much feared in his household for anyone to risk his displeasure. Miss Holbrook tried sometimes to turn the conversation to love, marriage and money, usually citing a play or novel as an excuse, even adding once, 'You see, I don't have a mother to guide me.'

'I'm sure the mothers of your friends are far more capable of advising you than I am.'

Miranda shook her head, watching her own graceful reflection in the mirror. 'They're so old and staid, as though they've never been in love at all. But you must have been, I'm sure, or you wouldn't be able to do it so well on stage.'

She looked so beseeching, so like the portrait on the wall behind her, which must have been painted at least five or six years ago. Elizabeth laughed.

'My dear Miss Holbrook, you must be aware that I am not married and you know, according to the precepts of all those novels you read, no lady allows herself to fall in love until a gentleman proposes marriage.'

'Oh, that is all stuff and nonsense and you know it. They all do it – Harriet Byron and Miss Sydney Biddulph and even Betsy Thoughtless, even if they have to hide it and think they have lost their lover forever, through reckless behaviour, or because he has a prior engagement.'

Memories flooded back. By the time she was Miranda Holbrook's age, she had fancied herself in love at least three times with unobtainable men. One had even been married.

But since then it had been all fussing and worrying, being told how eligible or ineligible a bachelor was before she had had time to get to know him and sometimes before she met him, being manipulated by well-meaning but heavy-handed matchmakers, being adored by naïve young men who would have adored any woman they imagined resembled their impossible ideal.

Nothing could be guaranteed to make her turn against a gentleman so quickly as being assured he was the greatest catch she could hope for with her dowry and she had deliberately sabotaged more than one proposed match by her contrariness.

But love? No, she had never been allowed to learn to love in her own time. The men who lived nearby she had known since babyhood and lacked the excitement of a new discovery. And those who passed through didn't stay long. It was a quiet little backwater and the frequent rain, which made the fields green, washed the beef cattle and turned the red clay into clinging mud, depressed visitors.

But in the meanwhile, her pupil was badgering her with questions and suggestions. She even hinted there might be someone in Mansfield she might care about. It was like a bucket of icy water thrown in her face. The smile vanished and Elizabeth sat forward.

'Firstly, Miss Holbrook, although I hope we have become tolerably good friends, my private life is none of your business. And secondly. . . .'

She stopped. Miranda's hands were clenched, the knuckles white. Without meaning to, the girl's face revealed how much store she set by Elizabeth's answer. She suddenly felt sorry for her. Of course she did not want her father to make a fool of himself over a woman not much older than herself.

'And secondly, there is no truth in any rumours you might have heard concerning me.'

Relief flooded through the girl's stiff body. Her fingers unravelled. Her hands fell apart, palm upward, the fingers curled, in her lap.

From that day, governess and pupil had got on much better and, as it was their last day, Elizabeth allowed herself to join in the silliness. When Mr Holbrook entered, they were both laughing over a story Elizabeth had been telling about one of her music masters.

The lines seemed more marked in his forehead today and it was with a distracted air that he hitched up the skirts of his frockcoat and sat down. Elizabeth felt his unhappiness ebb towards her, lap round her heart, tug it out towards him.

'You will take a dish of tea, won't you, Papa? To celebrate my

117

freedom.' Miranda lifted the creamware teapot and held it poised over the third cup.

'I see you were expecting me,' he said, trying to smile.

'You or Mrs Morris. She does step in sometimes about this hour,' the girl continued chattering, 'and then, you know, you will have to pay Miss Hathaway, even though you wouldn't dream of paying me and I think my work was much harder than hers.'

She went on in the same strain and the others managed bursts of sporadic cheerfulness. But still Elizabeth could feel the tide of melancholy pulling her in deeper, deeper. I am going away and he is sorry. I didn't mean to hurt him. I didn't want this, I should have withstood it.

Oh, but he will forget me soon. Mrs Tallant – she would be there to talk to him. Much more suitable, his own age, respectable. . . . But I like him too; I'll miss him. He has been a good friend to me and now I must face the world on my own again. But I will get used to that; it is no different than before I came here.

But it *was* different somehow. Will, for one thing; yet it was not quite Will she meant. She could not quite put her finger on what ailed her. Maybe it was only because here at Woodlands, although it was on top of a hill on the edge of a forest, she was constantly being reminded of her home amid meadows and gently rolling countryside. For three years, after all, she had dwelt almost entirely in towns and cities.

They did not have a moment alone. Their hands touched briefly as Mr Holbrook counted out her money. She put her purse in one of the pockets she wore tied round her waist beneath her gown.

'I ought to go,' Elizabeth said. Replying to the 'must you?' in his eyes, she added, 'I still have my trunk to pack and Mrs Boxall is always grateful for a little help.'

She held out her hand to him, but though he took it, he said, 'I'll see you to the door.'

Elizabeth shook hands with Miranda, who showed no inclination to come with them, then passed through the door he held open for her. Without thinking, she glanced up at the staircase. There was the woman swathed in flowing white draperies, the supercilious man she had made a face at that first night. There seemed to be no sound left in the world apart from their footsteps.

He flung open the front door. The wind whirled, throwing up a handful of dry leaves, loose sand and wisps of hay. The carriage was waiting. The horse nearest to her tossed its head so the harness jangled. He seized her arm.

'Don't go.'

'But the horses. . . .'

'Stay here. Marry me. Don't leave me here alone.'

The servants were almost within earshot. It had to be done quickly and quietly. But his hoarse whisper made a lump rise in her throat.

'You know all the reasons why it is impossible. You have your duties and responsibilities. And I still have my ambitions.'

It was scenes like this I was trying to escape, she thought. It pained her to see him look so drawn and old.

'I will come back,' she added, but her heart plummeted at what those words implied. A failure to achieve her ambition, to reach London, to join a better company.

'No, I don't believe you will.'

His cheek was flushed, as if he felt he had made a fool of himself. He dropped her arm, then in confusion took her hand again to help her into the carriage.

'You'll come tonight, won't you?' Elizabeth managed a cheerful tone and a cheerful smile for the benefit of the servants as she leaned out of the window.

His face had become a mask of stone, only his eyes alive and burning.

'Miss Holbrook will insist on it, no doubt,' he replied coolly.

For a moment she wondered if it was possible. She tried to picture herself the mistress of this house, Miranda's stepmother, a pillar of society. The house of cards fell down.

She was too young to be trapped like that, to do nothing but ensure the house ran smoothly, to rear children, to satisfy herself with cards and long letters instead of dancing and music, acting and applause.

But it was too late anyway. The carriage was moving and, arms folded on his chest, he watched it lurch out of the gates. And she guessed, even if he came to the play that night, she would not see him again.

PART II
1778

Chapter 10

*A*utumn crept past, slow and dreary, and both Edward and Miranda Holbrook considered themselves to be the greater sufferer.

Edward was irritated by a thousand calls upon his time and patience. There was a case of bastardy, in which a young woman refused to name the father of the child she was visibly carrying. Undesirable vagrants, to be sent back to whichever parish they could claim poor relief from, were numerous since some had found casual work in the area at harvest time and were quite content to be moved on at the expense of the authorities.

The rents had been hardly gathered before he was obliged to attend the Quarter Sessions at Nottingham, though temptation pulled him in other directions. The weather made journeys wearisome, but at full moon every month Miranda had to be taken to the Mansfield assembly, not to mention various other entertainments.

From notices in the paper he could follow the progress of Mr Boxall's company. He scanned them for any mention, however brief, of Miss Hathaway. Even hearing one of his fellow magistrates utter her name in Nottingham made a scalding wave wash over him.

Miranda was unhappy at being left alone so much. She had never seen her father so intent on his work. Some bizarre questions Mrs Collingham asked about Miss Hathaway made her uneasy, though she couldn't say why. She lost interest in taking charge of the house. It was dull work for a girl in her teens and all her closest friends were exempt from such responsibilities.

And there was the continued thorn in her side of Mrs Tallant.

Papa, far from honouring his promise, had apparently forgotten he had made it. Whenever they attended a social gathering, sooner or later she would see those two together.

Mrs Tallant did her utmost to make friends in order to pump her for information about her father. Miranda had the impression the widow suspected Mrs Holbrook had been unworthy of her husband, that he deserved someone better, more compassionate. More like herself.

You'll never be my mother, Miranda resolved. She began quoting Mama whenever Mrs Tallant offered an opinion or a suggestion. She tried to convince the widow Papa had been devastated at his wife's death and would never love anyone again. She drew attention to the mourning ring Papa always wore.

It amused her for a while to feed Mrs Tallant false information, in the hopes she would do or say something unforgivable, but the results were, on the whole, disappointing. Miranda did not insult her opponent's intelligence by expecting her to believe her father liked boisterous women and Papa was polite enough not to contradict a lady.

Mrs Tallant soon discovered from her own observations that she had been misled. She learnt her lesson thoroughly and never asked Miranda's advice again. Instead of being relieved, the girl felt obscurely annoyed. It robbed her of some of her power, now the war was out in the open.

The letter from Mrs Lester, inviting them to stay with her in Nottingham at Christmas, was a relief to both father and daughter. Filled with inexpressible hope, each glanced at the other with exaggerated casualness.

'Christmas will be strange without Mama.' Miranda's voice wobbled, remembering last Christmas. Mama had already been gravely ill and had barely lived to see the new year.

Her father agreed, then added, 'If you like, we could invite the Collinghams and the Parrs and a few other friends to dine and spend the evening with us.'

A few others no doubt included Mrs Tallant and her daughter, if she came home. Miranda pointed out they saw those friends frequently, whereas she hadn't seen her cousins for months.

'And we could go to the theatre in Nottingham, or have private theatricals or play charades; maybe even hold our own masquerade. They're all the rage in London.'

Mr Holbrook smiled, running his fingertip along the top edge of the letter and refusing to catch her eye.

'I'm glad you like the idea,' he said. 'The fact is I have to make a long journey and I'm not sure how long I will be away, so if you had something to look forward to, it would ease my conscience a bit.'

Miranda stared at him, stunned. Where on earth could he be going in *November*? It was a duty, he said, but he did not elaborate. Changing the subject, he offered her money for a new gown or two so she wouldn't look a dowd among the fine ladies of Nottingham and a little something for presents.

But when he was gone and the days went by without bringing him home, she wandered round the echoing house and murmured to herself, 'So this is what it is to be an orphan.'

They had already gone through the scene seven or eight times and still Mr Boxall wasn't satisfied. Elizabeth's head was humming like a spinning-top and she wondered if she had any energy left. It was as much as she could do to remember her lines in the correct order, much less put any feeling into them. Somehow, without an audience, it seemed artificial and hollow.

Unexpectedly, Will had approached her that morning, while she was waiting in the wings.

'I must speak to you.' His voice was gruff.

She shuddered, partly because she was cold. There was only enough light in this draughty cavern of a building to rehearse by and no heating at all.

'Not now,' he said, 'later. When we're alone.'

'Will, I really think. . . .'

'It's not what you think. It's for your own good.'

There was no time to wonder what he might mean. Mr Boxall called them to order and frowned briefly at the younger children. They had been running about the auditorium, climbing over benches and frightening each other in the dark, in an attempt to keep warm. They stopped for a moment before beginning to whisper, bicker and push each other and soon the game was in full swing again.

Mrs Boxall settled in the warmest corner she could find to feed the baby, who was nearly a year old now and able to propel himself along on his bottom, in spite of the long gowns he had inherited from his siblings.

The scene resumed. Even so, Elizabeth found memories straying through her mind between speeches. Her relationship with Will had remained strained since summer. Once and once only she had suggested he share Mr Holbrook's carriage with her and Nan. He started back as if she had thrown burning coals in his face. She knew it was tactless, but it was raining and she thought if she could get him safely to his lodgings, maybe he wouldn't drink that night.

She had grown used to smelling alcohol on Will's breath and clothes. According to Samuel, Will got drunk most nights in Mansfield. She gathered he drank her health with ironic emphasis more than once and made unpleasant remarks on women and womankind in general.

In the mornings, he looked haggard, and replied with a sneer if anyone commented on his appearance. It distressed her to see him like this. Only once had he come to a performance so intoxicated that Mr Boxall threatened to dismiss him. The threat appeared to work. From then on, Will only drank after the show and was often left to sleep until just a few hours before the next one.

Since leaving Mansfield, however, he had been almost entirely sober and though he watched her, he rarely came near her except on stage. But his acting had grown more and more wooden, especially in love scenes. There had been a few threatening murmurs from Mrs Boxall and even her husband was beginning to lose patience.

'You're a good-looking young fellow, Ramsay,' he cried out, slamming down his book, 'but how the devil are you going to make every woman in the audience swoon if you stand there as stiff as a – as a mantua-maker's dummy?'

Will glared at the actor-manager. 'Maybe I don't care to have so many fools swoon,' he muttered between gritted teeth.

Either Mr Boxall didn't hear or he chose to ignore his words. Instead he demonstrated how to throw yourself on one knee and clasp a lady's hand to your bosom with a languishing air.

Recently the Boxalls had been beset by misfortune. Since coming to Nottingham, most of the children had been ill. One of the boys was still in bed, with only the landlady and Charlotte to take care of him. Amid the scamperings in the audience, a hollow cough was occasionally audible and the baby fretted and gnawed anything he could find, particularly Bessy.

Mrs Boxall had thawed towards Elizabeth and allowed her and Nan to take their turns in nursing the invalids, amusing the convalescents and taking the healthy children for walks to keep them out of mischief.

Elizabeth winced as a disturbing memory crossed her mind. She had taken Johnny and Bessy (currently the only healthy children, though both succumbed later) to look at the shop windows, sniff newly baked bread, eye cakes and sweetmeats of all sorts and, naturally, to admire drums, trumpets, dolls, wooden soldiers, kites, carved animals and spinning-tops.

Bessy's little legs got tired on the way back. While Elizabeth stooped to pick her up, Johnny's patched coat, inherited from his older brother, vanished in the Christmas throng. For a moment Elizabeth panicked. But no, the boy was not a baby, he would be eleven soon and knew the town from previous visits. And, above all, she must not frighten Bessy.

She pushed past an old lady, who was taking up the whole pavement with her old-fashioned hoop, and cast her eyes round for Johnny's fair head, reassuring herself by talking to Bessy.

'You must help me look for your brother. He can't be very far, can he, Bess?'

She had not realized Bessy had grown so heavy. Her back ached, her shoulders ached, her arms ached. She could hardly drag herself along. Suddenly a man with a florid face and a coat so covered in braid and embroidery it must have been a bad imitation of French fashion barred her way.

'What a pretty child.'

Bessy buried her head on Elizabeth's shoulder.

'Yes, she is,' she agreed, trying to pass him and looking round again for the lost boy.

'She's not your child, is she?'

'No.'

She put every ounce of effort into forcing herself on. The man kept by her side, playing with a delicate cane that could be of no possible use, either as a walking-stick or as a weapon to chastise the uncouth. 'Won't you let me carry her for you a little way?'

'Thank you, no. She's shy with strangers.' Why on earth did she think she needed any excuse? Her straining muscles sobbed for relief.

'You're Lady Macduff, aren't you?' the man persisted. 'What, all my pretty chickens and their dam, at one fell swoop? Eh?'

'Excuse me, I must rescue young Macduff from his own valour,' Elizabeth murmured, spotting the familiar overlong coat and fair curls, tied at the nape of his neck with black ribbon.

There, at the crossroads, stood a group of soldiers, two privates, a sergeant and a trumpeter. All save the latter wore scarlet coats with white trimmings, white waistcoats and knee breeches. The trumpeter's coat might have originally been white but was so decorated with red and green, Elizabeth did not quite dare swear to it. All four wore cockades in their tricorne hats.

The small group gathered round them included several dirty-faced, open-mouthed boys, two tittering young women with whom the sergeant was flirting and rather a heavily built man with a look of doubt on his face and a sweetheart or young wife clinging to his arm. Young Boxall was examining a musket with a curious eye. He didn't hear her coming and started violently as a heavy hand was laid on his collar.

'Come along, Johnny. Your mother will be wondering where you've got to.'

The lad flushed indignantly, not wanting to appear to be ruled by women in such gallant company. 'I reckon me mam'd be proud to see me in such a uniform.' He drew himself up to his full height and slapped away her hand.

'I daresay she would, but they can't take you till you're five foot and an inch. That's the law.' Elizabeth deemed it unwise to mention

Johnny's oft-expressed ambition to be the new Garrick and reluctantly the boy dragged himself away from the dazzling spectacle and
dawdled along behind her.

But once or twice when she turned to wait for him or when she
let Bessy stretch her legs, she noticed the man with the lurid coat
following them from a distance. Since that time she had seen him
often, each time clad in garish colours which made him stand out
amid the more practical and sober clothes of those around him.

When she stepped out of the theatre after the rehearsal, he was
loitering in St Mary's churchyard on the opposite side of the narrow
road. He was taking a pinch of snuff, though goodness knows there
were enough reasons to sneeze without that.

Will attached himself to her side and they hurried past the
imposing façade of the newly rebuilt Shire Hall. Somewhere behind
that building was the County Gaol. Mr Holbrook must have
frequently passed those columns, sprung up those steps into the
mysterious interior.

The proximity of those ominous buildings – the oldest church in
Nottingham, the County Gaol – made her shiver suddenly. Only
weak sunshine struggled through wispy grey clouds and the wind
trickled through her cloak.

'What is it?' She instinctively lowered her voice, as though they
were surrounded by a thousand ears. Not even Nan was present.
She had excused herself by having to talk to Samuel, who had
promised to mend the broken heel of her shoe.

When Will finally spoke, his native accent was much stronger
than usual. 'They've sold you for money.'

'What on earth do you mean?'

He gulped audibly, his neck straining against the constraint of his
cravat. 'I've heard them talking. Mr and Mrs B. There's a gentleman
who's sent 'em money and they used it to pay t'doctor and 'pothe-
cary's bill and they can't pay him back and now he wants you instead.'

Elizabeth protested at the absurdity of his suggestion but dread
picked at her heart like a boy at a cake he has been forbidden to
touch. Mr Boxall's heartiness now seemed a little forced and even
Mrs Boxall seemed apologetic and helpful, as though to make
amends.

129

And somewhere behind her was that man. She had begun to be haunted by him, to imagine he was present whenever she glimpsed bright colours or heard footsteps behind her.

'They're supposed to trick you by sending you on some errand or something – I didn't catch that bit – and he'll see to the rest.' Much of what Will said passed over her head, but another phrase leapt out at her, 'He's threatening to have them arrested for debt if they don't do it.'

Elizabeth was baffled why any man should go to such lengths about a woman he only saw briefly on stage and with whom he had struck up a single short conversation. She glanced up at Will. His eyes were fixed straight ahead of him, as though he didn't dare look at her, but strong emotions tugged at the muscles round his mouth.

'Are you sure of this? No, I don't distrust you. I suppose I ought to thank you for warning me. I'll be careful.'

'Nay, that'll not stop him or them. But maybe if you was married. . . .'

She stiffened, but thrust the suspicion aside as unworthy of them both. Will would not invent such a story just to frighten her into marrying him. He grasped her by both hands.

'Don't you see, Lizzie' – he had not used that name for such a long time – 'if you married me, I'd have a right to protect you, maybe go to the law about it.'

Elizabeth shook her head. 'Poor man's justice, as like as not, is no justice at all.'

'We could leave Boxall's company and you wouldn't have to travel alone, looking for work.' He added in heartbroken tones, 'I've borne a deal for you, Lizzie Hathaway, and I'd bear a sight more if you could only love me a little.'

Unbidden, the memories of her last proposal flashed before her. The feverish grasp, the urgent whisper. Marry me. Don't leave me here alone.

How many more men can I go on rejecting? How many more hearts am I doomed to break? Does he really want me as I really am – proud, stubborn, independent, ambitious? And lonely and afraid. Didn't Will's loyalty deserve some sort of return?

'I must have time to think. My head is in a whirl.'

'But you're not saying no this time?'

'I'm not saying no.'

They went on in silence for a few minutes. Then Will, unable to contain himself any longer, began telling her how quickly he could get a special licence. It would make less fuss than having banns called or eloping. They could slip out during a rehearsal and into St Mary's and be back before they were missed, especially if they asked Nan to look out for them or. . . .

In a more light-hearted mood, Elizabeth would have delighted in ridiculing these plans with mock-serious questions and extravagant embellishments. One thing she was determined on, though she made no mention of it to Will in case he should object, was that she would tell Nan everything as soon as they were alone together.

Nan had a common-sense head on her shoulders. She would be detached from the problem in a way Elizabeth could not hope to be. She knew from experience that tiredness addled her thinking. She hadn't talked about That Man before, thinking it might be only her imagination or that it would sound like vanity, imagining every man was in love with her.

Since they were staying in Nottingham for a good while, they had taken lodgings on the third floor of a narrow brick house, which opened directly on to the street without an intervening garden. Today the stairs seemed never-ending.

Nan did not seem to doubt Will's story for a second. She listened, wide-eyed and chewing her hat ribbon. When Elizabeth began to describe the man who had been following her, Nan uttered a slightly hysterical giggle.

'You mean the Parrot, don't you? That's what I call him,' and she added more occasions when she had seen him take an interest in Elizabeth which she herself had not noticed.

But more than ever, Elizabeth recoiled from the idea of marrying Will. She couldn't help herself. Why on earth had she let herself be frightened into promising him as much as she had? Why hadn't she contradicted his plans?

Will was a changed man that night at the theatre. Mr Boxall congratulated himself on his foresight in going over that difficult scene so many times, though he had some doubts whether Will had not swung too far towards the opposite extreme. When Will kissed her fervently on stage, it was all Elizabeth could do to stop herself from pulling away from him. It reminded her of another place, where the wind rustled the leaves along the river-bank.

She was unaware that Nan had already written a letter, no light decision for one to whom writing was a heavy labour. She waited and waited, but there was no answer and nobody came. As the days went by, Nan watched the woman she admired drift towards marriage with an ordinary and rather jealous man.

Nan knew from Samuel quite how violent Will could be when he was drunk. The younger actor had hauled him upstairs to bed more than once during the last fortnight in Mansfield. And she had never told Elizabeth that Will's older brother had been killed falling from his horse in a drunken stupor, nor that Will secretly sent money to his mother because his father drank away every penny he could find in the house.

She had been proud of the way Will withstood the bad influence of his family. It was one of the reasons why she had loved him. He begged her not to tell anyone and she had only found out this much by accident, when his mother had come looking for him. Nan didn't want to degrade Will in Elizabeth's eyes by revealing that his family was so far beneath hers.

But if Elizabeth discovered this dangerous secret now, Nan was afraid she would see only the nobility and modesty of his behaviour and not see it as a warning of what her future life might be with Will.

His pretensions to being a gentleman had vanished on the day Nan met a real gentleman, on the day they went to Southwell. Little things that were a matter of course to Elizabeth had sunk deep into Nan's consciousness.

But she was doomed to disappointment. When finally amid the sea of faces in the streets, she found the one she was looking for, he was not alone. She could not catch his eye and it seemed to her he did it deliberately. Unconsciously she turned to gaze after him.

'What is it?' Elizabeth asked, feeling the tug on her arm.

'Nothing,' she murmured, heart sinking. He was in Nottingham; he must have received her letter, but he intended to do nothing about it. She was alone and would have to protect her friend as best she could from Will as well as the Parrot Man. And Nan could have bitten out her tongue or cut off her hand for saying or writing too much to the wrong man.

Chapter 11

Will would hardly let her out of his sight. At first it was comforting, knowing she had only to look up and he would be there. But as the twelve days of Christmas rolled by Elizabeth began to feel stifled. This was not why she had run away. What had become of her freedom now?

And Will, as only a man could, assumed that he had already won. He was more careful than he had been in the past. He didn't say anything to her, but every aspect of his behaviour, his looks, his actions showed he considered her his private property.

He deluded himself that he understood her and it dawned on Elizabeth he actually liked her to be frightened. She was conforming to the image he had always had of his ideal woman. It put him in the role of protector. She found herself tempted to disobey when he ordered her not to go anywhere alone. She knew it was for her own safety, but the rebel streak in her was aroused.

The Parrot Man had made no advances since Will warned her about him, but she still saw him watching her on occasions. She was sometimes tempted to believe Will had invented the conspiracy, that Mrs Boxall was kinder not from guilt but from gratitude that Elizabeth had sat up a whole night nursing Augusta and still performed the next evening.

But when she finally lost her temper with Will, he was so bewildered, so hurt, she bit her tongue. She felt her choices narrowing and if she became impatient with Nan, it was because one evening she voiced the fear that haunted her in the dead hours of the night.

'He's sure you'll marry him, by and by. And if you wait till the danger's past, he'll think you've only been using him as a tool. You can't marry him out of gratitude.'

It startled her that Nan, who had always been Will's advocate, had changed her stance and she made some sharp comment to that effect. Nan did not reply and Elizabeth felt too irritable to apologize. She spent a feverish night rehearsing possible conversations with Will, even dreamt about it till she hardly knew where waking thoughts ended and dream delusions began.

Will himself gave her an opening as they waited in the green room while the scenery was adjusted, by blurting out the question, 'You will marry me soon, won't you, Lizzie?'

'Oh, Will, I don't know how I can,' she murmured, mustering all her abilities as an actress. 'When I think of your devotion and all the scandal with Mr Holbrook. . . .'

'I don't care tuppence for that,' he intervened. He flushed but went on, 'I – I got the truth from Nan. She told me nothing happened between you and him and I know she'd never lie.'

She was frozen to the core. Her beautiful plan of pretending to be unworthy and inflaming Will's jealousy lay in tatters. For a moment she was overwhelmed by fury towards Nan. How could she betray her trust like this? Nan, who seemed so very much against the match now.

But if she was fair, she had to see the situation in another light. She had never known Nan to wilfully harm anyone. At that time, she, too, had been anxious to clear her name. Nan's influence had probably prevented further scenes, maybe even stopped Will's drinking.

He was still protesting his love. She sank on to an empty trunk in despair. She didn't want to alienate Will entirely, but oh, how she longed to get away somewhere, anywhere. She was not as naïve as she had been when she first ventured out into the wide world alone and, knowing what she knew, she was amazed by her former temerity.

The idea of making her way to Drury Lane or the Haymarket Theatre and asking for employment, which had seemed so simple a few years ago, now terrified her. She knew now there was no loneliness so vast and absolute as being in a strange city and knowing that not a single soul was aware you existed.

'But Will, I don't love you enough. I—'

'I don't care, Lizzie. I have enough love for both of us. I'm sure it's happened before that love grows after marriage.' He cast around wildly for an example. 'What about the king and queen? Wasn't King George in love with a Lady Sarah Something-or-other before he married? But they say there's no happier couple now than him and Queen Charlotte, and look how many children they've got already and very likely more to come.'

Elizabeth felt unable to explain the difference. The king and queen had not known each other before marriage, so naturally they could not love one another. But though she liked Will, she knew she could never be happy with him. He would never see her for what she really was.

Her levity had disturbed him in the past. That was the only way out she could see, but she still had not summoned the energy to play that part when she returned to her lodgings that night. The maid, who sat up to let them in, thrust a rectangle of paper towards her.

'Came 'alf an hour after you left,' she grunted in reply to Elizabeth's questions, 'by private messenger. 'E said there was no answer 'spected.'

Elizabeth turned it over and stared at the writing, unable to believe it was addressed to her. Her first thoughts were of her family – to compound her misery there was still no news from Herefordshire – but it was not handwriting with which she was familiar. Could it be a lawyer writing on their behalf? Disowning her? Seeking reconciliation?

Her heart full of dread, she followed Nan up narrower and narrower flights of stairs. The lowest steps were carpeted, the rest bare boards. Vaguely she heard snoring behind one door and a baby crying behind another.

'Who's it from?' Nan whispered, when at last they reached the safety of their shabby room with its paper-thin walls.

Elizabeth was still turning it over in her hands, looking at every mark in the candlelight. The seal had been applied hastily and was too smudged for her to make out. The handwriting, large, clear and very black, looked like a man's.

'I don't know.'

She could not bring herself to open it. The knot of dread grew larger, tighter. She wouldn't be able to sleep until she knew the worst.

Nan sat down at the green-flecked mirror and by touch alone removed her cap and hairpins. The sole candle stood by Elizabeth's side on the wooden seat of a chair, tilted because one leg was shorter than the others. They were so still, the mice began rustling beneath the floorboards.

The noise roused her. She tried easing the seal open, but it cracked in half. The note, it turned out, was very short.

Dear Miss Hathaway

I flatter myself you will guess who this is from. I have news of your family. I shall be in Mr Slater's bookshop tomorrow at eleven o'clock and at the same time the following day in case you cannot come.

It was simply signed 'a well-wisher'. The letter fell from her hand, but she did not stoop to pick it up. She knew even without looking that Nan had turned towards her.

She realized now she had never fully believed in the conspiracy against her. But this was the final proof. The trap had been set and she felt a wave of revulsion at its cruelty. Everyone in the troupe must be aware she had not received any letters for nearly five months. No names were mentioned, no places, since no one but Nan knew anything specific about her past.

Worst of all, she knew beyond a shadow of a doubt that if Will hadn't warned her, she would have gone to the bookshop. Even now the thought nagged her. Suppose it was genuine. Suppose there was news.

The night was long and restless, full of caterwauling cats, scuttling mice, wind and rain rattling the window, the night watchman's heavy tread and querulous call, the drunk reeling past, singing tunelessly.

There was a moment of oblivion, and then, once the creatures of the night had fallen silent, there was the stir of servants rising, the clank and gush of the pump far below in the street, the creak of wagon wheels.

The actresses agreed to say nothing to Will about the letter. It would serve no purpose. He would undoubtedly keep the appointment in Elizabeth's place. It was also equally obvious he would lose his temper.

But all the time uncertainty gnawed at her. Suppose someone had come all the way from Kington to deliver a message which could not be conveyed in writing. Suppose he had to leave in two days' time. What if someone was ill, dying, and she had been sent for but she would never know. Or maybe Lucy had got away and – but no, it was not Lucy's handwriting. But someone with her or from her, because her letters had been intercepted.

The bookshop was a little out of her way, but she passed by the end of the street on the way to and from the theatre. Each time she went by, she turned to look down the sloping street, half-wondering if she would catch sight of anyone she knew. Once she even took two steps in that direction, but Nan snatched her back by the arm. It was like standing on the edge of a precipice, her head spinning, half-wanting to hurl herself down it.

Will sensed her unease and tried to soothe her. Elizabeth felt the prison bars closing in on her. On the second day she was unable to bear captivity any longer. She took advantage of the fact Will was late for once and persuaded Nan to go with her alone to the rehearsal.

Across the city the church bells were chiming the hour as Elizabeth hurried along, clinging to Nan, head bowed but eyes darting one way and the other. Ten o'clock. One hour more, or two maybe, and it would be over. Until some new scheme was hatched against her.

Nottingham was built mainly on and between two hills. St Mary's, the centre of what had been Anglo-Saxon Nottingham, stood on one hill while the Norman castle, or rather, its seventeenth-century successor gazed down from the other. It was a stiff climb to the theatre, the wind channelled down the street by the high houses.

They reached the theatre without incident. Vaguely Elizabeth noticed the Boxalls showed no emotion at seeing her there, neither relief nor fear nor surprise. A few moments later, Will burst in through the doors. His eyes flew blindly from face to face until he caught sight of Elizabeth. 'Why the devil didn't you wait for me?' he demanded.

'Don't make a scene, Mr Ramsay,' Elizabeth hissed. 'I was not alone – Nan was with me.'

He dismissed this with an angry gesture. 'Did you never think I would be frightened in case something had happened to you?' he persisted, 'I don't want you to take unnecessary risks.'

'Nothing happened.' Her head was throbbing, beating out each passing minute. There was still time. She could still go. And he would surely wait in the bookshop. How long? Fifteen minutes? Half an hour? Maybe longer if it was important. What would his next step be? When would she be safe? When would she have some news?

Her first scenes were quickly over, but any hopes she had of studying her lines were frustrated by Will's persistence. He would never let a matter drop and she did not dare hide in the ladies' dressing-room, out of earshot of the stage. She tried to ignore him. Raising her feet on the rungs of a second chair, she leaned her script against her knees and covered her ears with both hands. Without warning one of her hands was wrenched away.

'Do you know why I was late?' he hissed. 'I went to get our marriage licence.'

'What?'

He seemed to repent his words, but Elizabeth cut his mumbled excuses short. 'You had no right to do that.'

'Yes, I did. I knew you'd never set a date if I left it to you – all women hesitate about things like that, what with maiden modesty and. . . .'

The script slapped noisily on the floorboards. There was a moment's silence on the stage and she felt as though accusing eyes turned towards her. The voices picked up where they had left off, but in the brief interval, Elizabeth had time to steady her breathing and her mind.

'Modesty has nothing to do with it.' She heard her voice quiver

139

with suppressed emotion. 'I never promised I would marry you, William Ramsay, and I won't let you force me into it. This attempt to tyrannize me when you have no right to demand my obedience, shows me the sort of husband you would make.'

Her eyes glimmered dangerously, but he had apparently not yet grasped her full meaning.

'Someone had to do something,' he muttered. 'You know it'll happen sooner or later. Delaying it is pointless.'

'No, getting a licence was pointless. I won't marry you, Will. Is that clear enough for you?'

For a moment all he could do was stare. Then his voice came out in a hoarse whisper, 'No, Lizzie, don't say that. You don't mean it. I can change. Don't cast me off like this.'

Desperate times called for desperate remedies. She could hardly believe it was her own voice that spoke. 'The fact is, I can't marry you, even if I wanted. I am already married.'

He had been flushed and angry, but every drop of colour drained from his face. She trembled at what she had done, but she couldn't go back.

'It isn't true. I don't believe it. You would never – I don't believe it,' he stammered. 'Who? When?'

'Didn't anyone tell you in Mansfield that Mr Holbrook and I were married?' Now the words were out she would have given worlds to recall them. Will was shaking his head in disbelief.

'Nan said. . . .'

'Nan didn't know. He wanted it kept a secret until—' Her inventiveness failed her. The lie lay heavy on her tongue. How could she hope to keep up this fiction?

Will uttered a cry like a wounded dog. Elizabeth shut her eyes. From a great distance she heard Mr Boxall's voice. For the first time in her career as an actress, she had missed her cue.

She stepped out on to the stage, but no words would come. Old Mr Wallace, who was kept on as the prompter and a player of minor roles, was repeating her lines over and over again, but Elizabeth found herself staring blankly at Mr Boxall's face. What had she done?

And the voice which, eventually, spoke was distant and high-pitched, and the words it uttered seemed totally meaningless. With surprise she observed her fellow actors, as though she had never seen them before and she could hardly stop herself from laughing.

What were words after all? Just a random collection of sounds. She uttered them and people thought they understood her and replied, and she could do it so automatically no one appeared aware she no longer understood herself.

The hallucinogenic effect wore off by degrees. There was time for her to be silent during the scene. Things settled back into their usual places. Bizarrely, Mr Boxall congratulated her on her performance, though chiding her for the time she had taken to begin. So he had noticed nothing.

The actor-manager had given his watch to Nan so she could dangle it in front of the baby and keep him amused. Sitting down beside her friend, Elizabeth saw the time. Midday. It was over then. The messenger would be gone. And now the opportunity was past, Elizabeth was irrationally convinced the message had been genuine.

'What on earth have you said to Will?' Nan whispered.

'Don't ask me.'

She moaned. Will would not keep quiet about something like this. How on earth would she explain why her supposed husband did not claim her? Will threw her such a look before he left by the stage door. Somehow it would have been easier to bear if he had been angry with her, not broken as he was. She heard Nan draw in an unsteady breath behind her.

'He'll start drinking again,' she breathed, 'and this time, I'm afraid he won't be able to stop.'

Elizabeth could not explain what made her look across the street as she stepped out into the wintry sunshine. For a moment, between the bobbing hats and hoods, she thought she caught sight of a familiar face. Then a horseman cut off her view and when she looked back, Mr Holbrook had gone. If he had ever been there at all. Her guilty conscience was capable of conjuring him up. What would she say to him if he ever found out what she had done?

It was impossible for him to be there. He was celebrating Christmas somewhere with his daughter, attending dinners and innocent diversions of all sorts. The next Quarter Sessions were not till the first Monday after Twelfth Night.

Elizabeth felt unable to settle. The confession was on the tip of her tongue, but she was too appalled by what she had done even to tell Nan. A dozen times she abandoned her sewing – she was making a new costume for herself – and prowled about the narrow space of their garret. The floorboards creaked. Nan did not seem in a much better state, but neither spoke much.

Unable to bear inactivity any longer, Elizabeth hunted in her trunk for her bundle of letters. She must re-read the last letter from Lucy, though she almost knew it by heart. There must be some clue in it, some little detail she had overlooked. There must be some reason why the letters had stopped.

Her fingers trembled so much, she couldn't untie the ribbon. Letters scattered in all directions, over the curtainless bed with its threadbare blanket, on to the bare floorboards. Nan put down the cap she was making and started gathering up the letters on the bed while Elizabeth scrambled about the floor.

Suddenly she sat back on her heels with a low cry, staring at the letter in her hand. Her left hand fell limply in her lap, the letters she had collected slid out of her nerveless grasp.

'What is it, Lizzie?'

She sprang up and started pushing aside the collection of plays on the dressing-table, hunting for something.

'Oh, Nan, Nan, I've been such a fool. What am I going to do now?'

Her voice gave out. She stared at the letters side by side, the anonymous note in one hand, the letter she had picked up from the floor in the other. Nan's face appeared in the spotted mirror beside her, but she didn't need confirmation from her friend.

'It's the same handwriting, isn't it?'

'Whose is it?' Nan faltered.

Elizabeth sank on the rickety chair, 'He found out something about my family. He wanted to tell me himself; he waited for me and I didn't come. And now he'll give up.'

'Who, Lizzie?'

The question surprised her. 'Mr Holbrook.'

Nan hugged her, murmured reassurances. But it was far worse than Nan knew. She didn't know about the snatched proposal. She didn't know what she had said to Will. What would Mr Holbrook think of her? Would he think she did not care about her family? Would he think she was deliberately avoiding him? She did not deserve his kindness.

It *had* been his face she had seen in the crowd. Maybe that had triggered an unconscious memory of the note he had sent with Miranda's gown. Maybe he would return home today or tomorrow and she wouldn't see him. It was too late, too late, too late.

She thanked God for *Macbeth* that night, despite the fact that in the fourth act, there was barely time for her to throw off her witch's robes and catch her breath before emerging resplendent as the virtuous Lady Macduff.

She was in the right mood to distort her voice into a cackle so hideous, Mr Boxall had once said her own mother would not recognize it. In London, the witches were played by men, but that wasn't possible in such a small company. Her fingers were all thumbs, even with Nan and Mrs Boxall, in her flowing nightgown and robe, helping her.

Johnny glared at Elizabeth, when the women swept out of the dressing-room. The three smaller children were holding hands, Augusta taking care of Bessy like a little mother. 'Hurry,' Mrs Boxall panted, 'and take the children with you.'

Johnny looked insulted. The proximity of the stage and a healthy fear of his mother prevented him from protesting out loud, but Elizabeth heard him mutter, *'I've* never been late. Not even when I was five years old.'

Bessy panicked in the wings and tried to pull away. Augusta threw Elizabeth a look of mute appeal and she held out her arm to the younger girl. Bessy hesitated a moment, then ran up to Elizabeth and pressed close by her side as she took her seat.

Her head in Elizabeth's lap, Bessy peered at the audience sideways, provoking admiring murmurs. This was precisely the effect Mr Boxall aimed for. The more innocent the children looked, the greater the tragedy of their sudden annihilation and the pathos of Macduff's grief.

Only Johnny was killed on stage. The rest had been taught to scream and scatter into the wings or be carried off by Macbeth's henchmen.

143

No matter how many times they rehearsed the scene, Bessy had never grown used to it. Her shrieks for her mother were real.

It took Mrs Boxall and Elizabeth some time to calm her, before the former had to do her sleepwalking scene. Elizabeth was relieved to have some distraction from her thoughts. She and Nan had come to the theatre with Samuel, who had brought back Nan's mended shoe. Will only appeared in the green room fifteen minutes before the so-called Scottish play was due to begin.

Through the walls, they could hear Mr Boxall's lecture, but Will listened in silence. Indeed, he said very little backstage the whole evening, although she sometimes caught him gazing at her. But Nan's prediction had not come true. There were no signs that Will had been drinking.

The afterpiece was the usual bit of nonsense, involving young lovers, fusty guardians, a fop, a braggart and a resourceful maid. By the time they had changed, Will had gone. The two young actresses walked back to their lodgings with the Wallaces, a middle-aged couple and the old prompter. The maid greeted them at the door, a half-frightened, half-gleeful look on her face.

'Eeh, I don't know what t'missus'll say if she finds out,' she whispered. 'There's a man up there in your room, miss, says he's engaged to you.'

'And you let him in?' Mr Wallace demanded. Elizabeth swallowed but was unable to speak.

The maid looked defiant. 'I've seen 'im with you before and 'e said 'e was one of the players. And he had a bit of paper as he showed me he said was a marriage licence.'

'It's Will,' Elizabeth said, her heart still pounding so loudly it drowned out all other noises.

She was far too tired for another scene, but she refused the help of the Wallaces and sent them home. Nan followed as she dragged herself up staircase after staircase to the upmost floor. The candle flame danced in response to her quivering breath.

A long black shadow swung out at her from the darkness. For one insane moment she wondered why she had never noticed Will was so tall. But at the same time, the true meaning of the scene before her exploded in her mind.

Her voice wouldn't come, though she knew Nan was on the landing. She was as immobile and silent as her opponent for a moment. Then she snatched up the fallen chair, clambered on it, stretched up as high as she could reach, trying not to look at the distorted face, the mouth fallen open, the staring eyes. But she couldn't help touching his still warm neck and she realized it was a woollen stocking, her own, wrapped round his throat. Nan tapped at the door.

'Elizabeth? Is there anything wrong?'

She realized she was making strange choking noises, little sobs that refused to come.

'Nan' – her voice was too loud, but she couldn't control it – 'fetch a knife. Will's hanged himself.'

Chapter 12

They found the marriage licence and a rambling letter to Elizabeth in Will's pocket. Nan was more than a little frightened by the calmness with which Elizabeth had behaved from the moment she found her trying to release the body until the two actresses were given shelter in the garret of one of the maids.

The master of the house was roused, parson, doctor and magistrate sent for, though there was nothing anyone could do. Several other lodgers in the house had woken up and stood about on the landings talking to each other, although they were merely nodding acquaintances by day.

By morning the news had spread through the town. The actors were regarded as public property, even by those who could afford only the cheapest and most uncomfortable seats.

At midday, Elizabeth was still sitting by the window of the garret, staring into the yard with sightless eyes. Now and then she had begun to cry, but that made Nan cry, too, and Elizabeth felt obliged to dry her tears and comfort her friend.

Breakfast had grown cold, untasted. Once or twice she had got up restlessly and then sat down again. Where could she go? They were all talking about her, looking at her. Somebody, no, several somebodies, men, gentlemen had asked her questions and she had answered them as patiently and carefully as she could.

Nan was crying again, but Elizabeth felt numb. The door opened but she felt no interest in who it might be. It wasn't Will. It would never be Will. But she couldn't seem to make her head understand that. It was her fault. If she hadn't lied to him. If she had told Will the truth during *Macbeth*. If she had been back a few minutes earlier. If. . . .

'Thank God you've come,' Nan gulped.

Elizabeth turned her eyes, surprised by her tone. She rose out of habit at the sight of yet another gentleman. And then she found herself clenched tight in Mr Holbrook's arms, her face pressed against the warm roughness of his waistcoat, so very different from the dead flesh she still felt beneath her fingers.

There was much to talk about. In the same dead tone as before, she began repeating the things she had already said a dozen times, then she broke off.

'Why did you come?' She added hastily, 'I'm not ungrateful, don't be offended, but. . . .'

'Don't talk such nonsense, child. I wouldn't be offended, even if you tried throwing me out of the window.'

Elizabeth began an unsteady smile, then wiped it suddenly from her face. Smiling would be inappropriate at present. Instead she looked down at their clasped hands in her lap, right hand enclosing right hand, left hand left. She could feel his arm across her back, his shoulder against her ear, his leg pressed tight against hers.

She didn't deserve his kindness. She had abused his name. She had killed a man. She made a half-hearted attempt to draw away from him, but he wouldn't let her go and, in an obscure way, she was grateful to him for it. Grateful to feel the strength and warmth of someone who, unlike poor Nan, was not as shocked and upset as she was. But she would have to tell him. Soon.

He was speaking and she forced herself to concentrate, to treasure each kind word before he spurned her. It was something about a letter which hadn't reached him in time because it was sent to Woodlands and had to be forwarded to his sister's house, where he was staying.

'The truth is, child, I wanted to see you, but I didn't know where to find you, except at the theatre.' He spoke hesitantly, but in spite of his tact, his words triggered a memory in Elizabeth's mind. She turned to look up at his face.

'The letter – I remember. You had some news for me. . . .' Her voice died. He looked so sad and serious and he gave her waist a squeeze which made her heart plummet.

'I wish I didn't have to tell you now,' he murmured, 'but the uncertainty must be gnawing at you.'

'Who's dead? Tell me, I must know.'

He would not meet her eyes. The room became chill and silent as a tomb, save for the voices of children calling to each other somewhere beneath the window.

'I'm sorry, Elizabeth,' he said. 'Your mother died last September.'

She bowed her head. She knew if she tried to speak she would howl. He said nothing for a while, only held her, and after several attempts, she managed a coherent sentence.

'Why didn't Lucy tell me?'

'Without penetrating the heart of your family I cannot tell you for certain. But it is common knowledge that even before your mother was taken ill, your cousin was in disgrace. Her father confined her to the house, so presumably she was not allowed any letters. All those I talked with assumed she had been caught corresponding with an unsuitable lover, but since they couldn't decide if it was a groom, a blacksmith or an impoverished soldier I drew my own conclusions.'

'And Mama is dead? How?'

'There was an outbreak of typhoid fever in the village and she tried to help. I'm sorry.'

Elizabeth didn't think to ask him how he knew all this. She struggled to assimilate the facts, but they wouldn't fit. She couldn't believe it, no matter how she tried. He explained he had chanced to be in Herefordshire and so made a few enquiries based on the little she had told him. Even in her confused state of mind Elizabeth couldn't help suspecting he had gone solely on her account, but she let that pass unchallenged.

'I didn't want to tell you this in a letter,' Mr Holbrook murmured.

'I can't thank you enough. . . .' But her voice broke and the torrents of tears finally came. He drew her head on to his breast. Even the metal buttons on his coat seemed warm. He waited till she had calmed down a little before he spoke again.

'I wonder if I should tell you something which might amuse you.'
He ran his forefinger down her damp cheek. She shivered.

'What is it?'

'Your family has tried to salvage their reputation and yours by
telling their neighbours you went to stay with a distant relation – in
every sense of the word, I gather – where you married without their
consent and that is why they have cast you off.'

An insane laugh escaped her. She couldn't help herself. The one
thing she was adamant she wouldn't do and her family had used it
as an excuse to disown her. But then the laugh cracked and her eyes
filled with tears again.

She had been very close to marrying Will, a man her family would
certainly disapprove of. A strolling player and nothing more. Only
now, because of her, he was dead.

He cradled her in his arms and she cried till she was exhausted.
She was vaguely aware that Nan was in the room – she must have
been absent before, she supposed – and that Mr Holbrook had gathered her up and carried her to the narrow bed. Propping her on his
arm, he insisted she drank a sleeping draught a doctor had left her,
though she didn't remember consulting one.

And as she began to tumble into a well of darkness, she felt a kiss
upon her lips and fingertips on her cheek and something kind
murmured to her and then nothing more.

The coroner's inquest returned a verdict of suicide and Will Ramsay
was buried quickly and without the usual Christian ceremonies.
Elizabeth was not told till it was over and she shrank from asking
where the grave was. She was not usually religious, but in her
morbid state of mind it preyed on her that she had been responsible for an action which Catholics at least thought caused the eternal
damnation of the soul.

After a decent interval, Mr Boxall opened the theatre again and
with an effort, Elizabeth forced herself to go to the first rehearsal.
Before then she had been leading an artificially enclosed life, seeing
few people apart from Nan. Once a day, if possible, Mr Holbrook
came to see her and when he didn't come, she felt sick and
depressed.

149

She still had not told him about her lie. There was nothing in the suicide note which referred directly to her supposed marriage, but she understood the hints even if no one else did. Mr Holbrook had found new lodgings for her and Nan, but it hadn't stopped public interest nor her nightmares. She still started at shadows.

There was some sympathy for her in the troupe. More than one person told her, now it was too late, that they had seen Will was not in his right mind some time before he died. But Elizabeth also detected covert hostility and couldn't even bring herself to be indignant about it.

Her attitude to acting had changed. For the first time it struck her how trivial her profession was, pretending to feel what she did not feel in exchange for money, while outside in the real world, real people lived and died and suffered. Comedies or tragedies jarred on her equally.

She struggled through her first scene before she started crying and found she was unable to stop. Mr Boxall drew her aside afterwards and gently suggested she shouldn't try to go on for the present.

'We'll manage without you for a while. Or maybe Charlotte could try some of your roles.'

So Mrs Boxall has won after all, Elizabeth thought, without rancour. Mrs Boxall had been pinning her hopes on her oldest child for years, though she showed none of the natural talent of Johnny or Augusta.

But she couldn't bear to stay and watch. She took her cloak, drew the hood over her eyes and plunged her hands deep into her muff. She had no clear idea where she was going. A flash of colour caught her eye.

She looked up in alarm. No, it was only a nurse carrying a little girl, clad in a bright pink gown and red cloak, to a children's party. But it put her in mind of the Parrot Man. She could not remember seeing him since Will died. Had he really intended to abduct or seduce her? Had he found some new object for his admiration, now she had all but disappeared from the public? Or had Will invented the whole thing, to try to frighten her into marrying him?

She didn't want to think ill of the dead. She walked faster to stop herself from thinking at all. Instinct led her to the bookshop where she had failed to meet Mr Holbrook. The wind made her bones ache and she was grateful for shelter.

She wouldn't admit to herself she had been half-convinced Mr Holbrook would be there until she heard a familiar voice. She looked up eagerly, but though the man talked with the same accent as Mr Holbrook, he was a complete stranger.

She spent as much time there as she dared, glancing into books and newspapers without the slightest interest. But inevitably she was forced out into the cold again to stare at shop windows. She even wondered if she should toil up the steep steps into the grave-yard of St Peter's Church. Maybe the church was open – but did she dare set foot inside?

For the first time, as she hesitated outside the iron gate beneath the steeple, Elizabeth acknowledged to herself that she was looking for Mr Holbrook. She thought about him constantly when he was absent. She remembered his words in the quiet of night, imagined he was holding her, kissing her, when thoughts of Will became unbearable.

Mr Holbrook had come less frequently of late and he often seemed in a hurry to leave. Of course he had social engagements, she understood that, and then on Monday there had been the Quarter Sessions. She wasn't unreasonable. She knew that, despite those hastily uttered words on the doorstep of Woodlands, a huge gulf separated them.

Maybe over the last days he had become more and more aware that there was blood on her hands. She had disgraced her birth by her profession. Now not even that profession was left. She had been good at it; it made her happy; she had been able to move others to cry or laugh.

Now what was to become of her? Unless she could rouse herself, Mr Boxall would not be able to keep her on. She did not want to stay as a sort of crippled limb. Her ambition, London, Garrick, still called to her, but from a very long distance. She could not help questioning the value of the success she had craved.

Was it, after all, a worthwhile cause? So many people did unpleasant things because they were necessary – surgeons pulling teeth and sawing limbs, scavengers removing refuse from the streets, small boys and girls climbing chimneys. . . .

What was the use of leading a butterfly existence? She had thought herself superior to her natural duties – to run a household, raise children, work for the good of the poor. Wasn't she more worthless now? Maybe that was why Mr Holbrook had sheered away, afraid she might become a burden on him.

Now her mother was dead, she couldn't even go home. There was no one to intercede for her any more. While her mother lay dying, she was no doubt flouncing about the stage, making the unwashed populace laugh.

A sudden burst of hail seared her face. She hurried up the incline of St Peter's Gate, not sure where she was going. She was reluctant to return to the theatre or the loneliness of her lodgings, but she dreaded the throng of the more respectable shops. Her teeth were chattering and the pain of the cold was excruciating. A carriage drew up alongside her.

'Can I take you anywhere, Miss Hathaway?'

Her heart thudded against her stays. Mr Holbrook was leaning out of the window. But then it struck her how formally he had addressed her and she gripped her fingers inside her muff.

'Thank you, no,' she stammered. 'I – I wasn't going anywhere in particular.'

Her skin was being flayed off her face. It was as though she could feel the ice penetrating her blood, killing her by inches. No one could endure this weather for long.

'Get in, now, Elizabeth Hathaway, or I shall take you by force.'

He had to raise his voice to make it audible above the drumming of hail on the roof. It danced and bounced off every surface. She could see muscles twitching in the horse's flank where the hail struck it. Her face stinging, shivering with cold, Elizabeth crawled inside.

The interior of the carriage was dark. The tall houses, the narrow streets, the grey clouds shut them in. She discovered she was soaked to the skin, strands of hair plastered to her face, water running down her forehead, nose, cheeks.

For a few minutes they were forced to stay silent. The hail on the roof was deafening. She was suddenly overwhelmed by a wave of shyness. She had not thought out the logical end of her train of thoughts. He, and the hail, had come too soon.

'What brings you out alone in such weather?'

Elizabeth pondered her answer as if her life depended on it.

'Loneliness,' she said.

Mr Holbrook uttered the bitter laugh she hadn't heard for a very long time. 'Oh yes. I know all about loneliness.'

They were both silent again, so close in the confined space they were nearly touching, yet infinitely far apart. Feeling it was her turn to speak, she asked when he was returning home.

'Tomorrow,' he replied heavily. 'The Quarter Sessions have adjourned to East Retford, so there is nothing to keep me here. I was going to come and bid you farewell later. How long before Mr Boxall plans to leave?'

'The company is going at the end of January.'

Two and a half weeks yet for her to make up her mind. But she was earning nothing, only living off her savings. Soon, if she were not careful, she would be a drain on the resources of her friends. Maybe she should go when Mr Holbrook did, where she didn't know. Nottingham would be desolate without him.

'And when are you going to illuminate the stage again?'

'I don't know.' She added in a whisper, 'Perhaps never.'

Her head drooped. Everything seemed too much for her at present. Tears gushed into her eyes, but she blinked them back.

'What nonsense is this? I won't hear of it. What on earth do you intend to do?'

His bracing tone was too much for her for once. Instead of rousing herself, she began to cry out loud, 'I don't know. I don't know anything any more.'

He sighed impatiently as she hid her face in her hands.

'You make things very awkward for me,' Mr Holbrook said in an aggrieved tone, the surprise of which instantly dried her tears. 'I had intended to beg and plead with you to give up the stage and become my wife. I shouldn't like to feel I influenced you while you don't have your full wits about you.'

His face was blurred behind a film of tears, yet she thought she saw an uneasy little smile twitching at his mouth.

'I – I'm not sure what answer you expect from me,' Elizabeth stammered, convinced he must be able to hear her heart lurching.

'No, neither do I.'

His tone was still unrelentingly grim, but he took her hand and began examining her oval nails as if he had never seen anything remotely resembling them in his life. There was another long pause. Elizabeth was dimly aware of sounds, the creaking of wheels, the thud of hoofs, voices of children and hawkers, beggars and coachmen. She felt giddy and it took her a moment to remember why she could not accept his offer.

'I know all the arguments against our marriage as well as you do,' he resumed after a little while, but she interrupted him.

'Don't say any more – there is something I must tell you.'

He listened in silence as she blurted out the incidents leading up to Will's suicide. His face remained rigid, only the eyes burning behind the mask. Unable to endure his gaze, she looked down at the hand he still held, motionlessly, on his knee.

'I know I should have said something sooner. . . .'

'If I were unscrupulous,' he interrupted her, 'I would use this incident to force you to marry me to try to cheat your conscience that way. Only I don't suppose it would deceive either of us. Don't sit there, looking so humble; I've no patience with it. It was a very rash and foolish thing you did, but it can't be undone and you couldn't guess what it would lead to. The fellow need not have done anything so—' He broke off.

'I wish I could believe that. I try so hard to convince myself.'

'Yes, well, that will take some time, I grant you. But it doesn't alter the fact that I want to marry you, if I could be sure you'd accept me for the right reasons. And I don't want you to be grateful either, so you can take that pious look from your face too.'

The word 'gratitude' had indeed been on the tip of her tongue and Elizabeth's cheeks grew scarlet. His fingers grasped hers tighter and she noticed he still wore both rings. If she did give way to temptation, she would take on the burden of his past as well as her own. And his daughter, too.

What was the alternative? Her mind shrank from her black shapeless future. If she left him now, she would never see him again.

There was nothing to keep her in Nottinghamshire. She ought to go home, or try a different provincial company. Maybe Mr Wilkinson would still be willing to take her.

The idea of being separated from Mr Holbrook sliced through her like a knife. Every nerve jangled, like a rotten tooth. The more he argued against the marriage and tried to set her free, the more she felt bound to him. She could sense the strength of his passion battling against his logical mind.

'I don't care about Miranda, or what people will say, or your age or mine. I don't want you to marry me to appease your family, or because you don't know what else to do. All that matters is whether or not you can bring yourself to be fond of me, old, scarred and bitter as I am.'

'You're not old,' she exclaimed; then moderating her tones she added. 'At least, you don't look *very* old when you don't frown.' She let herself do what she had often longed to do and ran her fingers across his forehead, trying to smooth out the lines.

'You little minx.' He could not keep the earnestness out of his voice. His eyes burnt the icy flesh of her face. 'You haven't given me an answer yet.'

'Haven't I?'

It was a struggle to resume her mock-innocence. Every time she tried to return to her old, carefree self, the image of Will, hanging from the curtain rail at the window interposed between her and the light.

'Then you will?'

'Yes.'

The whisper had scarce crossed her lips before he had gathered her in his arms.

'Come here, my poor drowned rat,' he murmured. 'I can't bear to see you like this. I want you to chatter and laugh until you drive me to distraction and this is the only way to silence you.' And with that he kissed her.

Chapter 13

There had been a great deal to talk about in Church Street. The news filtered through in a variety of ways. First there was a vague rumour when, day after day, the Holbrooks failed to return. Then a mysterious letter arrived for Mrs Morris from Mr Holbrook that no one quite liked to believe until barely legible scrawls from Miranda to Ruth Collingham and the Parr sisters followed and, on the same day, the *Nottingham Journal* finally reached Mansfield.

The newspaper, with its brief announcement of the marriage between Edward Holbrook, J.P. and Miss Elizabeth Hathaway, brazenly advertised as 'actress with Mr Boxall's company' for maximum effect, was the final proof necessary.

Mrs Collingham scuttled off directly to see Mrs Tallant. But the latter had for several days behaved in a renunciatory manner, assuring everyone who spoke to her that there had never been anything between her and Mr Holbrook, that it was too soon after Mr Tallant's death (although, to be sure, she had been widowed a full year longer than the magistrate, but it was different for men) and that she wished the couple the best of luck.

A few days later, Miranda returned to Woodlands in a blazing temper. She was half-tempted to accept her aunt's invitation to go and live with her. Mrs Lester and her daughter accompanied her and they, with Mrs Morris, were under instructions to prepare the house for its new mistress.

The reason Miranda publicly gave for her return was her wish to say goodbye to her friends and take one last look at her childhood home. If she did go, she was determined to take with her every item, down to the last pin, which she could claim either as her own or as her mother's.

Privately there were other reasons. For one thing, during the blazing row between her and her father, he had forbidden her to stay with her aunt. This roused all Miranda's stubbornness and contrariness and she defied him and railed against her stepmother.

Once her temper cooled, Miranda secretly acknowledged she was afraid of her father and what he might do. But she also loved him and didn't want to give him up without a fight. If she left Woodlands, it would seem like an admission of defeat. If she stayed, however, she could expose her stepmother for the fortune-hunter she was, cause dissension between the newly-weds and generally bring her father to admit he had been duped by a devious woman.

Miranda had only the vaguest idea how it would all end. If it had been a novel, she supposed That Woman would elope with a lover, fall into bad company when he deserted her and die, of consumption or in childbed (in which case, she supposed, the child ought to die, too), quite possibly deeply penitent and absolving her husband of all blame. And, though Papa would pity her, he would be cured of his embarrassing infatuation. But Miranda couldn't help suspecting life was a lot messier than the books she read would have her believe.

The newly-wed couple had, despite January weather and January roads, set off on a wedding tour about which Miranda resolutely took no interest. The whole thing had been sprung upon her so suddenly, she was still in a bewildered rage.

She refused point blank to attend the wedding, even before her father said anything about it. She was frustrated by the fact he made no effort to persuade her and only sighed, murmuring it was what he and 'Lizzie' had expected.

She thought she would have time to use her influence, with tears and tantrums, pleas and protests and reminiscences of Mama. But he had got the licence before he told her and with unseemly haste they were married the next day. She could not forgive them for that.

It was That Woman's fault. Those singing lessons had been part of her plot and the scandal with the suicide lured Papa back into her trap. One thing was certain – she would never call her Mama. Nor Mrs Holbrook. That too was Mama's name. But she wasn't sure she would dare call her to her face all the names she gave her in private. Papa was too daunting a proposition.

The reunion was uncomfortable enough. Papa tried to sound cheerful and Miranda *was* glad he was home – the place did not seem right without him – but she hid it and was as cold to him as she was to The Interloper. Several times she saw Papa frown and bite his lips. And then She would touch his hand or look pleadingly at him, and he made another effort to pretend nothing had changed.

But it *had* changed. The final straw was when The Interloper leaned over his chair in passing and kissed the frown from his forehead. Tears gushed into Miranda's eyes. She fled to her room to hide her anger and, buried deep, the knowledge that it should have been Mama who brought that radiant look to Papa's face, but it wasn't and, as far as she could remember, it never had been.

The return to Woodlands had also unnerved Elizabeth. Things had happened too quickly for her too. The tearful farewells from Nan and the children were still vivid in her mind. Mr Boxall kissed her and pinched her cheek for the last time, before suddenly embracing her and telling her he looked on her as a member of his family.

Edward's sister was polite and awkward when they were introduced. But when, in the traditional manner, she came to prepare the bride for bed, Mrs Lester suddenly announced, 'Look here, child, I won't hide the fact I was against this marriage when Edward first told me about it. But I haven't seen him so happy for a long time, so there must be something about you worth knowing. Though I warn you, if you ever, *ever* do anything to disgrace him or make him unhappy, I'll have my revenge on you, one way or another.'

Their reflections smiled at each other in the mirror. Elizabeth promised to do her best and thanked her for her good wishes.

'Hmm, well, it seems to me things will be hard enough for you without my adding to your problems,' the older woman replied, removing the last hair pin and spreading Elizabeth's dark hair with a speculative air. 'And if ever she becomes too much trouble, Miranda is always welcome to stay here.'

The following day they set out for a country house lent to Mr Holbrook, Edward (she was still not used to that name) by a friend. Edward did his best to make that short time together a haven, away from all the troubles of their past and the uncertain future.

There had been bad moments. A fold in the curtains, a sudden shadow looming up when the candle flickered, a portrait or mirror on the wall where she had not expected it – all made her start violently and brought back the horror.

She had nightmares about Will. Only sometimes it wasn't him hanging from the window; it was Nan once, her mother, her father, Edward and, worst of all, Bessy. She was glad when her tossing or sleeptalking woke her husband and he held her in his arms till the horror receded.

Once she woke from a nightmare that Edward was dead and when she turned to him, he was so motionless and cool to her touch, she was seized by panic. With a cry of anguish, she started shaking him, pleading with him to be alive. He struggled out of sleep and looked so wan, she couldn't stop apologizing for disturbing him. That was the only time he lost his temper.

'Damn that man! He had no right to be so cruel. He knew you'd be the first to find him.'

'And I had precious few stockings left,' she tried to laugh through her half-dried tears. 'But maybe that wasn't why he did it. Maybe he only wanted to feel close to me in the last moments of his life.'

Gradually the images of Will grew fainter and less frequent. If Edward was asleep when she woke, she would lie gazing at his face, the lines smoothed out by his smile of contentment.

She started to laugh and chatter again and she saw him gaze indulgently at her sometimes. When she thought he was absorbed, reading or writing, and not even aware she was in the room, he often surprised her by catching her round the waist as she passed and drawing her to his side.

They made a silent pact not to think about the future during that delicious fortnight alone. When either one sighed or looked grave, the other would exert him or herself to shake off the mood of depression. But the journey home was increasingly silent and Elizabeth clutched Edward's hand when they finally turned off the Nottingham road.

Though he said little, Elizabeth saw the coldness of Miranda's welcome wounded him. At breakfast the next morning Edward proposed a visit to Mrs Green's shop to buy summer clothes, but Miranda refused to come with them.

It must have quickly become obvious to onlookers that Edward Holbrook was besotted with his young wife. Elizabeth was embarrassed at the spectacle he made of them at the draper's shop. He insisted that they were served by Mrs Green herself and made her assistants fetch all the most expensive and fashionable silks down from the shelves, even though he had already bought new clothes for her in Nottingham for the wedding.

When Elizabeth ventured to protest, he countered with, 'Hang the expense. I can afford to clothe my wife in nothing but silk, if I choose. And I won't let you leave till you have picked out five or six patterns, whichever you like best.'

With some haggling, she beat him down to three. New clothes were essential for her new position in society. There were all the wedding visits to and from Edward's friends and acquaintances to endure yet. Everything about her, from her manners to her appearance, would be minutely analysed. It would not be easy to avoid accusations of extravagance, Edward was so determined to spoil her.

Behind her back, he returned to the draper's shop, bought several more lengths of silk and persuaded the mantua-maker to make them up without Mrs Holbrook's knowledge, using the measurements she had taken of the bride.

Elizabeth was surprised by her husband's good taste. He accepted her compliments and kisses with a smile, forgetting to add that the amount he spent had made both the tradeswoman and the seamstress his staunch allies and his best advisers as to what would suit Mrs Holbrook's pale complexion, blue eyes and raven hair.

It seemed to Elizabeth she had never enjoyed new clothes so much. The deprivations of the past years played a part, of course, but most of all, she liked to be admired. She was amused and flattered when Mary and Nettie Parr copied her hats and even Mrs

Tallant started wearing the longer sleeves which were becoming fashionable, and changed the trimmings on her gown to match Mrs Holbrook's, before travelling to London to attend her daughter's wedding.

Edward showered his wife with silk stockings, worsted stockings, gloves, hats, caps, jewels, muffs, shoes, lace cuffs and even – a recent innovation – a parasol. Elizabeth began to feel a little over-whelmed, as though she was only a doll for her husband to dress.

Moreover, she viewed the degeneration of Edward's relationship with his daughter with anxiety. True, he bought her a new velvet muff and a parasol at the same time as he bought similar items for Elizabeth, but the young stepmother saw Miranda felt neglected.

Initially, Elizabeth was rather taken aback by aspects of Edward's character which emerged when he was with his daughter. For one thing, she was surprised at how strict he was. Miranda flinched whenever her father replied to one of her earnest remarks with an ironic comment.

The more open hostility she showed towards her stepmother, the more disapproving and distant Edward became. It was as though, having taken the risk of marrying a woman so much younger than himself, he had lost his sense of humour on the subject.

Elizabeth was rarely alone with her stepdaughter. There was so much to do to set the house in order that she was rather grateful that Miranda frequently vanished, to visit her friends or ride with James the groom for company.

Mrs Morris only stayed long enough to hand over her great bunch of keys and pass on general information about the household before taking genteel lodgings in her native town in Yorkshire and return-ing to her role of impoverished but respectable widow.

Most of the maidservants had been at Woodlands for less than a year and therefore Elizabeth escaped comparisons with the first Mrs Holbrook. She knew from her mother's experience that maids generally did not stay long with any mistress, being liable to get married, fall pregnant or simply rebel against being treated as infe-riors and leave without warning.

There were signs of rebellion in the cookmaid's uplifted chin when she went to confront her. Elizabeth guessed that, in a house left effectively without a mistress, this woman had been used to a great deal of freedom, provided the meals were on the table in good time. She feared her master, but defied Mrs Morris and – so Jenny informed Elizabeth in a breathless whisper – had even made the housekeeper cry on occasions.

Elizabeth had no intention of crying or of putting up with unnecessary waste in the kitchen. She was aware that two of the maids were listening attentively, while pretending to polish the silver. If she did not quash this insurrection, she would have a full scale rebellion on her hands.

'T'master's never complained about t'tradesmen's bills, and he'd a better right than the likes of you.'

'Mr Holbrook has enough to trouble him outside the house,' she smiled politely. 'As for my past, I learnt how to keep myself fed, clothed and lodged for a few shillings a week and I don't intend to take lessons in economy from you, Molly, now I have a little more money in my keeping. If you cannot keep within the bounds I set, I suggest you find yourself another place.'

Elizabeth was generous in the perks she allowed the servants – tea, coffee, cast-off clothing for themselves and their families – but suppressed any attempt to encroach on these privileges. She didn't want the servants to think she was bribing them or unable to maintain discipline. Molly and one of the other maids stayed, Elizabeth judged, chiefly because of these perks. The youngest maid stayed because she admired her mistresses, or rather their elegant clothes, which might be passed down to her eventually. The fourth maid Jenny, however, stayed out of loyalty, after her mistress bandaged her hand and sent her home for a few weeks when she scalded herself with some boiling water.

On the eve of her wedding, Elizabeth had written to her father for the first time since she left home and Edward added a note of his own. Since then a tentative correspondence had been resumed, though the distance between Herefordshire and Nottinghamshire was used as an excuse why visits were not possible.

Mansfield society was another hurdle. No one was rude to her, though most kept their distance. She sensed Mrs Collingham was lying in wait for some social *faux pas* in order to inform her that

that was not how things were done. She seemed to forget Elizabeth was a lady by birth. As a result, she felt obliged to be constantly on her best behaviour, unless she was with her husband.

What she missed most was company of her own age. Inevitably Edward's friends were of his own generation. Once, out of loneliness, she spent a whole afternoon chattering to Miranda's friends and only afterwards noticed Miranda's scowl. She had enough tact to back off, so her stepdaughter wouldn't accuse her of stealing her friends, but Miranda was not forgiving.

Nan wrote to her, but they were the stilted letters of someone unused to writing. She found it was impossible to hear Nan's warmth in the carefully penned sentences about what play they were doing, where they were staying and how healthy, or otherwise, the children were.

Edward's duties took up most of his time. In his capacity as a landlord, he had to settle disputes between tenants and supervise repairs to fences or roads. As a magistrate, he had to consult other justices, attend clergy meetings and supervise the overseers of the poor.

Even if Edward was at home, there was every chance he had taken over the dining-room to examine witnesses and fine petty criminals. He had to make sure fathers of illegitimate children married the mothers or had sufficient funds to take care of the child if it ever became dependent on the parish. There were poachers to question, pickpockets and thieves to send to the House of Correction, beggars to return to their last permanent parish, drunkards to reprimand.

On one such occasion, Miranda strayed into the drawing-room where Elizabeth was sewing and did not notice her stepmother till it was too late to retreat unnoticed. She was about to go anyway, but Elizabeth spoke first.

'I'd like to talk to you, Miranda.'

The girl glared at her, then shut the door and walked across to the sofa where Elizabeth sat.

'I wanted to ask your advice. Won't you sit down? It will give me a crick in the neck to keep looking up at you.'

Her stepdaughter made no response to this friendly suggestion.

She folded her hands meekly in front of her, as though about to receive a rebuke from her schoolmistress, which she was prepared to endure before ignoring everything that was said to her.

'Well?' she asked in uncompromising tones.

'I was in the blue bedroom yesterday and I noticed the curtains were growing shabby. I wondered if you had any opinions on what I should do – find some new curtains to match, or redecorate the whole room?'

Miranda's body grew even more rigid. Out of respect for the girl's sensibilities, Elizabeth had made a point of not changing any of the rooms so far and contented herself with cleaning the house from top to bottom and making detailed inventories of every cupboard, wardrobe, closet, linen press, chest, box, drawer and trunk that was under her jurisdiction.

During her first week as mistress of Woodlands, her husband announced that she had the right to redecorate the whole house if she chose. Elizabeth sensed he was sometimes oppressed by the continued presence of his first wife in the house.

Maria Holbrook's taste did not match Elizabeth's either, being rather old-fashioned, but her courage failed her. She had heard references enough from Miranda and Mesdames Collingham and Parr that certain minor changes she had instituted were not how 'Mama', 'Mrs Holbrook' or 'Poor dear Maria' had done things.

'Do what you like. Papa does not begrudge money to *you*.'

The bitterness was unmistakable. She turned to go, but Elizabeth got up. They were both about the same height now and Miranda showed promise of growing still taller.

'We cannot go on living in this way. Don't you see how unhappy it makes your father?'

Her hand was on the door handle, but she turned to face her stepmother. Elizabeth was startled by the livid hue of the girl's face. Even her lips were pale, barely visible.

'I'll pack my things then and go,' she said. 'My aunt told me I would be welcome there if. . . .'

'For God's sake, child, you know that is not what I meant.' Elizabeth flew across the room and leaned against the door to prevent the girl from going. The clock nearby began its solemn chime. It seemed to her almost like a death knell.

'Why not? I know you don't want me here and Papa will not notice I have gone.' Miranda blinked back her tears and tried to steady her voice.

'Oh, fudge. I don't want to come between you and your father. And I am not trying to replace your mother. I couldn't even if I wanted to.' Elizabeth felt a sudden pang of guilt, though she attempted a smile. 'I am only ten years older than you.'

Since returning to Woodlands, memories of the conversation she had had with Miranda after the singing lesson had come back to haunt her. She had, indirectly, promised the girl she would not pursue her father. But things had not turned out that way.

'And I suppose you want to be my friend, my sister,' Miranda sneered.

'I think we could live tolerably together, for your father's sake.'

'For your father's sake, for your father's sake,' she mimicked in a high-pitched tone, backing away from Elizabeth into the room. 'Oh, save me, dear Edward, my wicked stepdaughter is being unkind to me. Lock her away in her room and feed her on bread and water.'

Elizabeth tried to intervene, but Miranda was in full rant by now and nothing could stop her.

'You may fool Papa, pretending to be in love with him, but I know you only married him for his money, and I'll make him see you as you really are, even if you kill me for it.'

Elizabeth's first indignant impulse to deny everything was suddenly swallowed by the desperate urge to laugh. But there was a pathos in Miranda's exaggerations because, in some ways, she believed what she was saying.

'I know things look pretty black to you, especially after I promised you that none of the rumours about your father and myself were true. But if you let me explain. . . .'

'I don't want your explanations. Papa and I were happy before you came, just us and Mama. We don't need anyone else.'

'Don't you think *I* should have some say in the matter?' The door to the library sprang open so suddenly both women started. 'Remember, Miranda,' Mr Holbrook went on, 'a true lady never raises her voice.'

'And a true lady does not show off her legs on a public stage either,' Miranda retorted.

The remark hurt her father more than its intended target. Elizabeth felt a knot of dread. She did not like to see Edward frown like that. She was afraid he might, in his eagerness to defend her, say or do something which would cause a permanent rift between him and his daughter.

'I won't have such talk under my roof.'

'And I've already told *her* I'd rather go and live with respectable folk like my aunt than stay here with her.'

'I hope my sister Lester will teach you some manners, because God knows I must have failed to bring you up properly.'

He did not seem to see the wild-animal glare in Miranda's eyes. He didn't see how much he hurt his beloved child.

'Don't, Edward, don't say such things.'

He ignored her. 'Your mother spoilt you and I never took time to put things right.'

Miranda was nearly crying, but Elizabeth knew that even if she tried to defend her, she would get no thanks for it.

'At least Mama loved me. *She* never wished I'd never been born. She never called me a changeling. My nurse told me what it meant.'

For some reason, Edward staggered at the word and sank into his usual armchair. 'Go to your room, Miranda. I can't talk to you when you are like this.'

Without warning he looked old. Though Elizabeth's heart went out to him, she held back, hoping Miranda would make amends. She wondered if she ought to leave them alone together.

'I won't trouble you much longer,' Miranda's voice trembled. 'I'll go and write to my aunt.'

Nevertheless, the girl hesitated by the door, hoping her father would call her back. He didn't even glance in her direction, though he winced at the click of the door. Elizabeth, feeling invisible, approached him and instinctively, he reached out and twined his arm round her waist. She perched on the arm of his chair, but for a long time he didn't speak.

'You've had a bad day,' Elizabeth suggested, stroking his shoulder.

'Yes.' He did not elaborate. There was another long pause. 'I loved her so much.'

She did not stop stroking his arm and shoulder, but she felt a surge of jealousy. She realized for the first time that secretly she harboured the wish that he loved her best, better than he had loved his wife or his mistress. She was not sure which of them he was talking about.

'She was such a beautiful child. I thought I wanted a son, but when I first took her in my arms and she smiled at me and looked at me with those big blue eyes . . . Miranda – we called her after Shakespeare's heroine because she was our little miracle.'

Elizabeth let him talk, adding murmurs of sympathy at intervals, but Edward did not seem to hear her. His eyes were staring at the dancing shadows on the lawn outside. The warmth crept through her again. Would he love her babies as much as he loved Miranda?

Edward had insisted on settling the same amount of money on her as he had on his first wife, despite her lack of dowry. But the question of what would happen if Elizabeth had children was still open. She feared her stepdaughter's reaction, especially if she had a son who would, theoretically, stand to inherit the majority of his father's wealth, including Woodlands.

The words now were tumbling out. He told her about an incident he had witnessed between Miranda and a playmate which had opened his eyes to her real character. His forehead crumpled into deep lines; he bit his lip. Elizabeth even suspected there was a glitter in his eyes, but maybe it was only the way the sunlight fell on his face.

'I couldn't bear it, Lizzie. I couldn't bear to think my perfect little daughter was a liar.'

She pressed his head against her breast and he clung to her, like a drowning sailor to a mast.

'You are too severe on her. How old was she?'

'Five, six. I don't remember.'

'Oh, Edward, of course she lied. All children lie to protect themselves. Only a mature person is not afraid to admit his or her faults. Some adults never learn to do that.'

He grew so still in her arms, for a moment she was irrationally afraid he might have stopped breathing. His eyes were puzzled, doubting, as he raised his face.

'Lizzie Holbrook, how did you come to be so wise?'

'I was the oldest child in my family. My mother made a confidante of me. Besides which, it is easier to be wise about someone else's problems than about your own.' A momentary thought of Will brushed its wings against her.

'You'd better go to her,' she said. 'She was nearly crying when she left. She'll want to be comforted now.'

He demurred, but she pointed out the letter would be ready soon and, if he didn't want Miranda to go, he had better hurry or she would be too proud to change her mind. She followed him into the hall to make sure he went, accused him of being as wilful as his daughter and gave him a gentle push, which propelled him forward a few steps. Then he turned back.

'I forgot to ask what Miranda said to you. Was she rude to you? I won't stand for it.'

'Now don't, for God's sake, say anything rash. In fact, don't say anything about me at all, do you hear me? You cannot force her to think or feel as you do, and you must not antagonize her at present. Why don't you tell her she is your little miracle?'

He sighed. 'Have you done lecturing me yet as if I were a foolish schoolboy?'

She pulled his head down by both ears and kissed him on the forehead. 'Bless you, my son. Go forth and conquer.'

Elizabeth never knew what Edward said to his daughter. But as the weeks passed, Miranda grudgingly tolerated her. On occasions they even managed to achieve something like the good-natured ease of their early acquaintance.

Then something would remind Miranda and, without warning, her voice would grow chilly or mocking. She steadfastly refused to succumb to anything she suspected was a ploy by her stepmother to gain sympathy or to make them better friends.

Poker-faced she listened to the exchanges of nonsense between her father and stepmother. Nonetheless Elizabeth clawed her way back to her buoyant frame of mind. She was less guarded in society and uneasy smiles were beginning to greet her attempts at wit. Mrs Tallant was the first of the older ladies to take her under her wing. Elizabeth felt she had misjudged her and warmed to her.

Her position in Mansfield society was sealed by Mrs Lester. She had been brought up in the town and when she came to stay at Woodlands and openly championed her sister-in-law, the women took notice.

Elizabeth was relieved her original impression of her sister-in-law was not mistaken. Mrs Lester bore unmistakable signs of being Edward's sister but was less embittered by her experiences. Children, husband, house notwithstanding, Sophia Lester had a relish for life and took her pleasures whenever she could. Elizabeth frequently forgot she was not bantering with one of her contemporaries.

Edward watched their friendship blossom with satisfaction. He had a double motive for inviting his sister. As well as wanting the two women to make friends and for Sophia to act as a sort of chaperon for his young wife, he had become anxious about Elizabeth's health lately. He didn't want her to be left alone with Miranda for the two or, at most, three days he would have to spend in Nottingham at the Easter Quarter Sessions.

As far as Miranda was concerned, the truce was over. She had consoled herself during the months since her father's ludicrous second marriage that at least her aunt was on her side. The betrayal rankled. She cursed herself for letting her guard down for a single second and redoubled her efforts to show her stepmother she was not welcome.

But worse was to come. One morning, Miranda successfully provoked a quarrel with The Interloper and, to her amazement, reduced her to tears. Her aunt was present, though her father was not, but it came to the same thing, she supposed. Half-triumphant, half-guilty, she sprang to her feet to leave, throwing one last contemptuous glance at That Woman, weeping in Aunt Lester's arms.

'Miranda, apologize immediately to your stepmother.'

The last dredges of guilt drained away. Only defiance remained. 'I'll cut my tongue out first,' she retorted. 'She may be my father's wife, but she is nothing to me.'

She flounced up to her bedroom. It was a virginal room, all white and pink and more suitable for a little girl than a young lady. Mama had promised to let her choose new curtains and modern paper hangings for the walls. The latest fashion was for all things Chinese, she had read, and she dreamt of a blue and gold room, full of shimmering silks.

But then Mama became ill and there hadn't been time or money and Miranda herself lost enthusiasm for the project. She thought of petitioning Papa once she was out of mourning, but then he had got married. If she said anything now, he was sure to tell her to talk to The Interloper, and Miranda would rather have died.

She brushed away hot tears and resumed her hard expression at the tap on the door. She refused to answer, but her aunt came in nonetheless. She drew up a chair next to the bed on which Miranda was sprawling, her right arm across her face.

'You really shouldn't talk to Mrs Holbrook in that way.'

'I don't see why not. She has stolen everything from me. She only married Papa for his money.'

'I don't know where you got that idea and I don't care. You say you are tired of being treated like a child, so I think it is high time you stopped behaving like one. I had such high hopes of you last summer in Buxton.'

Miranda sat up. Her hair was dishevelled and her cheeks flushed. It made her look like a child recently roused from a midday nap. Even her lip trembled like an infant's, despite the sophisticated, low-cut gown she wore.

'It isn't fair. She's taken Papa away from me and – and now she's stealing you, too.'

'Oh, Miranda, Miranda, you're old enough to know better than that. I'm quite capable of being fond of several people at once and so is your father. From what I hear, you haven't even tried to befriend Elizabeth.' Mrs Lester frowned, as though balancing something in her mind.

'I can still come and live with you, can't I?'

'I'm beginning to think that might be for the best.' The older woman suddenly sat forward and took her niece's hand. 'Now, I'm trusting you because I think you ought to know. You must be gentle with Mrs Holbrook for a while. She's – she's in a very delicate situation at present.'

170

Horror rolled down Miranda's spine in cold beads.

'Do you mean. . . ?'

'In half a year's time, all being well, you will no longer be your father's only heir.'

Chapter 14

'Take care of yourself,' Edward murmured.

'Don't fret about me.' Elizabeth picked a hair off the collar of his greatcoat as she kissed him farewell. She felt a pang of apprehension as he stepped into the carriage, but she wouldn't have shown it for the world. So far Elizabeth felt she had managed pretty well, despite feeling uncharacteristically weepy, and the worst of her sickness seemed to be over now.

She had been very ill in February, when the children of the tenants overran the kitchen to toss pancakes under Molly's watchful eye. On Lady Day, it was the turn of the tenants' wives to drink tea in the drawing-room, while their husbands were treated to ale by the master. Easter passed without incident. They went to church, gave alms to the poor and dined with friends.

Edward would be only gone two days. Miranda was subdued and kept herself to herself. In theory, she shouldn't have any problems, especially as Sophia Lester was at Woodlands. But even so she felt darkness descend over her as the carriage rattled away. Spring weather, rather than cheering her, had left her exhausted and enervated.

There was no one in the drawing-room and Elizabeth wandered upstairs. While she was on her honeymoon, the dressing-room had been stripped of all the feminine trifles she had noticed on the night she dined there with Edward. It was a relief that here at least she was free from her predecessor. She had introduced a few little items of her own, chiefly presents from Edward, like the footstool and the pretty new rug, but a few bought out of her pin money.

So far she had trusted only Edward and Sophia with her suspicion that she was pregnant. Miranda would have to be told soon, reassured that it would make no difference to her father's love or her financial position. After all, Miranda was sure to be married long before her half-brother or sister could become a serious rival to her.

Should she talk to Miranda about her mother? Her predecessor must have had her good qualities, especially since she had obviously been close to her daughter. Maybe too close.

Elizabeth gathered, mainly from Sophia, that Miranda had become a pawn between her warring parents. Unable to command her husband's love to the exclusion of everything else and tormented with jealousy, Maria Holbrook had set out to buy her daughter's love, not only with gifts and treats, but by indulging and flattering her.

Naturally Miranda took advantage of the situation – what child wouldn't? – and her father grew increasingly concerned about her unruly behaviour and poor grasp of the value of money.

His way of trying to win his daughter back, through severity alternated with bursts of repentant generosity, was far more uneven than his wife's and was just as damaging to the child. Several times he gave up totally in despair and hardly saw her for months on end. During those times her mother's influence over her must have been strengthened, Elizabeth judged. They must have had common interests, secrets, games.

Unconsciously she found she had wandered into the old nursery. The room had a ghostly air, the carpet covered in drugget so it wouldn't fade, the shutters closed and the furniture shrouded in dustsheets.

Elizabeth pushed back the shutters. The window looked down on the courtyard and the gates through which, maybe only half an hour ago, she had seen her husband disappear. Whether Miranda liked it or not, something would have to be done with this room before the baby came.

The floorboards creaked and her steps seemed unnaturally loud. Tentatively she lifted the corner of one of the dustsheets. There was nothing remarkable underneath, only a wooden chair, rather scuffed about the legs where it had been kicked by little swinging heels.

Emboldened when nothing untoward happened, Elizabeth went on examining the room. Most of the furniture was old, possibly dating back to Edward and Sophia's childhood, the sort of things which could not be put to use elsewhere.

As she stooped to examine the clothes press for possible wood-worm, however, a glint of silver behind it caught her eye. The gap between the press and the wall was just wide enough to insinuate her hand into it and her fingertip touched something covered in fluff.

It took some time to tease it out and the dust made her cough. A chain unrolled as she edged it closer. Gingerly, Elizabeth picked it up and blew the sticky, grey trail of a spider's web off the object. With a guilty glance round, as though afraid she was being watched, she rubbed it with the corner of a dustsheet.

It was tarnished and black, but even so its beauty took her breath away. It looked like a Tudor pomander, heart-shaped rather than round as she had at first thought, with a tracery of delicate leaves across the front. She prised it open. It was empty, but the faint scent of something rich and dizzying wafted up to her.

Something was engraved inside. She had to take it to the window to decipher it. 'M.H. 6th Nov. 1768.' The date looked familiar, but it took her a while to recall that it was Miranda's birthday. Her sixth or seventh – she couldn't work it out so quickly.

It seemed an astonishingly extravagant present to give such a small child and it occurred to Elizabeth that Miranda shared her mother's initials. Either way, it must have been sorely missed. Maybe this was a way of pleasing Miranda before she told her about the baby.

She found her in the drawing-room, tangling her sewing as usual. For a moment, Elizabeth watched her, fair curls drooping over her shoulders, scissors glinting in her lap, the cat playing with a skein of silk at her feet. Her figure was still lacking in womanly curves and she was growing so rapidly Elizabeth feared she might, like her cousin Lucy, become prone to fainting fits. If she touched on such subjects, however, all she got were sulks and rebuffs.

'I've found something that belongs to you. You'll never guess where it was.'

Miranda caught her lip beneath her teeth and began unpicking stitches. Elizabeth felt a twinge of impatience at her studied show of indifference. 'You might at least look at it.'

Her eyes darted up. She stiffened, then dragged her eyes away and, pretending to compare different coloured silks, she muttered, 'It isn't mine.'

What was wrong with her? Why wouldn't she let her do her a good turn? Elizabeth had seen the fascination in Miranda's gaze. She recognized the object. Elizabeth let the pomander drop into the girl's lap, the chain running through her fingers. Miranda started as if it were a viper.

'It isn't mine, I tell you.'

'It contains your initials, or your mother's.' Her reaction was so different from what she expected, Elizabeth hardly knew how she should behave.

'You'd no right poking about the nursery.' Miranda jumped to her feet so the chain and locket rolled away, under the sewing frame. The cat made as if to pounce on it.

'You seem to forget I am mistress of this house and can go where I like.' Disappointment made Elizabeth speak more sharply than she intended. 'You might show a little gratitude.'

She stopped. Her stepdaughter had been very pale, but now her face grew carnation red.

'You've no right to pry.' The girl panted between each word, pushing aside her sewing and sending the cat scampering for safety. 'I hate you! You're as bad as her, pretending to be my friend when all the while. . . . You – you insult Mama and you expect me to—' Words failed her.

'What on earth is wrong?'

'Oh, don't pretend you don't know. You did it on purpose and I'll never forgive you, never.'

She swept off, slamming every door she passed, and thundered up the stairs. In numbed stillness, Elizabeth heard Sophia's voice on the landing, but Miranda rushed on, unchecked. She stooped to retrieve the pomander from the cat, which had crawled out of its hiding place. She was standing by the window holding the innocuous-looking object when Sophia entered.

175

'What on earth is the matter with Miranda?'

'I've no idea. Perhaps you can tell me. I found this in the nursery.' Elizabeth held out the trinket to her sister-in-law.

Sophia's brow puckered in a way which reminded her of Edward. She turned the locket over several times and held it up to the light, but she shook her head. 'Where did you find it?'

Elizabeth went over the whole story in detail, while the older woman continued examining the trinket, especially the inscription. But in the end she admitted defeat.

'I have seen something similar to this, though why anyone would give something like this to a child, I really couldn't say.'

Sophia advised her to let Miranda calm down in her own time. The girl did not come down to dinner. When Elizabeth sent Jenny to enquire after her, she returned with the message that Miss Holbrook had locked her door and said she was not hungry. Elizabeth wondered aloud if they should send something up to her, but Sophia replied, 'Leave her be. Fasting might do her temper some good. Not that she isn't thin enough already.'

As they returned to the drawing-room, Elizabeth was almost certain she heard steps on the landing and she hoped Miranda might join them. She did not, though at supper-time she asked for a tray to be taken up as she did not feel well. Sophia, too, looked uncomfortable by now and admitted that when she had passed Miranda's room, she heard her crying violently.

'I can't help feeling there is something important about that locket, something I've forgotten,' she said. 'May I see it again?'

It was not till halfway through supper that the penny dropped. Mrs Lester's exclamation of 'oh!' startled Elizabeth, but she said nothing more until the servants had been dismissed.

'I think I remember now,' she said slowly. 'I knew the year 1768 was important somehow, but I was on the wrong track. It was the year,' she paused, choosing her words carefully, 'well, I suppose I can be blunt with you, dear. It was the year Edward fell in love with Julia Elton.'

Elizabeth felt the bitter surge of jealousy sweep over her again. She hadn't dared ask about that episode in Edward's life.

'She was a friend of the family, you see,' Sophia went on. 'She adored children. I've seen Miranda clamber into her lap and fight with my own children as to who should hold Mrs Elton's hand when they went for walks.'

'She was married?' Elizabeth asked in a low tone.

She nodded. 'Yes, and she had children of her own. That was what made it so difficult. Well, it occurred to me that that was where I'd seen a locket like this before. Julia had one and she often wore it. I think I remember Miranda climbing on her knee to look at it and begging her to give it to her. I wasn't here on Miranda's birthday, but it looks like Julia let her have her way in the end.'

'But if she loved Mrs Elton so much. . . .'

'Don't you see it was a guilty reaction? Maria had a deal too much influence over that child. When she discovered how Edward felt about Julia, I wouldn't put it past her to have done her utmost to poison Miranda's mind. The poor child didn't know any more who she was allowed to like in her desperation to be loyal to her mother.'

Elizabeth shuddered. Miranda must have hidden the locket because she could not bear to be torn between her parents any more. Uncovering it had woken unappeased demons. And now that Maria Holbrook was dead, it would have seemed the height of disloyalty for her daughter to question the correctness of her judgement in the slightest thing.

Before going to bed, Elizabeth tapped at her stepdaughter's door. There was no reply, but she apologized as best she could through the closed door. As she reached her dressing-room, she thought she heard a door behind her. She glanced back, but saw nothing.

She took half-a-dozen steps into the room before, in the dim light, she realized something was wrong. She glanced up at the curtains, gripped by her old fear. She almost dropped the candle. This time she wasn't mistaken. She stared at the bulk which should-n't have been there and uttered an inarticulate cry. The light flickered.

No, it can't be. I am imagining things. I am upset because Edward is away and I have unintentionally hurt his daughter. Trying to conquer her fear, Elizabeth took a step closer and held up her candle. Against the blood-red curtains, the white-and-pink striped gown showed up like a silhouette on a cameo.

177

'Oh God, no, not again, not again.'

She slid the shaking candle to the nearest table. She couldn't bear the thought of touching dead flesh again. What on earth would she say to Edward? He would never forgive her for killing his only child. She should have followed Miranda, talked to her. She should – but maybe there was still time. Sophia had heard her crying. She must have been alive then. Why had no one gone to comfort her? Maybe she was not dead yet. Oh, God, what shall I do?

The thoughts flashed across her mind like sheet lightning as she backed away, unable to take her eyes off that pink gown. She tripped, fell and for a moment lay stunned, unable to move.

She must save Miranda. She must get help. But as she tried to rise, Elizabeth felt a sudden wrenching, pulling, grinding inside her. Pain drenched her in an instant. One hand against her abdomen, breathing in painful gasps, she dragged herself across to the bell-rope.

She must do this for Edward, for Miranda, for Will. It couldn't be allowed to happen again. Her legs, trembling and leaden, would not obey her. She pushed a chair ahead of her towards the window, simply to keep her balance, and grasped its back as she climbed on the seat.

She had had so many nightmares like this. A fresh spasm of pain made her double up. Why didn't anyone come? It would be too late. Raising her arms tore something inside her. Her hair clung to her forehead in damp wisps. She could see her fingers shaking.

A pin jabbed her fingertip. The sleeves of the pink dress hung limply. The head, under a cap so large it hid her curls, seemed remarkably upright. The body swung round in her grasp and she shrank from the crudely painted face on the linen-covered bolster.

The door was thrown open, there were voices, steps. Elizabeth felt something thicker, warmer than sweat ooze down her thigh.

'Oh God, oh God, oh God,' she moaned.

'Lizzie, come down, come here, hold on to me.'

She recogized Sophia's voice, but the gulf between the chair and the floor seemed so deep and dark. The pain ripped through her again. She crumpled, fell into an abyss.

'Jenny, send Isaac for Doctor Litton. Molly, help me.'

And after those words, Elizabeth was aware of nothing more than black waves of pain and confusion. . . .

Longing for Edward welled up inside her. She needed to feel his arms around her, to lay her head on his breast. She needed him to kiss her and tease her, to call her his drowned rat and threaten to lock her in the wine cellar.

Someone was mopping her brow and talking to her. It took an effort to understand. 'As soon as Isaac returns, I'll send him to Nottingham. Edward will be back by morning, I promise.'

Slowly Elizabeth remembered. The pain was easier now she was lying still.

'No. Don't send for him. They need him there.'

'You need him, too. He isn't the only magistrate in Nottinghamshire, you know.'

She shook her head, but even that slight movement brought back the wrenching pain. 'He'll only worry. Don't send for him. He'll come as soon as he can.'

He won't be back till Tuesday, her feverish mind whispered. Two or three hours left today, twenty-four hours tomorrow. Even if he rose at six or seven and hardly ate any breakfast it would take him – how long? – to get home. Fourteen miles from Mansfield to Nottingham, one mile less to Woodlands that would take – how long? Four hours? Five? Six?

Maybe the sessions would end early. Maybe Edward would come home on Monday night. He would come if she sent for him. But, oh, he would be so tired and how would she explain to him about Miranda?

With an effort she reminded herself it wasn't Miranda hanging there. It was the baby that was dead; she knew it without being told. It never occurred to her that, in her present state, it was likely she would be confined to bed and so it would fall to her sister-in-law to explain.

Her mind wandered again and she began counting the possible hours until Edward would be home. She strained her ears for the chiming of the clock to give her some clue as to how much longer she had to endure.

And when she slipped into an uneasy slumber, it was not the bolster in a dress and cap, but Miranda herself who hung from the

curtain rail and Edward turned away his face, withdrew his strong
arms as she struggled to explain, her tongue larger and clumsier than
usual, her words slaughtered by the feelings in her heart and the
fatal locket fastened round her neck.

'Good heavens, Miranda, what are you doing here?' He made as
though to open the door of the chaise, but she shied away like a
wild pony. 'You haven't come to meet me for years,' Edward added,
softened in spite of himself.

Whenever he was obliged to be away, even for only one night,
Miranda had always come part of the way down the hill, with her
nurse when she was little and alone when she was older. He had
joked she only did it because she wanted to search his pockets for
presents, but the little mite had declared stoutly that Papa's kisses
were better than any present.

Miranda's face was paler than usual and there were dark smears
round her eyes as though she hadn't slept much. 'I had to see you
first, Papa.'

Her voice too was different, strangulated.

'Climb in, princess. I'll take you home.'

Still she held back. Her hands were systematically tearing the
petals off a fat, yellow dandelion she held, but she hardly seemed
aware of what she was doing.

'I wanted to—' She glanced at James on the box of the carriage.
'I didn't mean it, Papa. They won't let me see her; they won't let
me talk to her. Tell her I'm sorry, Papa. Please, please.'

Ignoring his questions, she darted away. Dread gripped him. He
started forward to follow her, then changing his mind, he urged
James to drive as fast as he could back home. He recognized the
doctor's horse being walked about the courtyard. He did not have
the patience to wait till the steps were lowered and leapt instantly
from the carriage and into the hall.

'What is it? What's wrong?'

The iron hand round his heart tightened. Sophia was just coming
downstairs with Dr Litton. In his mind, the presence of the doctor
could only mean one thing.

'Now, now, Mr Holbrook, calm yourself,' Dr Litton said in soothing tones. 'You won't do your wife a scrap of good if you see her in this agitated state.'

She was alive, then.

'For God's sake, tell me what's wrong with her.' A black wave washed over him. A thousand possibilities flooded his mind and all pointed to imminent death.

'Mrs Holbrook has had a bad fright.' How could the man sound so calm? 'She is out of danger, as far as I can judge, but I'm afraid she has lost the baby.'

Edward let his breath out with a hiss. His hand reached for the newel post for support. Elizabeth was safe. That was all that mattered. 'And I may go and see her?'

'Certainly, as long as you do nothing to alarm or disturb her.'

He dismissed this with an impatient gesture and, forgetting to thank the doctor, he began bounding up the staircase. A thought stopped him. 'When did this happen?'

'Sunday evening,' Sophia confessed in an undertone.

The hand clenched his chest again. 'And you did not see fit to send for me?'

'Believe me, Edward, I wanted to and God knows Elizabeth called your name often enough in her sleep. But when she was awake, she was adamant you should not be made to choose between her and your duties.'

Remembering his manners, he retraced his steps, shook the doctor by the hand and, ignoring the anxious looks with which his sister was signalling to him, he leapt up the stairs.

The doctor's warning made him slow his steps as he neared her room and he eased the door open. The damask curtains were shut at the foot of the bed. Silently, Edward motioned to the maid to go. He waited for the door to shut before he stole round the bed. The curtains were open at the side of the bed so the invalid could watch white clouds stream across the pond of the sky.

She did not perceive him at first and he watched her for a moment. She looked tiny, dwarfed by the vast bed. The blankets hardly even showed the swell where she lay. The bed might almost have been empty apart from the decapitated head in the lace-trimmed cap on the pillow.

She was always pale, but today she seemed paler. By contrast, the black-fringed eyes and sensuous lips stood out. She raised her eyes suddenly and with an exclamation, she sat up and stretched out her arms to him.

'Oh, Edward, I've been listening and listening for you, but that stupid doctor *would* keep talking and I couldn't be sure if I heard the carriage or not.'

He gathered her to his breast. 'Why didn't you send for me at once, you foolish girl?'

'Because I was afraid you wouldn't come. And I was afraid you would.' Her arms wrapped around his neck, her breasts against him felt warm, soft. 'In future, sir, if you come to me directly after returning home, I'd thank you to warm your hands ere you touch me.'

She was clad only in her shift and he felt her trembling in his arms, but despite her words, she pressed more tightly against him. He wrapped the folds of his cloak round her.

'Minx! I ought to punish you for that,' he murmured against her hair. 'I am glad what has happened has had no ill effect on the rapidity of your tongue.'

A shudder passed down her and he heard her lashes brush against his shirt. He knew she was about to cry and that she did not want him to know.

'You had best lie down and let me tuck you in, or the doctor will scold me for letting you catch a chill.' His voice quavered less than he had feared it would.

Reluctantly their arms untangled. Edward drew the covers up to her chin, but remained stooping over her, stroking her cheek and tugging her earlobe. 'What on earth could frighten you so much, child?'

'Didn't Sophia tell you?'

'I didn't give her time.'

Her lowered eyelashes quivered like butterflies in a breeze.

'It wasn't the fright,' she murmured, 'it was the fall.'

He was not sure he had heard her correctly, but he persisted, 'Well, but what caused it all?'

'It – it was a silly prank by Miranda. I'm sure she didn't mean any

182

harm by it. Sophia says she is penitent, but that she would only disturb me if she were allowed in here.'

He teased the details out of her, haunted by the memory of Miranda's strange behaviour on the road. He had been badly frightened and could hardly control his rage. He alone had seen the devastating effect Will's death had had on Elizabeth. Despite her attempts at cheerfulness, he could see unshed tears in her eyes. The unborn child was dead, his wife's life placed in jeopardy and he was in no mood to listen to excuses for his daughter.

Several times he was on the brink of going to confront Miranda, but Elizabeth grasped him tightly, first by the skirts of his coat, then, when he sat down beside her, by his hand which, he noted absently, was growing warm.

'It was my fault she did it,' she whispered. 'I reopened old wounds without meaning to. You see, I found something she did not mean to be found in the old nursery.'

His heart contracted. It had never seemed quite real to him that he might become a father again, until now that it was too late. She would not meet his eyes and seemed reluctant to go on.

'I believe Sophia put it on the dressing-table,' she said. 'We didn't know what else to do.'

He strode across the room. His impatience drained away, however, when he pushed aside a lace-trimmed fan next to the jewel box. She should have warned him. Silently he sank into the chair and picked up the pomander. He opened it and Julia's scent enveloped him.

He raised his head. In the mirror in front of him, he could see the deep lines in his face and the damask curtain which separated his past and his present.

'Edward?' she called, but he didn't reply. The covers rustled. 'You do understand, don't you? I didn't know if I should tell you or. . . .' Her voice broke off.

He knew the silence lasted far too long. He could not help it. He thought he was perfectly happy with Lizzie, but he still had not exorcized Julia, neither the love, nor the pain, nor the shame, nor the glory of it all.

She called his name again and this time he rose and went back to the bed, still clutching the trinket in his fist. She was in the act of tossing back the covers to come and find him, but she drew back when she saw him.

'You're not angry with me, are you? Or with Miranda?'

'No, I'm not angry.' He felt as if he could never be angry again, he was so tired. Still she did not remove her eyes from his face. She shouldn't be sitting up like that. The locket clanked on the bedside table. He took her by the shoulders, pressed her down on the pillows and kissed her.

'And you'll forgive Miranda too?' she asked, withholding a kiss from him. 'I won't kiss you again till you do.'

He demurred and a tap at the door interrupted them. Edward frowned, but before he could cover her mouth with his hand, Elizabeth called out, 'Come in.'

It was only Sophia. Her mind had obviously not been easy and she scolded her brother for tiring his wife, contrary to the doctor's instructions.

'I'll go as soon as she agrees to kiss me.'

'You know my condition. Do forgive her. She didn't know this would happen. And she didn't know about the baby.'

Sophia's voice startled them by its coldness. 'She knew. I told her.'

Elizabeth could do nothing to prevent the storm which burst over Miranda's head. If Edward hoped to shame his daughter with his reproaches, he was a poor judge of her character.

She was genuinely penitent and had been tormented by guilt ever since she heard Isaac ride off for the doctor. But her father's accusations roused her stubborn streak. She cried only in the pink and white bedroom, when she was woken in the middle of the night by her stepmother screaming in her sleep.

Once she lit her candle and got as far as the door of her father's room. There, trembling in the dark, she listened to Elizabeth weeping and her father's hushed words of consolation. Lonely and desperately unhappy, she crept back to bed, but it was a long time before Miranda could get warm again or push aside the things she had heard.

Her Aunt Lester, too, had scolded her, but her tempers had a tendency to flare up and then subside. She took pity on her niece long before her brother could bring himself to acknowledge openly that Miranda was suffering for what she had done. He never admitted he had overreacted because of his memories of Julia.

It was Sophia who, taking advantage of his absence, allowed Miranda to see her stepmother. The meeting was awkward. Miranda's confessional impulse had wasted away from being long suppressed and, though she tried to be reasonable in front of Edward, Elizabeth had moments when she convinced herself she hated Miranda for what she had done to her.

Nevertheless, she managed to gloss over her feelings and for once Miranda did not reject her attempts at friendship. An uneasy truce was sealed between them and when Edward returned unexpectedly and caught them together, he showed no sign of hostility.

Elizabeth recovered rapidly, at least physically. The day came when the doctor overruled Edward's wish to keep her cocooned and she regained the freedom of movement she had begun to miss in the close atmosphere of her rooms. Trembling, she took her first steps outdoors, leaning on her husband's arm, to sit in the sunshine of the walled garden and admire the roses. The wound to her peace of mind took longer to heal. Under stress the nightmares returned long after Will's death was relegated to the back of her mind. Julia could not be similarly dismissed. Edward did not speak of her and she was afraid to raise the subject. He must have taken the pomander, since she could not find it anywhere. She had not known what to do with it, but it made her uneasy, knowing he kept a memento of his former mistress.

The tensions between Edward and his daughter eased, but tacitly it was agreed it would be better for Miranda to go to Nottingham for an extended visit. Mrs Lester stayed as long as she could, but her own family required her attention. Elizabeth was glad her absence made it necessary for her to resume the reins of the house. Sometimes Edward's care seemed a little too smothering and she began to long for the independence she had given up.

185

PART III
1780–1781

PART III
1750-1781

Chapter 15

'I believe I met your father and stepmother while I was in Buxton,' Mr Prestwick remarked, to fill the void. They were not alone in Mrs Lester's drawing-room, though they were apart from the others, so any private conversation ran the risk of being interrupted.

'Papa took Mrs Holbrook there for her health,' Miranda replied stiffly.

For two and a half years now she had lived chiefly in Nottingham and, apart from the separation from her father which still rankled, she had to admit it was the best thing that could have happened to her.

Inevitably, the county town was livelier than Mansfield, where the main industries were beer and worsted stockings. In Nottingham, there were always regiments billeted, or simply passing through. Assemblies in winter were larger and might be attended occasionally by the nobility, local Members of Parliament, passing dignitaries and army officers. There were assizes and executions, horse races in summer, concerts and plays. Fireworks, bonfires and illuminations followed good news from America, even if it proved to be false or exaggerated a week later.

There were drawbacks as well, of course, like prostitutes, beggars and sporadic riots, usually by the framework-knitters, at low pay or high prices. But since Mr Lester was a lawyer rather than a hosier, Miranda reassured herself that there was no direct threat to them and enjoyed the excitement instead.

It was 3 June, the eve of the king's birthday. Mr and Mrs Holbrook had just arrived at Mr Lester's three-storey, red-brick house, to witness the celebrations and take Miranda and three of her cousins back to Woodlands, away from the heat and rancid smells of the city in summer.

Their brief stay in Nottingham could not have come at a less opportune time for Miranda. Since they met at Buxton nearly three years ago, Mr Thomas Prestwick had cultivated the acquaintance of Mrs Lester. Whenever he was in Nottingham, he called at her house in St Peter's Gate. So far he had not proposed, though he spent a good deal of time talking, walking, singing and dancing with Miss Holbrook.

There were several reasons for this state of affairs. The chief ones included Mrs Lester's vigilance, Mr Prestwick's caution and Miss Holbrook's flirtatiousness. Mrs Lester was convinced her niece was too young and giddy to get married and the others were half-inclined to agree with her.

Miranda liked the notion of wedding clothes, flowers and a nice gold ring to show her friends, especially since Mary Parr was now a Mrs Forbes and she and Ruth were next in age in their little group.

On the other hand, she still remembered with a shudder the tediousness of trying to be the housekeeper of Woodlands. Not to mention the fact that being married might put an end to her gadding about, wearing fashionable clothes and flirting with as many gentlemen as possible. She discovered quite young the influence she had over men and she had not yet finished experimenting with that power.

These experiments were not always to Mr Prestwick's liking and she often saw him frown and become jealous. This, too, had its charm, to see how far she dared venture before pulling back, winning his forgiveness and carrying on as though nothing had happened.

And Mr Prestwick was a good catch. Everybody said so. He was good-looking (though not as heart-stoppingly handsome as Frank Collingham, whose image she still carried in a private recess of her heart); he was well-off (she knew she had expensive tastes); and, most of all, he was intelligent.

That was what fascinated her most. Though she did not put it in precisely those terms, she was curious to see how foolishly a clever man would behave under the influence of love.

Miranda had no pretensions to being a bluestocking and he often talked of things she was too lazy to understand, but all manner of people admired Thomas Prestwick's abilities and that counted for a good deal. There was even talk he might stand for Parliament.

He had only been in Nottingham for a few weeks and Miranda was reluctant to leave him so soon. Yet she was more than a little scared he might find an opportunity to talk to her father. It would ruin the delightful suspense and indecision she was basking in at present.

'Is your stepmother always so pale?' he asked, looking across the drawing-room.

Miranda would not admit it in a thousand years, but Elizabeth looked utterly bewitching at present. She refused to follow the fashion for high towers of hair and wool, as sported by the Duchess of Devonshire, declaring such a monstrosity would make her head ache.

Instead she piled her unpowdered hair up just high enough to emphasize her aristocratic forehead, with soft curls clustering round her neck to make it look whiter. Her figure was still girlishly slim, despite being quite old, nearly thirty, which in itself was an offence in Miranda's eyes.

'Yes. Papa won't let a breath of wind or a ray of sun touch her without his leave.' She choked down her bitterness. 'Tell me honestly, what do you think of her?'

Mr Prestwick considered the matter for a moment. Or maybe he was only counting his waistcoat buttons, Miranda thought with a twinge of irritation. Thankfully, he did not seem tempted to look at her stepmother again.

'She seemed very well informed when I met her,' he said at last, 'but there is a sadness in her eyes. Is it really true she was an actress before she married your father? I could hardly credit it, but everybody said so.'

'That is because she can play the devoted wife so charmingly,' she replied.

His frown warned her she was on dangerous ground. Clearly he had been impressed by the second Mrs Holbrook. For the most part Miranda thought she had grown indifferent towards her step-mother, but at moments like this the old antagonism returned. She was glad she had stayed with her aunt. Living under the same roof as a woman with a tarnished reputation might have impaired her chances of marrying well.

'Her sadness is easily explained,' she went on. 'She's pining for her vagabond life. She can hardly bring herself to set foot in a theatre any more, she is so sick with envy.'

There was also the matter of a second miscarriage, but Miranda chose to ignore that. She was in no way to blame for this tragedy, but still she did not like to think of it because it brought back memories of her father's voice shushing the broken sobs behind the closed door.

'I would not have guessed it,' Mr Prestwick muttered, 'but then, I hardly know her, whereas you. . . .'

Hastily, Miranda changed the subject. Nonetheless, she noticed her admirer's eyes turned towards Mrs Holbrook several times before they separated to dress for dinner.

Miranda was not the best judge of character and rarely spent time at Woodlands. For that reason she was unaware of subtle changes in the relationship between Mr and Mrs Holbrook. Edward, for instance, had relaxed some of the smothering care he lavished on Elizabeth in the first months when he lived from moment to moment, terrified his happiness might be snatched away from him.

His life had inevitably lapsed into its former pattern of duties, habits and traditions. But in general his mood was lighter, things seemed easier, more interesting than in the days he had sought to escape from his first wife's reproaches, his daughter's wilfulness and his guilt over that business with Julia.

Busy as he was, he was unaware of the growth of a vague but insistent longing in his wife. Elizabeth had introduced more and more changes at Woodlands, but still she felt the brooding presence of her predecessor, not quite daring to begin afresh till Miranda's future was secure. But it was more than that, Elizabeth mused as she wriggled out of her riding habit. The trip to Buxton, this visit to Nottingham revealed to her how much she missed travelling. She dreaded returning to Woodlands for the long autumn and winter months, fearing she would be trapped there forever.

Miranda was correct in her dismissive assessment of Elizabeth's feelings about the theatre. Her ambition was dormant, not dead. As her stepdaughter had observed, she could not enter a theatre without being agitated. If the actors were mediocre, she was sharp-tempered all evening, but if a play seized her imagination, she unconsciously imitated gestures, expressions, intonations until she went to bed.

She hardly dared talk to members of Mr Boxall's company when they returned to Mansfield, so scared was she of damaging her hard-won reputation. She was shocked to discover Bessy no longer remembered her and had to be coaxed back, though Augusta's rapturous welcome soothed her soul somewhat.

In secret she mourned when David Garrick gave up the management of Drury Lane Theatre to the playwright Sheridan and his business partners. When the great actor died a year later, a part of her dreams died, too. Now she would never see him, nor would he ever see her act.

Even reading emotional scenes in novels upset her. Her inner ear heard how she would have pronounced those speeches on stage. Unconsciously she tossed her head, turned her eyes upward, played with her cuffs or raised her hand to her throat.

Reading plays was impossible. She did not look at that shelf in the library, or even allow the hem of her dress brush against it. Her collection of scripts had been hidden away, in the bottom of the linen press. She could not bear to look at or touch those handwritten pages, let alone read them or throw them away.

Once when Edward was away from home, she locked the door, emptied the press and spread the whole collection across her bed. For a long time, she simply stared at the black ink on the yellowing paper and finally nerved herself to choose one. But she only managed to read two lines before the longing welled up in her.

She wanted that happiness again, the feeling she controlled others, moved them as she was moved, made them admire her against their better judgement. She gathered up the plays and pushed them back into their hiding-place. It was dangerous to wake such powerful emotions.

Edward was not expected home that night. She tossed and turned for hours. In desperation she began to go over her lines in her head. To her horror she realized that words she had thought indelibly fixed in her mind were fading, leaving only faint echoes. She could feel the rhythm of blank verse, but not stray words in the middle of a line.

After that she became almost afraid of being alone. She was relieved at Edward's proposal to fill the empty bedrooms at Woodlands with guests when they returned from Nottingham. 'After all, we must give Miranda every opportunity to meet suitable young people,' he said, raising his eyes from the letter he held. 'Sophia tells me one gentleman in particular has been paying her marked attention. If we had him under our roof, we could observe him, and he and Miranda would have a better chance to get to know each other.'

Elizabeth agreed, trying to smile, and he leaned across the table to draw his finger down her cheek. 'And you, dear child, might start to laugh again and behave like a young creature.'

He didn't say so, but she knew he was thinking of the miscarriages. She struggled with her tears. Of late, it seemed like the whole world was full of babies, many in conditions far worse than those her child would have enjoyed. Maybe a child of her own would have given a new direction to her thoughts. And he was so kind to her, she redoubled her efforts and, sometimes, contrived to be as content as she pretended to be.

She was conscious that in public she was still playing a role, striving to make people forget her disreputable past. She could always tell when new acquaintances were told about her past by some busybody. Ladies grew stiff and distant. Pompous men became disapproving in their behaviour towards her, while libertines tried vulgar jokes or attempted to seduce her.

On the whole she thought she was winning the battle. Every year her reputation remained unsmirched made her more and more welcome in society. She didn't know it, but her position was greatly strengthened when one notorious rake lost his bet with his drinking companions that he would make her his mistress in less than three months.

Elizabeth had never been really tempted. The motives of her most vocal admirers were all too transparent and the mixture of irony and tenderness in Edward's character meant that, in spite of the age gap, the Holbrooks were well matched. Naturally there were disputes and quarrels, but none that lasted long or inflicted irreparable damage.

Elizabeth was favourably impressed by Mr Prestwick when they met at Buxton. Edward had taken her there to recover from the last miscarriage. Since she looked no older than she had a few years ago, she was addressed as 'Miss Holbrook' by someone who believed Edward was her father. Mr Prestwick overheard the familiar name and so they began to talk.

She judged him to be about her own age, old enough to have had his character formed. They had had several interesting conversations on the arts, politics and the progress of the American War and she looked forward to renewing their discussions in Nottingham.

At dinner, they started comparing their childhoods – dim memories of the books from which they had learnt to read and the coronation celebrations of George III, consisting of fireworks and plum pudding. They talked and laughed and it was not till afterwards that Elizabeth realized Edward had fallen silent and the puckers had appeared in his forehead.

Miranda, too, was alarmed to see her on such easy terms with her admirer. Although she had learnt to manage her quarterly allowance so she could afford all the stylish clothes she wanted, Miranda was insecure about her appearance. She was tall and fair-haired, as was fashionable, but she had to resort to false rumps and extra wadding at the top of her stays to enhance the rather meagre curves she had been endowed with. Her stepmother's hourglass figure had never seemed so obvious before.

Once in the drawing-room, Miranda tempted Mr Prestwick to her with a tearful gaze. By being on her best behaviour she kept him at her side all evening, flattered by her deference to his wisdom.

'Don't frown, Edward,' Elizabeth murmured, when at last they were alone together and passed her fingers over his forehead to smooth out the creases.

'Was I wrong to marry such a young creature as you?' he asked, gazing at her.

She took both his hands and wrapped them round her waist.

'Better an old man's darling than a young man's scorn,' she said, but the frown deepened. He worried about her, she knew. 'Besides which, if I'd wanted to marry a man of my own age, I had opportunities enough. It was you I chose.'

She kissed him and he smiled, but she couldn't destroy the worm which gnawed at his heart, that she *hadn't* chosen, that she had accepted him only because her life was falling apart. She would still be comparatively young when he grew old. By the time he left her a widow, it might be too late for her.

'You know I am not interested in Mr Prestwick for my own sake.' Elizabeth laid her head on her husband's breast. 'It is all for Miranda. You do approve of him, don't you?'

'He seems very sensible and amiable.'

'She needs someone to indulge her and scold her alternately. And she was so sweet and grave and hung upon his every word tonight, I really believe she is in love with him.'

'And I, of all people, ought not oppose true love, is that what you mean? Well, I shall invite him to Woodlands, but whether or not he accepts is his business – and Miranda's.'

The bells in every church in Nottingham began ringing early in the morning. Mrs Lester, with a sigh, scolded her husband again for choosing a house where they ran such grave danger of being deafened on Sundays and holidays, and blithely ignored his protests that it was she who had fallen in love with the capabilities of the house.

Thomas Prestwick called at about half-past eleven and soon afterwards, the ladies clad in their most gossamer-like gowns and the younger Lester boys dashing hither and thither, the entire party strolled out to join the crowds gathering in the market-place. Elizabeth had been told it was the largest market-place in England and had further claim to importance as the site where Robin Hood was arrested while taking part in the archery contest at the Goose Fair.

The largest of the bonfires in the town had been stacked there and at noon precisely, three troops of the Horse Guards Blue fired volleys and uttered deafening cheers. To add to the confusion, swarms of lads, mostly apprentices, let off guns, squibs and crackers of their own and Elizabeth clung to her husband's arm to prevent being separated from him in the crowd. Glancing round, she noticed Miranda and Mr Prestwick at a little distance from them.

'Don't be frightened by the noise,' Elizabeth heard him shout above the din, 'I'll protect you from any danger, Miss Holbrook.'

Miranda, to Elizabeth's trained eye, did not look the least bit frightened, though the throng was the perfect excuse to press against her protector as tightly as she could.

On the rare occasions Elizabeth had seen her stepdaughter with one or more of her admirers she had wondered at the girl's stratagem of pretending to be sillier and weaker than she really was. It wasn't something Elizabeth generally resorted to, except in a mocking way. But Miranda made no attempt at irony.

It baffled Elizabeth, moreover, that intelligent men could be deceived in this way. Some seemed genuinely moved by female helplessness. She noticed that at one moment she and Mr Prestwick might be deep in conversation, but at some nonsense from Miranda he would turn aside, his expression softened, and he listened as if she were pouring out pearls of wisdom.

However, it was none of her business and she was proud of Edward's superior judgement. Although it troubled her on occasions that he indulged Miranda as though she were not old enough to be a rational being.

Mr Prestwick spent the rest of the day with the Lester-Holbrook clan. In the evening, they ventured out again, to look at the illuminated windows in every house and the grand display of fireworks in the market-place. A crowd of some 12,000 people had gathered and the explosions mingled with shrieks and exclamations. Once, in a lull, Elizabeth was aware of the long wail of an infant in a nearby house, woken by the noise.

The market-place was barely two minutes' walk from St Peter's Gate under normal circumstances, but this time Edward Holbrook had to break their way through to Wheeler Gate, like a ship struggling through ice in the Baltic Sea. Elizabeth followed close behind and she could hear Mr Prestwick's voice at her shoulder, encouraging Miranda.

She paid little heed to the raised voices until suddenly there was a surge in the crowd and a clash of metal. Two or three bodies pushed themselves between her and her husband, but her cry of alarm was lost in the din.

Some dispute had arisen between some of the officers of the Horse Guards and local inhabitants. Swords were drawn on one side; the others snatched walking-sticks, paving stones and anything else that came to hand.

Elizabeth lost sight of her husband in the crowd, though she thought she glimpsed his hat a short way ahead. She did not dare glance back, for fear of losing that beacon. She was buffeted both by the combatants and those striving to escape. The mob was growing incensed.

She cried out and struggled when an arm wrapped round her, but Mr Prestwick urged her, 'Come with me, Mrs Holbrook. There is not a moment to lose.'

He was dragging Miranda by one arm, who was clinging to her hat with the other. Each step was a battle, yet such was Prestwick's determination that it could not have been long till they were out of the market-place and in the narrower street leading directly to the church.

She caught sight of Edward, fighting his way back to find her. She sprang towards him, utterly forgetting Mr Prestwick's arm encircling her. Mr Holbrook took charge of his wife, but his face was grim. Elizabeth discovered she was wheezing and shaking by the time he thrust her and Miranda inside Mr Lester's door.

The disturbance continued a good while longer. News drifted back to them, through servants and neighbours. The mob followed the officers to their lodgings and, lacking a vent for their energies, broke the windowpanes, frames and inner shutters of the Blackamoor's Head Inn.

As a result, an order was issued to the General of the District from the King in Council, allowing the military to act as they saw fit to disperse dangerous mobs, without having to seek the permission of local magistrates. Edward shook his head when the news reached him.

'It doesn't surprise me in the least,' he muttered. 'What with the news of the war and what is happening in London, it's hardly likely they'll stand for any insurrection here.'

News was just reaching Nottingham of the Lord George Gordon anti-Catholic riots in London. Moreover the East India fleet, valued at several millions sterling, and a thousand troops on board had been captured by the combined fleets of France and Spain, and other northern powers seemed braced to change their armed neutrality to open hostility against Britain.

For her husband's sake, Elizabeth put off leaving Nottingham day after day. In the county town important news would reach him sooner. Her stepdaughter, too, seemed content to stay, despite the fact Thomas Prestwick was to follow them to Woodlands.

After an additional fortnight, their departure could not be delayed any longer. Mrs Lester's two oldest sons and only daughter accompanied them and Elizabeth had to set the house to rights before any more guests arrived. On her return, she was greeted by a letter from her cousin Lucy. She had also been invited, but discovered she couldn't come after all.

Miranda's cousins and friends filled the house with noise and merriment. Elizabeth struggled to orchestrate the smooth running of the household from her dressing-room, the only room in the house where she could, occasionally, snatch a quiet moment to sit down.

Sometimes, passing the drawing-room on her way to or from the kitchen to superintend, scold or settle disputes, Elizabeth paused to listen to the laughter. The pang was even more acute, however, when she found the room empty and eerily still because, while she had slipped out to attend to some duty, the young people had been tempted outside by the weather.

She was not so very much older than her guests, yet she was thrust into the role of matron and chaperon, if they remembered her at all. She found herself being called upon to sympathize with Mrs Collingham's ailments or gossip with Mrs Parr, when her ears were straining to hear the latest news of 'Perdita' Robinson, the actress who was refusing to return the Prince of Wales's love letters until he paid the sum of money he had promised her.

Mr Prestwick was expected on the twenty-third. Miranda, who had not visibly pined for her absent lover, insisted on staying home all afternoon, but he didn't come. Dinner was delayed to no avail. At suppertime there was still no sign of him, and when Elizabeth went on her rounds to ensure the house was locked up for the night, she found Miranda sitting at the foot of the stairs.

'You might as well go to bed,' Elizabeth said, 'he won't come tonight.'

Miranda shivered. 'I'm sure something has happened to him. He would have written if he could, I know it.'

It was true Mr Prestwick was a punctilious man, but Elizabeth did her best to console her. 'If there had been some accident, don't you think your father would have been informed?'

Miranda rose and went across to the door. She opened it and, when she went to stand beside her, Elizabeth saw the sky was still light at the western edge.

'The nights are going to grow longer and longer now,' Elizabeth murmured, and she meant her own life, too. At thirty, it was popularly believed a woman reached her peak and, though summer would stretch a few months longer, autumn could not be far behind.

I am only twenty-eight, she thought. I had such aspirations and I have been consigned to the role of a middle-aged woman before my time. I have failed as an actress; I have failed to escape the destiny my parents doomed me to from birth; I have failed even as a mother. At my age, Mrs Boxall had five children and Bessy on the way. She was my age when I joined the troupe.

I have even failed as a stepmother. I am no nearer to being Miranda's friend than I was three years ago. I don't know what she is thinking, though she is standing so close to me that we are nearly touching.

Sometimes when they were alone, Miranda would forget herself and talk or laugh naturally with her. But in public her irritation would resurface and Elizabeth had decided it was better to remain aloof and allow her to pursue her own course.

'Maybe I will go to my room,' Miranda broke the silence at long last.

But when Elizabeth went to bed, there was a light still showing underneath Miranda's door. Unknown to the young stepmother, the candle was allowed to burn away to its socket while Miranda sat and waited. Maybe if Elizabeth had tried to probe her feelings, Miranda might have confided in her, but the moment passed and the word remained unspoken.

Suspecting Miranda had passed a poor night, Elizabeth gave the servants instructions not to wake her the following morning. There was enough to do, what with it being rent day.

One of the young Lesters had gone riding. The other, for want of a better occupation, went with his sister to feed the swans. Amid the bustle, the hoofs of yet another horse went unnoticed. Elizabeth, hurrying to the drawing-room to greet the tenants' wives and daughters, was brought up short in the hall. A tall figure in a bottle-green coat stood there, hat in hand.

'The servant has just gone to look for you,' Mr Prestwick said. 'I appear to have come at an inopportune moment.'

'Oh, it's quarter day, that's all. We didn't expect you for some hours yet. Or is it later than I thought?'

'No, no,' he reassured her, holding out his hand. 'I ought to apologize for failing to send a message yesterday. I couldn't drag myself away from Nottingham as early as I wished and it was late when I reached the Hutt near Newstead Abbey, so I spent the night there.'

'I suppose we should be insulted that you could not bring yourself to come to us.'

He started forward, taking her joking words for earnest. 'You must not think that, Mrs Holbrook. I stayed only to get the latest news. I thought Mr Holbrook might like to know Sir Henry Clinton has captured Charlestown. The whole town is celebrating.'

He went on to give her a full account, so carried away that Elizabeth did not have a chance to invite him into the library, or excuse herself with her waiting guests. He broke off suddenly.

'Miss Holbrook, I did not see you there.'

Miranda threw her such a venomous look, Elizabeth wondered how long she had been standing on the stairs and what it was she thought she had witnessed.

Chapter 16

*T*he end of June and the whole of July, save for two brief intervals, proved gloriously sunny. In town, the heat became remorseless and the roads were so dusty it was nearly impossible to breathe. But on the hillside at Woodlands, there was always a fresh breeze and cool shade.

Despite the presence of several admirers, who came and went, Miranda was listless and bored in the countryside. She had grown used to Nottingham, and Mansfield seemed dull and provincial by contrast.

She was still keeping Mr Prestwick at arm's length. Indeed, that gentleman hesitated a good deal before finally requesting a private interview with Mr Holbrook. It took Elizabeth a while to find her husband afterwards, sitting on a bench in the shrubbery, staring at nothing.

'I cannot believe my little girl is old enough to receive proposals of marriage.'

'You did not discourage Mr Prestwick, I hope?' Elizabeth sat down next to him.

'No. I told him Miranda was at liberty to do what she chose. But all the while, I wanted to urge him to consider he was risking his whole future happiness and Miranda's. I was younger than he is when I got married and Maria was about the same age as Miranda. I wonder if she'd been older if she would have made a different decision and spared us both a great deal of grief.'

They watched and waited, but Mr Prestwick failed to speak to Miranda. It was never the right time, or she made him doubt the wisdom of his choice by some freak of hers. Or else she found a dozen excuses to avoid a private interview, and when the couple were alone, she would turn the conversation into incongruous channels till her lover couldn't remember any of the beautiful phrases he had intended to dazzle her with.

'Surely she knows what Prestwick intends to say,' Edward exploded one evening, pacing Elizabeth's dressing-room like a caged tiger. 'If she means to have him, she should say so. And if she doesn't, the sooner she sends him about his business, the better for both of them.'

A memory of Will seared Elizabeth's conscience.

'It's possible she doesn't know her own mind, Edward,' she suggested.

'Or maybe she's a coquette and wants to exert her power as long as she can.'

Elizabeth was secretly more sympathetic than her husband. Miranda prolonged the period of uncertainty only to enhance the sweetness and excitement of the courtship.

Long engagements were almost unprecedented for people of their class. Once a maiden gave her consent, there was no logical reason to prevent the marriage from taking place as soon as the settlements were drawn up and the licence obtained. One week or a fortnight, and that was all, because, of course, no gentleman worthy of the title would dream of proposing marriage before it was prudent to do so.

And no one, Elizabeth reflected, could doubt Mr Prestwick's prudence, at least in worldly matters. If it was folly to love someone as giddy as Miranda, then it was a folly that young lady could not exactly throw back in his face.

Elizabeth did not hide the fact that she liked him. Since his arrival at Woodlands, he had been very attentive to his future step-mother-in-law and she had been included in many more of the young people's expeditions and conversations.

Even household duties seemed lighter now she had something to look forward to, whether it was a sketching party, a discussion about the newest novels, or a performance of *The Messiah* at St Peter's Church by the organist and choir of Southwell Minster.

A spell of dull, grey weather at the end of July confined what was left of the party indoors. Miranda couldn't stop yawning as she sat in the windowseat of the drawing-room, making no attempt at any occupation.

'I wish it was Christmas,' she suddenly announced with a good deal of viciousness, 'then at least we might have charades or a masquerade, or perform a play.'

The last words made Elizabeth's heart contract into a fist.

'Well, why don't you do it now?' she said quietly. 'It would be better than being bored.'

Irritably Miranda began listing reasons against the scheme. This attracted the attention of the various Lesters, who countered every objection. Mr Prestwick listened in silence, but he kept his eyes fixed on Miranda. It was clear her cousins' arguments had an effect on her. She was tempted to change her mind, but didn't know how to do it without apparently consenting to do what her stepmother suggested.

The idea of performing a play particularly appealed to the Lesters because they had never done so due to lack of time during the busy Christmas season.

'We could ask Miss Parr or Miss Collingham, or even Mr and Mrs Forbes to make up numbers,' George Lester suggested, 'and didn't Miss Collingham say her brother was coming home soon?'

'And you'll join in, won't you, Prestwick?' His younger brother Harry added his mite.

All eyes turned towards the grave young man.

'If Miss Holbrook wishes it, and if her father gives permission for this – enterprise.'

The chill of his disapproval settled on the three siblings. Elizabeth glanced at Miranda. This was clearly meant as a test of her character and the result was exactly what Elizabeth expected.

'I believe I *do* wish it,' Miranda replied, her natural perversity roused. She threw a nervously defiant look at her stepmother. 'I suppose, Mrs Holbrook, you could persuade my father if you chose.'

Like a spider's web, Elizabeth's past hovered in the air. As clearly as the voices around her, she sensed the unspoken question. What is your role in this? And maybe also the words – if you take part, I won't.

'I am willing to speak to your father when he gets home and then, I'm afraid, I'll have to leave everything in your hands, costumes, scenery and all. I shall be busy with all the jams and preserves, and the cherries from the orchard must be bottled if we are to have any at Christmas.'

Miranda's face cleared. Apparently she had no concept of what this cost her stepmother. In silence, Elizabeth bore the thorn in her heart. Without complaining, she wheedled Edward into compliance. He seemed to be growing mellow with age and made none of the objections she had expected, only gave her a look which made her flinch.

But after he was asleep, she stole across to the bedroom window to gaze at the moonlit garden and smother her sobs in the curtains.

Every single play was cleared out of the library and wherever Elizabeth went, she stumbled on young people skimming the pages. Mr Prestwick's sudden coldness towards his hostess was an implied reproach that she hadn't prevented this when she saw he disliked amateur dramatics.

But Elizabeth was more afraid of what Miranda might say or do if she thwarted her. She could imagine the comments if it got about. Dog in the manger. Of course *she* wouldn't want her stepdaughter to act – she is so jealous of her. Now, of course, she would be accused of being a bad influence. Either way, she couldn't win.

Finding a play was not easy, since most needed more male than female characters, and there was no one among them who felt capable of writing something to suit them all. The choice was narrowed down to *The Fair Penitent*, *She Stoops to Conquer* and *The Busy Body*, chief bones of contention being who would sacrifice themselves to play the older characters and servants.

In the midst of a discussion, the door opened and Ruth Collingham appeared, followed by a tall gentleman dressed in the height of fashion. His coat was tight-fitting, his waistcoat shorter than had been fashionable for the previous half-century and a starched cravat visibly restricted his breathing and the movements of his head.

In the absence of her stepmother, Miranda leapt to her feet and, regardless of appearances, flew towards him, both hands outstretched.

'Frank Collingham!' she exclaimed. 'When did you return home?'

His eyes rested on Miranda's pointed face, fair curls and elegant gown as if he had not heard her question. 'Oh, late last night. Faith, Miss Holbrook, when did you grow so tall and stylish?'

It was a long time since they had met. After Cambridge, Frank Collingham had decided to follow in his father's footsteps and had been studying law – as far as any young man in his situation ever studied when there was a whole metropolis to explore – at one of the Inns of Court.

Miranda felt the familiar flutter in her breast whenever she heard that voice again. He had plenty of news he was willing to share with them. Over the past days, Mr Prestwick had been gloomy and indifferent towards the project of the play. The contrast between him and the young attorney-at-law could not be more stark.

At times, Miranda even forgot the presence of her lover. She couldn't help glancing at Frank Collingham every few minutes. Frequently, she discovered him just looking away from her, or his eyes would turn towards her just before she glanced away.

Mr Prestwick was the only one of the group who wondered if he was embroidering his tales of the Gordon riots. In Holborn, distilleries had been blown up by the mob so the streets were flooded with spirits and the water supply to Lincoln's Inn Fields became alcoholic. It seemed to Thomas Prestwick the young puppy was still under the influence of that water.

Naturally the newcomers were canvassed on the subject of the play. Frank was eager, having trod the boards before at various houseparties he had attended with his friends, but Ruth shrank smaller than usual.

'Oh, no, I couldn't. I'd simply die if you made me do it. It would be awful to stand there and not be able to say a word.'

The others tried to encourage her, but not too much. Women's parts were scarce and everyone was more than relieved when Ruth offered to help with the costumes, act as prompter and generally make herself useful.

'And your handwriting is so neat,' Miranda added, thinking of her own rather dashing scrawl. 'Maybe, when we finally choose a play, you could write out everybody's part for them.'

It was Frank Collingham who settled the last doubts about the choice of play.

'Oh, by all means let it be *The Fair Penitent,*' he urged. 'Can you not imagine me as the faithless Lothario? And Miss Holbrook would be charming as poor lost Calista and. . . .'

He looked round at the rest of the company in some doubt but, following his example, the parts were quickly distributed. Mr Prestwick led the way, almost fiercely claiming the role of Altamont, Calista's virtuous lover. This rather surprised all those who gathered from his recent behaviour that he disapproved of the scheme and would not want such an important role.

George Lester good-humouredly undertook to be Calista's father, while the younger Lesters, much to their amusement, found themselves playing husband and wife, as Horatio and Lavinia.

'I'm sure Nettie Parr will play Lucilla if I ask her to,' Miranda went on, 'and maybe her brother-in-law would be Rossano and the servants can come on as servants if we need them.'

Now Frank Collingham had taken charge, the scheme gathered momentum. Ruth took the book home to begin her task and Mr Forbes cheerfully agreed to play Lothario's henchman.

Elizabeth, as an outsider, noticed that neither Parr sister was entirely happy with what had taken place behind their backs. Mary Forbes could only console herself with her most matronly air, while Nettie grumbled in an undertone at having only two scenes and muttered something about wanting to play a resourceful chambermaid in a comedy. She was the youngest of the group, however, and therefore her complaints were generally ignored.

When rehearsals began, Elizabeth found out the extent of her sacrifice. She was tortured by hearing familiar words uttered in what ought to have been Nan's voice, or Mr Boxall's, or Will's. . . .

She could not help wishing they had chosen any play but this. Rowe's 'She'-tragedy centred on Altamont's ill-fated love for Calista, who married him during the course of the play only to pique Lothario, the man who had stolen her virginity and then refused to marry her because he lost interest as soon as he obtained what he wanted.

It all ended in duels, suicides and grief, and Elizabeth was sometimes overwhelmed by a presentiment that the fraught situation at Woodlands would end equally unhappily, though probably less bloodily.

The abilities of the amateur actors varied greatly. Some mumbled, others declaimed and Mr Forbes, in particular, shouted. Miranda and Frank were undoubtedly the most talented, but watching them spurred on Mr Prestwick. He spoke with such earnestness Elizabeth was reminded of Will. He was not acting when he tried to win Calista away from his dangerous rival and swore to forgive her, without reproach, for her fall.

Mr Forbes admitted he had struggled to remember his Greek and Latin at school and his wife knew all his lines long before he did. All three Lesters quarrelled with each other, leaving Sarah in tears, George in a sulk and Harry in a bad temper.

Elizabeth was half-relieved that Edward was frequently absent. It would have troubled him to see Miranda so whole-heartedly immersed in her role that she became capricious and moody, now smiling at young Collingham, now tyrannizing poor Prestwick. But Edward would have been even more alarmed to see the low spirits into which Elizabeth allowed herself to sink when no one was watching. Despite her best intentions, she found herself drawn into the play.

When anyone was absent, she was called on by Sarah or Mr Prestwick to read the missing parts. Invitations had to be sent to the audience, which consisted of the half-dozen respectable families in the area. Ruth and Mary Forbes struggled with the costumes and enlisted her aid. While they sat sewing, Mary allowed her great secret to be teased out of her.

'Of course, I couldn't have trod the stage in my present condition, although it doesn't show yet,' she simpered. 'Mr Forbes would never allow it, and I don't think it would be quite proper.'

Elizabeth swallowed a bitter lump of longing and regret and congratulated her, promising to make some gowns and caps for the little stranger who was to arrive in five or six months.

The words of the play surrounded her. She could not escape them. It all came back to her so effortlessly. She lay awake at nights, playing the same scenes over and over again in her mind. Instinctively she wanted to correct Miranda if she forgot a word or simply emphasized a phrase differently than she had been wont to do.

Elizabeth discovered from the newspaper that Mr Boxall's company had been in Nottingham during the race week, and Nan had not written. Indeed, she wrote less and less as time went by, especially since marrying Samuel, who was a rising star in the company.

A week before the performance, the Collinghams arrived at Woodlands, bursting with news of an unexpected guest from London.

'Mr Cartwright and Papa have had some business transactions in the past,' Ruth explained with uncharacteristic energy. 'He's a Whig and he is friends with people who know the Duchess of Devonshire and Fox and Sheridan. And he goes to the London theatres and knows all the chief actors and playwrights.'

Half the actors were thrown into a panic at this news while the other half had sudden visions of being heralded as fitting rivals to the great Garrick or the beautiful Miss Farren. Elizabeth felt something shrivel deep inside her.

August proved sultry. The oppressive heat frayed tempers. Everything irritated Elizabeth, particularly Miranda. The girl had everything she could possibly want and still she complained because her costume wasn't ready, picked quarrels with her cousins and upset Mr Prestwick.

In his unhappiness, he started confiding in Elizabeth and she did her best to be sympathetic. But sometimes all she wanted to do was scream at him to come to a decision. Subconsciously maybe she wanted a violent misunderstanding to take place between her step-daughter and her lover. Honour, wounded pride, hurt feelings, convention would make him leave and without the hero the play could not go on.

He almost deserves to suffer, Elizabeth brooded. Even if he began a conversation by criticizing Miranda, he ended by excusing her and finding her faults endearing. And why, for God's sake, could he not confide in someone else? Elizabeth's relationship with her step-

daughter had deteriorated since the growth of her apparent inti-
macy with Mr Prestwick. Both women seethed under the load of
mutual jealousy, one for her lover, the other for her muse.

Frank Collingham was perfectly aware of what was going on. Far
from being concerned, he was amused by it. Sometimes when he
was flirting with Miranda, he could hardly suppress a smile of satisfaction when Mr Prestwick struggled to keep his temper.

Elizabeth was pretty certain that Collingham was toying with
Miranda, but she could not be sure. Rehearsals proved, if nothing
else, that he could alternate between cold cynicism and passionate
wooing at will, and then resume his ordinary manner as soon as the
rehearsal was over. Sometimes as he gazed at Miranda, he really did
seem to have a tender look in his eye.

Nor could she be sure how Miranda felt. If she were forced to
choose between her admirers, which would she choose? But the
situation was potentially more damaging to her reputation than
that. Mr Prestwick had declared his intentions honourably, if not to
the lady, then at least to her father. Collingham had not and did not
seem likely to. Prestwick was established in life; Collingham had to
work for financial security and probably had undeclared debts in
London.

Miranda's behaviour almost convinced Elizabeth she was in
earnest. The dangerous game of making Prestwick jealous worked
only too well, if it was only her intention to test her lover to the
limits of his patience.

But Miranda tried to push it further. By making matters up with
Mr Prestwick, she tried to make Frank jealous. The scheme back-
fired spectacularly. Far from behaving moodily or redoubling his
attentions, he retaliated in kind and started flirting with Elizabeth.
In spite of her better judgement, in her irritation with Miranda,
Elizabeth found herself responding sometimes. Opportunities to
display her wit had become so rare and Collingham made her feel
young again.

Even if she had retained a poker-face through all the compliments he lavished on her and refused his offers of help, Miranda
would have reacted badly. As it was, she was lashed almost into a
frenzy.

To add to her troubles, Elizabeth noticed her husband had grown quiet and was frequently absent from home. His description of his first marriage came back to haunt her. Suppose he was unhappy? Suppose that was why he stayed away and not because it was necessary?

But when she asked him about it, he only smiled wanly and said the weather was making his head ache. She snatched brief moments of happiness when he let her place cold compresses on his forehead while she perched on the arm of his chair, his arm round her waist.

He seemed so depressed and unlike himself, she couldn't burden him with more troubles. It was almost a relief to her when, in the privacy of her dressing-room, he let himself rant about the loss of his sanctuary in the library.

It would all be over in a few days, Elizabeth mused, as she stepped into the garden in search of a breath of air. All morning, hot and dusty, she had supervised the workmen putting the final touches to the stage. In practice, this meant that much of the furniture had had to be moved and half the room curtained off while the library next door would serve as the green room.

When the men had gone, she stood for a moment in the space that had been cleared behind the green baize curtains which, no doubt, she would make use of elsewhere once the craze for acting was over. For a moment, Elizabeth allowed herself to forget domestic cares and remember the last time she played Calista while Mrs Boxall's feet were so swollen she could scarcely waddle and her stomach too large for her to pick up Bessy when she became fretful.

Calista had been one of her triumphs. The words of the part echoed round her head. In vain, she tried to drive them out as she walked across the grass. It had grown crisp and yellow, only patches of clover showing dark green.

There had been a cool breeze earlier and the young people had decided to take advantage of it to ride a little after breakfast. Now it was nearly noon and there was a torpor in the air, but they were not back. She would have heard their voices, even above the clatter of the workmen.

Besides which, no matter how tired or dusty they were, they

would be eager to see the interior of the theatre as soon as they got back. They were probably resting in the shade in the wood before braving the heavy atmosphere and clouds of dust.

The shrubbery was shaded, but even there the earth was baked hard. In the still air, noises carried. An occasional stir in the leaves, the warbling of a blackcap lost in its own dream, James calling to someone in the stableyard nearby, the clatter of a bucket. The pods of broom bursting open somewhere in the woods.

And then, drumming hoofs. No one in their right mind would go at such a pace in this weather. Something was wrong. Elizabeth snatched up two handfuls of petticoats and ran, her train streaming out behind her.

She reached the stableyard in time to see James lift down Miss Lester from her horse. Its head was lolling, its flanks flecked with sweat. Sarah raised her face towards Elizabeth. She was white, trembling – and alone.

Chapter 17

'What is it? Where are the others?'
Sarah gasped out something, but Elizabeth couldn't
understand a word.

'Come inside. Sit down; have a drink.'

She shook her head. 'No time.'

Nonetheless, Elizabeth put her arm round the girl and led her
into the house. She was burning hot and Elizabeth wondered if she
had caught a touch of the sun. She made Sarah drink a glass of
water before she made a second attempt at telling her story.

'You must get things ready. They're coming behind me. Except
Harry – Mr Prestwick sent him for the doctor.'

'Doctor? Who's hurt?'

Sarah took another deep gulp before starting again. Elizabeth
gathered they had met Frank Collingham along the way and he and
Miranda had dared each other to more and more daring feats of
horsemanship, despite Mr Prestwick's pleas and warnings.

It culminated with Miranda accepting a challenge to leap over the
trunk of an ancient oak, toppled by the storms of the previous
winter. The horse cleared the obstacle, though bruising its hind legs
against the tree trunk. But Miranda failed to take into account the
branches of a nearby birch which knocked her, head first, from the
saddle.

'Poor Mr Collingham turned so white, I thought he would faint,'
Sarah continued as Elizabeth rang the bell for the servants, 'but Mr
Prestwick got down and examined her and – oh heavens! – she was
so still, I thought she was dead.'

Mr Prestwick sent the youngest two to fetch help and they contrived to make a stretcher out of some dead wood and their coats. When they lifted her into it, Miranda started screaming in pain and that was all Sarah knew.

Her nerves were in tatters and Elizabeth seriously considered giving the girl a few grains of laudanum and handing her over to one of the maids. The waiting seemed to last an age. Elizabeth flitted about, followed by a tearful Sarah, trying to anticipate everything Miranda or the doctor might need.

Her heart throbbed with dread. What would she tell Edward when he got home? What if Miranda died? He would be home soon, might even meet the three young men with their precious burden on the way. . . .

Oh, she shouldn't have hated and envied her stepdaughter. There must have been some way to earn her trust. She should have insisted that Mr Prestwick talked to Miranda herself. And certainly she should never have flirted with Frank Collingham.

Probing the murky depths of her heart, she wondered if she had enjoyed taking revenge on Miranda by stealing her lovers as well as her father. Wasn't there a malicious pleasure in putting yourself in the right by paradingly forgiving your enemies? No wonder Miranda hated her.

She had sent the menservants to help carry the stretcher and at last, standing on the doorstep, she heard voices approaching. She ran out as far as the gates. The scene was blurred by the sunlight in her eyes. She couldn't pick out one tall, white-sleeved figure from another, but her eye was drawn to a hand, raised from the stretcher, clutching the shirt sleeve of one of the men. Miranda was uttering low, sobbing moans, but a man's voice rumbled softly. Elizabeth felt a rock tumble from her heart. It was Mr Prestwick Miranda was clinging to, her ashen face turned in his direction.

She didn't notice Collingham among the number, but he must have been there. He was loitering in the hall, a little apart from the others, when she returned with the doctor's verdict. He was staring out of the window, tapping his crop in the palm of his hand behind his back.

'Miss Holbrook has broken her arm. I've sent for the surgeon to set the bone and we must thank God it is no worse. Unless she catches a fever, she should be quite well in a month or so.'

Her eyes remained on Collingham. While the others expressed their relief, he, ungracious in his remorse, took his leave, growling to Elizabeth to pass on his apologies to Miranda.

Mr Holbrook, meeting him at the door, was startled when he threw himself into the saddle as if it were midwinter rather than the heat of a summer's noon. He had barely time to register the crowd of guests and servants in the hall before Elizabeth tucked her hand through his arm and led him into the library.

'Of course there can be no question of our going on with the play,' Nettie muttered glumly.

She was only voicing what everyone else had been thinking for the past twenty-four hours. Now the floodgates were open, more and more tentative remarks were added to the collection.

'It seems such a shame, just as everything was ready, the stage, the costumes. . . .'

'Maybe we could try again at Christmas?' Sarah Lester suggested.

But it was promptly pointed out that Mr Prestwick or Frank Collingham might have other engagements and no one could guess where George would be, if his father bought him a commission. Nettie added she would be left in charge of Papa and the house while her mother and Mr Forbes were helping Mary through her dangerous time. Bad roads, bad weather, bad colds – a thousand things might impede them now that they were in a negative frame of mind.

They were sitting in the library. No one had had the heart to start dismantling the theatre and Sarah suggested the noise might disturb the invalid. And maybe they were not yet prepared to give up that one last hope which would remain as long as the arrangements were unaltered.

Elizabeth was sewing a shift from the scraps of a worn-out shirt for the baby of a war widow. She was reluctant to interfere, sensing that a straw would alter the balance of the mood in the library.

'Why don't you do the play anyway?'

They all froze in shock, glancing at each other as though each was afraid he or she had uttered the forbidden thought aloud. Elizabeth felt her whole body tingling. It was Edward who had spoken.

'Oh, but we couldn't,' Sarah breathed.

'Calista's the whole play,' George added. 'You can't have *The Fair Penitent* without a fair penitent.'

'Miranda would be mortified, don't you think? She'd set her heart on this.' Elizabeth felt she ought to say something.

'I've talked to Miranda. You don't suppose I'd suggest such a thing without doing that first, do you? I'm not such a fool as that.'

Edward's ironic tone had its usual effect of bracing Elizabeth's nerves. She felt hope beat again in her veins and struggled hard to crush it into stillness. She said nothing as the others clamoured to know what Miranda had said.

Having had time to think things through when pain kept her awake, Miranda decided she was sorry her actions had upset everyone's plans. When her father came to see her, she begged him to assure Frank Collingham that she at least did not blame him for her accident.

It was while she was in this heroic mood that she suggested the play should be performed without her. Even so, tears gushed into her eyes at her sacrifice. Although Edward did not say so, Elizabeth sensed he thought Miranda was relishing her present noble role. But Elizabeth knew from experience that such feelings were always short-lived, especially if you saw or heard others enjoying what you yourself had given up.

But the young people had returned to the great stumbling-block – the part of Calista.

'Do you think Miranda is the only actress in the world?' Mr Holbrook exclaimed, rising.

He gave his wife a penetrating look from the door. She didn't know how to interpret his expression. Had he guessed how she felt? She wanted to follow him out of the room, to reassure him that all her acting ambitions were over, and yet she could not bear to leave.

'Maybe Mary could do it,' Nettie said, blushing deeply, 'or – or I'm sure I could try if Mary took my role. It's only two scenes and—'

She broke off, breathlessly waiting for someone to agree with her and eyeing Sarah Lester as a potential rival. Elizabeth felt a pang. She might as well have been invisible.

The suggestion took on a life of its own and, though hesitating and sometimes drawing back from the brink, the new cast was soon arranged. Mary declined the role of Calista, claiming she only knew the scenes in which her husband appeared, but undertook to play Lucilla.

'You've been to so many more rehearsals than I have, Nettie,' she drawled, fanning herself, 'and in this weather, in my condition, I really think I ought not exert myself too much.' She bestowed a lazy smile on her husband, who obediently forbade her to lift a finger.

They fetched the book and crowded into the drawing-room. Sarah slipped upstairs to make sure Miranda had not – fearful of all fears – withdrawn her blessing and one of her brothers searched the garden for Mr Prestwick, who had not been in the library during the discussion.

Elizabeth found herself, at the pleas of the others, despatching a note to Frank Collingham. Next Nettie Parr cornered her to ask about altering the costume, since Miranda was by far the tallest of the actresses. That alone had made her so imposing as Calista.

The actors threw themselves into rehearsing with renewed vigour. Nettie in particular was sprightly and Elizabeth repressed a wince. Small and curvaceous as she was, Miss Parr would have been far better suited to a comic role and her glee at getting this part sometimes overrode the feelings her character was supposedly feeling. Still, that would wear off with time, Elizabeth supposed, and on the whole the cast seemed pleased with their first day's work.

Afterwards, Mr Prestwick was allowed an interview with Miranda, in which he repeatedly assured her of his admiration for her unselfishness and told her how afraid he had been when he saw her fall. Miranda's spirits had begun to flag, so the encouragement came just in time. She couldn't help letting a few tears fall, but Mr Prestwick wiped them away and gazed at her tenderly until he was told his allotted time was over and Miss Holbrook required rest.

He frowned when he met Jenny on the landing carrying a second bouquet from young Mr Collingham. He had also sent a bunch of flowers the previous day, with a self-accusatory and sentimental note. But still, Thomas Prestwick's prospects had never looked so bright and he was willing to be magnanimous to a defeated rival.

Relations between the two men had been frosty during the first rehearsal after Miranda's accident, but that was in keeping since Altamont and Lothario were enemies even before they became rivals for Calista. Collingham therefore looked suitably surprised, even suspicious, when Prestwick greeted him cordially the next day.

But just when it seemed that one source of contention might have been eliminated, another arose. Nettie struggled valiantly to memorize the part of Calista, but she did not feel secure and was liable to forget her lines if she became passionate, or to forget to be passionate when she concentrated on her lines.

Several times she broke down in tears and had to be consoled by the entire cast. Her round face began to lose its colour, dark bruises appeared round her eyes and – almost unprecedented, even in Mary's experience – she became snappish and bad-tempered.

Inevitably, the performances of the other actors suffered. Frank and Sarah managed to keep their heads, but Mr Prestwick in particular became rigid and cold. He did not need to pretend to be in love with Miranda; he could not pretend to love Nettie. It was as well that in the play kissing a lady's hand and kneeling were deemed sufficient proofs of devotion, because Elizabeth was certain nothing could have induced Mr Prestwick to come any closer to Nettie.

Two days before the performance, she broke down completely in the midst of spurning Altamont's pity.

'I can't do it – I can't do it,' she sobbed. 'Don't make me do it, please. My head is bursting. I'm no good.'

Reassurances did not convince her. Nor did Harry's tactless remark improve matters. 'You'll have to do it. There's no one else who can. It's too late to ask anyone – and beside, all the invitations have been sent out already.'

This last sentence made Nettie howl out loud. Sarah turned on her brother, lashing him with her tongue. Mr Prestwick, who was an only child and knew nothing about family squabbles, was ill-advised enough to try to make peace, till Sarah snarled at him and took herself off to the garden, saying she hated everyone and everything.

Harry was next to chide Mr Prestwick for interfering and he, seeing Collingham's smug grin, set out to provoke his rival. A promising three-way fight was brewing till Nettie drew attention to herself by crying even louder and declaring she wished she had never been born.

Elizabeth, Ruth and Mary had their hands full, offering the girl handkerchiefs, smelling salts, glasses of water and even a lie-down in a darkened room. The men meanwhile stood about, dismayed and reluctant to apologize.

Characteristically, Frank was the first to recover. He tugged the baize curtain, examined its folds and peered up at it with a critical eye, before announcing casually, 'It seems to me there is only one thing we can do – and would have been well-advised to do as soon as Miss Holbrook broke her arm.'

'Cancel the whole thing, I suppose,' George said glumly.

'Not at all. Tell me, who is the one person fitted to play the role at such short notice? The one person who no doubt knows the whole play by heart already?'

Elizabeth felt her face grow scarlet as all their eyes became focused on her.

'Oh, but I haven't done any acting for three years,' she protested faintly, 'and I am not sure it would be quite proper, an old married woman like myself.' Her fragile hold on respectability might suffer. But something stronger than that was pulling her towards her fate.

'I'm sure Uncle would give you permission.'

'And Miss Parr could take her old part again.'

'I'm sure you've not forgotten how to do it.'

The voices pressed round her. But in the midst of it all, she remembered Miranda and rose.

'I'm sorry, I can't do it. It must be nearly four years since I last played Calista,' and I know every word, her heart whispered. 'You must find someone else or give up the play altogether.'

Cries of dismay followed her from the room and she sought the kitchen as a sanctuary. But she found she left her commands mid-sentence and hardly heard or understood the servants.

Her heart was throbbing with the pain of renunciation. She had been so close. At the speed of lightning, visions of her triumphs had sped through her head. Would it really have hurt her to do this one last time? To please the young people. She had never said a proper farewell to her profession. One day she had been Lady Macduff, the next. . . .

She pushed the thought of Will aside. She tried to forget the old exaltation, the feeling she was flying when she was on the stage, the intoxicating sense of being someone else.

She didn't dare show her face till the guests had gone and she knew her husband was home. She scanned his face for signs that his nephews had spoken to him, but he was as inscrutable as he had been ever since the idea of the play was first broached.

The entire party was invited to dine with the Collinghams, in honour of their guest from London. Elizabeth tried to excuse herself, offering to stay with Miranda but she was overruled.

As soon as she entered the parlour, she felt a distinct chill in the air. Nettie's eyes looked inflamed and Elizabeth guessed she, too, had not been allowed to excuse herself from attending. Mr Parr tucked his hands under his coat tails and swung back on his heels as he eyed her and Mrs Parr and Mrs Forbes were as frigidly polite as they knew how.

Throughout dinner, Elizabeth could see Mrs Collingham was on the verge of speaking out. She was only checked by the presence of her guest and her son who, to annoy her, was particularly gallant to Mrs Holbrook.

It was with a sense of dread that she saw Mrs Collingham exchange nods with Mrs Parr and both ladies rose, signalling the exodus of the female part of the company. At the door, Elizabeth glanced back, hoping for a reassuring look from her husband. But Edward was already deep in discussion with Mr Collingham about the possible purchase of a horse.

The two mothers wasted no time, although the gentlemen would not join them for at least half an hour. Mrs Parr began by mourning in plaintive tones that there were so few innocent diversions for young people, whose parents could not take them to fashionable resorts.

Mrs Collingham interrupted her with a diatribe on selfishness and hypocrisy. Ruth, who looked unhappy at the charged atmosphere, suggested they should have some music. Her eyes darted between Sarah, Nettie, Mary, Mrs Tallant and even, tentatively, Elizabeth. She was overruled by her mother, however, and Nettie uttered a strangled sob and declared she believed she would never be able to sing again.

At first the onslaught made Elizabeth stubborn. She would gladly have done what they implied she ought to, but not if she was coerced in this manner. So far it was all done by insinuation and Elizabeth took refuge in pretending to misunderstand.

But Nettie's unhappiness touched her. The girl was unable to hide that she was terrified of Calista, desperate to try a little acting and guilty at the thought of disappointing the others.

'It's such a dreadful thing that has happened to Miss Holbrook.' Mrs Tallant tried changing tack. 'When I think how tragically it might have ended – well, it doesn't bear thinking about.'

'And such a shame it had to happen just before the play,' Mary suggested, fanning herself.

Nettie's eyes began to grow pink again.

'I had far rather it had not happened at all,' Elizabeth replied, 'before or after the play.'

'There won't *be* any after any more,' Sarah ventured. She grew bolder when none of her elders contradicted her. 'You could do it as easy as winking, if you wanted to.'

'I really don't think your uncle would approve.'

'Nonsense. You only want everyone to make a fuss of you and beg and plead.' Mrs Collingham rose with a rustle of grey-blue silk and strode purposefully about the room, though doing nothing of note.

'If you want to persuade me to play Calista, you are going the wrong way about it, madam,' Elizabeth said. 'I am tempted now to prove that no amount of pleading will convince me.'

Mrs Collingham flushed dark red and choked. Glancing round, Elizabeth was appalled by the hostility she felt emanating from every pair of eyes. Save only Ruth Collingham, maybe. Mrs Tallant refused to meet her eye. A deadly silence had fallen on the room. Elizabeth cleared her throat.

'Since you all feel so strongly about the matter – and such respectable pillars of society as yourselves seem to approve of my acting' – her voice seemed unnaturally loud in the stillness and it unnerved her – 'I *will* do it, not for all the begging and pleading in the world, nor from any sort of vanity, but for Miss Parr's sake.'

The clock began to beat again, the clink of glasses drifted across the passage from the dining-room. Several voices rose at once and stopped, abashed at having interrupted someone else. Elizabeth knew in her heart she had been too outspoken. Neither of the matrons would forgive her in a hurry.

She watched the scene across a gulf, picking out stray details. Ruth Collingham, for instance, looked more at ease and Nettie, still tremulous, dabbed at her eyes with a crumpled handkerchief. The candlelight reflected, red-gold, in Mary Forbes's ear-ring which swayed and danced at the slightest movement of her head.

Then the first gentlemen arrived and, to prevent retraction, Sarah Lester announced that Mrs Holbrook had agreed to be in the play. When Elizabeth caught sight of Edward, he was standing at the far end of the room alone, his head bent, examining a volume which had been left on a table. He was too far away and in the wavering candlelight she could not see his expression.

He was used to masking his feelings in public and she did not have an opportunity to speak to him until they were home. The young people vanished upstairs, but Mr Holbrook, taking his candle, turned towards the library.

'Are you not coming to bed, Edward?'

'Presently. There are a few letters I must write. I want them posted as early as possible tomorrow.' His hand was on the door and instinctively Elizabeth followed him.

'Edward, is there anything wrong?'

A shadow crossed his face, but, attempting to sound indifferent, he replied, 'What should be wrong?'

She hesitated a moment longer. 'You don't object to my taking part in the play, I hope?'

'I knew you were an actress when I married you.' He leaned forward to kiss her on the cheek. 'Now trot along to bed like a good child and don't let me catch you worrying or making preparations for tomorrow.'

Elizabeth shivered suddenly, unable to explain why she felt uneasy at being dismissed in this way. She tried to convince herself his behaviour was no different than usual, and yet. . . . Relief had crossed his face when she asked about the play, as if he had been afraid she would ask about something else.

His words also triggered another train of thought. Was she sure she knew all her lines? What would she do with the costume? She had only two days to prepare. Disobeying his orders, she took her old script out of the linen press and, huddled under the blankets, read through it till her eyes began to sting and she heard Edward's steps on the landing.

She whisked the script under her pillow, blew out the candle and pretended to be asleep. She heard soft rustling in the room, then the bed curtains opened beside her. She could feel the glow of the candle on her eyelids.

He stood there for a long minute. The curtain fell back into place and she felt the mattress dip as he eased himself in, near her but not touching. She wondered if she ought to pretend to wake, but he sighed wearily and a moment later his slow breathing told her he was asleep.

Miranda was still awake, but not because of pain. She had almost managed to forget the encumbrance of her broken arm, strapped tightly in pasteboard and stiff bandages, in the dark vortex of her feelings. She had been far too shocked and hurt at first to think and she could not bring herself to confide in anyone, they were so full of the damned play.

Her window had been ajar in the afternoon when she was resting, to let what little breeze there was ripple the curtains. Only soothing noises reached her – birdsong, rustling leaves. And then, as in a half-dream, voices. His voice. She would have recognized it anywhere.

She listened only to those tones at first, thinking it was a dream, but as she opened her eyes, she came to the conclusion it was real. He was in the garden, beneath her window. Curiosity aroused, she lay very still, trying to pick out words or identify the other voice.

'Don't despair yet,' were the first words she made out. 'I am sure it is possible to talk Mrs Holbrook round. I, for one, will use all the eloquence in my power.'

'Try your charm, eh?' Mr Forbes blustered, laughing heavily. 'Seems to work with Miss Holbrook, eh, what? Just like something out of one of those Greek tragedies, mother and daughter.'

Miranda stiffened and held her breath, waiting for Frank to defend her, at any rate to disassociate her from That Woman.

'What an absurd fellow you are, Forbes. *You'd* play the rake as well, if you dared, only that pretty wife of yours has you in leading strings. What odds will you give me that she'll put you into petti-coats when the little stranger comes, so you and the baby look alike?'

But Forbes was not to be shifted from his own more ponderous jokes so easily.

'I daresay Miss Holbrook would keep a close eye on you, if you were married.'

'I daresay she would. But I've no intention of giving that power to her, or any other pretty provincial miss. Why be satisfied with the love of one little girl, when you can be the favourite of twenty women of beauty and fashion?'

The voices drifted away, but Miranda felt an icy chill blow through the room.

Chapter 18

'*Mrs* Holbrook, may I speak to you?'

Mr Prestwick's face seemed to reflect her mood. The old joy and energy had returned to her, since she first set foot on the improvised stage. She could not imagine now how it was possible to live without this feeling. 'Certainly, Mr Prestwick.'

He glanced about him at the merry bustle. 'Maybe we could step out into the garden.' Elizabeth complied, but made a note in her head that if he kept her too long, she must excuse herself with her duties as a housekeeper and an actress. She opened her parasol as she stepped into the sun. 'Well, sir?'

'I could not wait till your husband was unoccupied. I must tell someone and you seemed the most appropriate person.'

The truth burst on her even before he uttered the words.

'I have proposed to Miss Holbrook and she has accepted me.'

'Well, I did not think you would look so happy if she had refused.'

There was a split second hesitation before he laughed, as if he had not initially understood her. She congratulated him, they shook hands and she listened as long as she could to his plans about where and how they would live and his ambition to stand for Parliament.

The post had just arrived when Elizabeth returned to the house. She was startled by the way her husband darted out of the dining-room and snatched the bag from the footman. He did not see her standing by the door. He unlocked the bag and searched through the letters for one in particular. After a moment's hesitation, he broke the seal.

The rigidity drained from his body. He leaned against the door-post for support, his eyes closed. She was going to speak but, without looking in her direction, Edward turned back into the dining-room and shut the door.

She remembered that scene as she sat in the library, the door half-open, listening to the mutter of voices as the guests greeted each other and chose their seats on chairs borrowed from the dining-room. She had received them with Edward, as she felt was her duty, before excusing herself to go and change into her costume.

Her stomach fluttered in the familiar way during the first act. Mr Prestwick's joy at being engaged matched Altamont's pleasure at his prospective marriage to Calista and thus far, all was well. How he would behave later, she couldn't judge.

She did not make her first entrance till the beginning of the second act, after her letter to Lothario proclaiming her guilt had been discovered by Altamont's friend Horatio. A profound sense of disquiet crept through her as she listened to Lothario's description of the way he had taken Calista by surprise and seduced her. Somehow from Frank Collingham's lips, it seemed almost too plausible.

It was both more and less acceptable for her to play a fallen woman than for Miranda to do so. More respectable because she could be safely assumed to know about the mysteries of marriage; less acceptable because if she followed Calista's example and fell from grace, her whole family would suffer.

She had met briefly the prestigious guest of the Collinghams, both tonight and at the dinner party two days previously. Mr Cartwright proved to be a portly, ordinary-looking man with a bob wig with short, unkempt curls and a waistcoat liberally besprinkled with snuff and sauces, despite the best efforts of his valet.

In spite of his unprepossessing appearance, Mr Cartwright was an astute man. The announcement that Mrs Holbrook was stepping into the breach led to a discussion, chiefly between him and young Collingham, on the merits of various plays and actors. Watched by so many prying eyes, Elizabeth kept quiet, though frequently some anecdote about Mr Boxall's company was on the tip of her tongue.

But that part of her life was over and it was better not to revive it. Edward knew her stories, but she had told them to no one else in an attempt to buy back the respectability she had voluntarily forfeited in her choice of profession.

Edward remained elusive. His ironic manner, which had once bound them together, had become a barrier. It struck her that it was a very long time since she had talked to him about her experiences as a strolling actress. The more painful her longings became, the less she dared talk about them. She only hoped he thought she did not speak of her past because she was content with the present.

All these thoughts vanished as soon as she stepped on to the stage. Miranda had begged her father for proper painted scenery, but even she had known in her heart of hearts that was too much to hope for. Instead, a number of plants in pots and a bench borrowed from the garden represented the outdoor scenes. Two chairs and a table symbolized Sciolto's house, with the sofa covered in a length of black cloth for Lothario's bier in the last act.

Elizabeth threw herself into her role with desperate enjoyment. This was her farewell to her profession. This was to be her cure. And therefore she must drink her happiness to the very dregs, relish every second.

She felt a ripple and stir in the audience. Whether they respected or despised her, Elizabeth felt she could command their attention.

The minutes flew past. She was soaring, her head light, her heart heavy, not with her own sorrows, but with Calista's. There was a look almost of awe on Mr Prestwick's face as she spurned his pity and chose to die gazing at the man she had injured.

Elizabeth's eyes shut. Distantly she heard Sciolto die, Altamont borne away and Horatio moralizing on the sanctity of marriage. It was over. It was all over. Her head was spinning as the curtains swished shut. Applause swelled in the drawing-room, like the rushing of waves across shingle. Throughout the play Elizabeth had avoided looking at the audience. Now she let her eyes run across the spectators, searching for the one face that was important to her.

As befitted the host, Edward was sitting amidst the most important guests. Everyone was so intent on applauding the actors or whispering to their neighbours, Edward had allowed his mask to slip for a moment. The old hunger was in his eyes, that look from before they were married. Her heart leapt towards his in response and she wished the rest of her might follow.

Instead, she was beset by guests, most praising and congratulating her. Only Mr Parr shook his head because such an immodest play had been chosen. His chief objection appeared to be that Elizabeth had played a flawed character too sympathetically.

' 'Tis a bad example to the young 'uns, to be flaunting her fall from virtue in that way,' he assured her solemnly. 'Far better to show young people a paragon like Sir Charles Grandison than to let them follow the lead of that scapegrace Tom Jones.'

'I rather think that is why Rowe includes Altamont's virtuous sister Lavinia,' Elizabeth suggested, craning her neck to find Edward.

But still Mr Parr was not satisfied and expatiated on the contrast between Goneril, Regan and Lady Macbeth with Cordelia and Lady Macduff. If you needs must have a villainess, paint her as black as possible so no one could possibly like or imitate her, he insisted. And for God's sake, relegate her to a subplot rather than the focus of the play.

At long last Elizabeth got away and managed to cross half the room. Edward was only a few yards away, and then Mr Cartwright pounced on her.

'Magnificent, madam, 'pon my honour. No other word for it.' He refreshed himself with a pinch of snuff. 'If I might make so bold, I'd almost say 'twas a pity you're so well settled in life. Could get you an introduction with Sheridan, or his manager. Take you, like a shot. Been looking for a fresh face since Mrs Robinson took up with the Prince of Wales.'

'Thank you, you are very kind.' She tried to edge away but to no avail.

'What's this I hear that you used to be a strolling actress?' he persisted.

Elizabeth swallowed, then somehow all the theatrical anecdotes she had suppressed two days ago came flooding out.

Supper was to be served in the dining-room. Elizabeth was delayed so long she was still in her costume and was forced to fight her way out of the crowd, leaving a trail of excuses and promises to talk later behind her.

It was eerily still upstairs, though she took Jenny with her to speed her transformation. The door of Miranda's room reproached her as she prepared to go down. Dare she enter?

Miranda turned her face away from her. She could not bring herself to come downstairs yet, using her broken arm as an excuse.

'I came to see if there was anything you wanted,' Elizabeth faltered.

'What, have our servants all eloped that you show such conde-scension?'

Apologies would not soothe her. If she had been willing to believe it, Elizabeth knew exactly how her stepdaughter felt at being excluded. She made one last effort.

'I also wanted to congratulate you on your engagement.'

She grunted. Nervously Elizabeth straightened the bottles and jars on the dressing-table.

'Hadn't you better go back to your admirers, *Mrs* Holbrook, instead of flaunting in front of me with your white silk and your pretended concern?' Miranda burst out.

'I do care what happens to you, for your father's sake, if not your own.' What was the point in replying so irritably? 'But you are right. I have guests to entertain. Goodnight, Miranda.'

Elizabeth paused at the foot of the stairs. A servant opened the door of the dining-room and, in the interval before it shut, she suddenly heard such hostile words that she flinched.

'Of course, no *real* lady would flaunt herself like that. I always thought that story about Hereford was. . . .' Mrs Collingham's voice vanished suddenly into the hum of the room.

Elizabeth lost her courage to enter. The mood had changed while she was gone. Again she was an outcast. Very little in this house was her own. Everything was a legacy from poor Maria, or an object Miranda had wanted and begged from her father.

This is the hardest role I will ever have to play. To pretend I do not care what they say about me. To pretend I left my old life with-out regret; to pretend to agree with these narrow-minded people, to like what they like. To stand condemned for anything I do differently, not because it is morally wrong, but because I will never be let back into the fold. They will always remember my past, when I most strive to forget. And there is no end to this, except death.

With a deep breath, Elizabeth opened the door and stepped inside.

The last of the guests had gone. Edward said he would lock up for the night and Elizabeth's candle burnt straight and serene on the table at the foot of the stairs. She took it, but loneliness overwhelmed her. What had she proved by her performance that night? Only that she missed aspects of her old life. Now it would be harder than ever to return to her domestic duties.

She went into the drawing-room for one last look before the theatre was dismantled. It seemed to recognize its fate. Why else would it look so forlorn? Chairs askew, petals from someone's flowers sprinkled on the floor, the funeral bier still in place on the improvised stage. Something stirred in the shadow of the curtains.

'I thought you would come here,' Edward said.

'You gave me a start.' Her voice rang false. 'I think everyone passed a pleasant evening, don't you?'

'I daresay they did.'

His mind was not on what he was saying. His face was in deep shadow. Elizabeth came closer, setting her candlestick on the mantelpiece, where its light was magnified by the mirror.

'What is it, Edward? I know something has been troubling you, you've been so distant.'

'Distant?' He seemed surprised, but after a moment's thought he added, 'Yes, I suppose I have. I've had a lot to think about.' Still he did not elaborate. Only a few yards separated them, but it might as well have been half the world.

'Edward, please, we cannot go on in this manner.'

'No, we can't.'

He looked up suddenly and held out his arms to her. She ran to him and was crushed in his embrace. She was startled at how tightly he held her, yet she was afraid if she reproved him in their old ironic way, the mask would be resumed and he would not speak openly to her.

231

'Oh, Lizzie,' he murmured, his lips against her hair. 'I saw tonight what I have long since suspected: I have kept you locked in my wine cellar far too long; it's time I set you free.'

'What on earth do you mean?'

'I mean, child, you were destined for greater things than this. And, God forbid, I should act like that scoundrel Sheridan who'd rather starve than let his wife sing in public, because it hurts his pride she should be more capable of earning a living than he is.'

He drew her across to the black-draped sofa and pulled her down beside him. He silenced her bewildered questions by laying the tips of his fingers on her lips.

'Don't say another word until you've heard me out. I want to take you to London to see Sheridan or his manager. If he engages you for the season, as I am sure he will if he has any sense, I'll settle you in respectable lodgings, with a paid companion to keep your reputation safe and anything else you could wish for. All I ask is that you wait till Miranda is married and settled, so as not to frighten Prestwick off.'

'Paid companion? What about you? Aren't you the best safeguard to my reputation?'

He was silent a moment.

'I didn't want to tell you. Sophia's husband is very ill. That's why she sent her older children here. I offered to take the younger two also, but they are staying with schoolfriends. I want to be near if she needs me and to settle the older boys in a profession so their parents needn't worry.'

'How could you keep this to yourself? I'm very fond of your sister, too. I could lighten your burden. How can you expect me to leave you at a time like this?'

'That's why I didn't want to tell you. You've been so unhappy this past year or so. Won't you let me make you happy again?'

His insistence took her breath away. Everything made sense now – his anxiety about the post, his distant behaviour, the look of long-ing after the play. He must have known about Mr Lester's illness since they were in Nottingham. And she had been afraid he might be running away from her, seeking shelter in the arms of Julia Elton's successor. Mrs Tallant, maybe.

'Edward, this is utterly unheard of. I cannot possibly go.' She refused to let herself think of what he was offering her. Yet her heart seemed to know and throb with suppressed excitement.

'No, I've never heard of a wealthy husband encouraging his wife to go on the stage either,' he conceded, 'but why should we be exactly like other people? *You* taught me to be unconventional.'

Elizabeth was silenced by this. How could she explain to him the conflicts she had endured, the loneliness that was the result of her unconventional behaviour?

Yet having chosen to break out of the mould of the genteel young lady, she recognized it would have been easier to stay outside society than to wheedle her way back in. If she broke out again there would be no road back, no forgiveness from the likes of Mrs Collingham or Mr Parr.

'Oh, but people would say I'd been unfaithful to you and that that was why we lived apart.'

'Do you still love me, Lizzie?'

'I never knew how much till now.'

'Then what does it matter what anyone says or thinks? We shall know the truth. And there are coaches to and from London twice a week which pass through Mansfield and more from Nottingham. I'd visit you as often as I could.'

She shook her head, struggling against her own inclination to yield.

'There is no guarantee they will want me at Drury Lane.'

'At least if you try you will not spend the rest of your life wondering what might have happened if you had not married me.'

'Oh, Edward.' She had never felt so close to him.

'For my sake, Lizzie, please. I couldn't bear to think I had blighted your life with my selfish love.'

He sounded so desperate, she pulled his head down and kissed him.

Miranda's wedding clothes became the excuse for their immediate trip to London. In fact Edward hoped to catch the manager of the Theatre Royal before the new season began and get an engagement for Elizabeth, even though she would have to return home until Miranda was safely married.

During the long, tiring journey, Elizabeth's thoughts dwelt on her sister-in-law. They hadn't told Sophia about Edward's plan. She had far too much to worry her at present. But it wasn't just that: Sophia was an enlightened woman in many ways, but she might draw the line at this.

And if I should fail, one less person will know about it, she thought. If I should fail. . . . The very concept of failure had been unthinkable when she had snuggled against Nan for warmth on winter's nights, when the sheets were damp. Now her secret conviction that she would succeed was to be put to the test and she was terrified. She had taken her collection of scripts out of the linen press and read and re-read them.

Like a spider dangling from a thread, she didn't know which way she wanted the wind to blow her. If she had not been married, how easy it would have been. She didn't dare trust herself to the waves of hope which lapped round her and tempted her to swim far out to sea. There would always be a watcher on the shore, calling her back with his mournful eyes.

In the last days at Woodlands, all Edward's distantness was gone. He could hardly bear to let her out of his sight. He refused to discuss the future and the house was so full of guests and servants, Elizabeth recognized the need for discretion. She only discovered he had a letter of introduction to the manager of Drury Lane when Mr Cartwright mentioned it at dinner on the day before they left. Clearly Mr Cartwright didn't know the purpose the letter would be put to.

It was a long time since she had stayed in an inn and she wondered if she would get any sleep at all. London was so much noisier than any town or city she had stayed in during her three years with Mr Boxall's company.

'Edward,' she said, when he crept into bed beside her, 'tell me truly – are you happy about this situation? We need not pursue it any further. We could just buy gifts for Miranda and. . . .'

'Don't tempt me in that way, now I have nerved myself for the inevitable.'

'But don't you see how far you are tempting *me* to behave contrary to my duty?'

'Duty be hanged.' The candlelight formed a halo round his head.

'I tried to use love and duty to keep a woman close to me before, when she had far rather been away. I don't want to make the same mistake with you. I want absolution.'

The insidious fear crept back into her heart. 'I am not the same sort of person as your first wife.'

'I didn't mean Maria; I meant Julia.'

Elizabeth recoiled. She could not help herself. She had asked no questions, merely accepted the fact that Edward had had a mistress for a while. Only once in the last years had she hinted something to Sophia, but her sister-in-law shook her head.

'Let his dead love be. It cannot change how he feels about you and it can do you no good to torment yourself about it.'

She no longer knew whether she wanted to know. The way he pronounced that name jarred her. She lay very still, her face averted, waiting.

'We knew from the start our love was doomed,' he said. 'She was married and I could not abandon Maria. Everyone would have condemned me and she was so – pathetic sometimes. I had no grounds to divorce her and it would have ruined me financially if I had. And I wasn't prepared to settle for a legal separation when the price would have been Julia's place in society.'

Elizabeth felt for his arm and drew it round her waist, but still she could not face him. His breast pressed against her spine, his breath tickled her neck, his cold feet got tangled with hers.

Unevenly he went on, 'Her husband was not a bad man, only a weak one. Like all weak men, sometimes he tyrannized her and sometimes he wanted her to mother him. He was jealous of the attention she lavished on her children and when they were frightened of his unpredictable temper, he accused Julia of turning them against him.'

'What became of her?' Elizabeth whispered after a long pause.

He did not seem to hear her words, but her voice was enough to make him go on.

'Rumours began, of course. Maria was the one who started them by her behaviour. She made me so miserable, I asked Julia to go abroad with me somewhere it wouldn't matter. But she wouldn't come.'

'And her husband?' Elizabeth turned towards him.

Edward hesitated. 'I don't believe he ever knew. He was incapable of concealing it if he had. Or if someone dropped a hint to him, he didn't understand. At any rate, Julia persuaded him their house was too small for their family and they moved elsewhere.

'But until they left, there wasn't a single argument or emotion I did not use to try to stop her from leaving me. I begged her to run away with me there and then, so her husband could say in his new neighbourhood that his wife was dead. I urged her that it was her duty to stay in Mansfield because her grandmother, who lived here, needed her to nurse her.'

His voice dropped low and Elizabeth distantly heard the screech of warring cats.

'We parted bitterly. She spoke out at last, angry that I was making the parting harder instead of sparing her feelings. She told me that though she loved me very much, she loved her children best and she would never leave them. I was fool enough to be angry with her for it. She accused me of being no better than her husband.'

'I suppose you both said a lot of things you did not mean,' Elizabeth suggested.

'I know. I knew it even then, I think, but I wouldn't make up the quarrel. She convinced her husband to leave a day early. They were gone before I could talk to her again. I was too proud to write at first and I thought it might be dangerous in case her husband found out and so. . . .'

'What became of her, Edward?' she repeated her earlier question.

'Two years afterwards, with such a look of triumph that I wanted to strike her, Maria told me she had died in childbirth.'

'I'm sorry,' Elizabeth murmured. He pinched her earlobe.

'You see now, don't you, why I want to let you go? I want you to have a chance of happiness while you are young, in the hopes you will come back to me someday.'

Every word he said made it harder for her to leave him, though he hoped for the opposite effect. She refused to think about anything other than choosing the prettiest silks for her stepdaughter. It was only through Edward's perseverance – and Mr Cartwright's letter – that they obtained the necessary interview with the manager of the Theatre Royal. Sheridan himself seemed to take little interest in the venture.

With the first words of Juliet's soliloquy, in which she prepared to take Friar Laurence's potion, Elizabeth knew her decision was made. Much as she loved Edward, her aspirations were more powerful. Without her acting, her soul might as well be dead.

'My dismal scene I needs must act alone.'

Juliet's dilemma was a twisted version of her own. For the sake of her peace of mind, she was taking a vast leap into the unknown. Only Juliet had the consolation that she did it all for love. Her emotion heightened her performance. Each moment she tiptoed closer to the brink. She knew as she let herself fall that, unless there was a full complement of actresses at the theatre, her fate was sealed.

The scene afterwards passed in a haze. Drifting on a tide of happiness, she barely understood the manager's words of praise, but they came back to her later, when she was alone.

Edward had slipped out at some point. She found him in the passage, staring out of a dingy window at a featureless courtyard. He turned as she approached and, wrapping her arms round his neck, she hid her face on his breast and whispered, 'Thank you.'

Chapter 19

*O*nly the drawing-room clock chimed the hour. The house was so still Edward could hear it in the library. The drawing-room was rarely used now. He wondered if anyone, apart from the maid who cleaned it, had set foot in it since Miranda's wedding. Even the cat, disconsolate, had cried at the door of the library till he took pity on her and let her in.

The light flickered on the gilded spines of his books, the cat purred as she licked her flanks, the fire crackled. Everyone seemed content to be indoors, save for himself and the howling February wind.

He did not mind the isolation. He saw now that he had always been alone. He had nothing in common with the Parrs or the Collinghams or any other genteel family in Mansfield, but that never troubled him until he met Elizabeth. In her he discovered an intellectual equal, someone able to talk in his own way. Now she was gone, for the first time in his life he felt lonely.

His duties as a magistrate brought him into daily contact with the ignorant or the narrow-minded. Only once or twice a month would he consult a fellow magistrate, a clergyman, a lawyer. And even then they merely discussed the business that brought them together or general topics such as the weather, the harvest or the latest news from London or America.

In September, the dissolution of Parliament had precipitated the wedding. Thomas Prestwick thought having a pretty young bride might influence some voters in his favour and he was reluctant to return to his potential constituency without Miranda.

Edward seized the opportunity to stay with his sister, on his way back from taking Elizabeth to London. He did what he could for Sophia. Sarah was visiting friends, the younger boys were back in school and Harry, who balked at returning to university, had obtained a place as a clerk in Abel Smith's bank. Edward put up the money to buy George the commission he wanted but he knew Sophia prayed every night his regiment would not be sent to America.

Edward tried to keep his brother-in-law's spirits up, but he was sinking rapidly. The bustle of campaigning beforehand and chairing, cheering and celebrating afterwards were distractions to the invalid, but he died a month later.

Edward did not really hope the election would be enough to occupy the gossips. For a while they talked of nothing else. But inevitably Mrs Collingham and her friends fell upon what they deemed Mrs Holbrook's abandonment of her husband with the relish of hungry wolves.

Edward had no doubt Mrs Collingham wrote to her son, begging him to discover what he could. In her latest letter, Elizabeth mentioned Frank had called on her at the theatre, though he had not yet, apparently, tracked her to her lodgings.

Finding a suitable home for Elizabeth was, mercifully, far easier than he dared hope. Her rebellious cousin Lucy had recently married a wealthy merchant and she was once more willing to embrace the disapproval of her family to help her kinswoman.

Edward tried to convince himself he was happy that Elizabeth's letters were so lively. She described life at the theatre, the foibles of her fellow actors, backstage squabbling, mishaps with stage machinery and a rather disreputable kitten she found starving in an alley and adopted.

She started with tiny roles and declared she was somewhat in awe of her rivals. However, the manager had a high enough opinion of her to allow her to play the lead in *Romeo and Juliet*, at least for a few weeks.

Hints that she disliked London almost as much as he did were muted but unmistakable, however. She wrote of the misery of the poorer districts, the shivering prostitutes she drove past on her way to the theatre, the beggars, the crippled soldiers struggling on crutches.

'Lucy has taken me, among other 'sights', to both the Foundling Hospital and the Magdalen Hospital. The former in particular is overcrowded. It is pitiful to think what straits poverty can reduce humans to. I cannot imagine being forced to abandon my child like that, and Lucy says she will never take me there again, for fear I'll take them all home with me.'

Elizabeth's voice, her laugh seemed to echo in the empty room. She was everywhere and nowhere in the house. Every room still bore the stamp of his first wife. It was as though Maria's jealousy had survived her, had kept the house intact, had been represented by her daughter. And in the end, she had stifled Elizabeth and driven her out.

Or rather, seeing how heavy-eyed she had grown, he had had to save Elizabeth while her vibrant nature survived. And he *had* saved her, he told himself. She blossomed even in the murky alleys and airy drawing-rooms, the fragrant parks and dingy dressing-rooms of London.

When he was settling his accounts or writing letters of complaint or recommendation, sometimes he thought he heard soft steps in the room, smelt the scent of roses, and he almost reached out to clasp the elusive waist.

He woke at unexpected hours of the night, his heart racing, thinking he heard Elizabeth cry out in her sleep. The first time it happened, he had not been able to fall asleep again, convinced that somewhere, far away, she, too, was lying awake, shivering beneath the covers, eyes staring.

Next morning her first letter arrived, so lively and affectionate. Even so his heart was not set at rest. That letter was written long before she had that nightmare. Later letters failed to reassure him. If she was unhappy, she would keep it from him to prevent him from worrying.

Miranda had departed for her first visit to London. In a stilted letter she informed him Thomas Prestwick had been elected and so they had hired a house for the London season. She left him in no doubt, however, that she would not seek out her stepmother and would cut her if they ever had the misfortune of being in the same place at the same time.

Miranda hinted she would have been only too willing to fly home and comfort her papa if Mrs Holbrook had deserted him, as rumour proclaimed. What she could not forgive was his complicity in the matter. He had embarrassed her and, still worse, embarrassed her husband. She thanked God she no longer bore the same name as That Woman. Why he had not insisted that she take a stage-name, she could not imagine.

That was something he had not calculated on when he let Elizabeth go. Somehow he had never brought himself to believe it would cost him his daughter.

From the day Miranda broke her arm until she was married, Edward had been closer to her than he had been for years. She clung to him when she cried in pain and he forgave her occasional invectives against her stepmother. He thought Tom Prestwick was a good influence on her and she made no attempt at flirting after her engagement became known. He had fooled himself she would be a comfort to him when Elizabeth was gone, that she would write to him, visit him. After all, she would only be in the neighbouring county.

He began to calculate if it was possible for him to go to London. It would confound the critics if he were known to be living with his wife. There were other magistrates besides himself to take care of things and Sophia was often impatient at his interference, now her first wave of grief was over.

He rarely went out now, except on official business. Parents with impressionable children looked askance at him. They would all be ready to sympathize with him at his wife's flighty behaviour, as long as he allowed them to drop a few gentle hints that he should have known better when he married a young woman, and one of dubious virtue at that.

'I suppose Mrs Morris will return to Woodlands now?' Mrs Collingham suggested once.

'Why?' he replied curtly.

'Well,' she simpered, 'you know yourself a house quickly goes to rack and ruin without a mistress and—'

'Woodlands has a mistress. I need no other.'

It was true, he supposed, the house had a neglected air. He had not found a replacement for Jenny, who had gone as Mrs Prestwick's personal maid, or the footman he had dismissed for drunkenness. But with neither wife, daughter nor guests to please, it did not matter much.

It occured to him he had become less fastidious about trivialities since Elizabeth's departure. He no longer cared if Molly burnt the meat or the shelves in the library were not dusted, or even if his shirts were less starched than usual.

The only person whose company he found even vaguely congenial was Mrs Tallant. He had avoided her, as he did all the other ladies of his acquaintance, but he had done her an injustice. There could be no doubt she deliberately waylaid him as he left the church, but instead of saying, 'I was so shocked or sorry (or whatever) when I heard about your wife', as the others had, she gazed at him earnestly and whispered, 'You cannot conceive how much I honour you for what you have done.'

'I'm afraid I don't understand,' he replied, still wary and wishing the dratted woman would let him get into his carriage and drive home, instead of keeping him there in the icy wind.

'I know I shouldn't say such a thing, and on the Sabbath too, but poor Mrs Holbrook was pining away amongst us old, dull folk.' She shook her head sagely and pushed aside the feather of her hat, which the wind had bent back against her mouth.

In a conspiratorial undertone, she added that there had been many a time in the early years of her marriage when she, too, had longed to escape for just a little while and be carefree again.

'And Mrs Holbrook is so talented. It's a shame the way a woman's accomplishments are all neglected after she is married, except to educate her own children. I simply must write to Clara to call on Mrs Holbrook.'

He talked to Mrs Tallant after that on occasions. Mindful of appearances, he took care not to seek her out. Even so, Mrs Collingham, when she managed to corner him, treated him to a panegyric on Mrs Tallant's virtues, hinting it was a pity it was too late now.

The first notices had appeared in the London papers, which strayed in Edward's direction, of the beautiful Mrs Holbrook's performance as Juliet. He both longed for and feared these snippets, longed for news and dreaded scandal. He refused to change his subscriptions, knowing any signs that he mistrusted his wife would be noted and spread like wildfire in the town.

Edward was beginning to drowse in his chair by the fire. The precious, closely-written letter slid with a sigh from his knee on to the rug. The wind hissed in the bare branches. Elizabeth's pale face drifted across his memory. He remembered the glint in her eye as she took her bow at the end of *The Fair Penitent*. He was right to do it, he was right.

The cat yawned and settled her chin on her forepaws. A twig snapped in the fire, a small avalanche of red and black whispered as it fell. A soft step barely touched the carpet. Silk rustled. The scent of roses wafted towards him.

> Is there no pity sitting in the clouds,
> That sees into the bottom of my grief?

Edward started awake at her voice, staring around wildly. But there was no one there.

'Lizzie!' he called out. 'Lizzie, where are you?'

For a moment he was convinced she was dead. Nothing could shake his unease. He lay awake long hours in the vast, empty bed until he made a resolution. I'll go to London tomorrow. I'll tell no one and stay in an inn and make private enquiries. If nothing is amiss, she need never know. And if it is, I shall be close enough to save her.

Travelling without ceasing, he would reach London in three days, as long as there were no blizzards like those of 1772 and 1776, which paralysed the Midland counties. In winter, coaches ran twice a week, on Sundays and Tuesdays and, thank God, it was Monday night.

His decision made, he promptly fell into a dreamless sleep. His mind was clearer when he woke at his usual hour and he had overcome all the superstitious nonsense of the previous night. Nevertheless, he persisted in his resolution.

Instinctively Elizabeth glanced at the house as she drove past. It differed in no way from its neighbours, with its stuccoed front, symmetrical windows with plain pediments and, between two pairs of columns and a projecting roof, three steps leading to the front door.

Lucy Warren, who made it her business to know everything, had pointed it out to her. 'That's where she lives.'

'Who?'

All Elizabeth could see was an undersized maid in a mob cap and ankle-length apron, showing the mended soles of her shoes to the world while she scrubbed those steps.

'Mrs Prestwick. Your stepdaughter.'

It was ironic she passed that house every day to reach the theatre. The Warrens' house was barely three streets away and looked almost identical. She had experimented with other routes, but this was undoubtedly the most pleasant and safe.

At this hour all that could be seen were the lighted windows on the drawing-room floor, suggesting the Member of Parliament and his wife had company. Or maybe Mrs Prestwick was entertaining alone. Parliament sat every night except Wednesdays and Saturdays.

She had made no attempt to meet Miranda since the latter's arrival in London, though she sent her a note. The result was what she expected. Miranda failed to reply. Elizabeth had seen her from a distance, once while out shopping. Another time Mrs Prestwick was stepping into a hackney coach with Frank Collingham as she passed.

More than once in the first homesick weeks she wandered past the Swan with Two Necks, where the Nottingham coaches stopped. Even the joy of returning to the stage couldn't outweigh the loathing she felt for London. It hovered like a malignant presence, threatening to devour her and a thousand other souls. Apart from Lucy, there was no one in the city who cared if she died.

Sometimes Elizabeth felt she had outgrown her friendship with her cousin. Lucy was perpetually restless and eager to go out, shopping, visiting, attending balls and masquerades, ridottos and religious concerts, drums, routs and cardparties, when Elizabeth had a few precious hours to rest, learn her lines and write letters home.

The letters surprised her when she ran her eyes over them before sealing them. There was so much she left unsaid and yet she dared not add another page, for fear of Edward's having to pay extra postage. Was there any point in telling him how unhappy she was sometimes? It would seem like casting his generosity in letting her go back in his face.

Thanks to Lucy there was always plenty to write about – a concert where she almost fell asleep out of sheer exhaustion, a duchess glimpsed in St James's Park, the latest scandal involving adultery, bankruptcy or gambling debts of astronomic proportions.

Elizabeth was grateful to her cousin for trying to amuse her, but she also suspected Lucy wanted to be seen in society as often as possible with a promising new actress, in the hopes that, between the two of them, they would claw their way into more genteel circles.

Possibly Lucy felt she had debased herself by marrying into new wealth rather than old blood – but since it was a love-match *and* a prudent one, Elizabeth not see she had much right to complain. Mrs Tallant's daughter, Clara Soper, had become Lucy's bosom friend and introduced them to her circle. Elizabeth was often startled at how similar Mrs Soper was to her mother.

Lucy's restless curiosity, which led her to spy out the novelist Miss Burney at the theatre, also made her interested in all Elizabeth's acquaintances, especially Miranda. Once the Prestwicks arrived in London, hardly a week went by in which Lucy did not unearth some news about them or urge Elizabeth to contrive a meeting.

Indeed it was growing difficult to avoid one another, as their circles overlapped. One night, Lucy waylaid Elizabeth on her way to bed and told her gleefully she had discovered for a fact that Mrs Prestwick had been obliged to go to Drury Lane when Elizabeth was performing.

'She dared not displease such an influential hostess by refusing to go, and she couldn't plead puritanical principles, since she has been to the opera and the theatre when you weren't there.'

'Well, and what good does that do me or her, or anyone?' Elizabeth asked, feeling for the next step with her foot. Nonetheless, she tried writing a second time to Miranda, but only received a frosty note in reply, repudiating any further connection with her.

The only person connecting her with her stepdaughter was Frank Collingham. He was unusually discreet, either on his own initiative or because Miranda had sworn him to secrecy. He rarely mentioned Miranda, but if his flirting became too outrageous, Elizabeth would ask, 'Tell me, how is Mrs Prestwick?'

He looked annoyed the first time she said it, but then he began to treat it as a private joke, a warning he was overstepping the bounds of propriety. His replies were always frivolous, but tonight she fancied she saw something uneasy in the way he shifted his eyes to the broom propped in a corner of the green room.

Maybe it was only her imagination. She had been unnerved by a strange sensation which seized her on stage as she was begging Lady Capulet to intercede on her behalf with her father. In the middle of a speech, she suddenly felt an icy shiver, a tug at her heart.

> Is there no pity sitting in the clouds,
> That sees into the bottom of my grief?

She went on with barely a hesitation. For a moment an image flickered before her eyes of Edward in his favourite chair, then it was gone. In vain she struggled to recall that sensation now in the hackney coach, though there was no one to interrupt her, save her sleepy maid.

She paid the coachman and as she mounted the steps to the door, it opened and a warm triangle of light stretched towards her.

'I wanted to catch you alone,' Lucy murmured breathlessly, peeping round the door as if afraid of seeing a stranger or an unwelcome, if very late, guest. 'Let's go to your dressing-room – there's a fire in there.'

She followed her cousin upstairs, watching their shadows drift backward and forward as the light flickered. Lucy placed the candle on a rosewood table before curling herself in a chair. Elizabeth wondered how soon it would be before the warmth would overcome the discomfort of her throbbing feet and she would fall asleep in front of the fire.

'Well, what great mystery have you to tell me now?'

'It's – it's about that friend of yours, Mr Collingham. And – and your stepdaughter.'

'They have been friends from childhood. I know they meet frequently.'

'Rumour has it, too frequently.'

Elizabeth laughed faintly. 'Really, Lucy, I am very tired and if you have nothing more important to tell me. . . .'

'Well, but he is always one of her party if she goes into society and escorts her whenever her husband cannot. And then, of course, someone – never mind who – gave me this.'

Chapter 20

Elizabeth took the scrap of newspaper. There appeared to be a poem printed on it. She was going to turn it over, thinking it was the wrong way up, but Lucy stopped her.

'No, no, read the ode. I have it on good authority it was written by Collingham himself.'

Elizabeth ran her eyes over the poem. It was entitled 'Ode to a Distant Star' and written, not in old-fashioned heroic couplets, but in lines of irregular length, full of feverish, Gothic imagery of untamed nature and all things supernatural.

But even if it was written by Collingham, Elizabeth failed to see how the goddess or captive princess the poem was addressed to could be identified as Miranda. Apart, of course, from a reference to azure eyes.

'I don't see that this proves anything at all.'

'Don't you?' Lucy, who had been so sure, wavered for the first time.

'The poem is anonymous and this lovely creature might be – oh, I don't know – the Duchess of Devonshire or Lady Melbourne for all I can see. Who told you Collingham wrote this?'

Her cousin pursed her lips a moment and leaned forward in her chair. 'Well, I heard it rumoured so I asked him and, after a good deal of teasing, he admitted it and then looked shy and swore me to secrecy, because he said he didn't want his father to hear of it.'

This was no doubt the truth as far as Lucy knew it, but Elizabeth had an uneasy feeling that Frank Collingham was capable of taking credit for another man's work, if he found it expedient or amusing.

It was a cheap way of flattering an acquaintance, by pretending to confide in her and making mysteries where there were none.

'Why should you think this is about my stepdaughter?'

'Well, I didn't at first,' Lucy admitted with her usual forthrightness, though Elizabeth thought she detected a blush. 'I thought frankly that it was addressed to you, just at first, you know, and that that was why he begged me not to tell you. But then, you see, I heard he'd been spending so much time with Mrs Prestwick and – and. . . .'

'And you came to a different conclusion.'

Though Elizabeth pretended to dismiss the matter, it recurred to her throughout the night. The ode had been published under the obviously false name of Launcelot Lovewell, which she thought she had seen somewhere else in a newspaper or magazine.

The thought bothered her so much, she glanced through all the periodicals she could find the following morning and discovered two or three more poems published under the same name.

These, too, were addressed to an impossibly beautiful woman, whose life was cast away on a dull, jealous husband, who would have locked her away from mortal eyes. One line in particular struck her. 'Seen too early, loved too late'. What else could that refer to if not to the fact he had not valued his beloved till it was out of his power to be anything more than a distant admirer?

Lucy did not stop foraging for gossip either. The next evening as Elizabeth was preparing to go the theatre, she announced triumphantly that the 'whole world' – or what passed for such in genteel society – was talking about the Prestwicks and Mr Collingham.

'Mrs Soper introduced me to Mr Prestwick. Rather a cold fish, he seemed to me, no sense of humour. Mrs Soper says Mrs Prestwick is always complaining about his meanness with money, at least to her private friends. And Mrs Soper once saw Mr Prestwick behave very brusquely when he came back from the House and discovered her and Mr Collingham and a dozen other guests in the drawing-room.'

'I suppose a man is entitled to be tired and wish for a little peace in his own home,' Elizabeth retorted drily, readjusting her hat in the mirror.

'Oh no, there was something *very* particular in his manner, Mrs Soper said. Especially when he was talking to Mr Collingham.'

It was likely enough. Frank Collingham had always been capable, in his most amiable manner, of riling Mr Prestwick.

Lucy's constant harping on this string made Elizabeth restless. Miranda might be risking her reputation, even her happiness, if she really behaved as rashly as Lucy reported. She considered writing to Edward, but she could lay no specific charges nor offer any evidence and he was so far away.

Miranda had refused to see her. Thomas Prestwick, however, had not. Miranda might not even have told him she had written. Elizabeth had had no communication with him since his marriage and she wondered how he regarded her return to the stage. But it might be worthwhile writing to him, to suggest a reconciliation.

It took her hours to phrase a discreet note, knowing that any suggestion of a connection between them, by blood, marriage or otherwise, might be misconstrued if the letter chanced to fall into the wrong hands.

After some debate with himself, Edward decided to take neither Isaac nor James with him. Leaving word with Molly that he would be absent for at least a week, he threw a few things together in a portmanteau and set off.

To avoid acquaintances, he preferred to drive thirteen miles to Nottingham in his chaise, which he then sent back, rather than riding the single mile to Mansfield. But even in Nottingham he was haunted by the fear of being recognized and his journey being delayed.

There was no difficulty in getting an inside place in the stage-coach. At this time of year few people travelled for pleasure, and business was more likely to be transacted locally than with the metropolis. The London season was well under way and Christmas visits had been returned before the end of January.

He was dirty, cold, tired and half-starving by the time he reached the Swan with Two Necks, in Lad Lane. His bones ached from the constant shaking of the uneven roads and, for the first time in a long while, he wondered if he was growing old.

The mirror in his room showed deeper lines pressed into his forehead and around his mouth. Despite the murky light, he thought he detected a single grey hair on his temple. Is it any wonder she should grow tired of you, an insidious whisper hissed at him.

It was too late and he was too tired to do anything that evening. But the following morning, he ventured to a coffee house to leaf through the London newspapers. If he hoped to find anything in the respectable parts of the newspapers, he was disappointed. Elizabeth might be the centre of the world to him, but in London she was only another soul trying to earn a living.

With a sense of foreboding, he glanced at the tittle-tattle in the long, narrow columns. A cluster of familiar initials chilled him to the heart. What, asked the anonymous writer, could be the meaning of a mysterious meeting between Mr P—, the Member for L—, and the promising new actress, Mrs H— in St James's Park? Could this be the reason the beautiful Mrs P— was seen so often in the company of the charming Mr F— C—?

Edward wasted the day, seeking out acquaintances and then not daring to question them too closely for fear of hearing something unfavourable or of giving rise to unjust suspicions in their minds if the rumour in the newspaper was without foundation.

Late in the afternoon, he summoned the courage to call on Mrs Warren and was relieved to discover Elizabeth had already left for the theatre. His suspicions were roused, however, by Lucy's embarrassed air, quite unlike her chatty cheerfulness at Christmas. She was expecting Mrs Soper and so she wouldn't feel obliged to invite him to join them, he decided to go to the theatre. After all, it was the one night of the week Elizabeth played Juliet.

He arrived at Drury Lane rather early by fashionable standards. Once he had paid his three shillings for a seat in the pit, he discovered himself chiefly in the company of liveried and powdered footmen, sent by their employers to find advantageous seats for them.

Edward had no intention of disputing their rights or those of their masters. He was not certain how much of the auditorium the actors could see, though Elizabeth would not, of course, be expecting him. The more obscure his seat, the better.

He was too anxious to look around him much, though he was aware of white and gold walls, and glanced, however briefly, at the geometric patterns painted on the ceiling.

The theatre started filling up soon after he had taken his place. The boxes along the two side walls, it was true, hardly contained a soul as yet, but voices and loud laughter were audible from the galleries above and behind him. His eye rested momentarily on the stage boxes, abutting the apron of the stage so it was almost possible to touch the actors. What was he thinking of? That was the last thing he wanted.

Edward began to feel invisible. Strangers in bright, striped waistcoats or low-cut gowns greeted each other and he wondered whenever a lady came close to him whether he would be able to see anything of the stage, between or above the towers of real hair, false hair, grease, hair powder, wax fruit and feathers.

He was probably the only person present who barely noticed the excited exclamations when Lord Such-and-such or the Duchess of Somewhere took their places, though to avoid singularity he sometimes craned his neck with the rest of the crowd.

A party of young girls with a tame chaperon in tow, who seemed more intent on attracting attention to her plunging neckline than she did on guarding the morals of her charges, sat ominously close to Mr Holbrook. Would they chatter *all* the way through the play, or would he be able to snatch a stray sentence here and there?

Fortunately he discovered from a chance remark from one of the ladies that she, at any rate, was new to London and therefore was more likely to listen breathlessly than to strive to appear fashionably bored.

At length the play began. It was, Edward noted, David Garrick's adaptation of Shakespeare which, among other things, omitted Romeo's unrequited love for Rosaline (on the grounds it made him appear fickle) and had Juliet wake before Romeo died to allow the pair a last tortured farewell before she killed herself also.

Time passed agonizingly slowly for the lonely watcher in the pit. Now he was so close to his goal, it seemed to evade him. Each minute seemed slower than the last.

And then there she was. The familiar voice spoke. She looked smaller than he remembered her. The stage was larger than any he had seen her on. Maybe that was also why she looked so young, so innocent, a little girl barely dreaming of love or marriage yet. Her unpowdered hair added to the illusion, in contrast with the sophisticated coiffure of Lady Capulet, with pleats and folds up the back and long, pendent ringlets over her shoulders.

But no, it was something more. Her old radiance had returned, the glow of happiness he had not noticed until he missed it.

He tried to hold the echo of her voice when she was gone, but other voices – actors', spectators' – intervened. The balcony scene drew gales of sighing from the party of young ladies and Edward was gratified when a gruff voice behind him muttered, 'Damned fine woman, that.'

A twinge of jealousy seized him. Why did she gaze at that fellow like that, instead of raising her eyes across the auditorium and discovering his hiding place? He had seen those affectionate looks, heard those shy, teasing tones before, but he had thought them directed solely at himself.

Rumours had never ceased during their marriage. Collingham was always a great admirer of hers, she and Prestwick had talked a lot . . . and both those gentlemen were in London.

> Goodnight, goodnight! parting is such sweet sorrow
> That I shall say goodnight till it be morrow.

She had sometimes uttered those lines in jest when he – fool! – chose to finish some business letter rather than follow her upstairs to bed. But she had rarely quoted plays in the last year.

'Remember, Edward, I am not I when I am on stage,' she murmured on the last morning, before he returned to Nottinghamshire. 'It is not I who feels the emotions I portray but a detached being at the top of my head, who loves or hates or fears.'

He felt ashamed of himself for doubting her, for believing the lies newspapers spread. He ought to know her better. It even seemed to him she had never been so tender in her love scenes before her marriage. He refused to believe she was in love with Romeo. It followed, therefore, that she had learnt to speak and listen and look like that from having been in love herself.

Thenceforward, it was he who was on the stage with her. He could hardly stop himself from stretching out his hand to touch her. The parting of the lovers on the morning after their wedding moved Edward unexpectedly. Elizabeth had gazed after him with those mournful eyes when he had left her behind in London. A real tear trickled down her cheek.

She had to gather her wits to go on with the scene with her nurse and parents, in which she refused to marry Paris and pleaded for forgiveness.

Is there no pity sitting in the clouds,
That sees into the bottom of my grief?

He had forgotten the precise words he had heard in his half-doze until he heard them again. It was not a well-known quotation. For a lightning flash, her eyes seemed to turn in his direction and he sat, rigid with shock, his ears ringing.

But no, her voice flowed on. She did not look constantly towards him nor studiously avoid that corner. There was nothing to indicate she had seen him.

Edward had never realized how rare it was for Shakespeare to focus so exclusively on the heroine in the central acts of a play. Juliet encountered Paris on her way to Friar Laurence, accepted the latter's advice, made up the quarrel with her parents and wrestled with the horror of premature burial until, for the sake of love, she drank the potion and fell limp upon the bed.

And that, save for the last scene, was all. While the Capulets mourned their loss, his mind turned back to Elizabeth's miscarriages. If she had died, he would have cursed Maria, as if it were her fault, maybe cursed Miranda too for being the only child he would ever have.

The last scene arrived. Edward noticed that, of the sixty-five lines Garrick had inserted between the point at which Romeo drinks the poison and his death, barely half a dozen were spoken by Juliet, and those were only reactions or exclamations of grief at her lover's ravings, caught between love and death.

The country-bred maiden in the row in front of Edward was

sobbing to herself. He felt less annoyed at this public display of sensibility than usual, it seemed so heartfelt. He braced himself for the bows. This would be the test. Throughout the play, he might have been misled, unable to tell apart Elizabeth from Juliet. Now she would be entirely herself.

She was radiant, glowing with pleasure at the applause, trying in vain to suppress the smile on her sensuous lips. She was no longer the sober woman he had grown used to, but the brilliant creature he had desired as he stared across a drab provincial theatre.

He was half-inclined to get up then and return to Nottinghamshire that very night, if there had been a coach to take him. She did not need him. But somehow he missed his opportunity. He stayed for the interludes and afterpieces, incapable of going while his ears strained to catch every drop of praise. And there was the small matter that Lucy Warren knew he was in London.

He found himself drifting after a group of strangers to the stage door, but only those with special permits were allowed to enter the green room. There, in the shadows, he paused.

He knew if he revealed he was Mrs Holbrook's husband, they would let him in, or at least send for her maid. But this was not how he wanted to see Lizzie. He had not decided what he would say to her. He could imagine the scene, the green room a clutter of costumes and props discarded in a hurry, to be put away at leisure. And Elizabeth in the midst of her admirers, flirting and twisting words in her old way, utterly unconscious that he was so close to her.

He drew back as a crowd of young sparks passed him.

'Where's Collingham tonight?' one called to another.

'Who knows? Maybe he's with that married lady he keeps drinking toasts to and celebrating in rhyme. Maybe she persuaded him to elope after all.'

'I thought that was our dear Juliet,' a third young lawyer remarked.

'No, no, she's a deal too shrewd to be deceived by him.'

Edward retraced his steps through the darkness and lamplight. Hackney cabs and private coaches still lined the street, chairmen and link boys loitered with sedans and torches. He threw himself into a hack. The second insinuation in the article recurred to him for the first time.

What kind of a father was he to lose sight of his daughter's welfare? He would pass by her house and he knew she kept late hours. There could be no harm in stepping in there on his way to the Warrens' house.

Mr Prestwick agreed to meet Elizabeth on the day after she sent her note, but he insisted it should be in St James's Park and in the presence of her cousin. She was startled by his iciness, both in his letter and face to face. He left her in no doubt that he disapproved of her separation from her husband and her return to her profession.

Elizabeth merely bit her lip, but Lucy was indignant and not afraid to show it. She defended Mr and Mrs Holbrook in no uncertain terms, much to her cousin's embarrassment.

'You are entitled to your own opinion, madam.'

'We ought to go, Lucy. People will stare if you do not moderate your voice.'

'I don't care. Let them stare. Their lives must be dull if they have nothing better to do.' She turned once more on Mr Prestwick, 'And you, sir, would do well to take care of your own domestic affairs, before you pass judgement on other people.'

The same maxim might have been applied to Lucy's fascination with other people's lives, but Elizabeth wisely held her tongue.

'I have no notion to what matters you are referring,' Mr Prestwick replied in his most pompous manner.

Lucy was right: he *was* a cold fish. Elizabeth could hardly recognize the pleasant, if grave man she had received as a guest only last summer. Was it really only eight months ago?

'Oh, nothing.' Lucy tossed her last words over her shoulder. 'Only, everyone says you should look to your wife.'

'Lucy, stop it. I'm ashamed of you. Pay her no heed, sir. Goodbye.'

Elizabeth bundled her away, but the damage was done. Mr Prestwick was incensed against both of them, but he harboured a dread which Mrs Warren's words served to confirm.

His jealousy intensified and, inevitably, alienated Miranda still further. She had resented the curbs he imposed on her when her pastimes had been quite innocent – buying pretty things for the house, flirting with men who knew better than to take her seriously, holding select parties or elegant dinners to amuse her husband when he was at home, and herself when he was not.

Miranda had long since lost her will to please him. She decided to please herself instead, as a much easier task, even if she paid for it afterwards in wrangling over bills and debts and countering his jealous accusations.

Jealousy in a lover, she discovered, was amusing when you could escape from it. Jealousy in your own home, however, was dispiriting. Yet rather than remove all cause for it, she squared her jaw and determined to cure him of the green-eyed affliction once and for all.

She punished him by flirting with Collingham, knowing that was the rival he feared most. But it was a dangerous game in which to indulge. Frank, even in the days when she nursed her broken arm and told herself she hated him, had never lost his glamour.

He was charming, handsome, witty. The fact that she had never succeeded in making him jealous became a positive thing in her eyes. *He* would not have stinted her money or made scenes, in private or public, if she had a little fun. *He* would have known she meant no harm.

She thought about him for hours when she had nothing to distract her, telling herself she was married and so nothing untoward could happen. The secret was so precious, she didn't even write to Ruth about it. She was her most trustworthy friend, but she was also Frank's sister and very moral. Talkative by nature, Miranda cast around in desperation for a confidante and finally turned to the one person to whom she should never have talked about her marital problems.

Frank Collingham surprised her in tears in the drawing-room on the morning after the meeting in the park. He urged her to tell him what ailed her and she mustered a faint smile.

'Isn't it too absurd of him, Frank? You and I are such old friends – almost like brother and sister – I don't know why he should be so jealous and unkind.'

Frank agreed and they discussed the matter, ignoring the feeling they shared that it was *not* absurd, that they weren't siblings, but two attractive, charming but rather lonely individuals. And, first tentatively, then more and more boldly, as though they could not help drinking from a poisoned well, they started speculating about what might have happened if they had married. Or how happy they would be if they could be together all the time.

He had only just gone and Miranda was still in happy dream when her husband, returning home from a coffee house to dress for dinner, burst into her dressing-room.

On the night Edward saw her at Drury Lane, Elizabeth sank down in front of her dressing-room mirror. She had been happy on stage and was reluctant to let the feeling go. But the situation with Miranda was oppressing her. Lucy, still intent on defending her, had trusted several friends with the secret that Mrs Prestwick was her stepdaughter and, she had no doubt, the news would be all over the metropolis tomorrow. The Prestwicks would be up in arms.

Elizabeth was nearly ready to go when a message came that someone was begging to see her. She sent her maid, who acted as her dresser and chaperon, to see who it was.

'It's a servant 'm. She says you'll know her when you see her, but she daren't give 'er name.'

It was late, but Elizabeth couldn't see what harm it would do to speak to a maid. She turned away from the door for her cloak and muff and she caught sight of the newcomer in the mirror.

'Jenny, how are you? How is your mistress? Did she send you? You are still with Mrs Prestwick, aren't you?'

Her voice trailed away. The girl was ash-pale, her fingers convulsively clutching the edges of her cloak. Her eyes darted about as though, even here, she was afraid she had been followed.

'Oh, ma'am, I don't know where to begin. I didn't know who to turn to. I don't think I should've come.'

'Of course you were right to come if you are in trouble. Why don't you sit down and tell me about it?' Elizabeth swept an armful of fripperies from one of the two chairs in the narrow, shadow-filled room. To her distress, the servant burst into tears and, crouching on the chair, covered her face with her apron.

'What is it, Jenny?' She knelt down beside her and put her hand on the girl's shoulder, 'Surely you can tell me. Have you lost your place, or had bad news from home?'

' 'Tisn't me, ma'am, it's – it's the mistress,' she sobbed. 'She – she's done something wrong and I don't know what to do.'

Chapter 21

It took some time for Jenny to recover enough to stammer out her story. The news was grim enough. Elizabeth gathered from stray hints that Miranda and her husband had been making each other unhappy to the point that they were rarely in the same room together, or if they were, it was amidst a crowd of Miranda's guests.

Mr Collingham, on the other hand, was a frequent visitor and offered Jenny money, ribbons, gloves, even a pair of metal shoe buckles to carry messages and letters to and from her mistress.

'Many a time I've stopped outside t'master's door and heard him sighing fit to burst, and all the time me with that – that Judas money or a letter in me pocket. But I didn't quite like to go to him neither an' tell him what I know 'cos – well, he'd be so cross and mistress'll suffer and – well, I'd be like to be turned off for bearing such tales.'

She looked so piteous, Elizabeth murmured a reassurance. Jenny was not much older than Miranda. It was no wonder the dilemma perplexed her, especially as Miranda showered her with gifts and cast-off clothing.

Even more binding to the tender-hearted maid were her mistress's tears. Eyes brimming, Miranda had sworn her to secrecy, told her that she, Jenny, was the only friend she had left and wished out loud she had been killed when she was thrown from her horse.

On the only occasion Jenny ventured even to hint there might be something improper in corresponding with Mr Collingham in this manner, she had been treated with such coldness for a week that it had devastated her.

'I'd far rather she'd turn me off than treat me like that again. She looked at me as if I was a snake or a spider and she wouldn't speak to me, 'cept to give orders, and then she was as short with me as she could.'

Though Jenny did not say so, Elizabeth guessed the only reason why Miranda did not dismiss her was because she was afraid her husband would demand an explanation and that the maid would betray her.

Instead, Jenny crept around the house miserably and, when Mr Collingham next approached her, she carried the letter to her mistress. Even that had not thawed Mrs Prestwick completely and Jenny was still trying to mend the breach between them.

'Master's a good master, but very strict,' she explained, dabbing at her eyes with the apron. 'I daren't go to him, and if t'mistress said I was lying, he'd believe her, not me. But 'tisn't right, what she's done now.'

'What on earth do you mean? She hasn't eloped, has she?'

Jenny started as though confronted with a ghost. After a second, she bobbed her head.

'Oh, Jenny.'

'There was a terrible row,' she faltered. 'T'master didn't want her to go to a masquerade tonight while he was at the Houses of Parliament and couldn't come with her, but she sent me to find a hackney coach and she stole downstairs. I thought there'd be no harm in it and it was a shame t'master wouldn't let her have a little fun, but she didn't go to the house she was supposed to at all, but to Mr Collingham's rooms.'

She broke off, apparently appalled by what she had said, but Elizabeth coaxed the rest out of her. Mr Collingham talked kindly to her mistress, though he looked put out, and eventually he suggested Jenny should fetch some of Miranda's belongings, since she had only a small bundle with her. However, under the pretence of giving Jenny her hackney fare, he whispered to her to fetch help, though he didn't tell her who she should turn to.

She stole back home to remove the farewell note Mrs Prestwick had left for her husband. Terrified though she was of her master, she would have gone to him, but he was not back yet. Not thinking it would be right to involve the other servants, she sought out the only person she knew in London who might be able to help.

Elizabeth reassured her, but all the way there, she wondered what on earth she was doing, travelling across London in a hackney coach at well after midnight, accompanied by Jenny and her own maid. She could not help fearing – or hoping, perhaps – that by the time she got there it would be too late and Frank and Miranda would be gone.

But it was an absurd hope. Collingham would not have sent for help if that was his intention. She left her maid in the hack, promising the driver an ample reward if he waited. The coachman shrugged. He had nothing to lose. The crowds had left the theatres. The exodus from gambling clubs had not yet started and many hardened gamesters would not go to bed till dawn.

Jenny led the way to Mr Collingham's chambers. Elizabeth could hear voices of bitter recrimination within, which were cut off by her knock. There was a scuffling inside, then the door was edged open.

'Oh, it's you.' Collingham gave a sigh of relief and allowed her to pass.

The room was more or less what she expected, sparsely furnished with tables, chairs and cupboards which had been badly abused in their time. The chair seats were worn, woodwork chipped and there appeared to be a scorch mark on the hearthrug.

Chaos reigned. Papers, playbills, books, boots, cards, cravats were scattered everywhere. A dirty plate, with a knife and fork resting on it, had been placed on top of a pile of letters and Elizabeth noticed most of the literature did not have much to do with the legal profession.

'You'd better come out, Mir— Mrs Prestwick,' he said heavily. 'Your maid has returned.'

The door to the bedroom opened. Miranda remained transfixed on the threshold. She wore her travelling cloak over her riding-habit and held her hat in her hand.

'Well, Mrs Holbrook, there she is. I hope you have more success in making her see sense than I did.'

That was enough to wake Miranda out of her stupor. She cut across Elizabeth's first words with an indignant cry.

'Oh, this is infamous! I have nothing to say to this woman and – and I'll never speak to you again, Frank Collingham. How can you treat me so shabbily and betray me into the hands of that viper?'

She threw a malignant look at Jenny too, who had shrunk into the shadows, and Elizabeth thought it wise to send her to wait in the hackney coach. Reasoning with her stepdaughter was an impossible task, however.

'You're not my mother,' Miranda snarled.

'No, but that is no reason to wake Mr Collingham's neighbours.'

Afterwards Elizabeth did not like to remember that scene. She could guess from what she heard what the earlier scene between the lovers had been, he urging prudence, she distraught at the betrayal but determined not to listen to any arguments to return to her husband. Though Frank loved her, in his own way, he was not prepared to risk everything for her sake.

'Of course, we cannot force you,' Elizabeth said at length, 'but what do you intend to do?'

'I'll go to Aunt Lester. She'd be glad of some company.' Her lips twitched as if she was about to cry.

'There aren't any coaches for three days. Where do you propose to stay meanwhile?'

It was as well their voices had sunk low at this point. The thundering knock shook them all.

'Collingham, are you there, you scoundrel?' Prestwick's voice demanded.

Miranda uttered a tiny cry of dismay. Elizabeth found herself being bundled into the bedroom, stepdaughter and all. Collingham struggled out of his coat and waistcoat and tore off his cravat. Understanding his actions, Elizabeth tumbled the bed, then took refuge with Miranda in the recess between the door and something tall, a cupboard or a bookcase.

For all her defiant talk, Miranda neither struggled, nor went out boldly to confront her husband. Elizabeth's argument that it would be her turn to be despised as 'that woman' had had the desired effect. Now Frank had failed her, it was imperative to save appearances by taking shelter with a kinswoman. Miranda was too fond of society to risk ostracism, except for love.

263

For what seemed like hours, Elizabeth's heartbeat drowned out the voices in the next room. Frank was his usual exasperating self, polite but protesting at being woken at such an ungodly hour and claiming not to have seen Mrs Prestwick since the previous morning.

'Do you see any signs of female habitation?' he added, presumably smiling at the mess.

'If you're alone, you'll have no objection to my glancing into your bedroom.'

'Oh, by all means, if you must. You won't find anything, though I must say this is hardly the action of a gentleman.'

Elizabeth felt a tight band across her chest. Did Collingham look as much at ease as he sounded? She pushed Miranda deeper into the recess, drawing in her breath as the door was flung open. They had been huddled in utter darkness and the sudden flare of lights dazzled her.

It was only then she realized that two men had burst into the room. Thomas Prestwick's back was towards her and his candle showed up the right hand side of the room. But barely a foot away from her, looking straight at her, was her husband.

Edward's eyes were riveted to her face for an agonizing moment, then he turned abruptly and said, 'There's no one here, Tom. We'd better go,' and he bundled Mr Prestwick out of the room, apologizing to Collingham for disturbing him.

Unspeakable agony gripped Elizabeth. She comprehended in a second all that her husband's recognition entailed. He must believe it is I and not Miranda who is an adulteress. He thinks I have betrayed him, yet he refused to expose me in front of his son-in-law. Why on earth did I disturb that bed? He will never forgive me. I have lost him forever, saving the reputation of his daughter, who will neither thank me for it nor lift a finger to save my marriage.

Days, months it seemed elapsed while she huddled in the dark with Miranda before Frank Collingham returned with a candle.

'Well, ladies, a miracle has occurred. Our prayers have been answered.'

Incredulously Elizabeth realized both he and Miranda, who had shut her eyes in resignation when her husband burst in, believed Edward's lie.

She heard her own voice from a distance, proposing to put Miranda up in her room at Lucy's house till she could go to Nottingham. At Collingham's instigation, she wrote a note for Jenny to deliver, explaining to Mr Prestwick that his wife had been taken ill at the theatre and therefore her stepmother had taken her home with her.

As in a dream, she found herself in the coach, with no memory of leaving Collingham's chambers. She discovered, when she alighted and paid the coachman's remarkably high fare without blinking, that Jenny had been left at Mr Prestwick's door, letter clutched in her hand.

She stood for hours on the doorstep till a sleepy servant unfastened the door. To preserve appearances, Miranda clung to her as though about to faint. The stairs had never been so numerous or so steep. Every footfall seemed a nail in her coffin, a reminder that Edward had seen her and would believe the worst. What was he doing in London? Why hadn't he written?

As soon as the maid was dismissed, with a bribe to make her hold her tongue, Miranda began pouring out her venom. Hurt and angry at the betrayal she had suffered, she needed a scapegoat. Elizabeth did not even care.

But after Miranda had grumbled herself to sleep, Elizabeth turned her back on her and lay awake for hours, her eyes open and smarting, unable to shed a tear.

She had the nightmare again. This time she was wandering through a maze of corridors, part theatre, part Inns of Court. She entered Frank Collingham's inner room and, as she turned to shut the door, there was the body, hanging from a hook. It was Edward's face, his eyes still open and gazing at her, more in sorrow than in anger. She cried out.

'No! Not this time. I won't let you go, I won't let you die.'

Her fingers fumbled, but she forced herself to go on. Miraculously he slid to the floor and she gathered him in her arms and held his head to her breast, crying and moaning.

She knew it was a dream then. She felt someone tugging her, tearing her upwards, away from that scene, but she didn't want to let Edward go.

'Edward,' she mumbled, her head heavy, her limbs stiff. She

wanted to reach out and touch him and Miranda's voice fell upon her naked face like cold summer rain.

'Wake up, wake up.'

'I'm sorry.' She struggled to remember any words. 'I thought he was dead.' And finally tears welled up in her eyes. It was not that her profession was any less dear to her, but that the months of missing Edward had culminated like this was more than she could bear.

Miranda was silent and watchful, feeling awkward at her obvious distress. Elizabeth made an effort to dry her tears. As soon as she was dressed, she sought out Lucy, bidding Miranda to wait where she was. Lucy, still wearing her robe, her hair half-dressed, dismissed her maid and urged Elizabeth to sit down and explain the meaning of her husband's unexpected arrival.

'You've no notion how terrified I was he would ask me about his daughter,' she confided. 'I wondered if I should feign a headache, but just as I was ready with my hartshorn and a pained smile, he sent a note that he had business with his son-in-law and would spend the night there.'

Elizabeth confessed Edward's arrival was a surprise to her also and distracted Lucy by telling her as much of last night's adventures as Miranda knew.

Thrilled, Lucy promised to swear blind that Mrs Prestwick had been with her at the theatre until she was taken ill. She even volunteered to enlist Mrs Soper in the deception, but Elizabeth quashed the idea, not liking to involve a comparative stranger.

Lucy had just trotted off gleefully to inform her husband of part of what had occurred before he left for his offices in the City, when Mr Prestwick was announced. Elizabeth had expected him as early as was compatible with consideration for others.

The message had had the inevitable effect. He was full of remorse, convinced Miranda's illness – once he knew it was not dangerous – must be the result of their argument. He seemed genuinely moved by the idea Miranda had taken their quarrel so much to heart that she had given up the masquerade, called her an angel and himself a monster and swore they would never disagree again if he could help it, even if he let her have her own way in everything.

In his enthusiasm, he apparently forgot he disapproved of Mrs Holbrook. Or maybe he was simply so grateful to her for taking care of his precious wife, he had forgiven her. Elizabeth listened to him almost in silence. He asked to see Miranda, but before she went to fetch her, Elizabeth turned back for a moment.

'There is only one thing I wish to warn you about,' she said. 'Don't take offence, but you must try to curb your jealousy. Miranda is like her father. Her love can be won, but can never be forced. Jealousy will only drive her away. And she is still so young. I wonder whether she wasn't too young and we were wrong to let her marry yet.'

I did it for selfish reasons, her heart whispered. I knew I could not escape till Miranda was married and so, if I had any doubts, I suppressed them.

'She would only have resented you as a jealous stepmother if you had tried to stop her.'

The voice made her spin round to the door.

'Edward!' The name passed her lips before she could stop herself. She even started forward to throw herself into his arms, as if no one else was present and nothing had happened, but she checked herself and scanned his face.

'What, no kiss for your darling husband?' he asked ironically.

Obediently she pecked him on the cheek, but his flesh seemed cold and she drew back. He looked worn and she longed to stroke the lines away from his forehead. Still, he smiled and reminded her she had promised to fetch Miranda.

'We can talk afterwards,' he added.

Elizabeth nodded. Her heart knocked against the ribs of her stays all the way upstairs. Miranda was apprehensive about meeting her husband and it took all her assurances that he was in a forgiving mood to persuade her to venture downstairs.

Mr Prestwick was waiting in the hall, unable to contain his impatience any longer. Before Miranda had a chance to speak, he was bounding up to meet her, apologizing and assuring her nothing like that would ever happen again. His carriage stood outside and, after making sure nothing ailed her, he suggested an airing in one of the parks so they could talk without imposing on the Warrens any longer.

Elizabeth left them and went quietly into the drawing-room. Edward was sideways on to her, studying a newspaper which had been left on a table. Her heart still hiccuped when she caught sight of him. She longed to run to him, but she did not dare.

'Edward,' she said, but stopped. What could she say to justify what he thought he had witnessed last night? The only way she could clear her name was by incriminating his daughter. If he was too angry, he might not listen or believe her.

He looked up.

'Everyone said I was a fool for marrying you,' he said.

She winced and bowed her head, clenching her hands to try to prevent herself from crying.

'You are so young and beautiful, so clever and talented – how could I hope to keep you?' he went on without a pause. 'Tell me, how many young women are capable of risking their own marriage to save that of another woman who doesn't even like her?'

Elizabeth looked up, startled. 'I don't understand.'

'It *was* Miranda at Collingham's chambers last night, wasn't it?'

She hesitated. Edward took something out of his pocket and put it on the table in front of her with a rap of his knuckles. She leaned closer and saw a lace-trimmed handkerchief with the entwined cypher M.P. embroidered in one corner.

'Yes,' she whispered.

'Oh, make no mistake, I was shaken to see you there,' he said, 'but you don't suppose I didn't see the second figure hiding behind you, do you? And the letter you sent Tom Prestwick confirmed my faith in you. If you intended to elope, you had nothing more to expect from me.'

He held out his arms to her. She snuggled on his waistcoat and they told each other everything. When Edward called at the Prestwicks' house, his son-in-law had just discovered Miranda's flight and was all for searching the house at which a masquerade was being held. His temper was so uncertain, Edward felt obliged to go with him to keep him in check. Extensive enquiries elicited the fact that no one had seen Mrs Prestwick that night, nor Mr Collingham. The rest Elizabeth could guess.

'What I don't understand is what you are doing in London at all.'

'It's simple enough,' he said, 'I miss you. I wanted to see you. So, what do we do next?'

'I don't know. All I know is that I cannot bear to be parted from you again. So if you want me to go back to Nottinghamshire, I'll go, once my contract runs out in summer.'

He took his time choosing his answer.

'Lizzie, I've seen how happy acting makes you. Surely there is no reason why I couldn't hire a house in London or Richmond, say. I even suspect I shouldn't let you return to Woodlands till you are so famous, the Parrs and the Collinghams will fall over themselves trying to win your approval. Unless you become pregnant – I insist you take every care of yourself if that happens, contract or no contract.'

He silenced her the only way he knew how, by kissing her.

'I can't believe Miranda was so careless as to leave her handkerchief where her husband might find it,' Elizabeth murmured as an afterthought, nestling against him.

'Can't you, sweetheart? Don't *you* leave your handkerchiefs scattered around Woodlands?'

She looked up at him, suddenly alert again.

'Didn't I tell you I found the handkerchief in Prestwick's house?' he continued.

'I assumed – oh, you know perfectly well you did not. That was a mean trick, Edward Holbrook, and I shan't speak to you again.'

'Shan't you? Then I shall have to find a different use for your lips.'

CENTRAL 20/12/01

NP